MW01165848

The Second Oldest Profession

A Spy Novel

CHERYL COSTA

BOORWORMS PRESS
An imprint of
DRAGON LADY MEDIA, LLC
ROCKY RIVER, OHIO
2024

This book is a work of Fiction. Names, characters, places, institutions, businesses and incidents are the product of the author's imagination or are used fictionally. Any resemblance to actual persons, living or dead, or actual events, locales, businesses, institutions or government agencies is entirely coincidental.

Copyright 2023 2024 Cheryl Costa & Linda Miller Costa All rights reserved.

Without written permission, you may not use or reproduce any part of this book in any manner. You must not circulate this work in any other form, and you must impose this same condition on any acquirer. You may not scan or digitize this book without authorization, except for fair use provisions of the Copyright Act of the United States of America.

Front Cover Art by Renee Reeser Zelnick
Rear Cover Art by Cheryl Costa
Linda Miller Costa - Editor & Publisher
Printed & Distributed by Amazon.com

First edition 2024

ISBN: 9798335382359

Publisher:
Boorworms Press
Dragon Lady Media, LLC
Rocky River, Ohio 44116
CherylCosta.Mystic@Gmail.com

DEDICATION

Since biblical times to present day, unassuming and nearly invisible women have been the backbone of the covert intelligence business. Women who many times just did their job with a friendly smile, good networking, their own smarts and sometimes pure guile!

This special breed of women usually took unthinkable risks with little or no recognition after their service. Many dying in anonymous obscurity in their elder years with their contribution to their home nation's security being conveniently erased because they were simply mere women.

The author of this book dedicates it to the tried-and-true former and present women spies among us, whom we never knew and will probably never know.

CONTENTS

A NOTE FROM THE AUTHOR

The Second Oldest Profession - The Spy Business

Modern spy movies like James Bond and Mission Impossible paint a picture of the spy business being glamorous, with handsome guys in tuxedos and vamped up women as eye candy. With plenty of breath-taking action sequences littered with gun fights, lots of hand-to-hand combat, high-speed chase scenes and, of course, plenty of gadgets.

The reality is that the lion's share of the job is simply quiet observation and report activity. Reading an adversary's media, listening to their comm traffic and casual public gossip. Another Trade Craft art is establishing friendships and creating informal contact networks.

The other side of the gathering of information is the sometimes hair pulling job of analysis. It's a detective's game of making sense out of the raw data and understanding the story it can tell, provided one can understand the context. Typically, people with training in language, history, and cultural understanding of a specific country or region of the world do the enormous job of analysis. Remember, Tom Clancy's character Jack Ryan was principally an analyst, who occasionally ended up in the field as a subject matter expert.

Many hundreds of thousands of people work in the business of intelligence gathering and analysis. No matter what they do, they are all bound by the bond of their personal anonymity and the silence of the secrets they keep. For some, carrying too many secrets can become a substantial emotional weight. It is a burden that they are oath bound to carry to their graves.

PART ONE
THE SOVIETOLOGIST

In the late Nineteen Seventies

Feb 5th 9:30 AM US Submarine Base, Groton, CT
Base Personnel Office

Electronics Technician-Radar second class Charles Stewart sat quietly, waiting for a first-class yeoman to finish typing discharge papers. The yeoman remarked. "I heard our state congressional representative got involved with your breach of contract case?" Stewart simply answered, "Indeed, he did." The yeoman scowled. "Didn't you use the chain of command?"

Stewart shrugged his shoulders. "Yes, thirteen chits up the chain of command from the bottom to the top over two years. No one ever acknowledged or entertained my breach of contract claim. They just rubber stamped what the last level of command said. My wife wrote to our congressional representative and his staff called the Bureau of Naval Personnel. They called me up on Christmas morning and told me I hadn't legally been in the Navy since Christmas 1976, when I reenlisted under a special program. They never took into consideration my previous Air Force service. That affected the signing bonus."

The yeoman rolled his eyes, "Oh my god! If you weren't qualified for the bonus. Then your contract wasn't valid!"

"Yeppers." Stewart answered. The yeoman lit a cigarette. "You went through three years of high-tech school and language school?" Stewart silently nodded. The yeoman closed his eyes, shaking his head. "Those schools must have cost two or three hundred thousand dollars." Stewart again just silently nodded. The yeoman took a long drag on his smoke and asked. "How much was the reenlistment bonus they screwed you out of?"

Petty Officer Stewart scowled. "Five thousand dollars." The yeoman, shaking his head, remarked, "Chump change by comparison." He slipped the discharge papers into a folder and slid it into a large manila envelope containing other papers, and handed it to Charles Stewart.

"Well, Charles, you are now officially a civilian! Good Luck." The yeoman said, shaking Stewart's hand. Then he added, "Before you leave, there are two civilian spook types that want to have a word with you."

Stewart gave the yeoman a troubled look. "Why?" The yeoman leaned into Stewart and remarked in a softened voice. "You've got a serious security clearance; you've been doing high-tech intel work and you've been to language school. It's my guess they're going to make you an offer you can't refuse." Stewart took a deep breath. "Good Grief." The yeoman led Stewart out of his office and down the hall to a conference room.

The yeoman opened the door. "Gentlemen, thank you for waiting. This is Mr. Charles A. Stewart, newly discharged from naval active service. He was an Electronics Technician- Radar second class and qualified in Submarines. I will leave you gentlemen to your business." The yeoman turned his back on the men in suits and gave Stewart a wink! After the yeoman closed the door, one of the two men addressed Stewart, who had just taken a seat.

"Charles Adam Stewart, on 7 November,1975, you sought the services of a small private psychiatric service facility in Hartford, CT, under the assumed name of Arthur Jurkowski." The man handed Stewart several photos of him entering and leaving the facility.

While looking at the photos, Stewart felt cold sweat running down his back. "Were you following me?" The other man in a suit spoke up. "No, that facility gets a lot of traffic from naval personnel who are having everything from marital problems, drug and alcohol and other conditions folks are trying to keep private from the Navy."

The first man added, "We ran your license plates, got your name, and discovered that you are stationed here in Groton and assigned to one of the submarines with a very high security

2

clearance. That flagged you, so we got a court order to see your medical report in the interest of protecting national security."

The second man grinned. "So, Chuck, do you really want to become a woman? You realize if you change, you will become a second-class citizen socially and legally?" Stewart initially looked embarrassed. "Yes, I understand that." He paused, seemingly deep in thought for a few moments, then added. "Ever since I can remember, I've been out of synch with my body and my gender role."

The first man spoke, "That clinic diagnosed you as a pre-transition transsexual woman." Stewart nodded. "Yep, that's about the size of it? I suppose you're going to take my clearance away from me and throw me in a federal prison some place."

They seemed to study Charles for a few moments. The second man held up his hand. "Whoa, the Navy put you through nearly three years of electronic and photo intelligence gathering training. Not to mention language school. They bungled your enlistment contract on a technicality which they could have wavered. The folks in your chain of command were idiots!"

The first man added, "Effectively you've been in the intelligence business for the past few years and, from all reports, you're talented at your job. How would you like to take your career up a notch and come to work for us?"

Stewart was stunned. "You're kidding? I might go through a sex change in the next ten years. Theoretically, I shouldn't be able to work for you. I'll be freaky queer in every sense. A respectable bunch of secret agency guys like you could never have someone like me within your ranks."

The first man answered, "Yes, you are right. It would be absolutely absurd for our organization to have someone like you or the woman you might become working within our ranks."

The second man added, "Yes, it's an impossibility for such an individual like you to work for us. But that would be the most amazing cover for a field officer. Because you couldn't possibly work for us or exist within our ranks!"

Both men sat grinning at Stewart. Their assertions overwhelmed him. After a few silent moments, the second man asked, "So, Stewart, do you have a feminine name picked out?" Stewart looked uncomfortable for a few moments. Then softly said, "Moira." The first man remarked, "Please say that again, louder." Stewart answered back loudly, "Moira!"

The second man smiled, "So, Moira Stewart, are you ready to go where no man has gone before?" Once again, Stewart felt overwhelmed by their proposal. "Wait a minute, you folks have had women as spies before and women as analysts. How would I be any different?"

The second man grinned. "Moira, you would be the impossible woman. Nobody would ever think you could work in our business." Stewart sat back with his hands over his face. After several minutes of silence, he spoke up, and asked, "Will I receive good pay and receive good medical benefits for me and my spouse?" The first man remarked, "Yes, comparable to the civilian job you have lined up." Stewart winced. "You know about those folks?" They just smiled and nodded. Stewart looked at the first man and then at the second man. "Gentlemen, where do I signup?"

Feb 5th 1:30 PM Navy Housing, Groton, CT

Charles entered the navy housing apartment and gave his wife Louise a warm embrace. As he hugged her, he whispered, "I'm a civilian again, but I'm in the active naval reserves so I'll be involved with one weekend a month and two weeks a year of duty. It's sort of the price of getting out early." He paused. "Let's grab a couple of beers from the refrigerator and have a long talk before we pack." Louise nodded and took a seat on the couch.

Charles got the two cans of cold beer, and after they opened them, he raised a toast. "For glorious adventures in the future." Louise raised a finger. "To glorious adventures in the future, no matter how they manifest." They gave each other knowing looks, nodded and toasted their cans of beer.

Louise raised an eyebrow. "Something's changed?" Charles regarded his beer for a few moments. "After they gave me my discharge papers, they walked me down the hall to a room and had me meet with two agents from a government intelligence service. They knew all about our visit to that psychiatric facility in Hartford."

"Shit!" Louise moaned, then she asked, "Are you...are we in trouble?" Charles shook his head. "Don't sweat it! They knew why I went there for my eval. They know all about my Moira side. It will not be an issue. They recognized my talent. Better yet, they recruited me, promised me more training and offered me a job suitable for my current job skills."

Louise whispered, "Are you going to be in the spook business?" Charles gently nodded his head and put his finger to his lips. "I'm simply going to be a data analyst for some defense contractor. That's our family story for the foreseeable future. I'm simply going to be a cube monkey in some corporation somewhere. Just an anonymous office worker."

Louise nodded. She understood. "Are we still moving to Norwalk?" He nodded. "Yes, actually. We'll be there for about a year, while I get some additional training. I might have some brief business trips from time to time. They will relocate us after approximately a year."

He said to Louise, "Our life and relationship are most certainly complicated. I'll have to travel from time to time, but not like those long Navy deployments. But like the Navy, you can't really talk about what I do and why I'm gone. I'm just away on business."

Louise put her beer down on the end table and crawled over to his side of the couch, and snuggled up into his arms. "All the wives of the submariners go into a private fear mode when you guys were on deployment. I think this will be different."

Charles kissed the top of her head. "Well, consider yourself blessed. Your spouse will never come home and bore you to tears with shop or office talk." She said nothing for a long quiet few minutes, content to be in her lover's arms. When Louise spoke up, she had a tone of resolve in her voice. "I've done a lot of reading in the library about the life you are about to lead. I understand the things that you might do and the things you'll know you must take to your grave with you." She paused and then added, "I don't care if you're Charles or Moira or a little bit of both. You are unique in ways words can't describe. Just stay in my life. I love you dearly."

She sat up. "Sweetheart, let's pack up our transfer boxes and lay out our traveling clothes and get ready for the movers."

Feb 7th 10:30 PM Navy Housing, Groton, CT

Louise and Charles Stewart quietly watched commercial movers under contract to the Navy dutifully pack up their household effects and had made fast work of it.

Of course, the couple had experience with military moves. They had two large wooden transfer boxes in their car with a small coffee pot, a hot plate and tables settings for each of them. In addition, there were kitchen towels and dish soap and scrubbing pads. In the other box, an air mattress, bath soap, bath towels and washcloths and a hair dryer. Each of them also packed a three-day supply of clean clothes, undergarments, toiletries, and a couple of sleeping bags. They were veterans of four military household moves to date and knew how to weather these transfer events.

Once the movers had emptied the Navy owned apartment. The couple and several friends cleaned the empty dwelling and finally handed the keys to the Navy housing representative. Afterward, the couple hugged their navy friends and said goodbyes. They got in their car and began their ninety-minute trip westward on Interstate 95 toward Norwalk, CT.

Feb 10th Norwalk, CT–The Carriage House

Charles and Louise Stewart found themselves mostly settled after their move from the Groton Submarine Base a week previously. The first two days after the movers delivered, their household items were challenging. Everywhere there was the clutter of half open boxes. But their five-year stint in Navy family living had taught them to keep their household furnishings scant for easy relocations. They knew they would be moved again in a year. Since Charles was starting the new job in two days, the couple relaxed and nested in their new dwelling.

Feb 12th 8:45 AM Greenwich, CT–New Job First Day!

Charles followed a map that was sent to him via a Federal Express envelope at his new residence. The location was a multi-use seven story commercial office building. As he entered the foyer, on the ground floor, he noted the building's directory signage that showed what floors the various businesses were on. He looked at the business card that had been paper clipped to the map. It was for Mr. Nathaniel Green, Field Service manager for North American Surveying. The building's directory showed that the business was on the seventh floor. Charles entered the elevator and pressed the button for the seventh floor. A few moments later, he exited the elevator and saw an ornate wooden door with an engraved plaque that read simply, North American Surveying.

Charles opened the door, and there was a receptionist who was perhaps in her thirties, sitting behind a desk. "Good morning. Welcome to North American Surveying. How can I help you?" She asked. Charles handed her the business card. "I'm a new guy, first day on the job here to see Mr. Green." Charles explained. The woman smirked. "Ah, a new chain dragger!" She pressed a button on her phone. "Good Morning, Mr. Green, your recruit, Mr. Stewart is here to see you." A voice on the speakerphone simply said, "Send him in."

The receptionist pointed to her right. "Third door on the left." As Stewart walked toward the door, he heard a buzz and a door unlocked. He opened the door and walked down the nondescript hallway to the third door. The name plate on the door read Nathaniel Green. Charles knocked once and heard a man's voice who said, "Come."

Upon opening the door, behind the desk was the second man who interviewed him back at the subbase. Mr. Green rose and extended a handshake, which Charles accepted. Green gestured for

Charles to take a seat. "Welcome to North American Surveying Mr. Stewart, or should I say Moira?" Stewart winced. "Let's save that until the day I present myself as Moira."

Green nodded. "I think I understand. Certainly, it's your call. We'll support your new identity when you reach that point in your personal evolution. That said, there are going to be people in our outfit that are going to have a hard time with it. But I suspect you already understand that." Charles took the commentary in stride and nodded in agreement.

Then Green asked, "We're pretty informal around here. So do we call you Charlie or Chuck?" Stewart closed his eyes for a few seconds. "I prefer Charles." Green studied Stewart for a few moments, remarking, "Most of us around here have served in the armed forces. Likewise, we had nicknames and monikers. Did you have a nickname or a handle on that submarine?"

Stewart casually offered. "Petty Officer Stewart." He paused for a few moments, closed his eyes and added, "Shipmates who seemed to sense me deeply called me Charleen. Everybody else casually referred to me as the seamstress. I was the ship's tailor as one of my collateral duties."

"I think I see why you are so formal with your personal naming." Green remarked. "Formality in naming can be very grounding. I get that, especially in our business. When as field officers, we might have multiple identities depending on where we're working."

Charles spoke up, "So, who exactly do I work for?"

"Care for coffee, Charles?" Charles nodded in the affirmative. Green got up and gestured for Charles to follow him. A few minutes later, the two of them were in a break area that hosted several high-volume coffee makers. "We have Dark Roast, Light Roast, decaf coffee and lots of hot water for use with tea and hot cocoa," Green explained.

Green pointed at a large piece of finished wood with spokes of dowel pointing out. "If you bring in your own distinctive coffee mug, you can hang it there. All the plain vanilla cups are for

8

anybody's use. Let's get our coffee and go back to my office and discuss who exactly you work for."

Back in Green's office, he closed the door and took a seat at a small conference table and gestured to Charles to do the same on the other side of the table. Green began, "I know we both remember the Cuban Missile crisis. I was in the seventh grade." Charles replied, "Yes, I was in the fourth and I clearly remember it."

Green continued, "In October 1962, the two world powers, the USA and the USSR, both had enough thermonuclear weapons to nuke us all twice over. But in the background, a Soviet attaché had a drink with a high-profile network news commentator and asked him to tell our leadership to cool the rhetoric!"

Charles intently studied Green with a questioning look. Then Green added, "By the same token, several former World War Two OSS operatives with still living Soviet counter parts started a similar effort to be an advising back channel to ease the proverbial Mexican standoff the two superpowers were having. In the end, those back channels helped cool the tensions caused by misunderstandings."

Charles gave Green a curious look. "Didn't the CIA have those sorts of back channels?"

"Yes, and no," Green commented. "Point one: the fifteen-year-old CIA was chartered to protect and defend and mitigate events," Green stated. "Also, while they had back channels, to use them would have destroyed deeply hidden intel assets that it took years to imbed."

Charles spoke up, "Okay Mr. Green, whom do I work for?" Green laughed out loud. "I like your persistence. Charles, publicly your employer is North American Surveying a corporate enterprise with offices all over the free world. You are simply a data analyst for us. That is all your wife, your family, friends and neighbors need to know. All our client details are confidential."

Of course, it's a front for the clandestine organization. Green paused. "After the Cuban Missile Crisis, it was determined that we needed another branch of intelligence that would gather information. Information of a softer kind. Our business is gathering undercover information and data related to relationships we can foster that will give us many paths of back channels in the future if needed."

Charles studied his new boss. "Mr. Green, it sounds like we're in the press-the-flesh and glad-hand, schmooze business?" Green grinned. "On one hand, that is accurate. We certainly do our share of schmoozing and establishing relationships. But on the other hand, we gather intelligence and we still do our own form of classic cat and mouse, cloak and dagger stuff."

Mr. Green turned to face his new employee and extended a handshake. "Charles Stewart, welcome to OSS62. Let's take you down to personnel and get your records, benefits and badging squared away."

Feb 12th 1:30pm Greenwich, CT–An Introduction to a Tutor

After lunch, Mr. Green took Charles Stewart down to the sixth floor. Green knocked on a closed door. There was no sound, so Green opened the door. The two men entered the room. Charles's first inkling as he entered the room was the impression that this looked like his grandmother's parlor.

There was a coffee table, a love seat style couch, opposite the love seat, an overstuffed chair in a conversational nook. On the other side of the room there was a small, dark wooden drop-leaf table and a pair of matching wooden chairs. On the wall was a blackboard.

Charles looked at Mr. Green. "Is this a briefing room?" Green smirked. "No, actually, this is where you will work this year, mostly." Charles gave his boss a curious look. "Is this my office?" Green simply remarked, "No, this is a classroom of sorts. This is where you are going to be tutored to become a Sovietologist." Charles cocked his head in a questioning manner. "Sovietologist?"

Green continued, "To do the sort of job we do, you need to be deeply immersed in the Russian language and Soviet Culture. In addition, you will sharpen up your conversational Russian with a native speaker." Charles looked surprised. Again Green spoke up.

"By the time Dr. Sidorov, your tutor, gets done with you. You'll be able to walk down the streets of Moscow acting and speaking like you were born there."

The door opened and an older man walked in and gave Green and Stewart a surprised look and a scowl. Charles's first impression was *'This guy looks like John Houseman'.*

Mr. Green spoke up, "Dr. Sidorov, this is our newest member of OSS62. Charles Stewart."

Charles greeted in Russian, "S uvazheniyem doktor Sidorov." (Best regards, Dr. Sidorov)

The academic tutor studied Stewart for a moment. Dr. Sidorov "Trying to impress the teacher, eh? Not bad, slight northern accent, but said like a clumsy foreigner. But we'll get that ironed out."

Dr. Sidorov looked at Mr. Green. "Nathaniel, I thought you were bringing me a young woman." Charles had a sudden sense of embarrassment and felt himself blushing. Dr. Sidorov squinted at Charles, noting his facial color had changed. "Well, he certainly blushes like a young lady. No matter, my friend, I will turn you into a first-class Sovietologist."

Dr. Sidorov looked at Mr. Green again. "Nathaniel, I think you have brought me a promising and intriguing student. Please leave this podmenysh (changeling) with me so we can start getting acquainted and start the studies." Green looked at Charles. "Welcome to OSS62, comrade!" Green turned and exited the room.

Sidorov gestured to Charles to go over and sit on the love seat. As Sidorov took his seat in the over-stuffed chair, he remarked. "Say comrade in Russkiy." Charles replied, "Tovarishch!"

The tutor grinned. "Well said! You sound like a good party man, and spoken like a Muscovite! My friend, we are going to work very hard this year, but I must say, I think you are going to be fun to work with. So tell me why you want to be a young lady? Please explain it in Russkiy if you can." Charles swallowed hard!

Feb 12th 6:15pm Norwalk, CT–Just an Ordinary Day at Work

Charles arrived home from work and gave his wife Louise a hug and a kiss. As they held each other, she whispered to him. "Well, how was the first day?" He nuzzled up to her ear and whispered. "Walls have ears! Day job looks mundane as hell. The job behind the job is George Smiley stuff."

Louise returned the endearment and snuggled up to his earlobe and began gnawing on it with alternate moments of little kisses and whispering. "So what is this year about?" Again Charles returns to nibbling on her ear, "Cambridge style tutoring in everything Russian." Louise gently pulled back and gave him a questioned look. Charles resumed the necking style whispering, "The class is less Smiley and more Lee Strasberg stuff. It's about becoming native." He could not see her eyes get wide with surprise and interest.

Then he whispered, "I want you to read up on Helen Keller." Louise leaned back and gave him a strange look. Then he spoke up, "Hey honey, let's go to Stew Leonard's dairy and get some frozen yogurt!"

After they got in the car, Charles took a moment to hold Louise's hand and pantomime scribbling on her palm. When she realized what he was conveying, she remarked. "I'm going to the library tomorrow and get a library card."

Before starting the car, Charles reached into his sport jacket pocket and retrieved his employee ID card and handed it to her. Louise examined the North American Surveying photo ID card with interest. "So you've gone from being in the Navy and nuclear submarines to being in the Surveying business?" He laughed as he started the couple's Chevy van. "Data analysis is data analysis."

The next day, Louise went to the Norwalk Library and got a library card and several books in both Finger Spelling and American Sign Language to read.

Six Months Later
Aug 12th 9:00 AM Greenwich, CT–North American Surveying

Nathaniel Green was reading his morning Profs messages when he heard a knock at the door. He simply said, "Come!" The door opened and Dr. Alexei Sidorov entered the office. "Good morning, Alexei! To what do I owe this pleasure?" Green asked as he gestured for the staff tutor to take a seat.

After Dr. Sidorov seated himself, he remained quiet for a few moments before speaking, which was his style. "It's about Moira." Green wrinkled his nose, "You mean Charles." Alexei gave the manager a perplexed look. "Nathaniel, I've lectured, tutored language, coached Russian culture and, yes, I've even had a few juicy and pleasurable philosophical and academic arguments with Stewart every workday for the past six months." Sidorov paused and remarked after a moment, "Nathaniel that's a young woman pretending to be a man." Green said nothing. Then Sidorov added, "That human being is going to be one hell of an operative when we're done with training him or her...or them!"

Green had a troubled look on his face. "Alexei, I can't possibly ask Stewart to change genders now. That's a deeply personal thing and, as I understand it, a profoundly personal evolution."

Sidorov softly pounded his fist on the arm of his chair. "Damn it, Nathaniel. She's among the best field officer candidates I've ever had. Frankly put, I'm trying to bring out the very best from her. But..."

Green gave the professor a concerned look. "But what?"

"Stewart is holding back that genuine self." Sidorov said earnestly. Then he added, "Actually, I came up here to get your permission to take Charles on the train to New York City and to Brighton Beach for a day or two to test his interpersonal skills in a Russian-speaking community."

Green looked puzzled. "You just told me Charles is projecting confusing femininity. Won't that be problematic?"

Sidorov shook his head gently with a smirk. "Nathaniel, I could put Charles in a Soviet sailor's uniform right now and pass him off as a nice young man from Murmansk tomorrow, and a catch for any young lady in the Russian neighborhood. He projects all that kind of charming male military bearing."

Green assumed a curious expression. "What about the feminine energy you spoke of earlier?" Sidorov smiled thoughtfully. "From our very first conversation, I told Stewart to relax and present the genuine self from within while in our private tutoring room. Moira is months ahead of every other candidate I've ever taught for you. Normally I wouldn't take a tutoring student to Brighton Beach or Sheepshead Bay until month eleven or twelve, you know that."

"Alexi, I'm ok with your proposed trip with one condition." Green said and added, "I want you to put Charles in a Soviet officer's uniform and pass him off as a Soviet Naval Lieutenant and member of the Soviet embassy staff. Let's see if the chicks all fall for him like you suggested."

Dr. Sidorov grinned, "I'll present him as my nephew Leytenant Charl'z Sidorov from Murmansk!"

"Alexi, as you know, much of this job is deep immersion character acting and impersonation. Let's see how the kid does! And tell him not to drop character for any reason whatsoever, no matter what happens."

Dr. Sidorov rose from his chair smirking and remarked in Russian, "Spasibo, Mister Grin. YA pozabochus' ob etom." (Thank You Mr. Green. I will see to it.)

Aug 12th 1 PM Greenwich, CT–The Tutoring Room

After lunch, Charles entered the Tutoring Room. As Professor Sidorov was already present. Charles offered proper courtesies speaking only Russian, as was the proper form in the tutoring room. "Good Afternoon, Dr. Sidorov." The professor returned the formal courtesy. "Good Afternoon Mr. Stewart"

Sidorov gestured for Charles to sit down. Sidorov began. "Normally at this stage of training, I like to take the student to a real-world Russian speaking community and let you immerse yourself as a visiting guest and just experience day to day conversational Russian and let you get comfortable interacting with just plain folks. Usually in a family style setting."

Charles smiled. "That sounds fun." In a more fatherly tone, Sidorov added, "There's a little kink. I need an excuse to tell these folks and for them to entertain us and perhaps show us hospitality and conceivably put us up for the weekend. Are you game for this?" Charles shrugged his shoulders. "Sure."

Sidorov continued. "So let's put your community theater experience to work for this effort." Charles smirked. Sidorov leaned in. "Moira, this is going to be an assault on your femininity, but this is necessary. I need you to go down to the corner barbershop and get a Navy style haircut. I need you to be clean cut, and squared away."

Charles raised an eyebrow. "What exactly are we going to do?"

Sidorov smiled, "I'm going to dress you in a Soviet Naval Officers Uniform and present you as my nephew Leytenant Charl'z Mikhailovich Sidorov from Murmansk! The people I am taking you to are all former Soviet citizens and they will want to roll out the red carpet to you."

Charles stood up. "Okay professor, I'll be back after I get the haircut." About an hour later, Charles returned to the tutoring room, appearing clean-cut and military in style. When he arrived, Dr. Sidorov was having tea with a young woman and addressed Charles in English, "Charles, this delightful lady is going to take you next door and take your picture." Emma led the way next door to the personnel office and to the photo area where he got his employee id six months before. "Can't we just use my old badge picture?"

Emma shook her head. "It's not military enough. Here, put this on." She handed him a white button-up shirt and handed him a dark navy-blue clip-on tie, then she helped him put on a dark navy blue uniform jacket with Lieutenant rank shoulder boards. Emma moved Charles in front of the camera and in front of a neutral background and took several serious poses and a couple of smiling. When she was done, and he was taking off the uniform jacket, he asked, "What was all that for?" Emma simply answered, "We can't have you walking around in a Soviet officer's uniform without proper ID now can we."

Charles walked back to the Tutor room. After entering, he addressed Professor Sidorov, "Was all that necessary?" Sidorov gestured for him to take a seat. "When you become a field officer. During mission prep, they will dress you in all appropriate clothing. Right down to your underwear. Everything you wear must be genuine. So on Thursday morning when you arrive here, a dresser will have you strip and put all your Charles clothing in a box or a plastic bag. Then the dresser will dress you from head to toe. And the staff will provide you with suitable ID for your field character, Leytenant Charl'z Sidorov, in this case."

"You mean like an ID card with the picture I just posed for?" Charles asked. Sidorov nodded and added, "and a set of Soviet dog tags."

Charles looked puzzled. "Seems like a lot of trouble for us to go through to just visit some local Russian folks." Sidorov held up a finger, "What if while you're there some little kid in the house wants to see your ID or your dog tags? Add to that, the staff here needs to keep up their skills at dressing and equipping field operatives. Besides, our brief visit gives them an opportunity to keep up their procedures quals." Charles got a troubled look on his face. "How do I explain the hair cut to my wife tonight and the trip later this week?"

Sidorov grinned. "You work for a surveying company and you will accompany a team to survey some land in marshland. The bugs are notorious for getting in your hair."

Aug 14th 9am Tutoring Room

A gentleman from the facility dressing team assisted Charles with stripping his work clothes and dropping them into a box. Once Charles was down to his underwear, the man from the facility dressing team turned away and waited patiently as Charles removed his underwear. The dresser with his back turned to Charles held out another pair of boxer shorts and a white T-shirt. Charles donned the new undergarments, then the dresser handed him a set of Soviet style dog tags.

Next, the dresser turned and faced Charles and handed him a pair of navy-blue trousers, which Charles quickly put on. The next item was a button-up white shirt. Once Charles buttoned up the white shirt, the dresser directed him to turn up the shirt collar.

Charles looked at the man. "What, no clip-on tie?" The man casually said. "Soviet Naval officers don't wear clip on ties." Then the dresser asked. "You do know how to tie a traditional tie properly, right?" Charles simply stated. "I've been tying my own ties since I was twelve." Then the man asked. "Do you require a mirror?" Charles casually said, "No."

After Charles had the necktie finished, he turned down the shirt collar. The dresser handed Charles a tie clip, which he studied for a few moments. "What's this about?" The dresser casually answered. "It's a memorial clip celebrating the 1917 October revolution. These kinds of fashion accessories items are common in the USSR." Next, the dresser held open a navy-blue dress jacket with Leytenant shoulder boards. Charles put his arms back into the sleeves and slipped on the uniform jacket garment. Once he had adjusted it, he buttoned it up.

The dresser handed Charles a service hat, then stepped back and looked Charles over. The dresser, speaking rough Russian, remarked. "Comrade, you look like a proper young naval officer."

Finally, the dresser held up a mirror to Charles. Looking in the mirror, Charles placed two fingers on his nose and adjusted the bill of the service hat. The dresser smiled at Charles. "You clearly know how to wear a dress uniform."

The dresser looked pleased with himself. He handed Leytenant Charl'z a wallet. "The wallet has your Soviet naval ID, your Soviet driver's license and your Embassy ID card as well. Please take a few minutes and memorize your military serial number on your Naval ID card. There are about 300 rubles of Russian currency and about $50.00 in small US currency bills." Leytenant Charl'z placed the wallet in the back of his pants pocket. Charles asked, "What do I do at the Russian embassy?" The dresser added, "You are a Jr. staff officer to the Naval attaché at the embassy."

Finally, the dresser handed him a handkerchief. "Most officers carry it in the uniform jacket pocket." The dresser asked to see Charles' right ring finger. The dresser pulled out a jeweler's ring sizing tool and placed it on his ring finger. "Ah, you're a size 10." The dresser opened up a wooden box that resembled a cigar box that was full of signet rings and removed a ring. The dresser placed the signet ring onto Charles' finger. "That's a Soviet Naval Academy ring. Class of '74, you are all set, Leytenant Charl'z Mikhailovich Sidorov." The dresser remarked proudly.

Then he walked over to the tutor-room door and opened it, and invited Dr. Sidorov in. The Professor stepped in and looked Charles up and down, taking a few moments to carefully inspect him. When he was done, he gave a smiling nod to the dresser. Then Sidorov remarked, speaking Russian. "My dear nephew, Leytenant Charl'z Mikhailovich Sidorov, it is truly good to see you again. You're looking fit."

Dr. Sidorov stepped over to a desk phone and dialed an extension. "Nathaniel, please come to the tutoring room. I have a young naval officer I want you to meet." The professor hung up the phone. "My friend, you look great."

A few minutes later, Nathaniel Green entered the tutoring room. Upon entering, he stopped dead in his tracks. Then Green slowly walked around the young Soviet officer, also giving him a discerning eye. Green looked at the dresser. "Sam, you and your folks did a wonderful job! The kid looks terrific!"

Mr. Green got into Leytenant Sidorov's face. "Lieutenant, I want you to remain in deep character no matter what happens! I don't care what knucklehead insults you on the train or subway. You don't understand or speak English, period! I don't care if Alexi gets run over by a truck! You do not speak or understand angliyskiy, no matter what, play it dumb. You grew up in Murmansk and you are a Jr. staff officer to the Naval attaché at the embassy, period! Got it?"

Leytenant Charl'z Sidorov shrugged his shoulders with a puzzled look on his face and remarked in a frustrated tone. "YA ne govoryu po-angliyski!" (I don't speak English!)

Green nodded and gave Dr. Sidorov a smile of approval and commented in Russian, "Otlichnyy" (Excellent) Sidorov simply smiled like a proud father! Then Green looked at Sam, the dresser. "Sam, could you get Leytenant Sidorov some shoes and socks?" All four men broke out laughing.

Aug 14th 11 AM Amtrak Commuter Train

Dr. Alexi Sidorov and Leytenant Charl'z Sidorov had embarked on an Amtrak Commuter Train bound for a 32-minute ride to Grand Central Station. Sidorov explained to his faux nephew. Once they arrived at Grand Central Station, they would take the NYC subway to the 16th street station, where they would catch the BMT Brighton Line for an hour-long train ride to Brighton Beach.

While on the Amtrak train, various passengers walking back and forth on the aisle seemed to note the smartly dressed military officer. Finally, two young men in their late twenties walked up to the two men and one of them asked what kind of military uniform is that?

Alexi Sidorov simply answered, "This young man is my nephew, and he is a Soviet Naval Lieutenant who works at the Russian embassy in Washington, DC." One of the two passengers remarked, "I thought so! He's a fucking Russki!" The young man bent down and got into the young naval officer's face. "We don't need you fucking Russians in our country." Lt. Charl'z assumed an expression of vacancy and smiled with a toothy smile. Alexi spoke up. "Gentleman, he doesn't speak a word of English."

The other male passenger commented. "Perhaps he should learn to speak some English before he visits America!" Dr. Sidorov pleasantly responded. "My nephew was recently stationed here for the next three years. It's my understanding that he'll be taking English lessons as part of his duties." The two abrasive men shook their heads and walked away. Charl'z responded in Russian. "I suppose those were the type of knuckleheads that comrade Green was speaking of." Sidorov simply remarked, "Indeed."

Once Alexi and Charl'z arrived at Grand Central station, they made their way to the subways and took a subway train to 16th St. Where Alexi led Charl'z to the BMT Brighton line where Dr. Sidorov purchased tickets for the train to Brighton beach. Since this was a midday train, it was virtually empty. Dr. Sidorov explained that the train would be packed to standing room only during rush hour.

Dr. Sidorov took this opportunity to discuss the folks he planned for the two of them to visit. "We are going to visit an old friend of mine, Ilya, and Galina Abramov. The couple has three daughters and a son. The daughters are Lara, Nina and Mischa and their young brother is Kirill."

Charl'z said nothing. Then, after a moment, he asked. "Does the family make American food or homemade Russian food?" Alexi simply responded. "I suspect Galina will make traditional Russian dishes. Perhaps a little bit of both."

Charl'z asked. "Is the Abramov family from Murmansk?" Alexi spoke up frankly. "Ilya and Galina immigrated here when Lara was a baby. But all the children essentially grew up in a Russian-speaking household and learned their languages on their mother's knee and on their father's lap. I dare say the daughters are Russian and English-speaking American kids who like rock'n'roll. The last I heard, at least two of the girls think Donny Osmond is a dreamy heartthrob."

Charl'z moaned. Alexi turned his head and gave Charl'z a questioning look. "May I ask who Moira had a passion for?" Charl'z said nothing. Alexi assumed an intrigued expression. "Oh, Come,

Come miss Soviet Naval Lieutenant. Who warmed your heart at that age?" Charl'z briefly assumed a sheepish, blushing countenance. "I had the hots for Barbara Streisand."

Alexi shifted his sitting posture and turned toward Charl'z and faced him squarely. "My friend, your secrets stays with me. I never imagined the depth of your complexity. Whatever you say to me will always stay with me." The still blushing Charl'z whispered. "Thank you."

When the train arrived in Brighton Beach, Alexi led the way for about an eight-block stroll to the Abramov household. The two men walked up the steps. Alexi remarked, "If they ask where you grew up. Say in the shipyard district, but don't elaborate." Charl'z curtly replied, "Got it."

Alexi knocked on the door. A few moments later, a teenage girl opened the door and immediately recognized Alexi Sidorov. Speaking Russian, she shouted, "Mom, Doctor Sidorov is here!" Then the young woman laid eyes on the handsome naval officer. "Who are you?" She said while looking at the handsome Charl'z with dreamy eyes. Alexi answered, "This is my nephew, Leytenant Charl'z Sidorov."

Galina Abramov appeared at the door and gave Alexi an endearing hug. "It's so good to see you, Alexi. It's been a long time." Then her eyes caught sight of the sailor. "Alexi? Who's this handsome young man?"

"This is my nephew, naval Leytenant Charl'z Mikhailovich Sidorov. He's newly assigned to the Soviet embassy for the next few years." Alexi said and made further introductions. "Charl'z, this is Mrs. Galina Abramov and her daughter Nina." Galina shook hands with Leytenant Sidorov. "Please come in and stay a while. Would either of you like coffee, or tea ...?"

Aug 14th 3:15pm - Abramov Residence

In the kitchen, Mrs. Abramov made tea for her two unexpected guests while carrying on a conversation with both of them in household Russian. Finally, she poured tea for the three of them. With a proud smile, Mrs. Abramov placed a small plate of apricot kolacky cookies on the table. Alexi looked at the cookies. "Are they bakery fare or homemade?"

Galina smiled proudly. "My two eldest made these and I'm quite delighted with how they turned out. Please try them." Both men tasted the kolackies. After a moment to savor the flavor, the two men gave Mrs. Abramov looks of approval.

That's when Galina gave Alexi a questioning look and asked. "Please stay for dinner." She said to Alexi. "Are you sure it won't be an imposition?" He asked. She shook her head. "Not at all. I've got more than enough for everyone. I've just made a forshmak baked casserole as an appetizer and a huge fresh pot of homemade borscht."

Then she turned to Charl'z. "Mr. Naval Leytenant, I'd bet good money it's been a good while since you've had a proper home cooked meal." Charl'z modestly nodded that it had been.

"Then it's settled." Mrs. Abramov remarked. Then she frowned at Alexi. "Please tell me you aren't planning on taking that train back to Greenwich tonight, are you?"

Alexi spoke plainly, "Originally, I had just planned to bring Charl'z down for the day to visit the Russian-American Club and introduce him around. We really had only planned a day trip and perhaps dropping by to say hello."

Mrs. Abramov hollered for her two eldest daughters, Lara and Nina. The teens promptly appeared in the kitchen. "Ladies, would you take the good Leytenant Sidorov for a walk down by the beach and be sure to show him the lovely shops along the beachfront?" Both of the young women lit up and agreed to take the handsome naval officer for a walk. Alexi Sidorov gave Charl'z a confirming nod to go with the teens. He stood up from the kitchen table and smiled at the teens. "Ladies, give me a moment to get my hat and we'll go see the sights." As Charl'z stood, he assumed an attentive posture toward his teacher and left the kitchen with the teens.

After it was clear that the three of them were walking toward the beach, Mrs. Abramov took her seat at the kitchen table. She removed a cigarette from a pack on the table and offered one to Alexi. He simply gestured no. She lit her smoke, took a drag, and seemed to study Alexi for a few moments.

"Is he one of your private students?" She asked casually. Alexi nodded in the affirmative. She took another puff of her smoke. "He's different from the usual types you train. He doesn't have the tough edge that most of your students have." She paused, seeming to ponder her next words. "The last five or six you've brought here; I was afraid to leave my children around them. This one is polite and ..." She paused and struggled for a word. Alexi spoke up, "Gentle?"

She nodded her head as she crushed out her smoke. "Well, we certainly aren't winning the Cold War with muscle and bravado, are we?" Galina remarked. Alexi commented, "I brought him down here to charm the pants off the intellectuals down at the club. If he succeeds. She's going to be a new kind of operative." Galina twitched. "She?"

Alex smiled. "A slip of the tongue." Galina leaned closer. "Alexi, be square with me." He nodded and remarked. "Colleague rules of privacy apply. Understood."

"Yes, of course, always." She said. He asked. "When you used to work for the KGB, who were the deadliest agents?" She uttered a slight laugh. "The men with their machine guns, or the women with smarts and pure guile." Alexi took on a thoughtful look. "I've worked with that young man every workday for six months. And I can only say she is the most talented person I've ever trained to be a Sovietologist. Can you imagine the implications?"

Galina lit up another cigarette. Took a few drags and seemed to be fascinated with the kitchen cabinets behind and above Alexi's head. After a few minutes, she looked at Alexi and asked. "What have you built?"

He simply shook his head. "I built nothing! She came that way. A healthy, smart and creative woman trapped in a man's body. I am simply her tutor in the Art of Sovietology."

Galina took several more thoughtful drags before crushing out her cigarette. "Alexi, you two must stay the night and take Leytenant Charl'z Sidorov to the Russian-American club. I want to watch him-her take some stuffy intellectuals apart in cultural debates!"

Alexi assumed a devious smile. "Did I tell you she plays a deadly game of chess?" Galina suddenly had the look of a kid on Christmas morning and began pounding on her kitchen table, and shouted. "YES, YES!"

Aug 14th 7:00pm - Abramov Residence

A lovely family dinner was over with. In the kitchen, the two youngest daughters, Nina and Mischa, were dutifully washing the evening's dishes.

In the living room, Galina quietly focused on a piece of hand sewing. Across from her were her husband, Ilya, and long-time friend Alexi, both men enjoying some after-dinner smoking. Ilya with his favorite pipe and Alexi with a pipe he borrowed from Ilya. The conversation was about everything and nothing, simply a catch-up between two old friends.

In the dining room, the Abramov family's nine-year-old son Kirill was quietly and intensely watching his eldest sister Lara doing battle with Charl'z on the family chess board. Deep into her third game, she was using every masterful move her parents had taught her. But no matter what she did, it always ended with Charl'z whispering, "Check and mate!"

She politely shook hands with Charl'z before whining, "Mom, he did it to me again." In the living room, the three older adults all gave each other knowing smirks and winks. Galina carefully put aside her sewing and stepped into the dining room and remarked to her eldest. "Lara, remember, each loss is another lesson in your chess journey."

Then she directed. "Lara, please go into the living room and close the pocket doors so we can have some game privacy." She looked at her son. "Kirill, please close the door to the kitchen and go upstairs and get into your nightclothes and do your bedtime reading. I have private chess business with the good Leytenant here." The two children giggled as they did as their mother asked, knowing that she was a chess master in her own right.

Galina stood behind the chair her daughter had been sitting in. "My eldest is very good at chess and you whipped her three times. As the Mother Bear in this family, it's up to me to defend this house's honor." Charl'z lowered his eyes and Charl'z said nothing. Then Galina challenged, "Alright, Miss Leytenant, are you ready for a serious chess game, woman to woman?"

Galina glimpsed sheer terror in Charl'z' eyes when he looked up at her. But then she watched as a look of calm and resolve returned to her opponent's face. Charl'z politely nodded his head and gestured to her chair. Galina stepped over to her dining room buffet and opened a drawer. She retrieved a chess clock and placed it on the dining room table next to the chess board. After Galina had taken her seat. She sat for a few moments and seemed to study Charl'z. Then, as if by magic, in a much softer tone and feminine voice, Charl'z stated. "You have white. You have the first move, Madame."

Galina made her first move and touched the chess clock button. Charl'z made the next move and returned the chess clock timekeeping back to Galina. Back and forth for the next 37 minutes, the war between the two chess aficionados ensued. When it was all over, Galina and Charl'z opened the pocket doors and entered the living room. Charl'z had a heavy look on his face and commented. "Mrs. Abramov whipped my ass!" Alexi and Ilya looked at Galina. So you triumphed! She shook her head. "Actually, Charl'z won. I had to play a defensive game. Charl'z was relentless. I can't wait to see him down at the club tomorrow!"

Aug 15th 10:30 AM–Brighton Beach Russian-American Club

Charl'z and Alexi had had a wonderful brunch at the Russian American club. The young man looked dashing in his Soviet naval lieutenant's uniform and it had attracted a great deal of attention from the former Soviet persons in the club.

As Doctor Sidorov had privately hoped, Charl'z received invitations to several large tables of conversation over coffee and donuts. He found it difficult to adhere to the rule of no English because of the mixture of conversational Russian with occasional English words dropped in. In order to keep up the façade that he knew no English, Charl'z found himself stopping the conversation to qualify the non-Russian word meanings from the English words used. He thought to himself that it was just an artifact of his performance.

Doctor Sidorov had written Charl'z's name on the chess game queue chalkboard. It was his understanding that the chess games did not begin until at least 11:00 in the morning. Several people had written their names under Charl'z's. At the club, when many people lined up and wrote their names under one person's name, it was a sign they assumed this new person was fresh meat for the gaming slaughter. The club's membership of chess players had absolutely no idea who they were going to be dealing with.

At 11:00 AM, a game referee made an announcement on the public address system that the gaming could now begin. Alexi led Charl'z over to a long club table. On the table was a chessboard. Next to the chessboard was a chess clock. Charl'z stood behind his chair and waited for his first opponent. A young man, perhaps 18 years-old walked up to the chair opposite Charl'z and, speaking English, stated, "I would like to play you Sir." Charl'z looked to Alexi, who was standing next to Charl'z and translated, keeping up the facade. That Charl'z spoke no English.

The young man pulled out the chair and took a seat. Charl'z looked at the man speaking Russian and said. "You have white. Please begin." The young man answered back in Russian simply. "Very well." He made his move and started the clock. Charl'z made his move and returned the clock. The game went on for about 12 minutes. When Charl'z called. "Checkmate."

The onlookers had intrigued looks. Two people who had watched the game walked over to the blackboard and scratched their names from Charl'z's queue list. The next person from the queue list walked over to the chair and greeted Charl'z in flawless Russian, and said, "Sir, I wish to play you." Charl'z nodded and politely responded. "Greetings welcome." Again, Charl'z began the game. "You have white sir. Proceed."

The man made his move and touched the button on the clock. The two men played their moves and back and forth, each touched the clock. 15 minutes later, they were done. Charl'z simply said, "Checkmate, my friend." They reached across the table and shook hands. As all well-mannered chess players often do.

Again, another man who had watched the game walked up to the chalkboard and scratched his name from the queue of perspective challengers. But two more people wrote their names under Charl'z's queue list.

A woman stepped up to the opponent's chair and said. "I've never played a naval officer before, especially one that's in the Soviet Navy. I would like to play a game of chess with you, sir."

Charl'z politely gestured at the chair for the opponent. "I look forward to it," Charl'z simply said. Charl'z did his customary speech. "Madame, you have white. Please begin."

The woman made her move and actuated the clock. The two chess aficionados played their moves and their strategies. 21 minutes later. Charl'z simply said. "Checkmate." The woman studied the board for a few moments. She reached across the table and shook hands and remarked. "That was amazing." She got up and left.

Alexi glanced over to the chalkboard for the next person who was on Charl'z's list, but that name was now scratched out. Charl'z got up and stated he was going to the men's room and would be right back. Alexi studied the board. There were five more names on the queue. Then a man in a three-piece business suit came into the club. He walked over to the chalkboard of different players and studied it, being especially intrigued by the list of Charl'z challengers. He walked over to another man and spoke to him for a few moments. That man walked over, scratched his name off the list and wrote in the name of the three-piece suit man who had just spoken to him.

When Charl'z returned, Alexi leaned into him. "My friend, someone has jumped to the front of the queue and I believe this is going to be a powerful player. Be on your best guard." Charl'z simply said, "Bring it on. There's been very little challenge, Lara Abramov could have beat most of them."

The next opponent was the man who jumped ahead in the queue. The man was perhaps in his 40s and he looked to be very professional in manner. He stood behind the opponent's chair and said, speaking Russian. "Leytenant, I don't think we've ever had the pleasure of hosting a Soviet naval officer here in our club. I wish to play a game of chess with you, sir. I might add that I am here to defend America on this chessboard." Charl'z smiled at the man. "Very well, you have white. Please begin."

The man pulled out his chair and slid it up close. He made his first move and started the clock. The game went on between the two players for 49 minutes. Finally Charl'z said. "Checkmate."

The man studied the board carefully. He looked extremely disturbed and almost angry. He dropped his fist on the table then he gained control over his emotion, reached across the chest board and shook hands with Charl'z. "That was a unique game, Leytenant."

Several hours later, when Alexi and Charl'z were leaving the club, Charl'z had played 18 games of chess, most lasting no longer than 10 or 12 minutes, a couple lasting nearly an hour. The list of players who chose not to play was upwards of twelve. Alexei was delighted with Charl'z's skill and how well he conducted himself and the quality of the Russian he was speaking in this conversational Russian environment. Charl'z had gained fans who applauded him.

He grinned and simply thanked them all as he put his naval service hat on his head. He followed Alexi out of the club. As they got out onto the sidewalk. Two men walked up to Alexi and flashed badges and said in English we are from immigration. One immigration man pointed at Charl'z and said. "He's a Soviet military officer, and he's not supposed to be here."

Charl'z did as he was supposed to do. He simply gave the men a vacant, non-understanding look. Alexi spoke up, "Gentlemen, he does not speak any English. He does not understand. I will tell him." Then quickly in Russian, Alexi remarked. "Relax, you know the rules about being captured!" Charl'z looked at Alexi and answered simply. "Yes, comrade." A moment later, one of the immigration agents put handcuffs on Charl'z and led him over to a car, put a hand on his head and helped put him in the back seat. A few minutes later, they drove off with Leytenant Charl'z Sidorov.

The club members, who were standing outside on the sidewalk, were shocked and dismayed at what had just transpired. All except for the man in the three-piece suit, he seemed to have a look of satisfaction. "Take that, you commie bastard!" He said under his breath.

The club members were asking Alexi about what had just happened. Alexi simply said, "I don't know." Alexi went back into the club and walked up to the day manager. He explained what had happened on the front sidewalk and asked them to use their office phone. The manager quickly obliged. Alexi called the offices of North American Surveying and ask for Mr. Green. A few moments later, the switchboard put Alexi through. Green answered the phone and said. "Nathaniel Green, this is an unsecured line. May I help you?"

Alexi said, "Nathaniel, this is Alexi. We have a problem. Immigration officers have arrested our Soviet sailor! They took him away in handcuffs!" There was a momentary silence on the phone line, then Nathaniel simply said. "Oh Shit!"

Aug 15th 2pm–Immigration & Naturalization Service NYC District

They led Charl'z through the front lobby and took him to an interview room. The immigration officer who had handcuffed him removed the cuffs. The INS officer remarked to the Soviet Naval officer, "You relax. Someone will be into speak to you shortly."

Charl'z gave the man a questioning look and simply said in Russian, "YA ne govoryu po-angliyski!" (I don't speak English!) The INS officer shrugged his shoulders and left the room.

Charl'z thought to himself, was this part of the test that Dr. Sidorov and Mr. Green put new tutor students through? But then he wondered, was this whole thing an unforeseen fluke? He relaxed. He knew Mr. Green and Dr. Sidorov would get him out of this predicament.

After about 20 minutes, a woman entered the room carrying a notebook and sat down. With her was a uniformed security guard. The woman began speaking in Russian. "Good afternoon. My name is Miss Popov. Who are you?" Charl'z simply answered,

"I am Leytenant Charl'z Mikhailovich Sidorov Navy serial ID number 37529338."

Miss Popov simply remarked. "Leytenant, you are not a prisoner of war." She explained, "Leytenant, we are detaining you because of a complaint that you disrupted the Russian American club and there is a suspicion that you are here illegally." Charl'z knew he wasn't supposed to speak English, he knew it was necessary not to break cover.

He simply answered. "I am Leytenant Charl'z Mikhailovich Sidorov Navy serial ID number 37529338."

Miss Popov opened a folder. "I have your naval ID card, your Soviet driver's license, and your ID card from the Soviet embassy. I know who you are. Leytenant, why were you at the Russian American club? Why are you not at the embassy in Washington, DC? Where you a courier to the Consulate-General of Russia here in New York City?"

"I am Leytenant Charl'z Mikhailovich Sidorov Navy serial ID number 37529338."

Miss Popov asked, "Leytenant, were you causing a disruption at the Russian American club at Brighton beach?" Charl'z simply said. "No, not at all." Miss Popov nodded and queried, "What were you doing at the Russian American club?"

Charl'z said simply, "I ate brunch with members and afterwards I played 18 games of chess with various members of the club."

Miss Popov gave Charl'z a questioned look. "Did you cause any trouble?"

Charl'z simply commented, "My victory over them disappointed several chess players. One man pounded his fists on the table because he lost. I cannot help that I'm a skillful chess player." Miss Popov gave Charl'z a curious look. "Did anyone shout at you or scream at you when they lost their game of chess?"

Charl'z nodded his head and with an innocent look on his face. "One man who was dressed in a three-piece suit. He lost; he pounded his fists on the table. The man told me he was going to defend America with his game of chess. He lost like everyone else. He was very bitter."

Miss Popov studied him for a few moments. "Are you saying you won all the games of chess?"

Charl'z nodded, "Yes, I did, all 18 games. The chess referee at that club can confirm this."

Miss Popov folded her arms, seeming to study him. "Leytenant, how long have you been in the Soviet Navy?"

He smiled at her. "I am a graduate of this Soviet Naval Academy class of 1974. Charl'z held out his hand and showed her his class ring. Popov inspected the Soviet officer's signet ring." She smiled. "Did you do well at the Naval Academy?" She asked.

Charl'z studied the table for a moment, then he remarked. "I ranked #20 of 400."

Miss Popov paused, then remarked, "We called the Soviet embassy. They told us they'd never heard of you. Can you explain this? After all, you have all the proper identification."

Charl'z gave her a puzzled look. "Did you inform them I was accused of causing a disruption and trouble?" Charl'z asked. The middle-aged woman simply nodded her head. Charl'z had a disappointed look on his face. "Then I suppose my home government has disavowed me. Perhaps I am now a non-citizen. I suppose that makes me a man without a country."

"Stop." She said. "No one said that you are disavowed. No one has said that you're no longer a Soviet citizen." Charl'z studied her for a moment. "But you said that they did not know me. That they said they have never heard of me, correct?"

"Yes, that is what they said." Miss Popov answered.

Charl'z explained. "In the Soviet Union, if someone falls out of favor or is an inconvenient problem. They disappear. In the coming days, weeks and months, records just disappear. They just cease to exist in all official records. The more prominent they are, someone simply paints them out of photographs. Anybody with a logical mind could assume they do not claim me therefore, they must consider me a disgrace. I have embarrassed them. Of course, it could be worse. I could have done it in front of my senior officers. They might have taken me out and had me shot. At least I am still breathing, but in the end, it is still the same thing. You're telling me my country does not want me and does not claim me; therefore, I must be a man without a country!" Charl'z said with a look of sincere sadness.

Miss Popov asked, "You were with a man at the Russian American club, correct?" He nodded, "Yes, Professor Alexi Sidorov. He is my uncle on my mother's side of the family. Uncle Alexi was introducing me to his friends at the Russian-American club. He thought it would be fun for me to have brunch with former Soviets and play several rounds of very challenging chess with the best among them. Perhaps I have said too much?" Charl'z shook his head with an expression of helplessness. "Are you going to put me in a cell? Am I going to be incarcerated in your facility?"

Popov expressed dismay at the Leytenant and stated, "I don't know what is going to become of you, but while you are with us, we will treat you well."

Charl'z stated firmly, "In my country they said that the United States puts on a friendly face, a pleasant face, but that they truly torture prisoners of war and other persons from countries they have deemed to be evil. Therefore, unless I am told otherwise, I will consider myself a prisoner of the Cold War and I will say nothing further. As I have stated, I am Leytenant Charl'z

Mikhailovich Sidorov, Navy serial ID number 37529338." Charl'z folded his arms, turned his head and seemed to just study the blank beige wall.

Miss Popov stood up with her folder and her notepad. Charl'z looked at her. "You say that I am not a prisoner of war?" Miss Popov replied. "You are not." "Madame." Charl'z remarked, "Appearances suggest that my country no longer recognizes me. Therefore, that makes me a man without a country. May I respectfully request political and humanitarian asylum in the United States of America?"

Miss Popov's eyes got wide. "Leytenant, let's not get ahead of ourselves. Presently, we truly do not know what your status is. But once we examine everything, if you truly are a man without a country, The United States of America will welcome you."

Aug 15th 4:17pm–North American Surveying

Back at North American Surveying, Mr. Green was calling in favors with the local CIA field office in New York City. Mr. Green attempted to find someone who would respectfully visit their facility and rescue Leytenant Sidorov. Of course, being August and a Friday afternoon, staff at the New York City field office was scant. Anybody with any authority was already gone for the weekend. Out of complete frustration, Mr. Green called the Commander's office at the Brooklyn naval yard. Following a brief conversation with the commanding officer, he established contact with the duty officer at the local unit of the Naval Investigative Service.

Aug15th4:17pm–Immigration& Naturalization Service NYC District

Dr. Alexi Sidorov, meanwhile, had gotten a cab to take him to the INS office in downtown New York City. After he arrived at INS, he spent time with various levels of bureaucrats trying to confirm whether Leytenant Charl'z Sidorov was present. After 30 minutes of pleading, he confirmed Leytenant Charl'z Sidorov was present and sequestered in the building. INS personnel requested that Dr. Sidorov wait patiently.

Finally, Alexi arrived at a case supervisor's office with an escort. Once in the office, the case supervisor instructed Alexi to have a seat. The INS supervisor stood up and announced himself as Peter Reynolds, the case supervisor. He introduced a case manager, Miss Popov, then he asked Alexi and another gentleman to introduce themselves. Alexi stood, and he introduced himself as the uncle of Leytenant Charl'z Sidorov. The other well-dressed gentleman stood up and said, "I am Mr. Anton Orlon, the assistant legal counsel of the Consulate General of the Soviet government. I am here to petition for the release of our naval officer." Alexi remained calm but privately swallowed hard. He thought to himself, how in hell are the Soviets involved? He raised his hand. The supervisor gestured to him.

"With all due respect, why is the Consulate General of the Russian government involved in a misunderstanding with immigration?" Alexi asked. Miss Popov raised her hand. "When we inspected Leytenant Sidorov's ID, we learned he was connected to the Russian embassy in Washington, DC. We called them and they said they had never heard of him. I told Leytenant Sidorov, and he became upset and concerned that he was being disavowed by the Russian government. He further feared that he would be a man without a country."

The Russian government attorney spoke up, "We contacted Moscow. They confirmed his identity and said that he was under orders to join the staff of the embassy's naval attaché."

Alexi said nothing. But in the back of his mind he thought, *Oh my God, those provisioning people are good.* The Soviet lawyer remarked, "I understand our officer was involved with a misadventure at a Russian American club. Was it a bar fight?"

Miss Popov remarked, "No, the Leytenant won 18 games of chess and it upset several patrons." The Russian lawyer smirked. "Americans are such sore losers."

Miss Popov added, "We suspected that the call to INS was, as you would say, a sore loser." Again, the attorney spoke. "I should take him with me. I can arrange transportation to your capital city and our embassy."

Miss Popov looked at her boss and lifted a finger. "There is a problem. Leytenant Charl'z Sidorov, thinking that the Soviet government had disavowed him. Considering that, he's asked for humanitarian and political asylum."

Doctor Sidorov smiled, thinking, *well played Charles.* He raised his hand and remarked. "As an American relative of Leytenant Sidorov, I will sponsor him for his immigration and give him a home and resettle him."

The Soviet lawyer, Mr. Anton Orlon, objected in no uncertain terms. "He is a citizen of the USSR and a respected naval officer. On behalf of my government, I demand the release of Leytenant Charl'z Sidorov to me."

Doctor Sidorov spoke up. "I suppose your government won't forgive him and will still send him to a gulag in Siberia. When your embassy said they never heard of him, it must have scared the hell out of him. Being here in the offices of a foreign government. Miss Popov, did the Lieutenant identify himself properly?" Miss Popov rose. "Yes, he did. In fact, he gave his name rank and serial number four times during my interview. Only when he thought he was being erased. He declared himself a man without a country and asked for asylum."

Mr. Orlan showed clear signs of irritation. "He is our citizen. We demand him back!"

Mr. Reynolds, the supervisor, tapped a small wooden gavel on his desk. Then he said, "Counselor Orlan, I have grave concerns about the treatment this citizen will receive if returned to the USSR. Your government has a clear history of erasing people who have fallen out of favor. I read the transcript of Miss Popov's interview thoroughly."

Reynolds continued, "Lieutenant Sidorov acted as a proper military officer when he thought he was a prisoner of war. He only asked for asylum after he realized the embassy was ignoring his existence. He clearly wondered what in the world would become of him. Wouldn't you? I know I would feel that way if it were me."

Reynolds paused, then added. "Mr. Orlan, if you care to take this matter up with the US Secretary of State, you may if you wish. But at this moment I grant his request for asylum and I'm handing him over to his American uncle. Doctor Sidorov, Miss Popov, will take you to Lieutenant Sidorov. Please take him home and get him settled. We will send you paperwork to arrange for proper documentation. And doctor, please tell him congratulations on winning 18 games of chess!"

An hour later, an INS vehicle dropped Dr. Sidorov and Lieutenant Sidorov at Grand Central station to catch the evening commuter train back to Greenwich, CT. The two men found seats away from prying ears. Still speaking Russian, Dr. Sidorov commented.

"Miss Popov, gave me a copy of the transcript of your interview. Your test weekend did not include any plans for this. The purpose of this trip was strictly to expose you to the Russian community. Obviously, someone had sour grapes about you beating them at chess. Or had an axe to grind about Soviet military personnel. In any case, I apologize for putting you at risk. You conducted yourself with grace under fire and you were smart on your feet. This could have gone badly if the Russian counsel had taken you back to the consulate or to the embassy." Charl'z said nothing and just listened. Sidorov continued. "You've remained in character and still are holding discipline and speak the Russian tongue."

Speaking Russian, Charles replied. "I suspected this went wrong badly. When they told me the embassy never heard of me, I played the man with no country card. And played on their lost soul sympathies."

Doctor Sidorov remarked. "Well, it worked!" Charl'z asked, "Does Mr. Green know what happened?"

Sidorov nodded, "Yes, he knows. He knows I'm your immigration sponsor, and you and I have to do some paperwork." Sidorov said. "And the job you did thrilled Mr. Green."

"What for?" Charles asked. Dr. Sidorov grinned. "My boy, you made Charles so real. We'll all have to do character maintenance. Complete with the immigration paperwork. Naturally, we will have to file taxes for Charles Sidorov to maintain appearances. You, my boy, have created a cover identity we can use in the future. Nathaniel Greene is going to love this."

Charles got quiet. "What happens when I become Moira down the road?" Sidorov got a grim face. "Alas, poor Charl'z will just regretfully die of a case of the flu. He should have gotten his annual shot!" Charles grinned.

Sidorov continued, "Usually my students have several real-life tests. The first one is a visit to the Abramov family and another family. We usually have you solve some sort of predicament. My boy, you just did that in spades. Perhaps your real-life test will be when you let Moira out-of-the-box!" In a soft and feminine tone, she answered. "Perhaps, professor!"

He returned to his male voice. Sidorov added, "The Lieutenant is a civilian now with a green card coming in the mail."

"Will I get to visit the Abramov's occasionally?" Charles asked. Dr. Sidorov stated. "Absolutely! I will let Ilya and Galina know you are out of the Soviet Navy. I'll send them a cover story where Charl'z asked for asylum, and he is now a former Soviet like them. Ilya and Galina will get the story into the local Grapevine and perhaps smoke out whoever called the INS."

"Is that important?" Charles asked. Dr. Sidorov remarked. "You could have easily ended up in the Soviet Navy for real or ended up in a gulag in Siberia. We need to have a word with whomever got you into trouble with the INS. Now, when we get to Greenwich, go home and take your wife out for a nightcap." After a few moments of reflection, Charles simply said. "Thanks for an interesting and adventurous weekend."

Aug 15th 10:25pm–Norwalk, CT–The Stewart Residence

A taxi dropped Charles Stewart off in front of his and Louise's carriage house. As Charles walked down the long winding driveway, Louise came out and met her husband halfway. As they met, they embraced and kissed endearingly. "How was your impersonation and deep immersion event?" Louise asked.

He simply said, "Let's go for a ride." The couple got into their Chevy van and drove around town. While they cruised aimlessly, Charles related his adventure as the Soviet navy lieutenant. After hearing the account, Louise had a look of shock but said nothing. Then, after a few thoughtful moments, she asked. "Are all these little training events preparing me for the day that you won't come back?"

Charles pulled the van off the thoroughfare and pulled into the parking lot of an all-night supermarket. After shutting off the engine, Charles commented. "Good grief, I hope not," he said frankly. Then he added. "Honey, you've seen enough spy movies to know some things can go like clockwork and other things can go really badly. On the other hand, I could get killed in the parking lot of a supermarket if the Fates wish it."

Louise nodded. "I get it. Everything in life carries a risk. When you really think about it, most of your work will be in an office or a cube some place. After all, your primary job is as a Sovietologist and as an analyst. I doubt you will ever see field duty very much."

Charles replied. "I suspect field duty will be very much about identity maintenance duty. To flesh out my cover persona. But honestly, I'm not expecting much experience as a field operative to be honest with you."

Aug 18th 9:30 AM–North American Surveying team meeting.

Charles entered the conference room. Present were five members of the provisioning team. A few moments later, Doctor Sidorov and Mr. Green and the site manager, Mr. Leo Hamilton, entered the room together.

Mr. Hamilton started the meeting. "Ladies and gentlemen, thank you all for coming. All of you have heard by now that Charles Stewart and Dr. Sidorov had a problem with the folks at INS. Even though our field agent trainee was in training, he was fast on his feet and played the INS authorities to give him an asylum green card. It appears the Lieutenant Sidorov persona might be dead for future use. Any thoughts?"

Mrs. Peterson, the manager of the provisioning department, spoke up. "We may need the Lieutenant Sidorov persona for Soviet eastern bloc countries and western European use," Mrs. Peterson suggested. Then she added, "Perhaps he might be useful in the Middle East related to USSR activities. Maybe in Afghanistan. There is a war going on there, after all."

Mr. Green visibly seemed to grimace. "His strengths are in Russian culture. I am not enthused about cross training him in the Middle East language or a laundry list of Middle Eastern cultural nuances." Hamilton spoke up, "Dr. Sidorov, do you have any thoughts on the matter?"

Dr. Sidorov gestured towards Mr. Green. "I concur with Nathaniel cross training Stewart for the Middle East work I believe would disrupt his strengths. He is talented enough to go down the streets of Moscow right now. Charles is going to be a fantastic Sovietologist. Let's keep him in his strengths."

Hamilton looked at Stewart. "Charles, do you have any thoughts about this?" Stewart thought for a moment. "When the INS people picked me up, they would not have messed with me if I had travel papers and transfer orders in my hand."

The provisioning team gave each other looks. Mrs. Peterson acknowledged, "We'll keep that in mind for Dr. Sidorov's future excursions with uniformed Soviet Operatives." Hamilton added, still looking at Stewart. "Charles, you were clear-headed and kept your eye on the ball. From what the documents suggest, you were inventive and adaptive. I, for one, think you are going to be one excellent field operative."

PART TWO
THE DEBRIEFING

May 16th, 1986, 9:30pm-John F. Kennedy International Airport

A government contract international airliner landed at John F. Kennedy International Airport (JFK). Security personnel escorted the aircraft to a vacant hangar at the outer perimeter of the airport property. A group of eight passengers and the aircraft crew exited the aircraft at the hangar. Personnel in hazmat suits and breathing gear escorted them to a screening area inside the hangar.

The team of six male university academics and the male members of the flight crew were all taken to a screening line. The authorities designated a separate screening line for the four stewardesses and the two women from the expedition team. As each woman approached the screening HAZMAT team, a woman Hazmat tech scanned each of the four stewardesses with the Geiger counter. When the Hazmat tech finished scanning each flight attendant with the Geiger counter, she announced, "Clean."

When Anya Gusev and Mashenka Petrova approached the Geiger counter scan, the Hazmat gal waved her wand over the two weary travelers and barked, "They're both hot as hell. Thorough showers and scrub their hair, NOW! And mandatory re-scan!" Then the hazmat team scanned both of the women's identification documents for radioactive contamination that the two of them had been carrying on the field assignment. Again the hazmat tech barked, "Bag all of it, it's all hot!"

Anya and Mashenka each carefully showered per the Hazmat tech's directions. While Mashenka and Anya were still dripping wet, the woman Hazmat tech scanned each of them again. She told Anya, "You're clear! Dry off and get dressed."

When the woman Hazmat tech scanned Mashenka again, there was still a loud sound of clicks from the Geiger counter as she passed the wand over Masha's hair. "Honey, your hair is still pretty hot. Please wash it again. Really scrub it." An obviously exhausted Masha just nodded in compliance. After another ten minutes in the shower shampooing Masha's hair, the woman Hazmat tech scanned it again. "Okay, honey, you're clean now." Go get dried off.

After Mashenka was all dried off. She sat quietly, wrapped in a bathrobe next to Anja. The Medical personnel drew half a dozen tubes of blood from both her and Anya. As well as stool samples from each of them. After showers and medical lab samples. The provisioning team provided the women with fresh, comfortable clothing. This was all irregular testing for both of the field officers and the OSS62 in-house hazmat and medical team alike, but the field mission had been, in a word, unprecedented.

Anya and Masha sat quietly, waiting for what to do next. A woman customs officer wearing disposable decontamination coveralls and rubber gloves walked up to the two women carrying two passports in separate zip-lock bags. She held up one of the zip-lock bags and looked at Anya. "What's your name?" Anya simply said in an accented voice, "Anya Gusev." The customs officer held up the other zip-lock bag, looked at Masha and asked, "What's your name?" She also answered in a heavily accented voice, Mashenka Irina Petrova. The woman customs officer smiled. "I know where you both have been. You two are the bravest women I've ever met!" She paused. "I will ensure the safe disposal of your passports, as they are heavily contaminated. We'll reissue your passports. Anya and Mashenka, welcome home!"

A few minutes later, Dr. Alexi Sidorov walked up to the two field officers. Alexi, with a cheery smile, greeted both Leila Blakely/Anya Gusev and Moira Stewart/Mashenka Petrova. Upon greeting the two women, he could see that they both had an unusual weariness in their eyes. Sidorov knew that the mission had been an unusually difficult one. Anya Gusev, looking very exhausted, simply said, speaking Russian. "Privet Professor" to her former tutor. Sidorov reached over and gave her an endearing hug and gestured towards an awaiting golf cart.

He looked at Masha, who slowly arose from her seat. Sidorov could see that Masha seemed to be worse off than Anya. He was especially sensitive to her situation, knowing she went on the challenging mission with a sick spouse at home. He stepped over to her and gave her a fatherly hug. "It's good to have you back." As he held her, he sensed she was trembling. Masha simply whispered in Russian, as was their custom. "Privet Alexi." Sidorov gestured towards the awaiting airport golf cart where Anya was already seated.

After Mashenka had climbed into the cart and took her seat. Doctor Sidorov climbed into the golf cart and sat next to the driver and, speaking in English, he directed the driver to the exit gate. After a brief ride in the golf cart, Doctor Sidorov invited the two women professors to follow him out of the airport and into a waiting limousine. After both women had fastened their seat belts, then Sidorov spoke to the driver and simply said, "We can leave now." Then he said, "privacy please." The driver pushed a button and a plexiglass barrier rose and isolated the passenger area from the driver.

Sidorov commented, "You are free to speak English, but I understand that if you are both deeply immersed and are still thinking Russian, you may do so."

Anya spoke up, speaking Russian. "We're both deeply immersed!" Mashenka simply nodded at Sidorov in agreement.

Sidorov explained, speaking Russian, "We'll debrief both of you when we get to Greenwich. We've arranged lodging for both of you. After debriefing, we'll get you some rest. Tomorrow, our provisioning team will give you back your real identities and we'll arrange flights back to your respective home cities."

Marsha simply nodded her head in silence. Anya softly told her former tutor, speaking Russian, "Thank You." After about 10 minutes on the road, Professor Sidorov watched with interest as both women simply laid back their heads and went to sleep. The noted academic simply reached into his jacket pocket and retrieved a paperback book, sat back and began reading.

In Greenwich, CT, at the North American Surveying facility, the front agency for OSS62, a dozen staffers met the limo at curb side. They clapped and cheered for the women as they exited the vehicle. Anya and Mashenka both did their best to force smiles. But everyone realized the women were not their usual bubbly selves. Once inside the building. They took the elevators to the offices of North American Surveying.

An awaiting staffer led each of them to separate debriefing conference rooms. Mashenka, after entering her debriefing room, sat down slowly into a comfortable executive style office chair.

Across from her was her boss, Mr. Nathaniel Greene and an OSS62 intelligence stenographer. The two of them faced Mashenka. Green spoke up. "Masha, you know the process. In your own words, start at the beginning. English if you can manage it. If not, the stenographer understands both Russian and English."

Mashenka took a deep breath, speaking English. "I received the phone call on the evening of 1 May 1986 that there was 'a fire.' Meaning that there was a potentially catastrophic event. I was told to leave immediately when a limo arrived at my home in Binghamton, NY. I was told to bring nothing except my emergency Masha purse with my Masha New York State credentials."

"A New York State police car escorted the limo to Cortland, NY. In Cortland, we picked up three scientists from Cornell University that the New York State police had shuttled over from nearby Ithaca. Once they were in the limo with their bags, we proceeded towards Syracuse International Airport. During the limo ride, I introduced myself as Professor Mashenka Petrova, and said that I was going to be one of their translators. They asked me what department I worked in. I simply said the theater department. At Syracuse International Airport, the other academics and I were escorted to an executive jet contracted for our use."

"When we arrived at JFK, provisioning folks took us to customs interview rooms. OSS62 personnel provided me with all the credentials I needed for an international field mission. They provided me with an updated passport, my New York State driver's license, my faculty ID card, as well as various ancillary materials, such as a library card and club memberships in the Ithaca area, as well as pocket litter. After the New York City team provisioned me with traveling bags and clothing, they escorted me to a meeting space to join up with Anya Gusev and the assembled team of scientists and engineers. The two of us introduced ourselves as colleagues, scientists, and translators for the mission."

"One scientist groused about whether we could translate the science stuff in Russian. I assured them we could accurately translate for them. One of the senior scientists didn't believe I worked at Cornell. I opened my purse and showed him my passport, my New York State driver's license, my ham radio license and my current Cornell faculty credentials. The man shut up. I politely remarked, remember, Cornell is a big place."

"At JFK, we loaded our entire team and all our materials onto a government contract international flight. A chartered Boeing 747 transported our team and all our materials to Kiev in Ukraine, USSR."

"Flying with us was an expert from the Atomic Energy Commission, who briefed the entire team during the flight over to Kiev about just how bad the situation was at the Research Center at Chernobyl. Also during the flight, Anya, who is a real-life scientist, familiarized me with any of the terminology I wasn't comfortable with. We each shared our familiarity with scientific terms. I now know more about nuclear physics, chemistry and engineering terms than I ever wanted to know."

"Upon our arrival in Kiev, government officials escorted us to a government office for the Soviet Emergency Bureau and provided us with a briefing on the situation."

"I will state this for the record. KGB in Moscow suspected both Anya and I of being intelligence operatives from the start. The State Emergency Bureau officials didn't seem to care. After all, we were there to help with the nuclear emergency that threatened Russia and perhaps the world. But while we were in Kiev, they ordered the two of us to submit to a medical examination."

"Since both of us are transsexual women, we both have had breast implants and both of us clearly had natural breast growth caused by our hormone treatments. Anya, of course, was post-op with her surgical transition and has female appearing genitalia. While I still have male genitalia, hormone treatments have significantly diminished mine. The Soviet doctor's opinion was that neither of us could possibly work for an intelligence agency. His opinion was simply 'what kind of intelligence agency in their right minds would have either of us working for them?' He commented that the USA probably sent us to this dangerous situation because we were expendable. No one questioned who or what we were after that. Both Anya and I minded our own business and simply attended to the business of translating."

"Hours later, they loaded us onto a Soviet army style bus and transported us to a command center about 20 miles from Chernobyl. For the record, the drive from Kiev to Chernobyl is about 59 miles or approximately 95 kilometers. On some very crappy roads it took about two hours and 46 minutes to reach there."

"During our first interface with Soviet engineers and scientists, our American team of nuclear physics experts and engineers felt uncomfortable speaking at a slower pace to accommodate translators. Anya and I, at first, had to repeat and coach everything with them. We had to teach them the art of the protocol of speaking through an interpreter. After a few hours, they had gotten the hang of it."

"Our Soviet counterpart translators were most gracious and were very helpful with subtle language variants between northern and southern dialects of the Russian spoken language. At first, this was a bit of a hindrance. The translators were most helpful in helping us understand these differences, mostly in the pronunciation of certain letters. We can only explain the difference by contrasting English spoken in Massachusetts versus English spoken in rural Georgia. There were some language differences in the pronunciations and inflections. Our northern Soviet translators referred to the southern Russian hosts as country bumpkins."

"It should be noted that it was a nuclear specialist from America working in concert with the Russian team, who came up with a chemical cocktail that was poured down into the pit where the nuclear material from the damaged reactor had melted its way deep into the earth underneath the previously damaged nuclear reactor."

"Part of the cocktail were chemicals that would react with the uranium and essentially make the uranium chemically impure, reducing its reactivity."

"The other aspect of the cocktail was large quantities of the elements hafnium and boron. These are elements that absorb huge amounts of neutrons. Because Hafnium is capable of absorbing huge amounts of neutrons, it effectively killed the fissionable reaction. Naval ships commonly use Hafnium in the control rods of their nuclear reactors."

Anya Gusev is the real-world scientist of the two of us. I will defer to her debriefing for a much more detailed and scientific explanation regarding the Chemical Cocktail, as that is not my expertise.

"Our mission was simple. We were there to support the Soviet team. Our American team was there to consult and help in any way possible. The American team leadership took the honorable and gracious position to allow the Soviets to save face. Therefore, our American team refused any requests for interviews by the western or Soviet press. Our posture was simply we were just advisors, nothing more."

"I make this statement for the record. The American scientist who designed the neutralizing chemical cocktail, by all rights; should receive a Nobel Prize for what he did. I am of the humble opinion he was the most noble man I've ever met."

"As I stated, the western press never would know what we did, and that is as it should be! The Soviet State Emergency Bureau and the Soviet Politburo knew exactly what the game was, as well as the Soviet media. Everybody played by the rules. None of how the American Science and Engineering team took part or what they did drew any press visibility, and that was by design on both sides."

"They did not regard Anya and me as nuclear engineers and scientists. So we could grant interviews because we were there simply as translators. The Soviet media presented Anya as a software engineer and a scientist who chases tornadoes. In that context, they carried out several interviews. I was simply an associate professor at Cornell University and I teach theater performing arts, and these facts turned into profiles on both of us as the translators. They simply profiled the nuclear team based on who they were, but did not mention how they contributed to solving the problem with the unleashed nuclear beast."

The Debriefing report signed,

Mashenka Irina Petrova,

Adjunct Professor of Theater Arts at Cornell University.

After the debriefing, the stenographer got up and left the room with her machine. Leila Blakely/Anya Gusev entered the room. Doctor Sidorov, who had quietly listened to Moira Stewart's/Mashenka's deep briefing, remarked, "You ladies did a remarkable job. I'm proud of both of you."

Mr. Green concurred and added. "Moira and Leila, the hazmat team read your TLD dosimeters. The hazmat people told me by OSHA standards you have both taken a lifetime dose of ionizing radiation therefore, you can never work in that field again. But I don't think either of you wanted to work in the nuclear field." He said. Moira and Leila thanked both men for their gracious compliments.

Then Mr. Green looked at Leila. "Leila, please head down to provisioning. Get some overnight clothing and your real-life identification documents. After I speak to Moira, we'll get you both over to a couple of suites, so you can get some well-deserved rest." Leila nodded and left the room.

Dr. Sidorov and Mr. Green sat quietly, looking at each other with troubled looks. Moira gave them both a questioning look. "Guys, what's up? What aren't you telling me? What's wrong? Did I take a fatal dose of radiation or something?"

Sidorov came over to Moira and stood behind her, and put his hands on her shoulders. Mr. Green spoke up. "Moira, it's my sad duty to inform you that your wife Louise passed away two days after you left. I'm deeply sorry."

What Mr. Green said seemed to roll off Moira for a few moments. "Wait, a minute. The doctors said they did the hysterectomy. She was recuperating and was on the mend. They said she was going to be OK." Green added, "Moira, they told our people that it was a complication from surgery that caused it. It was a surprise to her attending physician and her surgeon as well. Since we had a health proxy for both you and her. We made the arrangements. As you know, her wishes on the proxy were to be cremated. We addressed the situation. Again, I'm deeply sorry."

Moira sat quietly. Her expression was one of numbness. She closed her eyes in disbelief. After a few moments, Doctor Sidorov and Mr. Green saw tears slowly streaming down from her closed eyes and rolling down her face. Eventually, the tears began dropping off of her chin.

Green left the room, leaving Alexi Sidorov to attend to and support Moira. After about 15 minutes. Moira began sobbing seriously. She spoke up with a broken, choking voice.

"Alexi, I wish to ship her ashes to her blood family. They know I've been in the process of changing my gender. They want absolutely nothing to do with me." She paused and seemed to ponder her next decision. "I suppose I should write them a letter."

Doctor Sidorov handed her a small packet of pills and quietly suggested. "Moira, you are clearly seriously exhausted, and this is a deep shock. This will help you get to sleep. Let's get you to provisioning and over to your hotel room."

Sidorov added, "Also, in the morning, we'll have a grief counselor here to talk with you. After that, well put you and Anya into a limo and bring you back here to re-provision you for your real-life with your regular clothing. Then we'll put you on a plane to send you back to Binghamton, NY and Anya back to Virginia."

Moira said nothing, then she sat looking distant, staring at the floor. Then she remarked, "I'll be going home to an empty house. I don't know what to do. I'll be rattling around in that big empty house for some time to come. How much bereavement leave do I have?"

Sidorov spoke up. "Green told me to tell you. Take as much as you need. You've done a hell of a job under difficult circumstances. Take all the time you need." Then Moira began, "I think I'm gonna get rid of most of the furniture. I think I'm going to downsize to a one bedroom or perhaps a studio apartment. I don't need a lot of space." Doctor Sidorov whispered in a fatherly tone, "Give it time, my friend. Give it time. Make no major decisions until you've mourned."

Over the next year, Moira sold off most of her household items and began living in a rather recluse, minimalist lifestyle. She did her analysis work and Sovietology duties in a SCIF (Sensitive Compartmented Information Facility) area at a regional Defense Contractor Facility.

When called upon, Moira/Mashenka went on short missions graciously and did a professional job. But everyone who knew her had noted in her quieter moments that the light had gone out of her eyes.

In 1988, Dr. Mashenka Petrova received an invitation to be a translator for a team of Russian scholars who planned to tour various European and American cities.

Friends and colleagues alike say that when Moira returned from the four-month tour, she was again bright and full of life again. Not long afterwards, Moira moved to the Virginia-Maryland area and became pals with Leila Blakely.

PART THREE
THE CLEANING LADIES

In the Early Nineties
Jan 15th -Washington, DC

Moira Stewart sat reading the Russian language edition of Pravda, the former official newspaper of the Soviet Union. Customarily reading an online newspaper at work would be in poor form. But Moira was an agency attaché on temporary assignment to the Russia Desk team at the State Department. Reading the daily principle newspaper of record for the subject country was mandatory. Routinely performing OSINT, gathering Open-Source Intelligence; using information derived from publicly available sources.

Moira was enjoying this assignment as a well-deserved break from field duty in the now former Soviet Union. As well, the team was so accustomed to reading Cyrillic all day at work that both her and her Department of State teammates of Western Sovietologists simply spoke Russian all day, unless a non-Russian speaker visited the office.

On her desk were two telephones. One for state business and the other for casual office calls. The casual business phone rang. Moira paused a moment to think English, then answered the phone with a polite, "Moira Stewart, cultural analysis. May I help you, sir?"

A male voice addressed her, "Moira, Bob Akron here, sorry to interrupt your vacation over at State, but I need your expertise. I've got a sanitation issue. Everybody I would normally use is all busy prepping for Boris Yeltsin's visit next month. I need you to drop what you're doing and come over to the home office to get you read into a compartmented program."

"Your my boss, Bob, I'll be right over."

Sanitation Duty! Moira thought to herself in the elevator. *It's probably Ghoul's duty again. Some old spy probably died, and his or her grandkids have probably found some document artifact that should have been turned in years or decades ago.*

She thought to herself as she walked to the <u>Farragut West</u> station of the Metro's Blue line. After about twenty minutes, she got off her Blue Line train at Pentagon City. She took the escalator to the surface level and walked a block west and came upon an unassuming commercial office building. She took an elevator to the top floor. The elevator car doors opened across from a pair of mahogany doors with an engraved brass plate on the door that read, "North American Surveying."

Moira opened the door and, upon entering, a well-dressed, middle-aged woman sitting behind a reception desk greeted her, "Welcome to North American Surveying! How can I help you?"

Moira could see that the woman had one arm on the top of the desk and one arm under the desk. *No doubt she has her hand on an automatic pistol holstered under her file drawer*, Moira thought to herself.

"I'm here to see Dr. Akron about a flu shot." Moira stated plainly. The woman smiled. "The door on the left." Moira heard a buzz and a click as the door unlatched.

She entered the hallway beyond. As she did, the door behind her closed and had a mechanical latching sound. She walked down the hall to a door marked Robert Akron. She double knocked on the door. A gravelly voiced man called, "Come!" Moira opened the door and walked in. Bob Akron stood up and extended a handshake to her, "Great to see you Moira, how's things over at State?" She snickered, "All Russian all the time, but actually rather laid back especially considering how it used to be at the Russia desk." Akron gestured to her to take a seat, "Yeah, who ever thought we'd win the Cold War?"

As she sat down, she asked, "You said on the phone you needed to read me into a compartmented group?" Akron got a deeply thoughtful look on his face. "What do you remember from high school American history about the revolutionary war?"

Moira wrinkled her nose, "I suppose the usual, our war of independence, the continental army, General George Washington, I cannot tell a lie stuff."

Akron snickered, "You do know old George was an accomplished Spy Master?" Moira nodded in the affirmative. "Yes, they loosely covered it when they trained us at the Farm." (spy school)

He gave her a quizzical look, "Ever hear of Lady-355?" Moira seemed to ponder for a few moments. "If memory serves, the Culper Ring spy network had a code for a Lady-355. There's a myth that within the Culper Network there was a woman or perhaps a small network of women who carried encoded messages and intelligence information back and forth between George Washington and the Culper gang."

Akron nodded his head with a distant look in his eyes. "Ok Moira, what I am about to say is highly sensitive. The Lady-355 myth is just that, a well thought out and well-engineered myth."

Moira smirked. "If it's a myth, why is it a secret?" Akron looked at Moira squarely. "Lady-355 is the myth. Even though it may sound strange, the Ladies Secret Signal Society or L3S, which was the real secret women's intelligence network, continues to exist today. The sanitation job I have for you perhaps was a member of the L3S during WWII and collaborated with the OSS and the early CIA when they formed in the late forties. The L3S is America's oldest spy network staffed almost entirely by women!"

Moira sat staring at her boss, Bob Akron. "You've got to be kidding me. A network of American women spies has been operating since the American Revolution."

"It's no Joke." Akron remarked, "They supported Washington during the Revolution. Knowing how fragile the newly born United States was, the women stayed organized and grew. I mean, Moira, think about it, a plainly dressed or humbly dressed woman can virtually go anyplace unnoticed." Akron commented.

Moira spoke up. "Yep, Mrs. R. taught us that principle back in field operative school. We all found that we could go almost anywhere by simply blending in." She used to say, "The frumpier the better!" People didn't notice us or they considered us harmless.

Bob Akron took a sip of his coffee. Then remarked, "So here's the issue. Some clerk at the Library of Congress was going through some kind of Special Papers collection and discovered a substantial package of material. The package labeled not to be opened until after the death of one Mrs. Courtney Malone Davis. She passed away on the first of October in 1989. Anyhow, the clerk opened the package and found the next internal wrapping labeled Top Secret-L3S. The clerk, realizing that the material might have national security implications, contacted an agency liaison person attached to the Library of Congress. Who contacted my boss to arrange for a careful sanitizing of the material so the Librarians can put Mrs. Davis's papers in the historical collection?"

Moira grimaced. "Surely, something from WWII would be easily declassified by now. Even the most sensitive material is usually automatically declassified after fifty years."

"Ordinarily I would agree with you," Akron commented. "I did a web search for Mrs. Courtney Malone Davis and found that all the District of Columbia newspapers reported her obituary, which is unusual. Families usually only purchase one obituary notice. Likewise, the obituary was unusually terse. Through a further web search, it was discovered that Courtney Malone had a career in physics and had published extensively in scientific circles."

Moira gave her boss a curious look. "Did her widely published obituary mention anything about her being a scientist?"

"No! Only whom she was married to and that she was a mom, a grand mom and a great grand mom." Akron answered, "In fact after I reread her obit, it appears to me that her public obscurity as a researcher and scientist was by design!"

"My God, they scrubbed her professional career!" Moira hissed. Akron gently nodded his head. "Bingo! For all we know, she might have been on the inner circle of some sensitive program like the Manhattan Project or perhaps the H-Bomb. And nuclear stuff is exempt from automatic declassification."

"And being a woman, she probably didn't get any credit for her work in that era," Moira grumbled.

Akron answered, "Yes, that has crossed my mind as well." Leaning forward, he suggested, "Perhaps she left this package hidden in the Library of Congress archives as her way of having the last laugh and claiming her due credit."

"Your orders, boss?" She asked.

"Moira, I want you to get that package. Take it to a SCIF (Sensitive Compartmented Information Facility) and carefully go through it and make your best recommendations as to its disposition." Akron directed. Moira was quiet for a few moments. "I certainly have the clearance level for this job. But do I have the Need-to-Know?"

Akron nodded in the affirmative. "As the official sanitizer of this material, you clearly need to know. Understand it and come back and brief me." He opened his desk drawer, removed a business card, and handed it to Moira. "This is a liaison person to the L3S people. Hopefully, they will cooperate with you and assign an L3S person to work with you in this effort."

Moira stood, Bob Akron reached across his desk and shook hands with her. "Good luck. Perhaps this will be an E-ticket thrill ride for you, one where nobody will shoot at you!" Moira gave him a stare and just rolled her eyes before she left his office. As she walked down the hall toward the reception area, she looked at the card for the L3S contact person. It was for some woman at the National Arboretum.

Late afternoon Jan 15th -National Arboretum Complex

Moira called the woman at the National Arboretum, a Ms. Joyce Pemberton Anderson. Moira simply told the woman what agency she worked for and that she was dealing with some very old government documents, and that she might need the help from her network of associates. The woman, Ms. Anderson, specified a time and sent a map for a greenhouse at the National Arboretum facility out on route 50 to Moira's fax number.

Moira arrived at the appointed time, parked her car, and walked to the designated Green House. Upon walking inside from the January weather, Moira found herself in a glassed-in foyer area. As she opened the second door, she was met with a wave of warm tropical air, rich with floral scents and humidity. Sitting on a simple wooden bench was a red-haired woman dressed in dark seasonal slacks sporting a professional blouse and tailored jacket. Moira made the woman as perhaps in her late thirties.

"Are you Ms. Anderson?" Moira asked. The woman smiled, "Yes I am." She gestured toward a coat rack. "Please hang up your coat and let's have a walk through the greenhouse where we won't be disturbed." Moira hung up her winter coat. Ms. Anderson motioned for her to walk into the expansive greenhouse. "So, how can I help you?" She asked.

Moira explained that someone had stashed a package in a private collection area of the Library of Congress in the late 1970s. Then she commented, "The package had a Top Secret L3S marking." Ms. Anderson stopped dead in her tracks and asked, "Any idea who hid the package?" Moira looked at Anderson with a deadpan expression. "Yes, somebody named Courtney Malone Davis." Anderson put her hand to her lips. Then, after a moment remarked, "Dr. Courtney Malone! There's a name I haven't heard for a long time." She paused, then asked, "What has become of Dr. Malone?"

"I'm sorry to say she passed away in late 1989." Moira replied and added. "The double wrapped package is approximately a foot thick and has an outer wrapper that instructs to be only opened after Courtney passes away."

Ms. Anderson was thoughtful for a few moments. "I can take that package off your hands if you wish." Moira shook her head gently. "It's not that simple. I need someone from L3S who holds a traditional Security Clearance to help me go through the material in a SCIF location."

Ms. Anderson gave Moira a perturbed look. "You said the package's inner wrapper stated Top Secret-L3S. I wish to make the case that Ms. Malone's package is L3S property. And probably carries no more sensitive information than our sorority's information. Hell, Malone was probably just a chapter chronicler and that foot thick package may just be a historical narrative about the activities of her regional chapter from perhaps ten or twenty years ago. From our viewpoint, you'd have to be an L3S member to be privy to the materials."

Moira said nothing and continued to walk with Anderson amongst the lush green vegetation and flora. Then Moira stopped and made eye contact with Anderson. "I have received information about the compartment regarding L3S and its origins and long history. Sure, you may call yourselves a sorority, but the people in your organization have been spooks since the beginning of this country and your predecessors probably taught the CIA and my agency everything they know how to do. I'm offering L3S a professional courtesy to carefully review the material in my custody. I'm simply asking for the same professional courtesy from L3S."

Ms. Anderson closed her eyes for a few moments. When she opened them, she had a more relaxed, friendly expression. "If my superiors approve, I will propose offering you membership in L3S." Moira made a gesture as if she were going to speak up. Anderson simply said "Hush! Your membership would be on a non-conflict of interest basis. We expect you to keep our secrets and, in turn, keep those of your home agency."

"How would that work?" Moira asked. Anderson explained, "For instance, if there is a mutual need to work together. Sort of as we have now. Then we would exchange letters from our respective directors agreeing to this joint effort. Only then can we share the materials. For the period of the mission only."

"Would I stay a member of L3S after the mission?" Moira asked.

"Yes, you would, and you wouldn't be the first woman to be

a member of both organizations. We've been doing it this way since before you or your mother or grandmother were born!"

Moira looked thoughtful for a few moments. "Ok, I'll go back and make the proposal to my director." Anderson nodded. "I'll do the same, but remember, your director must provide a written agreement to my director." Refer to the mission as the 'Malone Materials' in the agreement letter."

Late afternoon -Jan 15th -Lobby of the Smithsonian Castle

Moira Stewart met with Ms. Anderson in the lobby of the Smithsonian Castle. In a quiet corner of the original Smithsonian facility, Moira handed a letter to Ms. Anderson. "It's from my director to yours."

Ms. Anderson, in kind, reached into her purse and withdrew a similar #10 envelope and handed it to Moira. "From my director to your agency's director. If all goes well, I'll call you on Monday and invite you back to our HQ. We'll then introduce you to L3S, make you a member, provide you with suitable identification, and pair you with a properly cleared archive specialist to analyze the Malone Materials."

Anderson glanced at her wristwatch. "I must be going." Moira piped up, "I thought I'd be working with you on this project?" Anderson smirked. "My job is to be a first interface person for L3S contacts with other agencies. I'm briefed on very little. I'm simply a go between. If I'm ever kidnapped and taken prisoner, I'd be useless to whomever were to capture me. Because I know next to nothing."

Moira frowned. "You will take these risks and know virtually little about what L3S is involved in. Why?" As Anderson walked away, she remarked, "It's my job to protect others, and it's my way of being a patriot. See you around, Moira!" She continued walking and exited the Smithsonian Castle building.

Morning Jan 20th -Deeper and Deeper

Moira was doing her routine reading of Pravda at her desk at the State Dept facility. Her casual business phone rang. She answered it. Before she could offer greetings, a familiar voice addressed her. "Good morning Ms. Stewart, this is Ms. Anderson. Your team's proposal has received approval. Please come over to Building #3 at the Arboretum Complex, at about 1pm. Our sisters are looking forward to initiating you into the sorority."

Moira was about to speak when the line went dead. Moira whispered to herself, "Geesh! This is like old school frat boy spy stuff. Initiate me? What are they going to have me do, swallow some goldfish and say cross my heart and hope to die or something? Good Grief!"

Moira arrived at Building #3 at the Arboretum Complex a little before the appointed time. As she approached the building, all the doors seemed to be utility doors similar to roll up garage doors. Finally, she approached the only door that appeared to be a public entrance, and she entered the building.

Sitting at a desk was a female sailor in her middle twenties, wearing a sidearm. "Good morning. Can I help you?" She politely asked. "I was told to come to this building for a meeting," Moira answered. The third-class yeoman asked for her identification. Moira opened her purse and removed her agency photo identification card. The sailor looked at it, and then she looked at a clipboard. "Ah yes, Ms. Stewart, they're expecting you."

She pressed a button; Moira heard a door unlatch, then the sailor directed her to the now unsecured door. Moira walked through the door. She quickly realized that she was in an antechamber room. The door closed and latched behind her. Moira glanced back and realized that the inside of the door that she had just come through had no door handles of any kind.

The antechamber room had two simple office chairs and a small nondescript table in the center. On the table were two glasses and a pitcher of water. A few moments later, a woman slightly older than her came through a door at the rear.

"Moira Stewart?" Moira simply answered. "Yes."

"Follow me." The woman replied. On the other side of the doorway was a hallway. She led Moira down the hall for several doors and knocked on one. Moira heard a woman's voice respond. "Come in." The two of them entered the room. Sitting there was a woman admiral having tea and muffins with a much older woman. The Naval officer gestured toward the comfortable chair across from the two of them. "Moira, please have a seat."

After being seated, the Admiral spoke up. "My name is Marie Jean-Baptiste. I command a branch of Naval Intelligence. I am a member of L3S and I act as a liaison to the group. This splendid lady next to me is the Director of L3S, Louise Peterson Hamilton."

We received a letter from your director requesting that you be a liaison to L3S from your intelligence agency. Moira spoke up. "One curious question. Why are you at the Arboretum?" The two of them laughed. The director woman spoke up, "The National Arboretum is simply a cover for what we really do. We've been here for nearly a century."

Again, Moira, being very forward, "I requested to be a liaison with L3S to support an investigation into one of your dead operative's and a pile of documents she's left behind. Do I really need to join to have L3S support for my investigation?"

Director of L3S, Louise Peterson Hamilton spoke up. "Yes, you must be a member. That's the price of admission. It's always been that way." "What if I say no?" Moira said cautiously. Hamilton stated plainly. "Then this meeting never took place, and you will simply go back to your duties at your agency, and that will stop your investigation mission." The admiral spoke up. "So, Moira, are you in, or are you out?"

Moira hesitated for a few moments. The admiral added, "Moira, I suspect you've taken security oaths before. This is just another one. Nothing more and nothing less."

"Ok, yes, I am in!" Moira responded. The two of them gave each other knowing glances. "Moira, please sign this letter." The admiral told her as she handed Moira a single sheet of paper.

"What is it?" Moira asked.

Hamilton smiled and said, "If you break our security rules and reveal what you know to unauthorized persons. They will find this letter next to your dead body. It's your suicide note."

Moira sat staring at both of them. "You are effectively making me sign my name in blood! Is this for real?" Hamilton remarked coldly, "As real as it gets, my dear." The admiral was gentler, "It's the price of admission, as previously stated." Hamilton added. "Think of it as an insurance policy for us."

Moira stared at the floor for a few moments. "But this won't be my full-time job!" The Admiral spoke up. "Moira, think of it as just another security oath before a field operation. In the future, we may reach out to your director and ask for your help. You'll already be part of the team and we'll feel secure knowing your loyalty is absolute!" Moira took a breath, whispered to herself. "Deeper and deeper," and signed the letter.

Early Afternoon Jan 20th -The L3S Forensic Archivist

After a quick lunch with Admiral Marie Jean-Baptiste at the L3S facility at the National Arboretum. The Admiral, with a beaming smile, introduced Moira to Fiona McKenzie. A woman whom she guessed was in her late forties or early fifties. She wore casual slacks and a loose-fitting laboratory jacket, not exactly a feminine shirt. Judging from her rather athletic look and very male short haircut style, Moira might have guessed that McKenzie perhaps runs in alternative groups, perhaps with the feminist lot or within LGBT circles.

After they exchanged pleasantries, the Admiral explained. "Ms. McKenzie is one of our Forensic Archivists. She can not only make sense of what the documents are about but, as need be, she can do the laboratory analysis on the paper, ink, type and anything else that might verify if a document is genuine or perhaps suspect or forged."

"Ms. McKenzie and Ms. Stewart," the admiral said, "I'd like to offer neutral SCIF space at a Navy facility in Northwest DC. The two of you will have exclusive sole access to the unit. The Admiral looked at Moira. This should prevent either of your agencies from having sole custody of the Materials during the investigation period. In addition, the site has a fully equipped forensic laboratory space for the testing of documents for validity and health risks."

Moira wrinkled her nose. "Health risks?" McKenzie spoke up, "It's an old school technique to protect very sensitive documents, by embedding the paper with certain toxins. It was also a poor man's assassination method back in the day." Moira rolled her eyes, mumbling, "Talk about cloak and dagger."

McKenzie added, "In the sixties, some agencies used to lace some documents with LSD and DMSO. An unsuspecting spy would handle the document, and the perpetrator's skin would absorb the LSD. Hours later, reports of an operative tripping were easy to track via police reports."

The Admiral offered, "My staff car is available to take you to where the documents are at present and then to the neutral SCIF in NW. Each of you will have an access key, and we have programmed the access door to require both of you to be present. That way neither agency can run off with the goods if this is something sensitive. I propose after each of you make your analysis and reports to your directors, they can make the final determination of the disposition of the documents after sanitizing them." Both Moira and McKenzie agreed to the proposal. McKenzie spoke up and remarked, "Let's go get the old gal's private treasure!" Moira gestured to McKenzie and the Admiral to lead the way.

10:17am Jan 23rd -The Cause of Death

Moira's agency boss, Bob Akron, called her on the business casual phone over at state. "Hey Moira, I had our research folks do as you requested. They've gotten police, FBI and medical examiner reports regarding Malone's death." Moira reacted. "Was it natural causes or murder?"

Akron answered, "First off, the obituary was so terse because they ruled her death as a suicide. Families and newspapers don't report suicides as a general rule." Again, Moira asked, "Was there anything unusual with the FBI medical examiner's report?"

Akron remarked, "I've always liked your intuition, lady. Yes, the medical examiner's report showed that Malone had all the classic health issues that suggested that she was suffering the health effects from long term ionizing radiation exposure, such as cancer and cardiovascular disease. The medical examiner noted he did not understand why a librarian at the Library of Congress would have all the long-term ills of a nuclear defense plant worker. Perhaps she really worked on the H bomb!"

Moira said, "I have become a member of the L3S sorority." The Navy has offered a neutral SCIF for our agency and L3S to research the Malone material jointly and perform the prescribed sanitation efforts. "Let me know if you need any other support as things move forward," Akron added.

"Bob, I'm becoming concerned that this effort is going to go down an interagency rabbit hole." Moira expressed. Akron soberly asked, "What's your concern?"

"Gee-whiz Bob, the L3S people put me under their own draconian medieval security oath. Cross my heart and expect to die kind of stuff! What was supposed to be a non-conflict of interest relationship has been anything but that. Everything you told me this morning is producing red flags." Moira explained and added, "What I'm concerned about is that I'm going to be put between a rock and a hard place at some point, in terms of loyalties, as I dig into the truth. Let's just say I have life and death sanction concerns."

"Really?" Akron questioned.

"Yes, really." Moira explained, "L3S has been around since before the American Revolution, as you told me. They really don't fall under constitutional authority or Congressional Control. Beyond a good-old girl handshake and wink-wink! It's like the old Soviet inner circle rules, if you get my drift."

Akron groaned, "Yep, they're the matriarchy's equivalent to Skull and Bones!" Moira remarked in a reserved fashion. "So, I think you understand my concerns if I don't speak plainly!"

"I received your message," Akron replied. "Keep me updated and be vigilant." Akron hung up. Moira let out a sigh and whispered to herself, "What I wouldn't give for a Masha assignment in some frigid valley in the Ural's about now."

Mid Afternoon 23 Jan -Opening Courtney Malone's Package

The forensic laboratory at the SCIF facility. Fiona McKenzie had placed the Malone package in an airtight plexiglass container and sealed it. Both she and Moira were wearing high end breathing masks. McKenzie placed her hands into two heavy duty rubber gloves and with a small box knife, she gently began cutting into the package wrapping. As she removed the wrappings, both of them noted a bound notebook and perhaps a dozen folders and another small cardboard box.

On the side of the Plexiglas box, there was a valve stem port and a large syringe seated in the valve stem. McKenzie withdrew her hands from the gloves. She turned the valve handle and drew the plunger off on the syringe, then closed the valve handle.

Moira spoke up, grinning. "Jeepers Fiona, what kind of poisonous gas do you think a librarian might have access to?"

McKenzie gave Moira a rather dull look, "Perhaps Cyanide or Sarin gas." "Malone was a librarian. Why would she have access to that?" Moira asked. McKenzie simply explained, "She was L3S as well. She had access to many chemical agents."

McKenzie stepped over to a Mass Spectrometer and placed the syringe into the port on the Spectrometer. Then actuated a switch on the device. A few moments later, there was a readout on the CRT screen. McKenzie carefully recited the read out, "Hmmm, ten percent ethylene oxide mixed with carbon dioxide."

"Is it poisonous?" Moira queried. "Yes... This is a product called Carboxide™ gas, its routinely used to fumigate paper materials that were even remotely suspected of mold or insect infestation. It's common for archives and rare book repositories. The Library of Congress would certainly use it. I suspect that Dr. Malone would have used it routinely for any archival pages like this one." McKenzie explained.

Moira remarked, "So we can open the container?"

"Not yet," McKenzie cautioned. "That box at the bottom of the stack of folders is suspicious. I'm going to open that next. If that tests positive for only fumigant, then we'll put the entire works in a ventilated out gassing chamber and then we can start pawing through it all."

"So, how do we proceed?" Moira asked. McKenzie seemed to study the stack of documents. "If we think like a devious bad guy or competent operative trying to protect something precious, I would most likely booby trap the box with some type of out gassing mechanism or a small anti-personnel device."

Moira wrinkled her nose and asked, "Do you really run into that sort of thing?" McKenzie gave her teammate a curious look. "You mean you don't? I thought you were an experienced field operative?" She remarked as she lifted the notebook and folders off of the box and set them down in the bottom of the examination chamber.

Moira casually commented, "Oh, I've disarmed a few bombs in my time, but I've never encountered an Improvised Anti-Personnel Device (IAPD) with a package from a Library of Congress staffer."

Fiona paused before she lifted the cover off of the cardboard box. "History has shown us that the moment you let your guard down is when you get bit!" She took a breath and lifted the cardboard lid off of the box. Inside the box were spools of wire. Moira looked at the spools of wire with a curious look. "What the heck is that?"

Fiona McKenzie stood looking at the spools for a few moments. "I think we're going to hear from Courtney herself, those my friend, are wire recordings circa WWII."

9:30am 25 Jan-Dealing with Fifty-year-old Tech.

The forensic laboratory at the Navy SCIF facility. Moira had spent half the day on Friday at a high-end stereo shop in Rosslyn, VA purchasing a couple of Broadcast Grade Cassette recorders, a stereo amp, Speakers wire and a crate of padded headphones and an eight-channel headset splitter suitable for supplying up to eight headphones with audio at once. Wanting no interruption on her and Fiona's effort to listen to the Courtney Malone wire recordings. Moira purchased an ample supply of hook up cable, two stereo plug adapters kits and two gender change plug adapters kits and two cases of high-grade cassettes. She hauled it back over to Northwest DC to the Navy SCIF center and waited to move it all into the SCIF unit. When Fiona arrived, she came to the SCIF unit carrying two industrial suitcases that looked sort of like high-end professional camera cases.

Fiona set the cases down, produced her SCIF key. With that, the two women went through the security ritual of opening the SCIF unit together.

Inside the SCIF, Fiona set down her camera like cases, removed and hung-up her winter garb. She sat down at a table, opened her purse, removed a pack of smokes and lit one up. After taking a satisfying drag, she remarked to Moira, who was carting in all the audio equipment she had purchased. "I had the most incredible case of good luck regarding the wire recorders." Remarked, Fiona.

"Do tell," Moira said, as she pushed several boxes through the SCIF doorway. While Fiona sat nonchalantly smoking her cigarette, she shared the story of her good fortune. "The folks over at Langley had a pair of refitted 1940s era wire recorders in their surplus facility." Fiona explained.

"So they loaned them to us?" Moira queried, as she carried in the last of the bags of hi-fi wires and assorted parts. Fiona crushed out her cigarette. "Hell no, they gave them to us!"

Moira groaned. "Do they even work?" Fiona snickered, "Sure, they work, but even better, they re-engineered both units back in the late 1970s, so all the electronics are transistors and not clunky old vacuum tubes. They are all the heavy-duty hardware from the forties and the quieter, lighter electronics from the seventies. They even changed the jacks for easy hookup to plug into commercial grade entertainment electronics like HIFI systems."

Moira remarked, "I bought a bunch of stereo stuff here. After I get it unpackaged and hooked up, I suppose we can plug in the Wire Recorders and see if those wire reels are still good."

For the next hour, Moira unpacked all her gear and crawled around on the floor under the table with the sound gear, fishing the cables and plugging in the jacks. Fiona mostly just smoked more cigarettes and watched Moira do all the sound gear tech stuff. After Moira was done, she stood up and seemed to stretch her back. "I'm finished. Do you want to plug one of those wire recorders in and see what old Courtney has to say?"

Fiona said with an excited tone, "You bet!" Fiona set up one of the wire recorders. She inserted a wire reel marked #1 into the unit and threaded a lead of the wire near the playback head, and attached the lead wire to the take-up reel on the other side of the machine.

Moira hooked up the audio output using a "Y" connecter, so the mono audio would go through both audio channels on the stereo system. She then put cassettes into both of her recorders and started the machines.

Moira looked at Fiona. "Fire it up." Fiona pushed the play switch, and the reels turned.

After a few moments, a woman's voice said, "Test 1 2 3 4" then there was silence briefly. Then the woman said, "This is reel one of the collection." After another brief silence.

"My name is Courtney...Courtney Malone. I grew up in Rehoboth Beach, Delaware, in the 1920s. Rehoboth Beach overseers frequently shunned the local kids and made us unwelcome, especially anywhere near the wealthy tourists. Yep, I was what they called a beach rat!"

"But I was enterprising. I made my spending money quietly, listening to the tourists lament about what they needed or wanted. Then, for a small commission, I would chase down the item or service that they desired."

"In 1929, when I turned sixteen, several out-of-town regular guests spoke on my behalf to one of the big beach hotels, and they hired me as a Jr. assistant concierge. The hotel gave me a slick uniform, and I plied my seeker skills for the benefit of the hotel. I quickly became highly respected by the hotel management. Though they would not tell me to my face. I found out much later that I was a significant asset to the hotel's reputation and amenities."

"My seeker talents brought me to the attention of one particular frequent visitor to the beach; we'll just call him the Commander. The hotel staff always gave this very soft-spoken gentleman and his wife the greatest respect and silver plate service. All I ever really knew was that he was a bigwig of some sort in Washington, DC."

"During the summer after I graduated from high school, the Commander's wife invited me to lunch on my day off. Of course, I was nervous, not understanding what she wanted. At lunch, she explained that both she and the Commander were very impressed with my hard work over the years. Then she dropped the big one on me. 'The Commander and I have arranged a college scholarship for you at William and Mary.'"

"I was stunned. This was a dream come true. The only condition was that my field of study was in the sciences. Of course, I accepted. The Commander's wife Edie visited me regularly while I was at school. She gave me advice and encouragement; she was for all intents a second worldly mother. During my time on the beach and through college, I never really knew their family name. It was always simply the Commander and Edie."

"When I graduated from college, the Commander and Edie were there in the stands to cheer me on. I celebrated my graduation with my blood family at dinner that evening. But it was Edie who invited me to breakfast the next day at the lovely

Williamsburg Hotel. At breakfast, the Commander shook my hand and finally formally introduced himself to me. 'Courtney, my name is Edward J. Clemson; I'm an Admiral in the Navy.'"

"During breakfast, the two of them told me how proud of me they were. They experienced the loss of a daughter about my age; she passed away in a car crash when she was fourteen. They told me that for years at the beach, they came to admire my industrious nature. That's why they wanted to send me to school to honor the memory of their daughter and because they liked me very much."

"Then the Admiral made me an offer. 'Courtney, if you don't have a job position yet, I have one for you that might be right up your alley.' Sure, I had a degree in physics, but being a woman, none of the people who came to recruit science graduates for major laboratories wanted to talk to me or another woman classmate. This was especially frustrating because we were both in the top five of our physics class. The recruiters only wanted to talk to the men!"

"Of course, I told the Admiral I was interested. He told me he had contacts at the Library of Congress, who were looking for someone with my training. I must have cocked my head strangely. 'A library? What would I do in a library? I'm a physicist.'"

"With a smile, he explained that scientific papers from literally everywhere came to the library for archiving and distribution to interested parties. He pointed out that the library needed a talented physicist who understood all the science jargon and the implications of the research. He paused, then added. Plus, there will be some laboratory perks offered to you down the road if you are patient."

"That got my attention; sure, I was good with that offer. I'm your gal. Let's do it. I said. That's when I mentioned my gal pal Corinne. After all, I was number three in my class and Corinne was number four by a half a grade point; we were among the best and brightest. I made my case to the admiral on her behalf. He thoughtfully listened to my pitch. Then he simply commented, 'I know somebody who could use her. Let me look into it.'"

"Needless to say, I went to work for the Library of Congress and yes, the job was interesting, and I got to read all the best papers and research from around the country from the greatest minds. End of reel one."

11:00am 25th Jan Courtney and L3S

At the forensic laboratory at the Navy SCIF facility.

After the first reel of wire had emptied, Fiona reached over to the wire recorder and re-looped the lead of the wire and pressed the rewind button. "Any thoughts so far, Moira?" Moira shook her head. "Maybe this package is just her autobiography. It's actually nice hearing her voice. It helps my mind accept her as a real person."

"I sort of thought the same thing, too. Let's get some coffee and come back and listen to some more of her reels." Fiona suggested. The two intelligence officers exited the SCIF compartment and looked at each other, held up their SCIF key to verify that each had it, and closed the door and actuated the locking mechanism.

An hour later, they returned with a box of donuts, a couple of cups of coffee and a box of Joe for follow on comfort coffee as the team embraced the audio collection of Dr. Courtney Malone.

After each inserted their SCIF key and turned together, the large soundproof door released. Fiona opened it wide so the two could carry in their morning snacks. After the SCIF door was closed, Fiona inserted a wire reel labeled #2. Moira pressed the buttons on the two cassette recorders and nodded; on that cue Fiona started the wire recorder. After a few moments, a woman spoke.

"Courtney Malone Journal reel #2," there was a pause. "Five years later, in the fall of 1940, the admiral's aide showed up in my office and asked me to come with him. He drove me to the National Arboretum field complex. He pulled the car up to a nondescript building amongst the heating facilities for the Arboretum's greenhouses and nurseries." The aide told me. "Go inside. Someone will greet you."

"I exited the car and entered the building. Sitting at a desk was a sailor in his late twenties said." 'Good morning. Can I help you?' "I let them know; I had been dropped off and they instructed me to come in. He asked for my identification. I opened my purse and removed my Library of Congress photo identification card. The sailor looked at it, and then he looked at a clipboard." 'Ah, Miss Malone, they're expecting you.'

"He pushed a button; I heard a door unlatch, then he directed me to the now unsecured door. As I walked through the door, I realized I was in an antechamber room. The door closed and latched behind me. When I looked back, I realized that the inside of the door that I had just come through had no door handles of any kind. Honestly, I felt trapped. The antechamber room had two simple office chairs and a small nondescript table in the center. On the table were two glasses and a pitcher of water. A few moments later, a woman slightly older than me came through a door at the rear of the room. Courtney Malone? I answered. 'Yes.'"

"'Follow me.' She replied. On the other side of the doorway was a hallway. She led me down the hall for several doors and knocked on one. I heard a male voice respond. 'Come in.' The two of us entered the room. Sitting there was the Admiral having tea and scones with a much older woman. He gestured toward the comfortable chair across from the two of them. 'Courtney, please have a seat.' Once I took my seat, the Admiral spoke up. 'Remember when you graduated from college? I promised you laboratory work. Well, this is it.' I gave him a quizzical look. 'But I'm not a gardener! I'm a physicist.' The two of them laughed. The woman spoke up, 'The National Arboretum is simply a cover for what we really do.'"

"'Who are we?' I asked. The Admiral glanced at the older woman and deferred to her. The woman spoke up, 'We are the Ladies Secret Signal Society or L3S; we're a very secret organization. Our roots go back to the revolutionary war. During the colonial period, women were virtually invisible to most men. In those days, we passed secret messages to General Washington and the Continental Army. In those days, our group was simply referred to as Lady-355.'"

"She paused for a moment. 'Even today, a modestly dressed woman can come and go unnoticed. We recruit talent like yourself because we make inquiries, monitor advancements and do research in almost every field of endeavor.' I looked at the Admiral for reassurance. He simply nodded. 'It's all true, Courtney, and we need you.'"

"Again, the woman commented. 'Germany and other countries have access to some extraordinary technology. As you already know from the literature, Otto Han and Fritz Strassman split the atom in Germany two years ago. They have other advancements all far and above anything our country has, or any other country has currently.'"

"I looked at her for a moment, then remarked. 'Look, our scientists are just as immersed in physics as are the Germans; I've read all the best papers. Where did all this special stuff you speak of come from? What did it do? Fall out of the sky?' They looked at each other and smirked. The woman spoke up, 'Yes, in a manner of speaking.'"

"For a moment, I let her remark sink in. After letting her remark sink in, I commented, 'Excuse me, but we haven't been introduced.' The woman rose from her chair. 'I'm Alice Pemberton. I'm the current director of the L3S.' She extended a handshake. After a hesitant pause, I embraced her hand and the two of us shook. Then she gestured for me to sit. 'Would you like some tea and a scone?'"

"The admiral spoke up. 'Courtney, please have a scone. They're really quite good.' I took him up on his offer as I thought about what Miss Pemberton had said. I poured myself a cup of tea and carefully picked up a scone."

"Pemberton continued as I sipped my Earl Grey tea. 'For the past 40,000 years, there has been evidence that some advanced species of beings have been visiting our world with regularity. Mostly, they have guided humanity and gifted our fledgling human culture with agriculture, mathematics, laws and other basic technologies.'"

"I interjected a sarcastic remark. 'I don't suppose somebody left a Buck Rogers ray gun lying around.' The Admiral's eyes got really wide as he looked over to Pemberton. 'I told you she'd cut to the chase.'"

12:00pm Jan 25-Courtney and L3S–Reel Three

At the Navy SCIF facility. Reel two of the Malone wire recording had just ended. As Fiona began rewinding the wire reel #2.

Moira gave Fiona a curious look and remarked. "People have painted flying saucers, UFOs, and alien beings as a silly, crackpot, and conspiracy theory notion for ages. If Malone's reels are going to continue in this direction, I have half a mind to write this sanitation effort off as a fool's errand and a waste of time."

Fiona lit a cigarette and thoughtfully took a few drags and puffs, seeming to consider what Moira had said as she half watched the wire reel rewind. As reel two finished rewinding, she remarked. "I'm content to not go any further if you are. Malone's narrative sounds like a typical induction to the Sorority. Perhaps it's really just her biography."

"Mine too!" Moira curtly replies. "The admiral and that Pemberton lady are just going to ask her to sign a suicide letter security oath."

As Fiona set reel #2 aside in a box labeled reviewed. She seemed to study Moira for a few moments. Then she asked, "As a field operative and analyst. Aren't you the least bit interested in the possibilities of off-world life and civilizations visiting us?"

Moira was labeling the cassette tapes from the reel of two sessions. She stopped and gave Fiona a raised eyebrow look. "As an analyst, I deal with facts and how those facts fit into a mosaic of a greater puzzle. I've seen no evidence come across my desk that hinted or suggested even remotely that any of this little green men nonsense is anything but a pipe dream," Moira said firmly.

Fiona gave Moira a studious look. "Are you content that this is all ridiculous stuff and just leave the sanitation effort to an L3S team?" Moira seemed to consider the issue with a perturbed look. "No, I'll go through it all with you. The fact is, I'm going to have to justify to my boss why I spent eight hundred bucks on HIFI gear on this project." She paused and reluctantly remarked, "Load up another reel."

Fiona smirked, "Ok, set up your cassettes and I'll load up reel three." Within several minutes, Moira pressed the buttons on the cassette recorders and gave Fiona a nod.

The audio on wire reel three began, "Reel number three—pause- As I was saying, The Admiral's eyes got really wide as he looked over to Pemberton. 'I told you she'd cut to the chase.' I gave them a surprised look. 'Are you telling me some Martian left a ray gun or something?' Pemberton spoke. 'Courtney, if you decide to join us, you are in the L3S for life. The things you will learn here will literally change your outlook on life and the meaning of everything.' There was a tense pause, then the admiral spoke up. 'Do you want to learn and explore physics at the next level, Courtney?' The admiral asked."

"'What if I say no?' I said cautiously. Pemberton stated plainly. 'Then this meeting never took place, and you will simply go back to your duties at the Library of Congress.' The admiral spoke up. 'Courtney, are you in, or are you out?'"

"'Oh, I'm so in, yes, yes, yes! I'm in! Bring on the Buck Rogers and Flash Gordon stuff.' I responded. The two of them gave each other knowing glances. 'Courtney, please sign this letter.' The admiral told me as he handed me a single sheet of paper. 'What is it?' I asked. He smiled and warned, 'If you break our security rules and reveal what you know to unauthorized persons, they will find this letter next to your lifeless body. It's your suicide note.'"

"I sat staring at both of them. 'Is this on the level and for real?' Pemberton remarked coldly, 'As real as it gets, my dear.' The admiral was softer. 'It's the price of admission, Courtney. Think of it as an insurance policy for us.' I stared at the floor for a few moments and then asked. 'Will this be my full-time job?'"

"Pemberton spoke up, 'Think of it as an extension of your day job at the Library of Congress. We have operatives over there who will grease things for you as needed. Presently on paper, the National Arboretum requested your services to consult with them on a research matter.'"

"'But what if my boss presses me?' I asked. 'She won't!' Pemberton said with a smile. 'My boss? Is she L3S?' I asked. 'Don't worry about who is and who isn't, at the present time. The fewer people you know, the better, for everybody's sakes. When war comes, you'll find out just how big our network is during the normal course of your duties. So let that topic just drop right now, OK?' The Admiral directed."

"I reached out for the letter; I read it carefully. Then I put it on the table and signed it. Pemberton extended her hand, 'Welcome to the Ladies Secret Signal Society and the biggest adventure of your life, my dear.'"

"'When do I get to hear about the Flash Gordon stuff?' I asked. Mrs. Pemberton picked up a little bell from the serving table and rang it twice. A woman entered from a door behind Pemberton. 'Yes, ma'am?' Pemberton spoke up and directed, 'Please give Agent Malone the standard briefing about our out-of-town-visitors.' The woman simply nodded. 'Yes, ma'am.'"

"With that, I left the room with the woman, and someone took me to another room down the hall. This quiet little room had floor to ceiling shelves full of books. In the center of the room there was a six-foot library style table with some chairs. The woman removed a large three-ring notebook from one shelf. As she set the book on the table. She spoke up. 'Ok Malone, if you bump into anybody that you meet here; do not engage us in conversation. If we approach you and start a conversation, we are simply occasional work associates. Nothing more, got it?' I answered simply, 'I shouldn't acknowledge you unless you acknowledge me first.' She confirmed what I had said, 'Yes, for now.'"

"In front of me, she opened the black three-ring notebook on the table. She smiled and commented. 'Welcome to Wonderland, Alice!' She left the room, and I began reading a long-involved history of out-of-town-visitors from other worlds influencing humanity since before biblical times."

"After my reading in, a few hours later, a Navy driver took me back to the Library of Congress. For the rest of the afternoon, I was deep in thought, thinking about all the wonders I had read about and imagining the incredible possibilities. To be honest, I was numb with the fascination of what I had read about and it distracted me for many weeks and months."

"In the spring of 1941, one of the Admirals' aids briefed me on an incident in Cape Girardeau, Missouri. L3S assigned me to visit a military foreign technology research facility in Ohio. They instructed me to evaluate the physics related to a crashed off world craft that the Army had recovered. My assignment was simply to learn all I could about the technology of our out-of-town visitors. End of reel three."

The wire from reel three rolled up onto the take-up reel. Fiona stopped the recorder-player and began setting it up to rewind. She glanced over at Moira. The intelligence analyst sat quietly, seemingly in a daze. Fiona smirked to herself with a knowing look. "Are you ok, Moira?" she asked.

Moira nodded slightly, speaking softly, "My dear Goddess, it's all real!"

9:36am Jan 27-Courtney and L3S–Details

Moira put in a few hours over at State to keep up appearances. She was deep into the financial page of Pravda when her casual business phone rang. The call was from her agency boss, Bob Akron.

"Moira, our information mining ferrets have found what we suspected," Bob said. "Remember how we joked that Malone's long illness might have been from nuclear work? Well, it turns out we were right. Courtney Malone worked on a compartmented aspect of the Manhattan Project."

Moira questioned, "How was this possible? Women were pretty insignificant back then!"

Akron remarked, "You have to remember the Second World War was on. Women were getting opportunities to contribute everywhere in the war effort. In June 1944, Oppenheimer moved William Teller, the father of the H-Bomb, out of the Manhattan Project's T Division and placed him in charge of a special group responsible for the Super. The Super was the early theoretical work that led to the development of the H-Bomb. Teller reported directly to Oppenheimer. Teller's Super group became part of Fermi's F Division when he joined the Los Alamos Laboratory in September 1944. It included Stanislaw Ulam, Jane Roberg, Geoffrey Chew, Harold and Mary Argo, and Maria Goeppert-Mayer and guess who, Courtney Malone. After the war, she worked for William Teller on the H-Bomb development."

Moira simply remarked that's amazing, "I suppose Malone, being a trained physicist within the Government, gave her an edge."

Akron replied, "Add to that she worked for the Library of Congress. She was reviewing and cataloging all the latest papers. Malone was current on all the best and current physics literature. She would have been a shoo-in at an interview. Add to that she had the Brass ring of being connected to the oldest Spook outfit in the country and the folks who could open doors for her."

Then Akron asked, "How is the review of the Malone wire reels going?" Moira hesitated and remarked, "Bob, this is not a secure line. But let me say it this way: it's profound and esoteric as hell. I can honestly say the further we get into these reels..." She paused, then added, "The deeper down a rabbit hole we go. Frankly, I'm thinking we might be able not sanitize this material."

"Is it still that sensitive?" Akron asked.

Again, Moira reiterated, "This is not a secure line. But let me state it this way. Imagine a man comes clean with an extra-marital affair to his wife. Then the wife asks, What else have you been lying to me about?" Again she paused and added, "In school they taught us that revealing Top Secret material could cause grave damage to our country. For the sake of argument, let's say that something above top secret could cause catastrophic damage to both our country and our human culture."

Moira's boss simply remarked, "You were right to do your sanitation work in a SCIF. I look forward to being read into the material. I'm sending over a few photos of Ms. Malone from back in the day."

Moira asked, "Have the ferrets found anything else I should know?"

"Yeah," Akron commented. "Our ferrets interviewed the medical examiner who did Malone's postmortem. He admitted to being pressured by dark government types to list Malone's death as a suicide. Someone asked him to hide the forensic evidence and lab work that strongly suggested foul play. Had it not been for the pressure that was applied, he would have listed her death as a homicide."

Moira sighed. "Oh shit. Cloak and dagger stuff."

"I'm afraid so," Akron grumbled.

"Bob, we're certainly not law enforcement. So there is not much we can do about her murder. But initially, I believed that someone murdered her to silence her about something," Moira hinted.

Bob moaned, "Moira, watch your back as you proceed." She muttered before she hung up.

"Yeah!" Moira stared at the ceiling for a few moments. "If you only knew Bob, if you only knew."

2:47pm Jan 27-Need to Know

Fiona McKenzie and Moira Stewart met in front of the SCIF module they were using. The two women went through the ritual of holding up their unit keys in front of them. Each inserted their keys and turned them together. They heard the hatch way door mechanism unlock the various securing rods within the door. After a moment, there was a slight whooshing sound as the hatchway opened slightly. The operatives opened the huge hatch. Upon first glance, the two intelligence officers both said nearly in unison, "What the hell?"

The table where the HIFI gear and the two vintage wire recorders/players had been, along with all the Malone material, was clear and empty. As they stepped up into the supposedly secure space, they saw a conference style tent card sitting on the table. It read; **You do not need to know.**

Moira sniffed, "Smell that?"

Fiona sniffed twice, "Alcohol?"

"Ya, no kidding, someone chemically washed the SCIF." Moira barked.

"Whoever took our stuff didn't want to leave any DNA around." Fiona remarked as she pulled out a chair and sat down. Moira could see that she was shaking and white as a sheet. Fiona anxiously opened her purse and removed a cigarette and nervously lit it. After two long drags, she seemed to compose herself and addressed Moira, "Are you open to an opinion?" she asked as she took another drag on her cigarette.

Moira had a disturbed look on her face. "Where we just played?"

Fiona slowly nodded her head. "I don't think they ever ensured the level of security they claimed for this Navy SCIF module. I'd lay money that they listened to everything we did in here."

"But who?" Moira questioned.

Fiona took a last puff on her smoke and crushed it out on the tabletop then she groused, "The bastards took the damned ash tray; they totally cleaned this place. Let's you and I go to a very public pub some place and sort this out. I'm not feeling very safe in this thing at the moment."

Moira put a finger to her lips. Then said, "Let's jump in my car and go to a joint I know on K Street." She continued to put her finger to her lips. "Let's hit the ladies' room, then drop the keys off with the front check-in-desk and sign out."

Moira then gestured to Fiona, who nodded and remarked,

"Sounds like a plan." They both left the SCIF module and walked down the hall toward the ladies' room and entered. They entered stalls, both women relieved themselves. As Moira was washing her hands she remarked, "I hope you like Chili." Fiona went along with the game, "Love it." Before leaving the rest room Moira pulled out her cell phone and sent a text message to her boss, "Going to K Street. Going to get a big helping of Chili." She pressed SEND. She turned her phone off. Fiona followed suit and turned off her phone as well.

Moira simply whispered, "Let's go." The two women walked to the front desk of the SCIF facility, handed over their keys to the Navy Security Guards and both women signed out.

As they turned to leave, Fiona briefly looked over her shoulder at the guards and remarked, "So long and thanks for all the fish!" One guard smiled and chuckled. The other guard looked puzzled.

Outside, Moira remarked, "Turn left." Fiona commented, "Our cars are back there in the parking lot."

Moira simply answered, "Do you have a remote car starter?" Moira asked.

Fiona simply said, "Yes."

Moira continued, "Let's assume the worst and that we're marked. Make sure your phone is off. Get the remote starter fob out, but don't press it yet. I want to get about a half of a block further down the street." As the two women got to an intersection about a block from the facility. Moira remarked, "I live by the motto, paranoia protects. On three with me, let's press our remote starters together. One, Two, Three." Both women pressed the button on their fobs. There was a deafening pair of explosions from the direction of the Navy facility parking lot. Fiona looked stunned.

Moira grimaced. "Let's head to the Metro station and ride around for a couple of hours." The two women heard the sirens of emergency service vehicles in the distance, heading to the Navy Facility Parking lot as they walked into the metro station. Fiona started to remove her metro hard card from her purse.

Moira commanded, "No, cash only! We'll get a couple of paper passes. Remember, we're both dead." Fiona got a surprised, horrified look on her face, but complied. Moira commented, "Doesn't L3S teach you folks any Trade Craft?"

Fiona whined, "I'm a forensic tech, not a damned field operative, for god sakes!"

Moira smirked. "Let's go!"

The two women went down the escalator and boarded a train headed toward Metro Center. They rode back and forth on several lines and switched lines at Metro Center. All of this happened during the afternoon rush. In a crowd of thousands of faces, they felt mostly invisible.

4:50pm Jan 27-My Uncle's Place

Moira and Fiona exited the north bound Metro Red line train at the Silver Spring Metro Station. Moira led the way, turning right onto Colesville rd. until the two women crossed Georgia Ave. Fiona followed Moira like a pet puppy. Moira turned and walked north on Georgia Ave until the two women were standing in front of an Ethiopian Restaurant.

Fiona looked puzzled. "I thought we were going to K Street for chili?"

Moira smirked. "It's a code phrase for a safe house location. Ok, here's our destination. Say nothing and let me do the talking. If all goes right, we'll get a clean, comfortable room and a splendid meal to boot," Moira stated. Fiona simply nodded in agreement. The two women entered the Restaurant. Moira walked up to the front counter and addressed the Ethiopian woman behind the counter, "Inidemini waliki" (good day) The woman smiled and answered "Mini liridashi?" (How can I help you?)

Then Moira stated, "Inē ye'āgotihi liji chēlisī nenyi, fok'i layi yalewini ye'āgotihini kifili ifeligalehu." (I am your cousin Moira; I need your uncle's room upstairs.)

The Ethiopian woman's face took on a surprised and then business-like expression. The woman simply nodded, speaking

English. "Come," as she gestured for Moira and Fiona to follow her. She led the two women back through the kitchen area and then to the rear entrance of the establishment. The woman took a small ring of keys off a hook on the wall. "Upstairs, turn right. The second door on the right." She instructed.

Moira accepted the keys. "I'm expecting my uncle. Send him up when he arrives." Then Moira spoke the foreign tongue that Fiona had heard previously, "Bet'ami āmeseginalehu." (Thank you very much).

Moira and Fiona climbed the dimly lit stairwell, turned right, and proceeded down the hall to the second door on the right. Moira inserted the key and unlocked the door. The two women entered the hotel like room. "This is a safe house for an agent on the run," Moira explained.

Fiona gave her a questioned look. "What was that language that you were speaking?"

Moira was poking her head in a doorway in another room. "Here's the bathroom!" She turned and faced Fiona. "I was speaking Amharic, the official language of Ethiopia."

Fiona cocked her head with a curious look. "You speak Ethiopian?"

"Nah, I know basic conversational phrases: police station, Public Rest rooms, restaurant, transportation queries like train station, buses etc. and basic greetings and pleasantries. At best, I speak Amharic like a clumsy foreigner." Moira casually said, to cloak her skill. A skill learned during two years of diplomatic courier duty, shuttling from the American embassy in Bahrain to a diplomatic mission near Addis Abeba during the Ethiopian Civil War, until it ended in '91. She looked at her watch. "I expect my boss to be here shortly to pick us up. My boss will buy us a nice dinner here and then he'll take us to more protected quarters. I suggest you hit the restroom just in case he gets here sooner than later."

About twenty minutes later, Bob Akron showed up with a casually dressed couple. As they entered the room, Mr. Akron introduced himself to Fiona McKenzie and exchanged pleasantries.

Moira gave the woman of the couple with Akron an inquiring look. She tapped her hand under her left armpit. The woman gave Moira a slight nod in the affirmative. This was a sign that the team with Akron was muscle and heavily armed. The woman reached into her purse, stealthily removed something and reached over to shake hands with Moira and palmed her a Snub Nose 38 caliber. Moira glanced at it and immediately slipped it into her purse.

Then the woman turned to Akron. "We should get these folks some supper." Mr. Akron piped up suppose I buy you all dinner before we leave. Moira and the couple spoke up, and all seemed to concur with the notion of an evening meal.

The woman spoke up, "I'll take Fiona down and we'll get a table for six." Akron answered back, "Sounds great, we'll be right down." The woman left with Fiona.

Akron spoke up, "Where the hell have you been?"

Moira simply said, "We rode on three distinct lines of the metro for nearly two hours, hoping to be lost in the rush-hour crowd."

Akron nodded, "Good thinking, let's get some supper, and get you gals some secure quarters, then we'll debrief both of you in the morning."

Moira flatly asked, "Are we dead?"

Akron coldly remarked, "DC police and DC emergency services have tentatively reported your identities to the media an hour ago as victims of a terrorist bombing. While the bombing occurred on Navy leased property, neither of you are Navy nor Marine personnel, NIS didn't claim authority. So the FBI and ATF are dealing with the issue and the forensics. We're liaised in with them. The public has been told that the intense flames of the burning vehicles virtually destroyed your bodies beyond recognition. Theoretically, nobody should look for either of you. It's all very sad," Akron said with a solemn smirk.

Moira stood shaking her head with an amused look on her face. "How long will we be dead?" Akron shrugged his shoulders, "It's hard to say, we need to figure out who pulled this stunt! Moira, you've been dead before. You know it takes as long as it takes."

8:30am Jan 28-The Hotel Flying Saucer

Fiona and Moira had adjoining rooms in a high-rise hotel in Crystal City, Virginia. Mr. Akron had a room next to Moira, and the muscle team had the room next to Fiona.

Moira was washing her face when she heard a knock on the door that the two rooms shared. Moira stood off to the side of the door. She humorously sang out, "Who's that knocking at my door?"

Moira heard Fiona bust out with a laugh on the other side of the door. Fiona responded, "Your friendly neighborhood, Lady-355!" Moira snickered, unlocked the passage door and opened it. Fiona was standing there in the hotel bathrobe. "What do we have to do to get some coffee in this place?" Fiona remarked.

Moira gestured for her to come in. "Well, that's actually a sticky point. Technically, we're both dead."

Fiona got a perturbed look on her face. "So you're telling me there's no coffee in the afterlife?"

Moira gestured to Fiona to take a seat in the room's overstuffed armchair. Moira pulled out the office style desk chair and took a seat. "Obviously you've never been in sequestered protection before," Moira remarked and then added, "That happy couple with Mr. Akron last evening is our muscle and firepower. If we need it, they are our protection. They will get us fed and watered."

Fiona groaned, "So, we're impounded guests and a couple of mafia hit men types are our concierges?"

Moira nodded in the affirmative. "That's about it."

"When do we get to be, not dead?" Fiona questioned with a facial expression most grave. Moira seemed to study the floor for a few moments, seeming to gather her thoughts. "I suppose it boils down to who is trying to kill us and why they wired both our cars with high explosives. That's the cat-and-mouse game, which I'm frequently up to my waist in. Put simply, someone trying to kill you amounts to the fact that you are a liability to them in terms of knowing something. In the spy game, knowledge is power over someone or a represents a financial opportunity. The more knowledge you have about something they are trying to keep close to their chest, the more you are a liability. In the intelligence business, the devil is in the details of the information you have gathered."

Fiona, in a whispering voice, commented, "That tent card said we do not need to know."

Moira pointed at her, "Bingo," and added, "The fact that they sanitized the room and wired our autos suggests we stumbled upon something we weren't supposed to know...and that made us a liability. The only question I have in my mind was, what was that key element?"

"What happens to us if your agency can't figure out who's after us?" Fiona said with a strained crackle in her voice.

"In your case, they'll resettle you in a program similar to witness protection. A new identity, a new location, a new job and a new chance at life," Moira explained. Fiona squinted at Moira. "What about your case?"

Moira seemed to stare at the ceiling for a few moments. "In the spy business, I have half a dozen cover field identities. I could slip into any of them and make that my real life from now on. Of course, that too has its drawbacks and risks, as well as some advantages."

Fiona shook her head, "When the frack are we going to get some coffee and breakfast?"

Moira looked at the alarm clock in the room. "Oh, hell, it's almost 9:30, we're supposed to be debriefed at 10!" Moira picked up the telephone receiver and listened for a dial tone. She winced! Then tapped the switch-hook buttons on top of the phone. "Frack, it's dead, Fiona. Get dressed pronto and grab your purse."

Fiona sat mesmerized and didn't move. Moira spoke up in a command tone of voice, "Fiona, get dressed now! We have a problem!" Within ninety seconds, Fiona got dressed and took her purse.

Then Moira directed, "I'm going to knock on the door of the muscle. If something is wrong, I'll yell GO NOW, you head for the fire escape, and we'll meet in the parking lot. If I don't show in five, or perhaps ten minutes, go flag down a cop pronto!"

Moira slipped out of the hotel room. Fiona stood next to the door open about two inches, so she could hear Moira, if needed. Moira walked down the hall and knocked on the door of the muscle. She didn't hear any response. She again knocked, but hard. "Sally, Jimmy, are you in there?" Once again, she encountered silence. Moira looked at the maid getting ready to enter and make up a room.

Moira asked politely, "Española" (Spanish). The maid answered. "Sí" (Yes) Moira, with an urgent tone in her voice, asked. "¡Por favor abre! ¡Mis amigos viajeros están enfermos!" (Please open! My traveling friends are sick!)

The maid reluctantly came over and put her key in the door and unlocked it and opened the door. Moira took two steps into the room. On the floor lay Sally with an ooze of blood on her forehead. When Moira glanced towards the bed, she noticed Jimmy lying there with half of the right side of his face blown away.

"¡Están muertos, llame a la policía!" (They are dead. Call the police!) Moira barked to the maid. In a loud voice, Moira closed the door and yelled, "Fiona, GO NOW!" Fiona ran out of the room and headed for the fire escape, with Moira right behind her.

As Moira was about to exit the hotel, she saw a fire alarm actuator. *We need distraction;* she thought. She pulled the lever down; sirens and bells began ringing in the building. As Moira exited the building, she saw Fiona and dashed over to her and grabbed her by the arm. "Walk fast with me!"

Fiona looked startled. "Where are we going?"

"Not sure! But we can't hang around here. We shouldn't run, but we must walk briskly," Moira said crisply. After a few minutes of walking, the two women arrived at the Crystal City Metro station. "Now what?" Fiona asked. Moira gestured for Fiona to follow her. Moira walked up to an outdoor pay phone. She opened her purse and removed a coin, then inserted the quarter and dialed a number. Moira heard a phone ringing on the receiver. A moment later, a woman answered and simply said, "North American Surveying, how can I help you?"

Moira calmly commented, "There's been a landslide at the Crystal mine. The Survey team may have perished. The Russian Princess has Georgie-girl, and is taking her to Vietnam for Pho!"

"No! Take her to the Temple," the woman's voice said firmly, "…and treat her to Masha Tea!"

Moira thoughtfully replied, "Taking Georgie girl for Masha tea!" The woman's voice said simply, "Enjoy!"

Moira motioned for Fiona to go into the metro station. "Let's go for another Metro ride." Again, with cash, they purchased metro tickets. Moira led Fiona to the side of the Metro line that read Franconia-Springfield. They stood quietly on the platform until a Metro train arrived. When the doors opened, Moira and Fiona got on to a mostly empty train car. After the doors closed and the train moved.

Fiona asked, "Where are we going?" Moira softly quipped, "I'm taking you to brunch."

At Franconia-Springfield, the pair left the station. As they walked, Moira remarked casually, "We have a bit of a walk, but where I'm taking you is safe and, I might add, delightful."

The two women arrived at the Hoffman Town Center after a long walk up and down several streets. Moira led Fiona to an establishment called Rus Uz. It was obvious to Fiona that this was a Russian Tea House. Moira leaned into Fiona, "When we enter this place you are my cousin Georgia." Fiona gave her a puzzled look. Then nodded, "Okay, I'm Georgia."

They entered and waited to be seated. From the rear area of the business, a short, heavyset, but elegantly dressed woman with gray hair walked toward them. Suddenly, the woman lit up with an excited, beaming expression and spoke Russian, "Privet Mashen'ka, proshlo mnogo vremeni!" (Greetings Mashenka, it's been too long!) Moira and the elder woman embraced like long-lost friends. Then Moira remarked in Russian, "Yes, much too long, old friend. English, please."

Moira stepped back, gestured toward the woman and introduced her to Fiona, "This is Madame Natakya Solovyova. We are old friends."

Natakya looked at Fiona and smiled broadly, "Da, we are very old friends!"

Then Moira introduced Fiona in her nom de plume, speaking Russian. "This is my cousin Georgia."

Madame Solovyova turned to Fiona, "Georgia, I am pleased to meet you." Solovyova stepped back and addressed Moira, "Masha, do you have time for tea?"

Moira responded cheerfully, "Actually, we're here for brunch, and do you still have some coffee?" Madame Solovyova laughed, "For you, old friend and your cousin, anything you wish. Better yet, I will make you both a nice brunch, a Natakya special. You both sit over here and I will bring you some coffee!"

Madame Solovyova went back to the kitchen after Moira and Fiona took their seats.

Fiona gave Moira a curious look. "So you speak fluent Russian and you two are very old friends?" Moira grinned. "In a manner of speaking, yes, very much so. Natakya and Mashenka have had some pretty colorful adventures together once upon a time."

"I don't suppose you'd care to share one of those adventures with me?" Fiona asked. Moira shook her head in the negative. "Nah, you don't need to know."

"Cloak and dagger?" Fiona queried. Moira just replied drolly, "...and then some. Mums the word!" Moments later, Solovyova returned with a carafe of coffee and cups and saucers.

As she set them down on the table, Solovyova asked Mashenka, "So Professor Petrova are you still teaching Theater at Cornell." Moira, while blowing on her cup of black coffee, commented, "Yes, but I'm on sabbatical."

Solovyova remarked, "It is good you take a rest from the teaching. I'll be back with your brunch."

Fiona gave Moira an amused look. "My, what an interesting life you have, Professor Petrova?"

Moira curtly remarked, "Drop it!"

"So? What can we expect for brunch?" Fiona asked.

"I suspect it might be an open-faced sandwich, with Russian-style smoke sausage or maybe boiled sausage called *Doktorskaya kolbasa*. Maybe wheat pancakes and a side of either boiled or perhaps scrambled eggs." Moira explained.

A bell rang as the front door opened and two well-built men wearing three-piece suits walked into the Tea House. The men looked around the teahouse and made eye contact with Moira. They nodded at her; she knew them and nodded back at them. The two men took seats at a small cafe table for two near the front door. Moira remarked to Fiona/Georgia, "We can relax. Our new muscle is here to protect us while we eat. After we finish our brunch, they'll transport us to a safe place."

2pm Jan 28-The Pillared Mansion

Maureen Henderson, Deputy Director of OSS62, conducted the debriefing for the agency. She sat in an overstuffed armchair, as did Moira Stewart. Next to both of them was an OSS62 stenographer. The three women were in a soundproof room on the third floor of a palatial mansion somewhere in Potomac, Maryland.

Moira commented, "Before we start, what's the status of Bob Akron?"

Henderson shrugged her shoulders. "We do not know. He wasn't in the room when our people went through it. There's forensic evidence he had been in the room and that he had spent time in the bed. We found a gym bag outfitted for perhaps a night or two worth of stay and his toiletries. Oddly, his shoes and socks were on the floor next to the bed. His service pistol was under his pillow set in a safe setting. He placed his shirt and pants, which he had been wearing, on the desk chair. It looks like someone entered the room and spirited him away literally in his underwear."

"Perhaps he's a hostage?" Moira remarked.

"Well, that's our current thinking. But why? Is the question." Henderson commented. "There's two lines of thought here. One: whoever sanitized your SCIF and wired both your cars thinks you are both alive and plans to hold Bob as a bargaining chip. Two: The other line of thought. They know Bob was your boss and had information about your progress. If they were sanitizing a sensitive data spill, it's logical for them to silence the last person who was on your reporting chain of management."

Moira spoke up. "Something doesn't add up here. That they killed Sally and Jim and took Bob but didn't kill either me or Fiona makes little sense. We were the bigger data spill, we're the genuine risk. I think we're looking at two different situations."

"Good point," Henderson answered. Moira sat pondering for a few moments. Then perked up, "Wait a minute, have Bob, Sally and Jim been in the field together on an operation?"

Henderson commented, "That's interesting, and we can check that easily enough. Let's finish your debriefing!"

After about an hour of Ms. Henderson finishing a debriefing of Moira about the SCIF incident and Moira's account of their experience on the run. The two intelligence officers sat down and observed afternoon tea. Moira sat sipping her jasmine tea. After a few minutes, she stated, "Maureen, I'm not a homicide detective, but the question arises. How were two highly trained security bodyguard types, the likes of Sally and Jimmy snuffed out so easily?"

Maureen grimaced. "That's an interesting point! Any thoughts?" Moira shook her head. "Logic says they both knew and trusted their assailant!"

"Are you suggesting that Bob shot them?" Maureen asked.

Moira studied the floor for a few moments. "If not Bob, then somebody else in our little clandestine family. Somebody whom they both trusted, and they thought had their backs!"

Maureen began to tear up. "Oh, god this is unthinkable. But what would be the motive?"

There was a deafening silence in the room as both women

considered the implications. After perhaps ten minutes, Maureen spoke up. "Let's say that L3S was completely honorable and would never hurt a sorority sister. After all, you and Fiona are both technically L3S sorority sisters."

Moira spoke up. "There is a risk of a sanctioned death clause in their security oath. But neither Fiona nor I had violated that Security Oath. In fact, our whole SCIF operation should protect those sorts of secrets." She paused. "But someone wired our SCIF for sound. Perhaps a third party."

Maureen sat quietly, pondering, then gave Moira a quizzical look. "What did you find that was mind blowing and earth shattering?" Moira studied Maureen for a few moments. "Ok, regarding my L3S security oath, no specific details, but a couple of high-level bullet points, OK?" Maureen nodded in the affirmative.

"First, Bob discovered that Courtney Malone's murder was covered up and made to look like suicide administratively," Moira commented. Maureen asked, "What else?" Moira continued. "Malone's wire recording revealed that UFOs and aliens among us are very real and that some covert sect has control of the information and will kill to keep it suppressed."

Maureen buried her face in her hands for a few minutes, then she spoke up, "It's got to be the Vatican's League of Under Guards." Moira had a shocked look on her face. "You mean those guys are real?"

"Oh, they are real, all right! They've been around for centuries and they are so ruthless they make the old Soviet KGB look like a troop of Eagle Scouts! They were a huge part of the effort that took out the Knights Templar on Friday, October 13, 1307!" Maureen described.

Moira hung her head and muttered, "Frack!"

10pm Jan 30-Glen Echo Park

Moira Stewart and Fiona McKenzie sat quietly in the back of a black stretch limousine, facing Maureen Henderson. "The DC office of the Swiss Guard wanted our meeting to be on neutral turf.

So they arranged our meeting in Glen Echo Park in a building called the Spanish Ballroom." Maureen explained, "Honestly, they were reluctant to talk to us and L3S."

Fiona gave Maureen a quizzical look. "L3S is sending a representative?"

Maureen gave her a gentle nod. "They were stunned to hear that you are alive. In fact, they expressed great delight that you are both safe. They agreed to send a representative to facilitate your rematriation, as they put it."

Moira grumbled, "I hope all three parties agreed to safe conduct?"

Maureen smiled at Moira. "Absolutely!" Moira muttered something under her breath in Russian. Maureen raised an eyebrow with a questioning look.

"It's an old KGB saying, Hope for the best, expect the worst," Moira remarked.

Fiona responded with a sober, "Amen to that."

Maureen had a thoughtful expression for a few moments. Then remarked, "Trust me, I get that we're going to be dancing with the devil and that we'll be dancing to his tune. But if there is any chance that Bob Akron is still alive. I'm willing to endure a few turns on the dance floor to find out."

Fiona looked at Maureen. "Do you really think the Sondergarde (Secret Guard) is going to be square with us?" Maureen slowly shook her head in the negative, "No, I don't."

Moira glanced at Fiona and remarked, "Of course, the first rule in this business is to deny everything!" Maureen simply nodded in concurrence.

The driver lowered the window separating him and the three women. "Ma'am, it looks like all the parties are here."

Moira remarked, "Once more into the breech." The driver got out and opened the limo door for the three women. Each of them quietly exited. Moira was the last to leave the vehicle. As she did, she leaned into the husky driver and softly said, "Please tell me you are packing?"

With a stoic look, the driver simply said, "Yes, ma'am!" Then he added, "There's plenty of high-end toys under my jacket in the front passenger seat...enough for a serious party." Moira gave him a wink.

As the delegates walked over to the entrance. Two men with metal detecting wands passed them over the two representatives of the Guardia Svizzera. Then they passed the wands over the L3S representatives, Joyce Pemberton Anderson and Fiona McKenzie. Finally, Maureen Henderson and Moira Stewart of OSS62. After scanning each of the women, all the organizational delegates entered the cavernous Spanish Ballroom building.

In the center of the expansive ballroom floor was a large round banquet table. On the table near each chair, there were tent cards that read.

Noah Brunner - Guardia Svizzera
Wagner Vincent - Guardia Svizzera
Joyce Pemberton Anderson - L3S
Fiona McKenzie - L3S
Maureen Henderson - OSS62
Mashenka Petrova - OSS62

Upon reading the OSS62 tent cards, Maureen glanced at a shocked Moira with a surprised look and whispered, "I never told them who was coming with me and I most certainly didn't tell them Masha was coming."

Moira groused quietly. "Shit, we've got a mole!"

Maureen moaned quietly. "Yep! Just roll with it, hon, just be Masha." Moira could feel cold sweat appearing on her back.

After all the parties were quietly standing behind their chairs, Noah Brunner spoke in a gracious tone, and said, "Ladies, please take your seats." Everyone pulled out their chairs. The women sat down, followed by the two men.

Again, Noah Brunner spoke. "It is good to meet all of you."

He paused and looked at Moira. "Professor Petrova, I remember you from a tour of Soviet scholars in the Sistine Chapel in 1988. I was that humble Swiss Guard you directed a question to."

Moira nodded and answered in a slightly accented voice, "Yes, I did. I'm honored that you remember me. After all, you must see thousands of people."

Brunner replied, "It's a strange thing. Some people just linger in one's memory. I'm delighted to see that after the fall of the USSR, you found gainful employment with the OSS62."

Moira gave him a beaming smile and remarked, still in her accented voice, "They've given me career opportunities that I never considered. Thank you."

After the pleasantries with Professor Petrova, Mr. Brunner addressed the entire body of the women present. "Dr. Henderson, my superior, informed me that you wish to discuss some possible operational overlap between the Guardia Svizzera and OSS62 and the L3S?"

Maureen responded immediately. "I wish to know if the Guardia Svizzera or the Sondergarde took the sensitive materials that Ms. McKenzie and Dr. Petrova were analyzing. In order to maintain good working relations between L3S and OSS62, we would appreciate a straightforward answer." Maureen stated.

Brunner leaned to his associate, Wagner Vincent. There were a few moments of whispering. Then, Brunner stated, "Yes, the material in question was most certainly stolen by Dr. Malone back in the nineteen fifties. The Vatican Library wanted it back. The material is culturally sensitive and its premature release would, in the Holy See's view would be catastrophically damaging to the spiritual view of the human family at large."

Then Dr. Henderson asked, "Were your agents responsible for the deaths of two of my security soldiers several days ago?"

Again, he consulted his associate, Mr. Vincent. Brunner took on a disturbed face. "Regretfully, yes, they were an impediment for the Sondergarde who were on a mission to extract Mr. Robert Akron, who was a Double Agent and was harming both our agencies greatly and had become troublesome to us. We will, of course, compensate the families of your two soldiers."

Maureen looked irritated. "Would you consider releasing Mr. Akron into my custody? We will make sure he faces consequences."

Brunner shook his head no. "Dr. Henderson, Akron was not doing your agency any favors, and he represented a tremendous information risk to our institution, regretfully we had to sanction him."

"You had no right!" Maureen said in a heated tone.

Brunner folded his arms and was silent for a few moments, then responded, "Life and death decisions are among the toughest things we do in this business. It was a hard decision, and I took full responsibility for it. Dr. Henderson, would you have made that decision to protect your OSS62 agency and sanction him?"

Maureen answered plainly. "No, I don't like to play God."

"Dr. Maureen Henderson, how did you ever rise to the leadership rank you have?" Brunner commented. Then he looked at Moira, "Dr. Petrova, would you have sanctioned Akron?"

Moira gave it a moment's thought, "Considering the risks to the agency and longer-term ramifications. I believe I would have sanctioned him. It's a very hard call every time you have to pull the trigger. I suppose in this business it's one of those things that tests your meddle. Weighing the options and do what's needed."

Brunner, with a resolved look, glanced at the other women. "Ladies, if Professor Petrova lives long enough. I would wager money she'll probably be running OSS62 in 10 or 15 years!"

Dr. Henderson gave both Moira and Brunner a disgusted look. "Mr. Brunner, will you compensate the family of Mr. Akron?" Brunner was silent for a few moments. "Yes, we'll compensate you for his family's sake. But he was a sewer rat and you know it now! If you call him a hero at his funeral, the lie will be on your lips. I believe we have concluded our business."

Moira raised her hand. Brunner nodded to her. "Who wired Ms. McKenzie's and my car?" Mr. Vincent shook his head. Brunner nodded. "We informed Akron that we stripped and cleaned the SCIF unit. It is our understanding that Akron ordered your autos wired to cover his tracks and the fact that you were even looking at that sensitive material and that it was now gone. We also believe that he was also very shocked that you two survived. How did you manage that, Professor?"

Moira thought for a moment, then answered, "I think it's like my old fencing instructor used to say, if in trouble always, return to the fundamentals. When I first received training, my instructor taught me that a governing rule of this game is personal intelligence guided by experience. I didn't panic, and I just reasoned my way to safety."

Dr. Henderson stood up and began walking away and remarked. "We have concluded our business, and we're leaving!" Moira stood and looked at Brunner, and gave him a polite nod. She looked at the L3S women and gave them a polite nod as well. "Thank You for your time, everyone," she said graciously. She turned and walked toward the exit. Brunner shouted, "I'll see you in 10 or 15 years, Professor Petrova!"

Moira Stewart and Fiona McKenzie together attended the memorials of the slain OSS62 bodyguards killed in Crystal City. To maintain appearances, Moira reluctantly attended the funeral of her former boss, Robert J. Akron. The burial of Robert J. Akron's ashes took place in Arlington National Cemetery. During the graveside eulogy, Dr. Maureen Henderson spoke highly of the fallen Akron. She praised him as a hero for the greater good of his country.

PART FOUR
THE DRAMA PROFESSOR

In the mid Nineteen Nineties
10:15 am March 9 -An Irregular Request

Moira Stewart sat quietly reading the morning edition of Pravda at her contractor position at the Russia Desk unit at the State Department. Her casual business desk phone rang. Moira paused a moment to think English, then answered the phone with a polite, "Moira Stewart, cultural analysis. May I help you, sir?"

"Hi Moira, Laura Boyce here, any chance you can drop over to my office this afternoon? I might have a field assignment for you." Moira frowned. "Laura, you said might. I never thought I would ever hear that word from your lips. Its sounds like I have an option, to say no."

Moira could hear her manager laugh, "Actually, no is an option. I think what I've got to tell you will intrigue you. Show up at my office about 1:30 and I'll fill you in on this unique assignment opportunity."

1:15 pm March 9-North American Surveying, Inc

Moira took the escalator to the surface level from the Pentagon City Metro and walked a block west and came upon an unassuming commercial office building. She took an elevator to the top floor. The elevator car doors opened across from a pair of mahogany doors with an engraved brass plate on the door that read, "North American Surveying."

A well-dressed middle-aged man sitting behind a reception desk at North American Surveying welcomed Moira upon her entry. He addressed her and asked, "How can I help you?"

Moira could see that the man had one arm on the top of the desk and one arm under the desk. No doubt he has his hand on an automatic pistol holstered under his file drawer, Moira thought to herself. "I'm here to see Dr. Boyce about a pneumonia shot." Moira stated plainly.

The man grinned. "The door on the left." Moira heard a buzz and a click as the door unlatched.

She entered the space beyond. As she did, the door behind her closed and had a mechanical latching sound. She walked down the hall to a door that had an aluminum plate on it that read Laura Boyce.

She knocked twice, a woman's voice sang out, "Come in." Moira opened the door and there was her manager, Laura Boyce. "Moira!" she cheerfully said, as she stood up to shake hands. Boyce was an African-American woman in her early forties. The two women had come up through the ranks together in the eighties. Laura motioned for Moira to close the office door and take a seat.

Moira sat down and simply asked, "What's up?"

Laura sat quietly for a moment before she smirked and began, "I got a call from the Chair of the Performing Arts department at Cornell University. They have received an invitation for your Mashenka cover identity to come and teach for a year at the St. Petersburg State Theatre Arts Academy in the Russian Federation."

Moira, with a stunned expression on her face, simply whispered, "What the hell?"

Laura continued, "Well, think about it. Professor Petrova has been on Cornell's books for nearly fifteen years as a resident professor. Over the years, you've taught a few classes and directed a few plays. Hell, you've even published academic papers on American Musical Theater history over the years. We need to further develop the character of Mashenka and maintain the illusion that Petrova is a real person." Laura paused, then asked, "Would you like to do it?" Moira had a strange stare in her eyes. Boyce could see that Stewart was considering all the ramifications. Then Laura spoke up, "I can handle all the complications for the contracts you are working on. That shouldn't be an issue."

Moira sat back with a serious expression and asked, "Is my cover blown? Is this a ploy by the FSB to lure me into the country and drag me off to a gulag in Siberia?"

Laura waved her finger. "I did some checking. The college's original founding was in 1779 at the Emperor's Theatre in St Petersburg, making it the oldest theater school in Russia. Apparently, over the course of its history, the institute went through several reorganizations and name changes. Moira, the institution is prestigious!"

"But there have to be a couple of thousand university grade theater arts professors out there more prominent than me and are the real deal! I can't see how they would find an obscure and, for God's sakes, a counterfeit one like me," Moira moaned.

Laura stared at her desk with a knowing smile. "Ok, I'd buy that, if they were just looking for a plain old theater arts professor to just teach. But what if they remembered an American theater arts professor who helped save their country during a disaster?"

"What the frack?" Moira remarked with a puzzled look.

"I looked at your service record. In 1986, you were one of two American academics that acted as translators with an American team of top nuclear physicists and engineers that were sent to help the Russians put a damper on the runaway nuclear reaction during the Chernobyl disaster!" Laura explained.

"Yeah, but all I did was translate. Besides, virtually nobody state side except high-level government people even knew we were there to advise. We had no media attention in the free world and, of course, that was by design." Moira said in an exasperated tone.

Laura put up her hands. "Whoa! I agree that the state side of the team got no visibility, probably to let the Russians shine. But

I had our research folks perform a Citation Index search. Guess what? The Russian press wrote many stories about a top team of American scientists who were helping the effort. Remember, this was all happening during the Mikhail Gorbachev era of perestroika political reform and Glasnost transparency. Pravda did several extensive articles about the American adviser team and their two translators, one of which was an American theater arts professor from Cornell University, Professor Mashenka Petrova."

Then Laura added. "Your service record also states that Professor Petrova received an invitation to travel with some Soviet Scholars to the Vatican when Pope John Paul was making overtures to Gorbachev for a papal visit to the USSR in 1988." Laura added. "Again, the Soviet press was writing nice things about you."

Moira laid back in her chair, looking like it had knocked the wind out of her. Laura sat quietly with a Cheshire Cat grin.

2:30 pm Tuesday 9 -March North American Surveying

As Moira poured herself a cup of coffee from the duty coffee pot in the staff pantry, she remarked to her boss, Laura Boyce. "If I do this faculty exchange thing in St. Petersburg, I'm going to have to sit down with Provisioning and have a hand in what clothing they're going to issue me."

Laura was pouring hot water into a cup for some tea. "You've had no issues before. What's your concern?"

Moira leaned up against the service counter and sipped her coffee. "Well ok, first off, Provisioning has usually given me resort casual and utilitarian clothing suitable for short-term field missions. If I'm going to be over there as Ms. Professor, I'm going to need daywear for non-workdays, professional attire for her teaching role, at least a small collection of eveningwear suitable for dressy faculty events, not to mention the theater and concert events. After all, St. Petersburg has a serious performing arts scene. Masha will be obliged to take in the performing arts."

Laura gestured for Moira to follow her back to her office. As they walked, Laura remarked, "You'll have an agency backed credit card. Why can't you just take a large suitcase with a basic rotation and purchase what you need in the local economy? After all, present-day St. Petersburg isn't the cold war Soviet Union you remember with nearly empty store shelves. From what I hear, St. Petersburg has great shopping these days and plenty of great clothing from the global market." As the two women entered Laura's office, Moira sat down and became quiet and seemed to be in a thoughtful fugue. Laura simply sat behind her desk, sipping her tea and quietly studying Moira's thoughtful stance. Finally she spoke up, "If you are worried about your expenses and purchasing the required wardrobe off the local economy. Don't sweat it, the agency will cover it. A suitable wardrobe for a yearlong assignment is completely justified. What's still got you concerned, hon?"

"Actually, it's not the clothes. I'll be arriving in the summer. St. Petersburg has really long daylight and even midnight sun in the summer," Moira answered.

Laura looked curious. "Do you mean white nights?"

Moira nodded. "Yes! St. Petersburg is far enough north to have white nights. In St. Petersburg they'll get midnight sun, for a few hours every day, but even when the sun is down May to July the sky is still white."

Laura simply nodded as she sipped her tea. Then she asked, "What else is on your mind?"

Moira grinned, "Nothing really. It's just been a really long time since I've spent time in St. Petersburg. I'll have to purchase some serious winter clothing." Laura chuckled at her comment. The two women sat in silence for a few minutes.

Then Laura spoke up. "Moira, you should have had my job. You're twice the field officer I am! In fact, last year all the smart money was betting on you for this position when the last Field Director moved on."

Moira smiled. "Laura, I'm happy for you. Believe me, this isn't sour grapes. I suppose I shouldn't be telling my boss this. But the truthful answer is I'm not terribly motivated to go out there on field missions. Supposedly, colleagues in our business see me as a rock star, but they passed me over for the management job. I guess my view is why I should even bother to stick my neck out there anymore."

"Moira, I'll level with you, but it can't leave this office." Laura remarked.

Stewart shrugged her shoulders. "Hey, I'm in the spy business! What's one more thing I can't tell a blessed soul about? Please level with me. Who did I piss off?"

"For starters, Congress." Laura frowned. "Back during the Reagan era, the far-right Republicans have been down on the LGBT community. Back then, they were purging the military ranks of anybody they could catch or out for being gay or queer. Now we've got Bush W. in office and the same old guard hardliners have their knives out and sharpened and pointed at the Queer community. Members of the Senate and House Intelligence oversight committees have been applying pressure to all the intel agencies to purge our ranks of LGBT personnel. We've pushed back hard, telling them that our operatives do a tough job and can go places straight folks can't."

Laura stared at her desk for a few minutes. "Moira, what I say next stays here!" Moira nodded and gestured, zipping her lips.

"OSS62 director Daniel Kramer has those anti LGBT leaning's and has the ears of folks in Congress. Kramer thinks you are out of your flipping mind being a transwoman and all that."

Laura paused and struggled to find the right words. "Moira, the director, would like nothing better than to see you go out on a mission and either screwup royally or get your ass killed in the field. He'd be happy to disavow you publicly. Or worse, stand up in front of the oversight committees and use you as an example of why LGBT folks shouldn't be in the intel agencies."

Moira lowered her head, and for a few moments, she buried her head in her hands. When she lifted her head again, Laura could see that Moira's eyes were wet and that her mascara was running. Laura handed Moira a handful of tissues.

"Moira, if you truly don't want to go to St. Petersburg and teach for a year, I'll support your decision with no prejudice." Laura remarked.

Stewart spoke up frankly. "You know, Laura, a guy like Daniel Kramer probably hasn't been to a stage play or a live classical concert in decades, if ever. I think that man has no fracking class and no culture. I'm of the opinion that he would just hate it if I were to go over and schmoozed the hell out of those upper crust St. Petersburg Russians who are patrons of the performing arts." Moira finished wiping her eyes and runny eye makeup. She gave Laura a look of resolve. "Laura, what the hell? Please sign me up and inform them I would be honored to come over there!"

"Moira, you know that Director Kramer will have to sign off on the mission?" Laura added.

Moira threw her arms back, remarking, "Hey, Laura, inform Cornell to let the Dept. of State know one of their professors has been invited to teach American Musical theater in St. Petersburg for a year at the prestigious St. Petersburg State Theatre Arts Academy."

"Let Kramer try to veto the project. He doesn't have the balls to veto something with this kind of positive visibility." Moira grinned. Laura broke out in deep laughter and laughed to the point of tears. As she regained her composure.

Laura snickered. "Moira, you really can be cold and calculating, can't you?"

In an expressionless manner, Moira articulated, "Fourteen years in this business. I've learned from the fracking best!"

Laura asked again, "Are you sure about this, Moira?"

Moira leaned forward and rested her elbows on the edge of her boss's desk and remarked. "Director Kramer still views me as a guy in a dress! So be it. I've got bigger balls than he has and mine are home in a jar!" Laura broke out into hysterical laughter again!

As Laura relaxed from her bout of laughter, Moira gave Laura an intense look. Speaking up, she clarified some expectations.

"Laura, I'm content to do the observe and report kind of stuff, but please refrain from giving me any cloak and dagger spy duties. Let's To be clear, this is simply a yearlong cover identity maintenance mission and schmooze the natives undertaking! Nothing more! Okay?"

Laura held up a hand. "Unless the Russians roll tanks into eastern Europe. On my honor I won't ask you to do anything dangerous. You just go over there, immerse yourself into Dr. Mashenka Petrova and be a Theatrical Arts professor for the next year. I imagine it will be fun, and I most certainly expect it will be nice to not get shot at for a change."

After taking a deep breath, Moira instructed, "Okay, call the chair at Cornell and have him convey to the St. Petersburg State Theatre Arts Academy folks that it would honor Professor Petrova to teach there for the upcoming academic year." Laura nodded with a smile. "Will do."

Then Moira added, "Finally, I'd prefer to fly on an American, Canadian or French airline going over. Aeroflot has had a dismal safety record in the past few years," Moira moaned.

Then Laura commented, "Before, I make the phone call, I want you to go downstairs and have our doctor give you a thorough physical."

3:45 PM-OSS62 Agency medical department.

Moira came down the internal back staircase from operations to the OSS62 medical dept. Kevin Rice, MD. met her "Hello Moira, long time no see."

She sheepishly lowered her head, "Kevin, I'm sorry I've been dodging your calls."

He folded his arms and gave her a perturbed look. "Well, I figured that you either didn't like my cheery smile, my choice of dinner wine at our last dinner date, or perhaps my deodorant isn't working."

Moira didn't acknowledge what he had said. She only commented, "Laura wants you to give me a full physical. I'm going on a yearlong undercover assignment." Doctor Rice led her over to a dressing screen and handed her an examination gown.

"You know the drill. Change into the gown open side out."

As Moira undressed behind the screen.

Rice remarked, "Alright, Moira, on a nonprofessional note, why have you been dodging my calls?"

"Sorry, it's been a matter of feeling out if you can handle the truth?" She remarked from behind the screen.

"Moira, I already know you're a trans woman. So what's the big secret? Because I think you are a talented lady and cool as hell," Dr. Rice stated. Moira stepped from behind the changing screen.

"Okay Kevin, the cold hard truth is that I'm into women."

He stopped dead in his tracks. "Did you know this before or after you changed?"

She sheepishly grinned, "Oh, sure, my shrink explained all this to me over twelve years ago. They thoroughly tested me with every sort of psych test and instrumental measurement. All biology aside; gender identity and sexual identity are two vastly different things. I identify as a woman and I'm attracted to other women. Kevin, it's nothing against you or other men. It's just the way I am."

The physician just stood quietly with his eyes closed, slowly shaking his head, "So you are telling me you spent fifty thousand dollars to become a lesbian?" As Moira climbed up on the examination table, she simply remarked, "That's about the size of it, Doc!"

He put his stethoscope in his ears. Kevin reached into her exam gown and listened to her heart. He stepped behind her and asked her to lower the back side of the gown and listened on her back to her breathing. "Okay, you sound great. My nurse is going to check your blood pressure, height and weight and such, draw some blood and get a urine sample. I'm going to the basement to warm up the MRI. She'll bring you down and stay while I scan you, okay?"

Moira simply nodded, "Certainly."

Ninety minutes later, Moira dressed and received inoculations for a dozen different diseases. She was now quietly sitting in front of Dr. Rice's desk. He carefully read her lab test results and then stated, "Moira, I own two horses, and you are healthier than both of them. I noted in your medical record you were at Chernobyl in 1986. During your short time there, your TLD dosimeters showed you took enough ionizing radiation to disqualify you for life from any further professional nuclear work."

"Yes, I am acutely aware of that." Moira acknowledged.

Dr. Rice asked. "Can you give me an approximate idea of what kind of mission you are going on or what kind of environment you'll be working in?"

Moira responded frankly. "I'm going to be teaching theater performing arts at a prestigious Russian theater school." He nodded his head a tad. "Alright, that's great, very little chance of further exposure."

She smirked. "I'm going to be lecturing about American musical theater and teaching my students to sing and dance. That's about it."

Dr. Rice gave her a strange look. "That's your mission?" She shrugged her shoulders, "It's called cover identity visibility and maintenance work."

He gave her a thoughtful look, "I suppose in your line of work that's a necessary task. Good Luck!" Then Dr. Rice gave her a caring look. "While you are gone, find someone endearing to be close to."

As she was leaving his office, she glanced back at him. "I'll see who walks into my life. Au Revoir Kevin!"

9:00am March 11-OSS62 provisioning

In the lobby of the North American Surveying building, a young man in his mid to late twenties greeted Moira. He held up his phone as he glanced back and forth between Moira and the phone. "Good morning, Moira. I'm Ishmael from Provisioning and I'm here to escort you to our facility. We've been told you have special needs; we decided you should meet our senior clothing curator for your mission clothing. Please come with me."

Outside of the building was a Black Town Car waiting. Ishmael opened the rear door and allowed Moira to enter the back seat. After he closed the door, he walked around the car and opened the rear seat door on the other side of the vehicle and climbed in. After he closed the door, Ishmael spoke to the driver. "The warehouse please."

As the car moved, Moira spoke up. "I could have driven there."

Ishmael glanced over at her. "Our warehouse facility is in a rough area of town. We prefer to bring our clients to us for their safety and ours."

After about a fifteen-minute drive, the limo pulled up to a red brick early twentieth century style warehouse building, an automated garage door opened up, and the limo drove in and the roll away door closed behind them. Ishmael exited the auto and quickly came around to Moira's side of the vehicle. He opened the door on Moira's side and helped her exit.

"Now we go see our executive curator and senior costumer." Ishmael stepped over to a modern elevator, pressed a button, and politely gestured for Moira to enter first. She initially felt herself to be in a threat situation. Then Ishmael stepped in and pressed a button for the eighth floor. Moira did her best to remain calm. In the back of her mind, she knew she could throttle this squirt if he posed a threat. "So are you folks' government?" she asked casually.

"We're contractors, but we support every manner of presentation environment." There was a ding. The elevator doors opened to a well-lit show room style space like Moira had seen in high end bridal salons when friends of hers were picking out bridal gowns.

Ishmael gave Moira a smile. "There is our senior curator. Please step over and make yourself comfortable. She'll be with you in a few minutes." Moira gave Ishmael a nodding gesture and stepped out of the elevator. There was a ding, and the elevator doors closed behind her. In front of Moira, perhaps thirty feet away, was a long wide worktable that was clearly a desk of sorts. Behind the desk was a somewhat athletic-looking woman, perhaps in her late forties. The woman had long black hair in a braid that clearly went the length of her back and she wore a brown turtleneck shirt. She seemed engrossed in some paper documents on her desk.

After several moments of silence, Moira spoke. "Excuse me."

The woman did not break her gaze from her materials. "Consider yourself-excused," the woman commented before falling silent.

Feeling perplexed, Moira was more direct and said, "My name is Stewart, and I'm here for provisioning."

There was a long pause, then the woman broke her eye contact with the work on the desk. She looked at Moira up and down. "Do you fancy yourself a lady of the court, or perhaps a courtesan?"

Moira simply blinked in surprise. "A what?"

Again, the woman spoke in a cryptic tone, "I would have figured you for a lady of the court type."

In a frustrated whine, Moira asked, "What are you talking about?"

"You are Moira Stewart, and they sent you to me. In order to plan a year's worth of clothing to support your mission to Russia. Your cover identity is as a Cornell University Theater Arts professor. Am I correct or do I have the wrong client?"

Moira spoke up. "Yes, I'm Moira."

The woman spoke directly to her again. "So Ms. Stewart, if we had both you and your Theater Arts professor standing in front of me; would you be the 'lady of the court' all about the rules and being proper or 'the courtesan,' who's smart, educated, artsy and a freethinker?"

Moira stood stunned that the curator had pigeonholed both her and her Masha persona so accurately. She spoke up and answered, "Just plain old ordinary me. I'm the lady of the court." She paused then remarked, "Masha is the artsy fartsy free thinker and let it all hang out type until she's called upon to do a job, then she's all to business, whether its jumping in bed with the king or cutting the throat of one of his evil henchmen, that's Masha."

The woman smiled. "That's an interesting dichotomy. In

your job, you obviously must become her for varying periods of time."

Moira considered what the curator said, then remarked, "Usually on missions I've been Masha for a day or two at a time. On some occasions, it was a few weeks. But never over two or three months." Moira went quiet for a few moments, obviously in deep consideration. Then she spoke up, "I'm going to have to be Masha twenty-four seven for a year or more. I've never done that before. Frankly, that is scaring me a little."

"It should scare you a lot. Your life depends on it," Barbara remarked. After a few moments, she gave Moira a thoughtful look. "A stage actor morphs into character each night in the dressing room during the stages of makeup and donning a costume."

Moira nodded. "I sort of go through that process when I dress for a mission. At each stage of taking off of my Moira clothing and slowly donning Masha's clothing. I begin mentally transitioning into her mannerisms and speech patterns." Moira explained, relating to what the curator had said.

Barbara continued her commentary. "If we look at television series and movie actors, they undergo the same transformation in the makeup chair and in the dressing area. Some actors are comfortable shifting in and out of character during their workday. But the most serious actors I've known once they get into character for a long day of filming. That's who they are for the rest of the day. Until they clean up and take a shower. Yet, if they are doing a series or a movie, it might take them months to get that character out of their head."

Moira responded, "I've noticed that. If I have been her for several months, I have had trouble shifting back to English and I hunger for the food she eats on missions," Moira commented.

Barbara clasped her hands in a thoughtful stance, "Together our challenge is going to be to define what Masha's wardrobe is going to be and only dress you in Masha's personal style, in order to keep you deep into character for the period of your mission. This is a deep immersion mindset. You cannot afford to shift out of that Masha persona during your mission year."

Barbara pushed her chair back, stood up and walked around the end of her worktable and came over to Moira and guided her to a small conversation area with several comfortable chairs and a coffee table. She gestured to Moira to take a seat. Once both women took their seats. Barbara gave Moira a thoughtful look. "This is going to take a few weeks. What we must do is dress your theater professor as your inner courtesan. We must make her professionally memorable, practical, and functional. Above all, a showstopper when she enters a ballroom or a concert hall! Last but not least, she must never be out of character and must never become the lady-of-the-court during her year on her mission. We are going to dress you in such a way that you will be so deep into character that Moira will not come out and break your cover," Barbara articulated.

9:30am Mar 12 -Moira's Apartment

Barbara and Ishmael from Provisioning showed up at Moira's front door promptly at 9:30am per verbal agreement. "Show us to your closets, your chests of drawers, any hanging storage bags. I want to see all of your current clothing, even what is in some other form of storage."

Moira shrugged her shoulders, "What's in my dresser and my closet and half of the guest closet is all my clothing? There's nothing else."

Barbara thoughtfully leaned into Moira and asked, "Please put on another pot of coffee." Then she looked at Ishmael and directed, "Lay out two outfits at a time on the bed, then step up on your step stool and photograph them with your camera. I want everything she's got photographed."

"I've got this covered boss," Ishmael cheerfully said as he climbed up a small stepladder and directed his camera at the clothing laid out on the top of Moira's bed. Barbara left the bedroom and walked out to Moira's galley kitchen.

"Is there anything else clothes wise you have stashed?

Perhaps a storage closet in the apartment complex or perchance a storage unit in the burbs?" Barbara asked.

"Nah," Moira remarked, "My upbringing didn't exactly encourage me to be a girly girl, and I definitely don't have a passion for fashion!"

Barbara seemed to frown at her. "I read your profile. You are a transwoman. I would have thought you would have been a bit more of an over-the-top gal in terms of your fashion."

Moira interrupted her, "Yeah, everybody has this idea that all trans women are some kind of all stylish woman all the time or that we turn into these ultra fem Vegas Show girl types. It's not about the clothes! It's about body identity. For god's sake, nobody raised me as a girl and nobody socialized me as a young woman. Barbara, the first thing I learned during my transition to becoming Moira, was to blend in. I watched other people I transitioned with get all prettied up on Saturday night. A lot of them got beat up or worse, ended up dead!"

Barbara gave Moira a studious look. Barbara mentioned that she had seen photos of her as Petrova, carrying out identity persona maintenance at Cornell. "As Mashenka. You dressed nicely, dolled yourself up, wore makeup, and looked like a polished professional."

"Hey, I clean up well." Moira remarked. "Like an actor, Petrova is a role I sometimes play because it's my job. Go outside and take a walk through the apartment complex. The average woman out there watching her kids or the neighbor's kids isn't wearing any makeup. Most of them are wearing jeans and tee shirts. Maybe a bit of lipstick or some mascara at the supermarket or at church on Sunday. The average worker bee woman these days is low maintenance. I just patterned myself after them to blend in!"

Barbara had a quiet smile on her face as she watched Moira's coffee pot stop perking. "Well, I was right about one thing." Moira was opening the refrigerator for some creamer, and queried, "Like what?"

"Moira is a lady of the modern workingman's court. She's dressed down and casual as hell," Barbara commented.

"Yep," Moira cracked! After the two women had poured coffee and did a short ritual of additives.

Barbara commented, "Moira, Professor Petrova isn't due over in St. Petersburg until early July. I have a concern," she remarked before sipping her coffee.

Moira perked up and gave the provisioning curator a questioning look. "Like what?"

"I suspect you've had firearms training, explosives handling, survival school, as well as hand to hand combat and martial arts training?" Barbara asked. Moira nodded in the affirmative. "Yes, basic and advanced spy school, to boot. I know my Trade Craft."

Barbara commented, "Moira, you said it yourself. Your mother didn't socialize you as a proper young woman."

Moira humbly whispered, "No, she didn't."

That's when Barbara stated, "Sweetie, I'm going to arrange four or five weeks of the toughest school you've ever been to."

Moira shrugged her shoulders with a bit of a swagger, "Hey bring it on, I'm up to it! So what's this new school?"

Barbara gave the seasoned field officer an expressionless look. "I'm sending you to charm school!"

Moira simply groused, "What the frack!"

10:00am Mar 22-An Arduous Journey

On the third floor of the Provisioning Warehouse Facility, Moira stepped out of the elevator, escorted by Ishmael. They walked down a hallway to a door that simply had the word "Behavior" stenciled on it. Ishmael knocked once and opened the door. Moira followed Ishmael into the room that appeared to have two halves. One side of the room had a small amount of furniture arranged like an elegant sitting room. In the other space was a lovely dining space, with a table and chairs for eight people. The room was reminiscent of old Dr. Sidorov's tutoring room.

Ishmael gestured to Moira toward the sitting room furniture. "Please have a seat and Mrs. Campbell will be with you shortly. By the way, Barbara said from this point forward, you must present as Professor Petrova. Likewise, she said to tell you that Mrs. Campbell is top security cleared and that you should tell her you will teach at a Russian Theater Arts School and will live in an entrenched academic culture for the foreseeable future."

Moira gave Ishmael a thoughtful look. "Thank you. I will conduct myself appropriately."

Ishmael smiled. "Good Luck with your class!" Then he exited the space. She walked around the dining room setup and then back to the sitting room side. She sat down in a wing-back chair, crossed her legs, and picked up a magazine that was on the coffee table. After about ten minutes, the door opened. An elegantly dressed woman, perhaps in her late sixties or seventies, entered the room. Moira did not get up from her chair. The woman walked over to the seating arrangement and set her purse down on the wing-back chair opposite Moira.

"Are you the new janitor on the third floor?" The woman asked, speaking with a strong British accent.

Moira contorted her face for a moment. "No, I'm not. I'm waiting for a Mrs. Campbell; I'm supposed to take charm and etiquette lessons from her."

The woman gave Moira a rather earnest look. "Please pardon my mistake. Given your athletic sneakers, faded jeans, Red Skins tee shirt, no bra and a headband in your hair. I naturally assumed you were part of the custodial staff. I sincerely assumed that you were not the esteemed Professor Mashenka Irina Petrova from Cornell University."

Moira closed her eyes and realized that she had just put both feet in it. She stood and assumed a respectful posture and extended a handshake. "I am dreadfully sorry. I am Dr. Petrova."

The woman accepted the handshake and introduced herself, "I am Mrs. Olivia Bailey Campbell, I am going to be your etiquette teacher for the next four weeks and from the looks of it, this is going to be an arduous journey for both of us."

Moira said nothing, with her eyes lowered. She had many a military instructor over the years and knew a dressing down when she heard one. Mrs. Campbell studied Moira for a few minutes.

"Your attire simply will not do if I am going to give you the proverbial crash course in charm and etiquette. Please go up to the eighth floor and see Ms. Barbara Hamilton and tell her I want you back here dressed suitably for tea in a gracious lady's outfit, wearing a bra and some hose or stockings and some suitable shoes!"

Masha assumed a military attentive posture and gave Mrs. Campbell a head nod salute. "Yes, ma'am!" Then she executed a proper reverse pivot and exited the room. In the elevator going to the eighth floor, she gently pounded her right fist on her forehead. At the eighth floor, she exited the elevator and walked over to Barbara's working desk. "Ma'am, Mrs. Campbell respectfully requests that you put this etiquette school recruit into an outfit suitable for tea. Specifically, a gracious lady's outfit, with a suitable bra, some hose or stockings and a pair of suitable ladies' shoes."

Barbara Hamilton fought back a laugh, "I see you've met her Ladyship. Very well, let's send her a properly attired Professor Petrova."

Thirty minutes later, Mashenka was riding the elevator back down to the third floor dressed in a dark green wool tweed suit with a white silk blouse. She was wearing hosiery and three-inch black pumps. She walked down the hallway and knocked twice on the door labeled "Behavior."

An accented woman's voice called out, "Enter."

Mashenka entered the room and gently closed the door behind her. She stood quietly for a few moments, then addressed Mrs. Campbell, "Good afternoon, your ladyship. I believe you've invited me to tea if the invitation is still open."

Campbell studied Mashenka for a few moments. "Yes, my dear, I would be happy to have you join me for tea. Please have a seat." Mashenka stepped over to the wingback chair she had been sitting in earlier. She carefully sat down on the edge of the chair with her knees together and her feet tucked back under the chair, one in front of the other.

Campbell raised an eyebrow. "Where did you learn to sit like that?"

Mashenka simply said, "I watch a lot of old movies. I saw a lady sit like this in an old film."

Mrs. Campbell cracked a smile. "Very good. You are obviously teachable!"

1:20 pm Mar 22-A Little Star Power

During tea, Mrs. Campbell spoke in a thoughtful tone. "Mashenka, in western society the concept of gentlemen is nearly extinct. In western society, there are men who have perhaps attended Ivy League schools, and maybe those who have undergone etiquette training to advance in their corporate careers. The military schools still teach the art of courtesy to their cadets so that they can be officers and gentlemen. But chivalry is dead in Western society." Mrs. Campbell remarked before taking a small bite of her Scottish Short Bread.

Mashenka nodded slightly as she sipped her tea. Then, after a moment asked, "Then why am I being given this training if courteous gentlemen are nearly extinct?"

"My dear, the training I'm going to impart to you will reinforce the appearances that as a University Theater Arts Professor you are a Lady and second a Lady of charm and grace. Ms. Hamilton told me of her costuming theme with you, the persona of a courtesan. I like the idea. I want the academics and others of high social standing people you meet in St. Petersburg to think that you are as graceful as any Lady in waiting at Queen Elizabeth's court." Mrs. Campbell stated.

"In modern Russia?" Mashenka questioned. Mrs. Campbell took a sip of her tea, then set her teacup down and nodded in the affirmative.

"There are many in the higher social circles who walked the Communist party line all during the Soviet years. But these days they are capitalists with lots of money and in the back of their minds they privately yearn for the mystique and prestige of Good Czarist times."

Campbell paused, then added, "Consider for a few moments. The St. Petersburg State Theatre Arts Academy is among the finest performing arts colleges in the world. Wealthy, powerful people like being patrons of the arts so they can show off their generosity. Now, here comes Professor Mashenka Petrova, and she's not some crude hedonist American arts person. Absolutely not. Mashenka is charming and has the social graces of a British Aristocrat. Add to that, Mashenka is a hero. She helped Russia during the Chernobyl incident, our country's most dire disaster." Campbell leaned toward Mashenka. "My dear, if you learn your lessons well, you'll have amazing star power and the connections any spy would ever hope to have." She sat back, lifted her teacup in a toasting gesture.

Mashenka put her teacup down, almost trembling. "A field operative isn't supposed to attract that kind of attention. It's usually an invitation to a poisoned glass of champagne, a bullet in the head or a first-class ticket to a gulag in Siberia." She paused, then she asked. "Does my boss know you are talking to me like this? The mission is just supposed to be a cover identity maintenance mission. Nothing dangerous and what you are describing has dangerous written all over it in bright neon letters!"

Mrs. Campbell, with a broad smile, answered, "I'm going to invite Laura Boyce over for tea tomorrow and we'll lay out the entire plan. Trust me, she has support from many levels of her management."

Her ladyship took another sip of her tea, then added, "I heard a story a few years ago that a prominent member of the Guardia Svizzera thought you'd probably be running OSS62 by now! This is that plum assignment that could put you at the top of your professional intelligence career."

"Madame, that's classified!" Petrova commented. "You aren't just some contract etiquette teacher. Who do you really work for?" Again, her ladyship lifted her teacup in a toasting gesture, "MI6." Mashenka's jaw dropped for a shocked moment before she whispered. "Oh My!"

1:00 pm Mar 23 -A Ludicrous Idea

Mrs. Campbell had directed Mashenka to enter the 'Behavior Room' precisely at 1pm, and she followed the instructions. Her Ladyship was already in the room, sitting in a love seat in the seating area. "Punctual, excellent," Campbell remarked and added, "Let me look at you." Mashenka walked over to within six feet of where Mrs. Campbell had taken a seat. She was wearing a knit plaid Pocket Dress with front pleats; on her legs were black leotards, and her shoes were a unique style of pump. Mrs. Campbell gestured for her to turn slowly. "Very nice. Please step closer." As requested, Mashenka complied and moved closer. Campbell softly commented. "A gentle touch of makeup. Subtle! Just enough to accent without looking overly done. What are you wearing?"

Mashenka respectfully explained, "A little mascara, a light foundation, and a touch of lip color."

Mrs. Campbell nodded slightly. "You look wonderful. That look is more than adequate for your day wear for teaching classes, faculty meetings, your rehearsals and stage craft workshops."

Mashenka spoke up. "I'll need your guidance for dinner parties and for a night at the opera or a concert."

Mrs. Campbell seemed to pause and think, then remarked, "We'll discuss evening events and looks later in the week. There are going to be three or four scenarios you'll need to consider, but we'll discuss it in a few days." She paused, then changed the subject. "Your handler Laura Boyce and your Director Daniel Kramer will be here at 1:30 to discuss your mission. I want you on your best behavior. Please, no open rebellion and complaining. Just listen to everything we're going to propose. I honestly think that everything we are considering will be well within your comfort zone."

Mashenka simply nodded in the affirmative, "Yes Ma'am."

1:30pm-OSS62 Management Arrives

Mrs. Campbell and Mashenka were casually chatting in the sitting room area when they heard a knock at the door. Mrs. Campbell gestured to her student. Mashenka rose, walked over to the door, and gracefully opened it. Standing in front of her was Ishmael.

"Good afternoon, Professor. Mrs. Campbell's guests are here." Masha stepped back to the side and made a welcoming gesture.

First through the door was her manager and handler, Laura Boyce, who paused as she walked in and remarked, "You look lovely."

Petrova nodded slightly. "Thank you."

OSS62 director, Daniel Kramer, entered and gave Petrova a look over. He snorted a laugh and remarked, smirking.

"My god Chuck, you look ridiculous." Petrova maintained her composure at being dead named by the Director. She glanced over at Mrs. Campbell, who simply and subtly lifted a finger to her lips. Petrova gently nodded and closed the door. Kramer walked over to the sitting area and stepped over to the seated Mrs. Campbell and extended a handshake.

"How the heck are you, Olivia?" Mashenka watched as Campbell politely forced a smile and simply answered,

"Never better Daniel. Please sit and have tea."
Kramer plopped himself onto one of the wingback chairs. He sat down with his legs spread apart and his clasped hands hanging down between his legs.

Mrs. Campbell spoke up. "Mashenka, would you do the honors and serve our tea?" Petrova quietly nodded and lifted the pot of tea and began pouring the tea into teacups.

Kramer snickered, "Olivia, I see you've trained Stewart for a suitable job as a transvestite server." Petrova bit her lip as she handed a teacup and saucer to the director.

A few moments later, she handed a teacup and saucer to her manager Laura, who politely said. "Thank you, Masha."

Again Kramer spoke up. "Olivia, what's this nonsense about sending Stewart to St. Petersburg to teach acting to a bunch of Russians? He's not a real drama professor and I think this whole proposed identity maintenance mission is nonsense. I mean, look at him! He's a guy in a damned dress! He's a freak." By this time, Petrova was sitting quietly in another wing-back chair; her legs together and her hands resting gently on her legs. She was expressionless and seemed to just be staring at the serving tray and the pot of tea.

Mrs. Campbell addressed Director Kramer. "Daniel, I think this is an excellent opportunity to connect with the nouveau riche of St. Petersburg. Professor Petrova will have the position of being a visiting academic and guest staff at the prestigious St. Petersburg Theater arts school. In addition, so what if a few people perhaps perceive Masha as a man in a dress? It's irrelevant! Actually, I think it just adds to her exotic potential star power."

Kramer took a slurping drink of his tea and remarked. "I do not know how his girly presentation won't make him a laughingstock in St. Petersburg."

"Aristocratic history, my dear Daniel," Campbell commented.

Kramer put down his teacup and picked up a Scottish Short Bread from the tray and took a chomping bite. With his mouth full, he simply answered. "Okay, enlighten me."

Mrs. Campbell gave Laura Boyce a knowing glance. "Daniel, we're trying to connect with the nouveau riche of St. Petersburg with their wealthy aristocratic elite from back before the Bolshevik revolution, back during good czarist times."

Kramer simply muttered, "I'm listening," while giving Petrova an arrogant glance.

Mrs. Campbell continued. "Back before the Bolshevik revolution, there was a very colorful royal aristocrat. His name was Prince Felix, Felixovich Yusupov. He was the noble who shot Grigori Rasputin. Yusupov also engaged in racy cross-dressing and had a reputation for stealing his mother's ballgowns and jewels for this purpose. I've seen pictures of him. He was lovely, actually. Similarly, he had a reputation for enthusiastically engaging in love affairs with both men and women. After the revolution, he lived in Paris. At Paris opera houses, they frequently saw Prince Felix in lovely feminine attire. In his feminine persona, they said he was the Toast of Paris."

Kramer sat shaking his head, "Olivia, you can't be serious. Do you expect Charlie Stewart to pull off a similar stunt and become the toast of St. Petersburg? Just because he's become a woman on paper and been through a bunch of medical shenanigans and has become the spy business version of Christine Jorgensen. I think that he's a joke and that this idea is ludicrous." There was a deafening pregnant pause in the room. Then Kramer spoke up. "I'm not signing off on this operation, period. Laura, as a sectional field director, both you and Stewart are free to partner with Olivia's MI6 people, but OSS62 officially isn't involved in this operation. Olivia, this is an MI6 operation. If it all goes south, it's on yours and MI6's watch. Am I clearly understood?"

Mrs. Campbell simply smiled and nodded. "Yes, clearly understood." She turned her head and looked at Laura.

Laura Boyce spoke up, "Director Kramer, I'm going to support MI6 and place Moira Stewart on long term detached duty for the foreseeable future. Helping MI6 with this project."

Kramer stood up, shaking his head. He walked to the door and as he opened the door, he paused and remarked, "Hey, Charlie, I hope you'll like the Siberian Hospitals (Prisons). You know what our old KGB counter parts used to say, 'Hope for the best, expect the worst!'" Kramer left the room.

Mrs. Campbell shook her head with a disgusted expression. She looked at Laura and then at Mashenka. "I will not say my only comment in the Queen's English!" Then she remarked in Spanish, "No cojones, señor Kramer! No cojones!"

11 am March 30-Courtesies chat over Tea

Mashenka and Mrs. Campbell were taking a break from the morning's lessons. Masha had filled an electric tea kettle and was waiting for the water to heat. She dutifully placed Lady Grey tea bags into the scalded tea pot and waited patiently.

She spoke up, "Madame Campbell, I was watching an old movie last evening. There was this acquaintance gentleman, and he was visiting a woman and upon greeting her, he kissed her on the cheek. Was this proper, or was he pushing himself on her?"

Mrs. Campbell smiled, "Oh my, you are certainly becoming courtesy observant!"

Mashenka smiled, "So far, everything you've explained to me in our sessions has made me acutely aware of both subtle and pronounced social customs and the lack thereof."

"Very good, my dear," Campbell remarked, "Etiquette wise. A gentleman must never presume to kiss a lady's right cheek, especially at their first meeting. This is always supposed to be up to the discretion of the lady involved."

As Masha poured the piping hot tea into each of the teacups, she asked, "Okay. Suppose they know each other well."

Mrs. Campbell held up her index finger to make a point. "If you are happy to accept a social kiss from the gentleman, then you would turn your face offering your right cheek, then both of your cheeks touch gently. One kiss on the right cheek is suitable and do not make any mwah noises, that makes a mockery of the courtesy!" Mashenka brought the two teacups and saucers over to the sitting area and placed them on the coffee table in front of each of their chairs. Both women took their respective seats. They each picked up their respective teacup and blew gently upon the tea, followed by sips.

Mashenka set her teacup down and seemed to be deep in thought. Mrs. Campbell noted the face and queried, "What's distracting you, my dear?"

"Well," Mashenka began, "Later in the movie she offered both her right and left cheek to another gentleman."

Mrs. Campbell sipped her tea, then nodded and asked, "Was the gentleman French?"

Mashenka's eyes got wide for a moment. "Yes, he was a Frenchman!"

Campbell smiled. "That is a French custom. In fact, you might see it in Russia as well. During the Soviet years, France and Soviet Russia were quite close." There was a long pause as both women enjoyed their tea and the quiet presence of each other's company.

Then Mrs. Campbell remarked, "Back in England, we often see Prince Charles kissing the Queen's right hand. Back in the day, ladies did this as part of the introductions by offering their right hand for a kiss. It is a lovely old tradition which few practice these days, but if you want to test the character of a gentleman whom you are meeting for the first time, offer your right hand. If he shakes your hand, he is too modern to practice such an old courtesy or worse, he's just ignorant of it. But if a modern man takes your hand and kisses it, he's something special. Make note of it." Mrs. Campbell paused in her conversation and took a tiny bite of Scottish Short Bread. After she swallowed her morsel, she remarked.

"While we are discussing gentlemen. Let's talk about how to spot a gentleman. When you, as a properly postured lady, walk into a room or stand to leave a room. Make note that a man grounded in his courtesies, therefore a gentleman, should stand for you, even when dining, it would be polite for a gentleman to stand out of respect for the lady. As well, the man on your left or right, especially if you've been sharing pleasant dinner conversation, should stand up and help with your chair."

"Really?" Mashenka remarked.

Mrs. Campbell nodded, "Yes really. Upon occasion I have risen from dining and neither gentleman rose."

"What did you do? It's not like you can demand that they should stand for you," Masha queried.

Campbell smirked, "I softly commented, 'Oh my chivalry must be dead!' Usually it wakes somebody up and one or both gentlemen gets up and assists me with my chair."

Mashenka snickered a bit. Mrs. Campbell simply lifted her teacup in acknowledgment of her humorous point. Then her face became a bit more serious.

"Mashenka, I'm going to take you to a society dinner party early next week. I will introduce you as simply a recent friend. I expect you to practice all the social graces I've taught you to this point. In addition, I'll speak to Ms. Hamilton and arrange for a dress suitable for the occasion. This is not an evening at the opera or concert, so your understated daywear makeup will be suitable."

Mashenka nodded in acknowledgement. Then asked, "How exactly are you going to introduce me?"

Mrs. Campbell nodded and raised her index finger. "Good point. We can't talk about your proper day job. Let's keep it general and simply use your cover identity profession as a theater professor at Cornell. Keep the conversation light and avoid getting into detail or time frames, vague is the rule of thumb! If you want to mention that you occasionally do Russian-to-English translations and vice versa as a freelance consultant, that would be truthful. If someone at the gathering comes up to you and begins a conversation in Russian. Exchange a few brief pleasantries but no long conversations. That would be impolite to the rest of the party."

"Noted Madame," Mashenka replied.

8:40am May 1-The Rogers Maneuver

Mashenka was pacing the floor of the 'Behavior Room' mumbling to herself and seeming to make panicked remarks about every four or five minutes. At 8:59 am, Mrs. Campbell walked in and found Mashenka nearly in tears and shaking like a leaf.

"My dear Masha, what is wrong?" The elder asked her in a concerned tone of voice. At this point the waterworks began to flow and Masha sat down in one of the sitting area's wing back chairs, sobbing. "Mashenka Petrova! I cannot help you if you don't tell me what is wrong," Campbell said in a command voice.

Masha picked up a couple of paper napkins from the coffee table, wiped her tears and blew her nose. Still choking a bit from her crying, she blurted out.

"Please tell me there won't be any dancing at the dinner party next week!"

Mrs. Campbell gave her a curious look. "Masha, you've shown that you are a social person. Why are you concerned if there is going to be dancing at the dinner party?" Masha sat quietly for a few moments, trying to compose herself.

Then she spoke in a breaking voice, "I don't know how to follow! Ginger Rogers did everything that Fred Astair did, but she did it backwards in heels! Olivia, I don't know how to follow!" At which point, she began sobbing again.

Campbell stepped over to the wet sink and filled the electric teapot with water, placed it back in its electrical nest and pressed the switch. She reached into a China bowl and withdrew two Earl Grey tea bags and placed one in each of the two teacups. Then Mrs. Campbell handed the sitting Mashenka a handful of napkins. She sat down and, with a mother's manner, remarked.

"You climbed tall ladders and fixed telephone lines in Vietnam, you've been on guerilla warfare missions, and at unbelievable depths in a nuclear submarine, you've endured a gender change and acted as a translator near the Chernobyl nuclear melt-down and now you're telling me you are terrified of dancing backwards in heels! Now I have heard everything."

Masha sniffed and coughed twice. "My mom taught me to waltz when I was in grade school, but she taught me to lead. I don't know how to follow! This was something I had never given a thought to after I changed genders. I was busy doing spy stuff! Ballroom dancing wasn't in the Spy School Training package!"

Then Mrs. Campbell stated, "Well, dancing is in your training package now. Before you leave my charm school tutelage. We'll get a security cleared dance instructor to teach you to waltz, do the tango and whatever it takes to get you comfortable with society dancing in St. Petersburg!" The teapot clicked off and Mrs. Campbell got up and poured the hot water and for the first time in

Masha's training, she served her tea. Slowly, over a few moments of blowing on her hot tea, Masha settled. Mrs. Campbell, sensing the easing of her stressed student's panic, commented.

"Masha, the dinner party this coming week doesn't involve any dancing. If the topic for some unforeseen reason comes up, I will quash it! Your only mission at the dinner party is to be your usual impressive friendly nature and charm the pants off everyone at the affair. Just be your chatty, bubbly self. That's your mission next week. It's just a dinner party with some of my friends."

Campbell took a thoughtful sip of tea. "Alright Mashenka, as a warrior I know you understand the term blooding."

Masha nodded. "Yes, it's a lightweight battle for unseasoned troops to get them ready for being part of a major offensive."

Campbell concurred, "Exactly!" And added, "In late May, there is going to be an embassy ball at the British Embassy. It will be sort of like a state dinner. I will have you all prepared to charm the hell out of the people there and yes, I'll have you well-tuned for whatever sort of dancing they typically do. You will be at the top of your charming game."

Mashenka tilted her head slightly, "Is the dinner party next week my society, blooding?"

"No, my dear, the dinner party is a war game. The British embassy ball will be your blooding," Mrs. Campbell explained.

Masha curiously looked at Campbell, "If the British Embassy is my societal blooding. Then what is the major offensive?"

Campbell took a sip of her tea and grinned. "The Russian Federation Embassy ball that's about three weeks later at their embassy in late June. That is where you are going to begin to charm the hell out of the St. Petersburg elite, who will be in town for the event. If you do this right. When you get to the St. Petersburg State Theatre Arts Academy in mid-July in prep for your fall semester, you will have already made a splash on both banks of the Neva River!" Mrs. Campbell smirked, "Welcome to the spy world version of the Miss Universe."

Mashenka, with a shocked look on her face, simply asked, "Has the Russian Federation Embassy invited me to their ball?"

"Not yet, my dear, not yet," Mrs. Campbell commented. "But they will!"

Masha simply whispered, "Oh my!"

4:15 pm May 7-Ernesto Torres

Mashenka was in her third week of charm school training under the tutelage of Mrs. Campbell, of MI6. She had just come down to the sixth floor from the eighth floor, where Ms. Hamilton had dressed Moira in a light cotton muslin copy of a ballgown that was in the works for her first ballroom appearance at the British Embassy in two weeks. The sixth-floor space upon first appearance was half basketball court and half fabric warehouse with rows and rows of industrial racks with huge bolts of fabric wrapped in plastic. She admired the immense amount of fabric, thinking, *This is a dream come true for sewing enthusiasts!* Masha heard the elevator doors open. She looked across the basketball court and saw a clean-cut Latin man exiting the elevator and walking toward the center of the court carrying a briefcase and an enormous boom box.

He spoke out, "Are you Ms. Petrova?"

Masha spoke up, "Yes I am." He gestured for her to meet him in the center of the court. As she walked toward him, she called out, "Whom do I have the pleasure of, sir?"

With a bright smile, he answered, "I am Ernesto Torres. I will be your dance instructor and I believe that we have Mrs. Campbell as a common friend?" Mashenka said nothing but simply shrugged her shoulders. He set his boom box and briefcase on the floor. Torres smirked at her. "My god your spy craft is showing. By not confirming or denying your affiliation with her Ladyship, Mrs. Campbell."

Mashenka comments, "I have no way of confirming who you are. You might be the local drug lord for all I know."

He gave her a considerate expression. "Olivia called me two weeks ago and told me her current charm school student is prepping to go to St. Petersburg for a year. She further told me that her student had a five-alarm meltdown; all because she doesn't know how to follow while waltzing because she used to be a boy and only knows how to lead." He paused, then asked, "Or did I get the wrong basketball court in the clothing warehouse?" Masha blushingly grinned. He gave her a look over.

"What's with the half-finished hobo ballgown?" Masha shrugged her shoulders, "It's a test of the dress design in the actual practice of dancing." Torres looked considerate for a few moments. "That sounds like a great idea to me. Ms. Petrova, let's get dancing." She raised a finger. "Masha please."

As he reached down to turn on his boom box, he commented, "Masha, it is." He gestured for her to follow him away from the boom box. He stood in front of her. "Ok, as I understand it, your mama taught you to slow dance and, of course, taught you to lead. Show me!" He reached into his pocket and withdrew a small control fob. He pressed a button. A movement of waltz music began. Masha put her arms around him as if he were a woman partner and stepped forward with her left foot and onto a step to the side with her right foot so that it was parallel to her left foot. She continued by moving her left foot together to her right foot. Then she gracefully stepped backwards with her right foot and stepped to the side with her left foot so it was parallel to her right foot.

"More," He said, "Show me more. Just how grand can you move the lady across the floor?" Masha took bigger steps and began moving into a grander circle. The two danced until the movement ended. Masha let go of Mr. Torres and stepped away from him. She had a sheepish, almost embarrassed look on her face. He walked around in a little circle for a few minutes, obviously in deep thought. "You have good timing," he said. He paused. "Masha, you have nothing to be embarrassed about. Your mama taught you well. How often did you dance with your mom?" He asked.

Masha remarked, "Every damned day after school."

Torres crossed his arms. "Do you know any other classic dance?"

Masha seemed to think for a moment. "Well, my mom simply wanted me able to take a girl to a school prom and not make a fool of myself or my date. But she introduced me to a little bit of tango dancing, but again, to lead only. My former spouse and I actively took part in the submarine base tango dance club. We would dance there twice a month when I wasn't at sea. It was splendid fun."

"Anything else you know how to do besides waltzing and tango dancing?" He asked.

Masha winced slightly. "I took two years of Oriental dance lessons from a terrific teacher in Silver Spring, Maryland."

Torres gave her an intrigued look. "Did you perform?"

Shyly, she answered, "A couple of class dance recitals at some senior center that was about it. But I was frumpy compared to all the skinny gals with the 'I dream of Jeanie' type bodies and outfits."

Torres walked over to his briefcase lying next to his boom box, reached in and shuffled through some CDs. He took a CD out of a crystal box and replaced the waltz CD already in the Boom box. Torres looked up at Masha. "Show me!" He pressed the play button on the boom box.

A moment later Masha heard a bongo style drum in a slow rhythm. After a few moments, Masha moved back and forth with her hips in a side-to-side swaying. The sound of zills joined the drums, and the music continued to build. She slowly grew with her rhythmic movements. As the music picked up faster and faster, so did Masha's grand motions and gestures with her arms and hands, all the while rocking and swinging her hips and undulating her stomach muscles. As the music ended, Torres stopped the Boom box with his control fob. Then Torres stood thoughtfully quiet for a few minutes before finally addressing her, "Masha, you are clearly an amateur Eastern dancer. But if you were to dance for some drunk Russian business executives, especially those who like Oriental dancing and its mystique. Honey, you could charm the rocks off of them!" Masha sheepishly looked at him, looking slightly embarrassed. "But I came here for ballroom dancing." Torres put his hands upon her shoulders, "Honey, I'll get you whipped into shape, and you'll be the toast of the ball with the classical stuff. But while you are on your yearlong mission, I strongly recommend that you keep yourself practiced up with your belly dancing because, honey, that could be an asset in the future!"

5:30pm May 7-The Simple Dinner Party with Friends

After the day's dance lessons, Mashenka showered in a dressing room style space on the eighth floor. After she dried herself, she left the bathing area in a terrycloth bathrobe.

Barbara Hamilton had undergarments laid out for her. "Mrs. Campbell suggested that I have a hair stylist available to make sure your hair is in order. She expects you to do your own makeup, per her suggestions. Likewise, she picked out your outfit for this evening." Barbara explained.

"Oh, my!" Masha said with an exaggerated look of surprise. Then Masha remarked sarcastically, "This is just supposed to be a simple dinner party. I feel like I'm walking into a minefield blindfolded."

Barbara chuckled, "It's never simple with her ladyship!" At 6:15pm Ishmael escorted Mashenka down to the first floor. The usual black town car was waiting. Mashenka walked over to the rear of the vehicle. A rear door was open. Mrs. Campbell was sitting in the rear seat and quietly reading the newspaper. She looked up from her reading and gave Mashenka an inspecting eye in her burgundy cocktail dress. "Perfect! Get in my dear." Masha walked around to the opposite side of the limo; the uniformed chauffeur dutifully opened the door for her. After she got in and buckled her seat belt. The chauffeur carefully closed the door.

As the limo moved, Mrs. Campell spoke up, "My dear, this is just a simple dinner party, a four-course meal."

Mashenka comments back, "Okay, a soup, an appetizer, an entrée, and dessert." Mrs. Campell responded, "Correct!" The two women were quiet for a few minutes.

Then Masha asked, "Is the British Embassy event a dinner or a ball?"

"It's a ball, hence our emphasis on your dancing. It's a nice evening, perhaps four or five courses and dancing. If it were a diplomatic dinner, the dining might comprise upwards of eight courses." Campbell explained and added, "Tonight, just focus on being your charming self and be sociable. All the men at the dinner table are members of the British diplomatic service. Our hosts are Lord and Lady Walker. We address them as your lordship and your ladyship upon initial introductions. If they tell you, address them by their first name, you may do so. The rest of the guests are Mister and Misses, whomever they are. I suspect everyone will invite you to use first names at some point. If you are in doubt, be formal. Don't get casual with any of them early on. Gradually, relax into it based on how informal they are being with you."

Masha thought for a moment, then asked, "Is anybody else in the room MI6?"

Her ladyship pursed her lips with a slight smirk. "That would be telling." When the limousine arrived at a gate to a mansion in Potomac, Maryland; the Limo driver announced to a call box that Mrs. Campbell's party had arrived. The gate opened.

Her Ladyship leaned to Masha, "Forget Moira, you are Mashenka, you are in deep cover. All your cover history is fair game, but nothing from your Moira life!"

Masha obediently responded, (Speaking Russian) "Yes, I am Masha." Campbell studied her for a few moments as the limo stopped.

"This is a cultured crowd. If someone addresses you in any language that you know; you are free to respond but keep it to light courtesies. No prolonged foreign language conversation at the dinner table. After dinner, it is okay to converse in another language if spoken to."

Masha simply remarked (Speaking French) "Yes, madame."

A footman standing in front of the house came to Mrs. Campbell's door, first opening it and assisting the elder woman out. Then he hastened around to Mashenka's side, opened the door and assisted her in exiting the vehicle. As the two women approached the stately residence, a dashing older man in a dark suit approached them. "Olivia, it is so wonderful to see you." She turned her right cheek to him and he kissed it. "Liam, it's been far too long."

Campbell gestured toward Masha, "Lord Walker, this is my delightful friend Professor Mashenka Petrova." Lord Walker turned to face Masha; she extended her right hand. The noble gently took her hand and bent over slightly and kissed it.

"Delighted to make your acquaintance, Professor." He gestured toward the mansion. "Please come in. Almost everyone is here." Lord Walker led the two women to a sitting room where five people were standing, chatting. Masha immediately noted that all of them were clearly her seniors.

Lord Walker made introductions. "Ladies and gentlemen, you all know Olivia. With her is Professor Mashenka Petrova." Everyone in the room gave her smiles and polite nods. Lord Walker gestured to a lovely, mature woman, "This is my dear wife, Lady Walker." The woman spoke up, "Esther, please." Then Walker gestured to another couple, "This is my longtime colleague William Taylor and his wife Emily Taylor, who is a former member of Parliament." William Taylor spoke up, "Good evening professor." Masha politely greeted them, "I'm pleased to meet you both."

Then Lord Walker gestured to a second couple. "These lovely folks are Harry and Anna Lloyd." Harry stepped over to Masha and extended his hand, palm up. She graciously placed her hand on his palm. Harry bent over and kissed Masha's hand and said, "We are very delighted to make your acquaintance."

Masha graciously responded, "I'm delighted to meet you both." Masha noted that Mrs. Lloyd, while looking pleasant, was openly looking daggers at her.

Lord Walker remarked to his guests, "Charles and Freya will be here shortly."

Masha leaned into Campbell. "I need to use the restroom." Olivia nodded; she stepped over to William Taylor. "William, would you be so kind to show the Professor where the upstairs amenities are?"

Taylor nodded. "Please follow me Professor." He led her back out into the open foyer and led her to a staircase that was wrapped in a curve upward along a wall. Part way up the stairs Taylor remarked, (Speaking Russian) "Welcome comrade." Masha smirked, (Speaking Russian) "Comrade has been out of style for a few years. Or didn't you get the memo?" She joked.

Taylor continued, (Speaking Russian) "You have a Northern Russian accent." Masha grinned (Speaking Russian) "So I've been told. But when a child learns language, it's usually at their mother's or father's knee. My parents were originally northern people."

Taylor pressed his nosey query further, (Speaking Russian) "You're cold war talent, aren't you?"

Masha ignored the question, (Speaking Russian) "I need a few minutes in the toilet." She stepped into the restroom and closed the door. A few minutes later, Taylor heard a flush, followed by sink water rushing. Then Masha opened the door and remarked (Speaking Russian) "A few minutes ago, you mentioned the Cold War. By some chance, have you heard of me?"

Taylor stared at the floor for a few moments. (Speaking Russian) "Back in 1986, during the Chernobyl event. I sat at a desk that was monitoring Russian comm traffic. You and another woman, Anya Gusev, showed up a great deal in reports back to St. Petersburg and Moscow. Orders back from Moscow to high-level persons dealing with the Chernobyl situation in Ukraine, cautioned that you women might be CIA or some other agency." Taylor explained.

She shook her head with a perplexed look, (Speaking Russian) "Both Anja and I were simply part of a team of academics pressed into public service to consult technically in the face of a catastrophic human emergency. Anja and I were simply translators, nothing more. In the end, everyone in our technical help team were all decorated with medals as a gift from the grateful people of the Soviet Union."

Then Taylor added, (Speaking Russian) "You realize the theater arts community in Russia knows the name Mashenka Petrova, the American Drama professor?"

Masha modestly nodded her head, (Speaking Russian) "I've been told it is probably half the reason I'm being invited to teach at the St. Petersburg State Theatre Arts Academy for a few semesters."

Taylor looked thoughtful for a few moments, then gave her a very direct look, (Speaking Russian) "My dear Miss Petrova. Some advice: play it close to your chest what every you are going to do over there...and watch your back. I don't know what Olivia Campbell and her crew are up to. You just go there and be a fantastic university theater professor...but nothing more."

She studied his face. (Speaking English) "Thank You Mr. Taylor for the delightful conversation. Let's go join the others for dinner." Then William Taylor asked her, "I don't suppose that you'd be willing to tell a colleague your real name?"

She winced at him, seeming to study his face for a few moments, "Good Sir, I am Mashenka Irina Petrova. My parents are from Murmansk and they immigrated to the United States in 1949 from Finland after leaving the USSR in 1947. I was born in 1951 in Rochester, New York. I attended Nazareth Academy, a Catholic school for girls from kindergarten to sixth grade, before attending regional public school. My father worked for forty years for the Eastman Kodak Company and retired in 1990. I work for Cornell University and I teach a broad range of theater arts. Perhaps we should rejoin the other guests."

Taylor gave her a curious smile. "Very good. Let's go have a lovely evening with friends."

When William Taylor and Mashenka Petrova returned to the sitting room, there were two more people present. Lord Walker introduced Mashenka to Mrs. Freya Gardner and Mr. Charles Lawerence. After a few courtesies, the Butler stepped in and announced that dinner was ready to be served.

In the dining room there was seating for ten people. There were small tent cards with each person's name. They positioned Lord and Lady Walker at opposite ends of the table. Masha sat to the right of Lord Walker at the head end, to his left sat Mrs. Anna Lloyd, to her left was the nosey William Taylor, to his left was Mrs. Freya Gardner and to her left was Mr. Harry Lloyd. To the right of Masha was a man in his late forties named Charles Lawerence. To his right was Olivia Campbell and to her right was the intimidating Mrs. Emily Taylor.

His Lordship rang a small bell and two attendants entered the dining room and placed a large tray on a lovely sideboard. One attendant served Lord Walker, and the other served Lady Walker. There after the attendants quickly served each of the guests. The first course was Consommé soup, a highly flavored broth. As the dinner party began dining on their soup. Lord Walker instigated the small talk. "Professor, Olivia tells me you are going to be teaching performing arts in St. Petersburg for the upcoming year. Are you excited?"

Mashenka finished a sip of her soup, "Masha, please! At first, I was hesitant to accept the offer, but I'm actually looking forward to the experience." Mrs. Lloyd, across from Mashenka, remarked, "I think it would scare me to go live in a police state." Mr. Lawerence next to Mashenka spoke up, "Come now Anna, almost every modern city is full of CCTV cameras these days. St. Petersburg can't be any worse than downtown London."

Mashenka looked at Lord Walker, "Your Lordship..." He spoke up, "Liam, please."

"Liam, I was loosely told that many of you work at the British embassy?" Liam nodded. "I've been remiss in my introductions. Please, let's go around the table and briefly say what we all do. Masha, I'm the Chargé d'affaires at the British embassy."

He gestured to Anna Lloyd. She spoke up, "I'm a magazine journalist."

William Taylor simply remarked, "I'm a foreign service officer."

Freya Gardner smiled at Masha. "I'm a retired Cambridge History Professor."

Harry Lloyd had just lifted a spoonful of broth, paused and comments, "I'm a commerce attaché."

At the far end of the table, her Ladyship Esther Walker humbly smiled. "I'm a writer. I write history books."

Emily Taylor glanced down at the table toward Masha. "I'm a former MP. These days I work behind the scenes for the Tory Party."

Olivia Campbell just faced Mrs. Gardner, seeming to smirk. "I serve the Crown in a variety of roles."

Across the table, William Taylor snorted a laugh at Campbell's description of her work.

Charles Lawerence leaned a bit toward Masha. "Officially, I'm a protocol officer and once in a while I get to be a diplomatic courier."

Masha addressed the dinner guests, "Thank You, I'm impressed by the variety of talents amongst you." A few moments later, the attendants removed the appetizer soup bowls and brought salads to his Lordship and her Ladyship and then the rest of the guests. Masha noted that the salad was a shrimp salad. It was chilled shrimp tossed with crisp celery and red onion. They coated the mixture with a creamy, bright herbal dressing.

Masha had just gotten a mouthful of shrimp salad when William Taylor addressed Lord Walker. "Liam, before dinner, I had a splendid chat with Mashenka. She speaks Russian like a native, with a strong northern accent." Masha felt a chill go down her spine. For a moment, she debated in her mind whether her serving knife was sharp enough to penetrate Taylor's chest.

Lord Walker spoke up, "Goodness speaking fluent Russian is certainly going to be a plus, since you'll be lecturing in St. Petersburg. You know, I never gave it a thought that the Russians have dialect differences."

At that moment, Masha took command of the conversation. "Liam, actually since the Russian Federation is so large, small local dialect differences are present across the Federation. For example, my parents are from the north in Murmansk and they immigrated to the United States in 1949 from Finland after leaving the USSR in 1947. I was born in the USA in 1951." Then she explained, "They say the lands north of Moscow have a northern accent. The lands further south from Moscow, the southern accent is more prevalent." Liam and most of the dinner guests were intently interested in what she said. Olivia Campbell was quietly enjoying how Mashenka had taken control of the conversation.

Liam spoke up, "What about Mikhail Gorbachev? I've spoken with him many times over the years. His grasp of English was very strong. What kind of accent does he have?"

Masha finished sipping some water and answered, "Mr. Gorbachev was born in the south in Privolnoye. It is a rural locality in Krasnogvardeysky District of Stavropol Krai, Russia, on the Yegorlyk River. Back during the Soviet era, Gorbachev's hometown region of Privolnoye was pretty much evenly divided between ethnic Russians and ethnic Ukrainians. I have heard from native Russian acquaintances that northerners considered Mr. Gorbachev a bit of a country bumpkin. His southern pronunciation of certain letters and therefore words with those letters made the poor gentleman the butt of many jokes with the northerns."

Liam sat transfixed on Masha. "Fascinating! Back before the Soviet Union ended. I read literally piles of intelligence reports and analysis about Mikhail Gorbachev." Liam looked at the rest of his guests. "Never once did I read even a hint at what you just told me. I am flabbergasted."

Masha shyly smiled. "Please remember, it was the USSR. To

speak of such things publicly was not suitable form."

Having finished her thought, Masha took a last mouthful of her shrimp salad and gave a stunned Mr. Williams a coy nod. A few moments later, the attendants again returned and gathered up the salad plates and spirited them off. Within minutes, the servers returned with the main course of steak and potatoes. They had cut the Yukon gold potatoes into smaller bite-sized pieces and, with similar sized pieces of sirloin steak, all of it roasted in oil. The whole thing seemed prepared with garlic, with hints of rosemary, oregano, perhaps kosher salt, and a bit of ground black pepper. It looked and smelled scrumptious. Masha savored every mouthful.

As dinner conversation settled to small talk between small groups of guests, Anna Lloyd comments to Mashenka, "Being a performing arts professor at a prestigious Russian Arts Academy could be a wonderful story hook for a magazine series. Masha, would you consider writing a monthly?" Before Masha could answer. Anna struggled for a word for a few moments, then blurted it out.

"A monthly love letter to the folks back home. People always hear about diplomats traveling to Russia or occasionally some loud rock band. But as a drama professor, you are unique. St. Petersburg's got a New York City, Broadway or the West End of London feel to it. Are you going to direct any performances?"

Masha took a sip of her wine before she answered, "The department chair and I have discussed via email some American musicals. I've proposed Rodgers and Hammerstein's musical, 'Oklahoma' and Stephen Sondheim's, 'A Funny Thing Happened on the Way to the Forum'; or perhaps. 'Into the Woods.' But we're still discussing it."

Anna Lloyd looked like she was going to jump out of her chair. "Mashenka, my darling, think of it as a monthly series of articles about an American Drama teacher teaching American musical theater in St. Petersburg."

"Anna," Masha said, "I'm going to be extraordinarily busy

teaching and directing these shows. I'll have training assistants, but I really don't think I will have the time to write this sort of thing." Mrs. Lloyd sat pondering the problem.

Liam looked at Anna. "Let me propose something. Our diplomatic service has a corps of talented journalists within the service. We must have some journalistic talent who are bilingual, English and Russian. Why can't we have one of them shadow Masha and share regular dispatches with your magazine's editors? Perhaps the magazine could get the series syndicated. I think it could be a tremendous goodwill gesture. Saying great things about the Russian arts community would make Mashenka a star over there and over here as well."

Liam paused, then added, "Olivia, she's your charm, school student. Do you think she's up to being the Russo-American darling who brings Broadway to St. Petersburg?"

Olivia spoke up, "Your Lordship, I don't have a doubt in my mind or my heart. Mashenka is certainly the woman for the job!"

The guests at the table broke into discordant chatter and discussed amongst themselves about what they had said. From across the table, Masha could see William Taylor with a concerned look on his face, slowly lifting his wine glass slightly in a toasting gesture.

A serving attendant placed a dessert plate in front of her. Masha was numb from the implications of what they all had just said. As she stared at the yummy fruit tart dessert sitting in front of her. Masha thought to herself, *Holy Shit! It just keeps getting deeper and deeper.*

5:17pm May 17   A Private Dance Recital

In the sixth-floor warehouse/basketball court space, Mrs. Campbell watched with interest as Mashenka and Ernesto Torres gracefully danced to a rendition of 'Tales from the Vienna Wood.' It fascinated her at how gracefully the two glided across the basketball court. As the music ended, Ernesto and Mashenka executed a proper waltz, bow and curtsy.

Mrs. Campbell smiled broadly and clapped excitedly, "You two were wonderful. It looked positively tender!" Ernesto and Mashenka gave each other glances and grinned.

Ernesto spoke up, "Madam, traditionally, a waltz is a romantic dance style. But for your purposes, do you just want Masha to look graceful and romantic, or perhaps fiery and passionate on the dance floor?"

The elder Campbell gave Ernesto a devilish look. "What do you have in mind, Mr. Torres?"

Ernesto gave Masha a knowing look. He walked over to his boom box and removed the CD inside and replaced it with another that he took from his briefcase. He walked back to a spot where he and Masha had ended the previous waltz. She joined him. They faced each other as he pressed a button on the fob in his pocket and moments later an enticing violin played, followed by an abrupt set of low cords on a piano. He reached forward and grabbed her, pulling her close. They took on a dancing posture, and the couple executed a Tango passionately.

Mrs. Campbell watched pensively as the couple danced a very stylized tango. She marveled at their overtly sexual moves that they made with entangled legs, glides, swaying and passionate bending, not to mention him dragging her for a musical measure. For a moment Campbell waved her hand near her face as she felt a long forgotten hot flash. She whispered to herself, "Sweet Jesus."

As the music ended, Campbell sat quietly, staring off into the distance to an unknown somewhere. The music and the dancing couple had transported her to half a lifetime before. Campbell experienced an overpowering occurrence that moved her to tears. She whispered to herself, "Perform that tango at the embassy ball and it's most certainly going to inspire some shagging."

After the dance, the couple walked over to her. Both of

them glistened with perspiration. Campbell took a few moments to compose herself. Finally, she spoke up and did so very much for business. "Ernesto, there is no way I am going to let her dance with just any clodhopper guy who thinks he's a gentleman. I need you to dance with her at the British Embassy Ball."

He gave her a perplexed look. "Ma'am I'm Cuban-American. I don't see how I'm going to mix in at a British Embassy affair."

"It's all about appearances, my dear Ernesto. I'll pull a few strings," Mrs. Campbell explained.

"But ma'am, I'm sure you can get me into the British Embassy event but it's the Russian event is where she has to blow their socks off! I can't see how some sleight of hand is going to get me into the Russian event."

He protested. She gave him a reserved look. "Leave that to me."

Campbell looked at Masha. "You did wonderfully. That muslin you are wearing is the test for the Russian event. How was it to dance in?"

Masha answered up, "To be honest with you, when he pulled my dress up for that calf-knee grab during the tango, I was tight. During two practices earlier today, it didn't slide up properly. It surprised me. It worked during our demo for you."

Campbell nodded, "Very well. Let the three of us go upstairs, so you both can show Ms. Hamilton the costuming problem right now."

Fifteen minutes later, the three were on the eighth floor showing the dance maneuver that was causing the problem. Ms. Hamilton and two of her seamstresses had the dance couple show the maneuver a half dozen times. They watched the dress fail four out of six times. Finally, on the last failure, with one of the seamstress's laying on the floor watching the dress, she shouted she saw the problem.

They led Masha behind a changing screen and had her take off the problematic dress. Masha donned a bathrobe and waited as they incorporated a temporary fix into the muslin ballgown. After about twenty minutes, they had Masha put the sweaty test garment back on. Again, the dance couple showed the maneuver that caused the problem a half dozen times and there were no failures. Ms. Hamilton was pleased; Mrs. Campbell looked satisfied. With that, Masha took off the dress and headed to the shower.

Mrs. Campbell sat down with Ernesto. "You look troubled, Mr. Torres. What's on your mind?"

He shook his head gently, paused for a thought, then continued. "Using me as a dance partner for her at two embassy ball events, with all the high-intensity photography, will burn me out for any kind of undercover field operative work, especially in Europe, perhaps globally."

"Mashenka needs to be confident when she's out there dancing," Campbell explained.

He gave her a perturbed expression. "Except for her short-lived fear of dancing as a follower, which she is very much over, she is as confident as any amateur dancer I've worked with. I assure you she'll blow the socks off of everybody."

"So what do you want me to do, Mr. Torres?" Campbell asked.

"Honestly?" he queried.

She nodded in the affirmative.

"Please use your connections and the favors you can call in to get two different semi pro guys to dance with her. A different one for each embassy event. It will seem less staged, and I'll still be relatively obscure for active field work," Ernesto stated.

"I'm not sure if we can find someone as talented as you, who's cleared on such short notice," Olivia remarked.

"Cleared!" He coughed. "All you need this guy to do is dance with her and make her look great on the dance floor. It's not a James Bond operation! You need to get a dancing date for the British ball, even if you have to hire him. Masha is deep into her mission character. If you tell her, he is not cleared. She'll keep it close to her chest. She's a pro, you know that," Torres pointed out.

"Mr. Torres, if I do as you say and hire her a dance partner for the British event. What about the Russian event?" She asked.

He laughed, "Look, the British diplomatic gentlemen are all stiff-upper-lip-guys. A semi pro American or Brit dancer will let her shine. At the Russian event, there will be all kinds of French, Spanish or Italian diplomatic sorts who are big peacock types who are avid dancers. Oh hell, some of the Russians are serious dancers, too. Any of them would love to be on her dance card. So what if they aren't as good as me? So much the better, Masha will dance rings around them. Trust me once she gets going, she's a big show off!" Torres declared.

"Alright Ernesto my old friend, I will try to find a suitable stand-in for the British event. But if I can't, you are it! I accept your opinion there will be suitable talent at the Russian event. Is that acceptable?"

"Yes, Madame Campbell," he replied as he took leave of her and left Ms. Hamilton's conversation space. Masha came out of the dressing room area in casual daywear Ms. Hamilton's team had made for her. She took a seat next to Mrs. Campbell and poured a small cup of tea from a teapot on the small table in front of them.

"Has Ernesto left for the day?" Masha asked.

"Yes," Mrs. Campbell answers. "Is he going to be my dance partner at one of the ball's?" Masha queried.

"Maybe one, probably neither," Olivia said. Masha took a sip of green tea. "Did I do anything wrong?"

Campbell turned to her protégé. "No, it's just one of the drawbacks of our business."

Masha took another sip of tea. "Ah, the old rule of visibility with other operatives."

Olivia nodded her head and let out an exacerbated moan. "High visibility of one may endanger the team. If we don't use him at either ball, we could still use him in St. Petersburg, down the road?"

There was somber quiet between them both. Then Masha remarked, "It's ok ma'am, I'll just accept the luck of the draw for dance partners at either ball."

Mrs. Campbell simply smiled, "Spoken like a trouper."

10am May 21-The Protégé's Hair

On the eighth floor of the clothing provisioning building, Masha quietly sat in a beauty parlor style chair. A hairdresser was preparing to test various hair styles for putting Masha's hair up for the British Embassy Ball the following evening. Of course, Mrs. Campbell was ready to state her wishes.

"Masha here is debuting at a British Embassy Ball tomorrow night. I want her hair elegant and classy, but not over the top."

The hair stylist gave Campbell a bewildered look. He remarked, "When I'm told someone is debuting, the young lady is usually fifteen or sixteen years old. This woman is thirty something. I'm confused."

Mrs. Campbell nodded, "You are correct, debuting is perhaps the wrong word. Mashenka here is a notable academic, and she is being introduced to the British, as well as the International Diplomatic Society. She needs to be elegant, but not stuffy." Olivia paused and held up a finger. "When Mashenka gets on the dance floor, she's going to have a charm like a thousand-watt lightbulb. Her hair must be elegant, fresh and sturdy enough for energetic dancing!"

The hair stylist folded his arms and seemed to study Masha. He took a few minutes walking around her to study his subject. While he gave her a careful scrutinizing, for a moment their eyes met, then Masha sheepishly looked away from him. Speaking to Masha, "The way the Senora talks about you. She gives me the impression you are a real firecracker on the dance floor." Demurely Masha lowered her eyes for a few moments. Again he looked her in the eyes, "So what is this energetic dance the lady speaks of?"

Masha simply remarked, "A Tango."

The hair stylist reacted with exaggerated surprise. "A Tango!? Hmmm, every self-respecting Mexican-American young _man in my hometown knows how to dance a tango. Some dance it respectable, still others dance it hot!"

He stood back from her for a moment. Both of them had their eyes locked on each other.

Then he spoke up, "So how does our thirty something senorita debutant dance a tango?"

Masha folded her arms like his, "Hot and very passionate, senor!" She said with a challenging tone!

Mrs. Campbell remarked, "People, we're supposed to be figuring out Masha's hair style for tomorrow night. Not posturing for a Mexican standoff!"

Masha got out of the chair and stood in front of him. She gestured with her finger. "Follow me, Senor, I want to see what you've got." She started walking for the elevator door, followed by the hairdresser.

Barbara Hamilton motioned for her seamstresses to follow her as she remarked to Mrs. Campbell, "I've got to see this!" Campbell quickly rose and followed them, "Me too. Wait for me!"

Masha and the hairstylist rode quietly down on the elevator to the sixth-floor warehouse/basketball court space. As they exited the elevator, the doors closed and returned to the eighth floor.

The man looked around. "So, what are we going to play, a game of basketball?"

Masha walked out to Mr. Torres's still present boom box. As she kneeled down to check the CD in the boom box, she pointed to the spot where she and Ernesto had danced earlier.

"We'll start over there!" The hair stylist looked amused and walked over to the place Masha had directed him to go. Masha picked up the control fob for the boom box. As she began walking to the starting position, the elevator doors opened and out exited Barbara, her two seamstresses and Mrs. Campbell, who took a seat in the chair she used earlier. At the starting spot, Masha joined the hairdresser.

They faced each other, Masha remarked (speaking Spanish), "Are you ready, sir?"

The hairdresser, with a smirk on his face, (speaking Spanish) "Yes, lady, if you are ready."

The enticing sound of a violin followed by an abrupt set of low chords on a piano filled the air in moments after she pressed a button on the Fob in her pocket. She reached forward and grabbed him and pulled him close with intensity. They each assumed a dancing posture and Masha, leading the couple, began the tango.

Mrs. Campbell was stunned to watch her protégé as she led the two in a very different tango to what she had witnessed earlier. She marveled at their explicitly sexual moves that they made with pronounced swaying and elegant glides. Masha executed a spin on the man and the two began with him now leading her with passionate bending, not to mention him dragging her for two musical measures, and finally him implementing a series of maneuvers with the two alternately trading entangled leg moves. As the music slowed to an end, they stopped their dancing motion and ended the dance as one. Both enveloped in a warm embrace.

Barbara and her seamstresses were clapping and cheering. Mrs. Campbell stood up and barked in a loud command voice, "You two get over here! Now!"

The couple, holding hands, walked over to her and stood respectfully in front of her. "Just what the hell was that?" Campbell demands.

The hairdresser spoke up, "Senora, from my perspective, it was an exceptionally well executed tango." Campbell sneers.

She gave him a perturbed look. "I wasn't speaking to senor...," she stumbled in addressing him, "Whoever you are."

He spoke up, "Javier Luis Perez at your service, Senora."

Mrs. Campbell gave Masha a stern look. "Give account of yourself, young lady!"

"Well, we can't use Mr. Torres tomorrow and Senor Perez

was giving us such great bravado about dancing the Tango! I took some initiative and auditioned him for the damn job, madame!" Masha replies.

There was a hushed quiet, one that could proverbially be called a deathly silence. Mrs. Campbell stared first at Mashenka. After giving her a stern look, she then looked at Perez, "You're hired, Senor Perez."

He smiled, "What? I thought I was just here to do Senorita Masha's hair tomorrow night?"

Mrs. Campbell grinned at him, "Tomorrow night you are going to do her hair, then you are going to get into a tux and be Mashenka's escort and dinner date to the British Embassy Ball! The two of you are going to blow everybody's socks off with your dancing!"

Perez was astonished. Masha took him by the hand. "Come on Senor Perez, let's go figure my hair out and we'll fill you in on the ball. Please tell me you can waltz?" A bit overwhelmed, he answered as they walked, "Well, of course I can."

"Great!" Masha replied, "Senor Perez, you and I are going to make all the news outlets. Won't that be fun?"

6:30pm May 22-Last-Minute Details

At the provisioning warehouse on the first floor, an elegantly dressed Mashenka Petrova and handsomely Black-tie attired Javier Perez stood quietly next to a limousine awaiting last-minute instructions.

Perez gave Masha a pleasant look and smiled. "By the way, you look terrific." She gave him a beaming smile. "Hey, I'm just a canvas. You did my hair and a remarkable job on my makeup. I could never have done it as wonderfully as you did it. To be honest, I'm too nervous."

"All part of the service. Can I ask you a serious question?" Perez queried. Masha nodded.

"That Mrs. Hamilton lady told me you are going to St. Petersburg, Russia, for a year to teach Theater Arts at an academy."

146

Masha nodded. He looked thoughtful, then asked, "Why are they staging this and having you show off your dancing at a diplomatic dinner?"

Cautious of mission security boundaries, Masha told him the simple truth. "Think of it as a goodwill effort, but with some splash. If I were to just go there as a simple theater professor. Hardly anyone would ever hear about it. But if we by some chance put on a show at a couple of embassy events, the diplomatic staffs will buzz, tongues will wag within diplomatic society circles."

"So, this is a publicity stunt?" He questioned.

She pursed her lips slightly. "Notoriety, opens doors and will get me invitations to the elite and the movers and shakers over there. I get to be a one-woman Good-Will ambassador to help US and Russian relations." She paused, then comments, "Since the Soviet government ended a few years ago. Many people have been working hard to mend fences with our old adversaries. I'm just doing my part, and so are you, my friend, by being my handsome dinner guest and dancing partner."

"Is all this hush, hush?" He asked. She shook her head in the negative, "Nah! But we need to keep it close to our chests so that we don't spoil the good thing we're trying to do. You and I are just occasional pals in the dance community. That's all we'll say about ourselves, ok?"

The elevator door opened; Barbara Hamilton stepped out. As she walked over to them next to the limousine. Hamilton came to a stop and directed her gaze towards them momentarily. She broke into a bright smile. "You two look smashing."

As she approached them, she remarked. "Some instructions from Mrs. Campbell. She'll be at a different table with some high society snots. If you bump into her, act as if you don't know her." She opened a file wallet and withdrew an envelope. "Mashenka, this is your invitation, Mr. Perez. You are her plus one! Do you both have your ID with you?" They nodded. She gave them a serious look. "Show me." Perez opened his wallet and produced his District of Columbia driver's license. Hamilton looked at it. "Great, everything is current."

She turned to Mashenka, who opened her clutch purse and produced her Petrova Maryland driver's license and passport. Hamilton nodded, "Excellent!"

Hamilton reached into her file wallet and withdrew a basic flip cellular phone. "This phone has two numbers. The number to your driver and the other number to the driver's dispatching service just in case something unforeseen happens."

Perez gave her a curious look. "Like what?"

Hamilton grimaced. "Year before last, one of our clients went to an affair much like this one. The limo driver died of a heart attack during the ball and nobody was there to pick up the guests. It was unfortunate and very messy."

Masha took the phone and slipped it into her purse. "Thank You. Any other tips?"

Hamilton thought for a moment, "Yes, two things. Mr. Perez, on the off chance some of your high-end customers bump into you, you are simply Ms. Masha's occasional dance partner and her guest." He nodded, "Got it."

"Dr. Petrova, if by some off chance you have contact with the British embassy staff you met at dinner, you are free to converse with them, but keep it to small talk about the evening," Hamilton stated.

"Finally, this is from me. You two, go be the talk of the town tonight with your splendid dancing. We know there will be at least one tango, perhaps two. Strut your stuff. Some of the stuffier British types might think you are being too undignified with the dance. It's none of their business. Of course, it's going to set tongues fluttering in the international diplomatic community, and that is the aim. Don't worry about what the stuffy Brits think! You two have a wonderful evening!"

She stepped over to the driver's side of the limo and knocked on his window. A formally attired driver got out and opened Masha's door. The driver closed the door after she had taken her seat, fastened her seatbelt, and ensured that her dress was inside the vehicle. The driver walked over to the opposite side of the limo and opened the door for Mr. Perez. Again, after he got seated and strapped in, the driver closed the door for him.

Inside the limo, Mashenka looked at Perez. "How do you want me to address you this evening?"

"My clients call me Javier, but my close friends call me Luis. As we are familiar dancing partners, please call me Luis." Masha gave him a smile, "Then my dear friend and guest, Luis, it is. If I have to introduce you more formally, I will call you either Mr. Perez or Mr. Javier Perez, depending on the situation."

He nodded, "I heard Ms. Hamilton call you Doctor. What about that?" Masha nodded. "We're informal friends. Call me Masha, if you must introduce me, I'm Professor Mashenka Petrova."

Masha tapped on the plexiglass barrier between them and the driver. The driver started the vehicle and pressed a button that opened the roll away garage door and drove the limousine out of the warehouse building. Masha reached over and grabbed Luis's hand. "We're off!"

7:15pm May 22-The British Embassy

Mashenka and Luis sat quietly as the limo driver made his way through early evening traffic. Luis asked, "I've heard of charity parties at various embassies all over Washington, but what is different about tonight's party?"

Masha gave him a pleasant look. "Okay, tonight's event is not a charity event, nor is it an official state dinner. An embassy ball is a formal dance party. I'm told there will be a four-course dinner and afterwards, dessert and drinks and an evening of dance and small talk with other guests." He gave her a questioned look. "Will there be VIPs?"

She grinned, "I've been told it's going to be a who's who of foreign dignitaries and Washington, DC elite." She glanced out of her window, "We're at Massachusetts Ave. it won't be long now we're coming toward Embassy row."

Suddenly the limo slowed, the limo driver lowered the plexiglass barrier between them. "Ma'am, there's a line of limousines in front of us. Cops are directing traffic. We'll wait our turn."

Luis asked the driver, "Where's the embassy?" The driver answered back, "That's it up there at the end of all these limos. 3100 Massachusetts Ave Northwest, it's one of the most storied diplomatic addresses in the district. Be patient, they are moving right along. Ma'am, I won't be getting out of the car. They'll have decked out valets to open your door and someone will direct you two inside."

Masha spoke up, "Thank you for the ride." The driver answered back. "Ms. Hamilton gave you a cell phone?" Masha answered, "Yes." The driver added. "Ok, ma'am, call me at the end of the evening. I'll come pick you both up. When I pull in for pickup, your name will be on a sign in the front passenger window."

Masha simply answered, "I will do that. Thank You."

Then the limo driver raised the barrier. They directed the car into a covered breezeway area. Two young men in period uniforms of some sort opened the doors of the limo and offered evening courtesies to both of them as they exited the vehicle. As Luis stepped around to Mashenka's side of the Limo. He offered his right arm, and she laid her hand on his arm. A valet directed the couple toward a line of guests waiting to pass through a security checkpoint. As the line briefly stopped, Masha noted the couple in front of her. It was Harry and Anna Lloyd whom she had met at Lord Walker's dinner party. Masha greeted them, "Harry and Anna Lloyd, is that you?"

Harry turned and looked at her. "Professor Petrova, how nice to see you again." Anna turned and did a quick scan of Masha in her burgundy, long-sleeved silk ball gown. "Mashenka, you look absolutely lovely. Visit our table once we get through all this security." Moments later, the Lloyds were called to go through security.

After they finished, the Lloyds moved on and Masha and Luis had their turn at security. The security personnel scanned Masha and Luis with hand wands and put Masha's silver clutch purse through an x-ray device, then cleared the couple to enter.

Again, Masha and Luis stood behind the Lloyds, as they were waiting to be escorted to their tables. Anna turned and leaned into Masha. "I love your dress. I might have known you'd be wearing a Russian designer." Masha gave her a puzzled look. Anna qualified, "Certainly, you knew you're wearing a Badgley-Mischka design! How did you ever afford that on a professor's income?" Mashenka rolled with the remark, "I have generous friends." Anna smirked, "No doubt!"

Masha asked Harry, "Will the embassy staff be sitting together in one area?" Harry leaned into her. "No, we're all mixed in with the other tables. I believe that William and Emily Taylor will be at your table. Her Ladyship asked them to shepherd you a bit." Mashenka smiled, "Won't that be delightful," as she remembered Emily, the woman who glanced daggers at her at Lord Walkers.

As Luis and Masha were being led to their table, she quietly remarked, "We're going to be seated at a banquet table with the Taylors. Be careful with William and Emily. My first impression of them was that they are slippery." Luis asked back, "Are they spies or snobs?" Masha about choked on his spy remark. "No, Luis, they are upper crust staff, and I'm not exactly sure where I stand with them." Luis gave her a grin, "Ok, we'll do this by old boarding school rules. Exceedingly polite until proven otherwise." She looked at him with a shocked expression. "You went to boarding school?"

Luis smirked, "Oh, here it comes! You thought I grew up on the streets in No-Where, New Mexico, didn't you?" Masha had an embarrassed look on her face. "Luis, please set me straight." Luis led her away from the table that had their names on it. "My father is a high-powered corporate lawyer in Albuquerque, New Mexico.

Instead of my last two years in traditional high school, dad sent me to a Prep School in Boston. I won a scholarship to the University of Massachusetts, Boston; and later I went to law school, and that made my father proud."

Masha stared with a surprised look, "How did you end up in the Beauty Business?" He walked her to their table, which still had eight vacant seats. Luis continued his private conversation. "But I was interested in fashion. The Commercial modeling business specifically. I started a small niche legal business specializing in handling the legal affairs of Modeling businesses, Beauty Schools and the Beauty business. Would you believe it was largely an orphan industry for legal representation? To understand it, I went to Beauty School and learned the business and along the way I became a commercial hair stylist. As it stands, I'm a specialized legal eagle and my beauty sideline has introduced me to some of the loveliest women I've ever known, including yourself."

Masha was stunned. "How do you want me to introduce you?" He grinned as fellow guests for their banquet table gathered around the table. "Introduce me as you see fit, Professor. After all, we're both in the entertainment business, aren't we?" Perez added. Mashenka smiled and found a tent card with her name and respective chair at the banquet table, as did Luis.

7:48pm May 22-The Banquet Table

With all eight guests standing behind their appointed chairs. William Taylor, a Foreign Service Officer, spoke up, "Welcome honored guests, on behalf of Her Majesty Queen Elizabeth the second. I bid you greetings and welcome you all to our Spring Embassy Ball. Please take your seats." The gentlemen around the table stepped behind the chairs of the women and pulled the respective chairs out and assisted the women with being seated. With the women seated, the men pulled out their own chairs and sat down.

Taylor spoke up. "Let's have a round of introductions. I am William Taylor. I am a Foreign Service Officer with the British Diplomatic service." He gestured to his right; a woman spoke up.

"I am Alejandra Romero; I am from Spain and I am an attorney." She gestured to the man to her right.

"I am Boris Baranov. I am an acting Diplomatic Air Attaché with the Russian Federation." Mashenka's head perked up. *Pavel?* She thought to herself. Baranov smiled and gestured to the woman to his right.

"I am Natalya Baranov and I am a pediatric physician. I am from Russia." She gestured to the man to her right.

"I am Felipe Romero and I am the Diplomatic Commerce Attaché for the government of Spain." He gestured to the woman to his right.

"I am Mashenka Petrova and I am a Theater Professor at Cornell University and I live in the United States." Before she could gesture to Luis... A man's voice remarked, (Speaking Russian) "Masha from Chernobyl?" She looked over at Baranov, nodded and remarked. (Speaking Russian) "Yes, Comrade."

Masha resumed the introductions and gestured to Luis to her right.

"My name is Javier Perez; I am an attorney here in the United States." Finally, Perez gestured to the woman to his right.

"My name is Emily Taylor. I am a former member of the British Parliament. I am a political Strategist." She gestured to her husband; he gave her a polite nod and addressed the table guests.

"The first course is about to be served. Please enjoy your dinner conversation, Bon appétit everyone."

A few moments later, a server was carrying a tray of appetizers. The server started with Mr. Taylor and made his way right around the table. The served appetizer was Atlantic Pompano Amandine.

Mashenka took a fork and gently probed her appetizer. Felipe Romero leaned toward her. "It's an almond-encrusted fish. It is tasty senora." She nodded and softly answered, "Thank you

Senor." He smiled and winced a bit, "Felipe, please." "Thank You Felipe," then she asked, "What does a Commerce Attaché do exactly?"

He picked up his glass of wine and held it up. "I do my best to promote the export products of my country, like wine and, of course, olives for which we are famous! Of course, there are many other things."

Then he asked her. "Do you teach stage drama?"

She cleared her mouth, took a sip of water. "Yes, I teach many aspects of theatrical craft. In fact, I'm going to be a guest professor at St. Petersburg State Theatre Arts Academy for the next year!" He gave her a surprised look. "Really?" She nodded. He turned to Baranov's "Boris and Natalya, Mashenka here is going to be a college professor this year in your St. Petersburg! Isn't that wonderful?"

The Baranov's gave each other surprised looks. Natalya leaned toward Felipe, (speaking Spanish) "Pardon my Russian."

Felipe smiled and nodded. Then Natalya (speaking Russian) "Mashenka, you must visit us in Moscow." "When will you arrive?"

Masha looked past Felipe, (Speaking Russian) "I expect to arrive in early July. I'll need your contact information."

Natalya opened her purse, removed a card, and handed it to Felipe, who a moment later joked, "Now it seems I now work for the Russian Mail service!"

There were giggles and snickers around the table as he passed Natalya's card to Masha. At that moment, the servers returned and removed the appetizer dishes, interrupting all the other conversations around the table. A few minutes later, other servers returned and placed the main course in front of each guest. This main course was roast squab, artichoke with vegetable puree. Masha quickly glanced around the table and saw smiles all around.

She looked at Luis. "What do you think?" He gave her a surprised look. "So far, this has been amazing." Then she whispered. "It's all lovely." Then Luis quietly asked, "It looks like you know Baranov." Masha gave him a perplexed look, "I met him back in 1986, but I haven't exactly met his wife yet."

As the main course was being taken away, another server came to Masha and handed her a small envelope. She thanked the server. She opened the envelope and quietly read the note inside. Luis leaned into her. "Is there a problem?"

"No, just some instructions." Masha comments. Luis gave her a curious look. "Instructions?" Masha quietly answered him, "There are going to be four sets of music for dancing. We are not to dance in the first set at all. It's mostly for notables and guest dignitaries. The second set will have slow dancing, swing, waltz and a restrained traditional roles tango last. They advised us to dance well but not-to-steal-the-show. In the third set, we can show off a little with swing and waltz. In the fourth and final set, we can go as over the top as we want with our waltz. The tango will be last in the final set, the gloves come off! Throw everything at it, duel leads, hot stuff, go for broke. End the night with a bang! Those are our orders."

Luis just folded his arms and gave her a stern look. "I was in ROTC while at the University. I know a military operation when I see one. This is a precision field operation, isn't it?" Masha dropped her eyes. "Yes." She raised her head and looked deeply into his eyes. "If you want to quit, tell me now."

He studied her carefully. "This is important, isn't it?"

She hesitantly said, "Very." Luis frowned and gently shook his head, "Just how important is it?" She shrugged her shoulders. "I told you what the mission is. I need to be the talk of the diplomatic town." Luis gave her a stern expression. "That Russian fella mentioned your name and Chernobyl in the same sentence. Were you somehow involved?"

Masha dropped her eyes. "Luis, this is, I'd have to kill you in the morning stuff." He shook his head and snickered, "Hell yes, I'm in. Ok we'll do it by the book. Whatever the old lady wants. Yes, I'm in."

Then she commented, "I'm going to dance with a couple of other fellas before our mission sets up. Ok?" He smirked, "Are you going to go dance with old Boris?"

Masha rolled her eyes, "Yes and only if Natalya says it's ok. And I'm going to dance with William Taylor too after I have a brief talk with his wife, Emily." Luis commented. "I want to chat with our Spanish folks."

After Luis pulled her chair back, Masha walked over to Natalya and Boris, (Speaking Russian) "Natalya, it is such a pleasure to meet you after all of this time." Natalya stood up and wrapped her arms tightly around Masha, expressing in Russian, "I am deeply honored to meet you. You are so well known in my country." Masha simply answered. "All I did was translate..." Natalya cut Masha off, (Speaking Russian) "Boris told me of some risks you took. You and that Anya Gusev lady. I'm proud to know you. I hope you will visit us in Moscow."

Masha answered. (Speaking Russian) "I'll be teaching and producing American Musical theater at St. Petersburg State Theatre Arts Academy. You and Boris will always be my guests at my show openings!" Masha told her sincerely. Natalya gave Masha another hug. Masha spoke up, (Speaking Russian) "Will it violate protocol if I'm seen dancing with your husband once or twice tonight? This place is crawling with an international press." Then Natalya laughed, (Speaking Russian) "Not at all my dear, you both will probably end up in the Pravda's society page, this week! Certainly, you can dance with him! He could use the visibility." The two women hugged dearly. After a few minutes Masha remarked, (Speaking Russian) "Tell him to ask me for the last dance of the first set."

Later, just before the last dance of the first set. Boris Baranov asked Mashenka Petrova to dance with him. It was a traditional slow dance. But it was something much more. For two people who had been to hell and back during an unthinkable nuclear disaster, and then not to see or talk to each other for eight years. This unexpected meeting and tender dance was like a cup of cool water in a cruel dry desert of time, distance, and the harsh complexities of world politics. As the dance ended, their friendly embrace remained for many minutes.

As they left the dance floor, Mashenka whispered to him, (Speaking Russian) "My dance with you tonight was real, my friend. Between us, the other dances you see me doing tonight are a performance. From this point on, I'll be working." He stopped walking forward, (Speaking Russian) "My dear, you do what you must. I understand. Natalya and I look forward to dinners and teas with you." She held out her hand. He took it and gently kissed it. "Rock the place, Mashenka!"

In the second set, Masha and Luis enjoyed several slow dances, expertly danced to some swing, whirled around the dance floor with the best of them during the waltz, and ended the set with a sanitized tango.

In the third set, they did as suggested. They showed off a bit during the swing music, only to tone it down for a waltz.

They sat out the first three dances of five of the fourth and final set. In the fourth set, Masha and Luis glided in grand style through "On the Beautiful Blue Danube." Their performance nearly cleared the dance floor and the guests of the ball applauded loudly at their expertise.

After a brief rest, the orchestra began with an enticing violin being heard, followed by an abrupt set of low cords on a piano. Masha reached forward and grabbed Luis and aggressively pulled him close with intensity. They each took on a dancing posture, and Masha, leading the couple, executed a passionate tango.

They transfixed the Embassy ballroom audience, watching a very distinct and exotic Tango, compared to what any of them had ever seen, let alone at an embassy affair.

Boris and Natalya marveled at what the steamy two dancers were executing in their highly explicitly sexual moves, their rhythmic swaying, and their seemingly effortless glides. When the couple stopped, they ended the dance as one presence enveloped in a warm embrace.

The ballroom audience erupted in an inter-twisted mix of both enthusiastic applause and outraged jeering at the couple's lewdness. Amid the cheers and jeering, two large embassy security officers came onto the dance floor after a few minutes, fearing a social disruption. They immediately escorted the pair out of the ballroom and took them to a private holding area. The pair sat quietly, cooling down from their highly energetic dance performance. Luis finally broke the silence, "Mrs. C. wanted us to make a splash! Honey, I think we brought the damned house down literally."

Masha considered what he said, then softly remarked, "Yes, the mission was to make a splash. I told you we're going to make all the news outlets! When they come for us, we must, of course, be very remorseful."

Luis nodded in agreement. "As our legal counsel, I assure you the worst they can do is throw us in the Tower of London. But on practical consideration, they won't want that kind of publicity. They'll probably ban us both for the season from the British Embassy."

Masha quipped! "Gee, that's a trophy worth having on the mantle!"

After twenty minutes, Lord Walker, the Director of Security, a security detail of eight guards, and Mrs. Campbell entered the room with the door being slammed.

With a fiery face, Lord Walker raised his voice. "What in fucking blue blazes were you two playing at? The Spring Embassy Ball is a shining gem in our season, and you two have destroyed that loving legacy with your sexy, enthusiastic and lewd display. I would throw you both in the Tower of London if I had my way! Do you realize the network camera crews and paparazzi are coming out of our ears and filling up our breezeway? I hereby officially ban you both for life from attending all events at the British Embassy! Security, go out and clear a path to our embassy limo and get this disgusting scum out of Her Majesty's embassy!"

"Aye, your Lordship the Director of Security barked, come on lads, we have a job to do." The security detail slammed the door as they exited the holding room.

Lord Walker, Mrs. Campell, Masha, and Luis remained in the room. Lord Walker spoke up with a grin, "Mrs. Campbell, as always, it's a pleasure and an adventure to work with you and your expert teams. Ms. Petrova and Mr. Perez, I am deeply sorry for the harsh language, but I had to put on a good front for the staff. I thought you both did a remarkable job tonight. If you didn't have an invitation to the Russian Ball, I dare say you will receive one after tonight. Because anybody who embarrasses the Crown and the British Empire, they will love. I'd wager you'll both be in the news cycles for two or three or perhaps four days. Enjoy it! Good Luck with your mission." Mrs. Campell simply smiled like a proud mother. "I'll see you both in the limousine." She left the room.

12:20 am May 22-The Hide Out

A few minutes later, two security guards escorted the couple past a sea of flashing cameras and video teams. Many of the news teams shouting questions to the two of them. Neither of them said a thing and just ducked the cameras and sometimes covered their faces until they had reached the refuge of the awaiting limousine. Moments after the doors were closed by the valets, the driver stepped on the gas and drove out of the Embassy breezeway.

The escape limousine provided by the British Embassy took a 45-minute, complicated route to lose any following paparazzi that might shadow them. Luis and Masha sat quietly with cool bottles of water, mentally decompressing from a busy evening. Mrs. Campbell praised the two for a brilliant set of dancing performances during the evening.

"Both of you sleep in, you've earned it. Have a private breakfast or brunch, whichever. I suggest that you both should avoid the hotel restaurant. That entire scene of you two being marched out to the limo will be all over the network news feeds by morning." Campbell paused and considered her next instructions. "I recommend that you both plan to hide out in the hotel for at least a few days." She handed Masha back her purse. "When you are ready to leave the hotel in two or three-days' time, use your cell phone to call your regular town car driver."

Masha spoke up, "What about clothing? We're sitting here in perspiration-soaked clothing…"

Campbell cut her off. "All taken care of. Ms. Hamilton arranged for a four-day supply of resort casual clothing. It's already up in your suites along with several burner phones in case you need to call out. The mission is to lie low for a few days."

Luis addressed Mrs. Campbell, "I've got a high-end hair salon to run?" She studied Luis for a few moments. "You must have an assistant manager or third key person who can open the shop?" Luis simply commented, "I do." Campbell added, "Have them clear your calendar for the next three days and have them reschedule the lot for a few days from now. You know Luis, this visibility is going to make your designer hair salon the chichi place to be!" Luis smirked. "Good lord!"

After the long stealth driving trek around the District of Columbia, the driver made her way to Georgetown and pulled into the Four Seasons Hotel. Campbell handed each of them the suite keys. "Charge your rooms for everything!" Mrs. Campbell thought for a few moments. "Remember to lie low. Your residences and Luis's business are probably staked out with news crews and paparazzi!"

Masha remarked, "But you told me you dealt with my apartment and stored my belongings securely." Campbell grinned, "Yes, and none of the media teams know that! They'll be camping outside Dr. Petrova's empty apartment." Campbell looked pleased with herself, knowing she just covered Masha's real identity. Then she added, "Sleep well. You both earned it, you did a brilliant job, both of you."

11:10 am May 22-A Hotel Suite in Georgetown

Masha awoke in her king size bed and looked around to orient herself. *Oh yeah, the hotel room.* She thought. She got up and went to the bathroom and relieved herself. As she looked at herself in the mirror, she saw a somewhat grotesque version of herself looking back. Her makeup from the previous night was now smeared and had a macabre melting appearance based on her intense dancing perspiration.

"I should have showered instead of falling into bed!" she said to the hideous woman in the mirror. She looked around at the bathroom vanity and found a toiletries bag provided by Ms. Hamilton. She opened the bag and found a small jar of cold cream. "Barbara, you are a saint!" She remarked as she began the ritual of removing the previous evening's makeup. After showering, she wrapped herself in a hotel provided terrycloth bathrobe.

She walked over to the door to the adjoining hotel suite and lightly knocked. A moment later, she heard the other door being unlocked; it opened and there was a refreshed Luis holding a cup of coffee. "Shall we order breakfast, brunch or lunch, senora?"

"Let's do breakfast." Masha responded. He nodded in acknowledgement, then asked, "My place or yours?" She closed her eyes for a moment. With her eyes still closed, "I don't feel like entertaining. Let's do your place."

"What do you want?" Masha responded without pausing, "Three eggs scrambled, double bacon, a croissant or toast. If they're out of croissants, then whole wheat toast, an orange and lots of coffee."

In a business manner, he simply told her, "Go make yourself presentable and I'll call in our order."

Masha closed the door and dug through the clothing Barbara Hamilton had provided her. After she laid out what she was going to wear, she considered turning on the television to see just how big the splash that she and Luis had instigated. Then, after a moment, she decided to wait and would watch it with Luis.

Thirty minutes later, Luis had a knock at the door. He opened the door and there was a room service server who politely addressed him, "I have your room service sir." Luis gestured for the middle eastern man to come in. "Please set up breakfast for two on the table by the window." The server nodded and pushed his cart over to the round table by the windows and arranged a breakfast setting for two.

The server glanced up at Luis several times. Then spoke up, "The news is talking about a couple who shocked everybody at the British Embassy last night. You sort of look like the guy they're talking about."

Luis picked up his wallet from the top of the chest of drawers and removed a couple of twenty-dollar bills and slipped it to the server, "I want my privacy, that wasn't me, ok?" The server smiled broadly, "On second thought you look nothing like him!" The server said with a wink. After the server left, Luis knocked on the adjoining room door to Masha's suite. "Senorita, breakfast is served!"

Masha opened the door wearing dark slacks and an emerald-green stretch top. She mumbled, "Coffee" as she entered Luis's room and made her way to the breakfast table setting by the windows.

Luis remarked, "The server mentioned I looked like the guy on TV all the news channels are talking about."

Masha stared at him, and simply whispered, "Shit!"

Luis waved a finger at her. "I slipped him a couple of twenties to keep his mouth shut." She took a deep breath and sat down.

After a moment, she noticed something irregular. "Hey, you ordered the same thing I did!"

He shrugged his shoulders, "What you ordered sounded good, so I got one too. Shall I turn on the television so we can take a peek at the TV news?"

She nodded as she bit into a piece of crispy bacon. "Do it!"

He turned the bulky large screen television toward their breakfast nook. With the remote in hand, he turned on the TV as he pulled out his chair and sat down. A quick local cable channels check showed that the local commercial channels were all running morning, daytime syndicated programing.

"Nada," he remarked, "We'll have to wait until the 5 or 6 pm local newscasts." Then, he changed the channel to CNN.

As the news story ended, the news anchor remarked, "In other news. Last evening in the nation's capital, a pair of guest dancers who performed a provocative tango rocked the British Embassy. The performance had international dignitaries' ballroom guests both cheering and condemning the provocative dance performance." (On the Screen was video of the two dancing with part of their movements blocked by video overlay.) "The dancers were Luis Perez, a noted high fashion hair stylist in the District of Columbia and Cornell University Drama Professor Mashenka Petrova." (Video showed the two being escorted to a waiting limousine by uniformed security officers, amid a sea of press camera's flashing.) The video cut to a British Embassy official Lord Walker deploring the incident and officially banning the two dancers involved for life from all British Embassies globally.

Luis clicked the remote and turned the television off. "There you go, Masha. We'll never get to go to another British embassy ball event anywhere on the planet. Now there's your trophy!"

Masha shook her head, "My god, I hope my handler and Mrs. Campbell can smooth things with the university folks up in Ithaca, NY!" Luis quietly sat back and gave her a considered look. After a moment he remarked, "You're a spook aren't you!"

1:20 pm May 22-The Credo Talk

Luis repeated what he said, "You're a spook aren't you!" Masha said nothing. Luis stated his position plainly, "Ok Masha, don't you dare clam up on me. Look at it from my perspective. I get hired to do someone's hair and find myself conned into dancing at an embassy ball for a principal world government. A day later, I am ensconced in a hotel in Georgetown, hiding from the global media and the freaking paparazzi, and I am banned from that afore mentioned country's embassies worldwide for life, I might add. Mashenka, or whoever you are, it would be damned honorable and polite if you would tell me honestly what the heck I've been dragged into. Listening to Mrs. Campbell, she's a Brit! That Lord Walker fellow running the Embassy, was in on the operation's con job too and he's a high-ranking Brit. I noticed that the clothing warehouse facility looks like quite an operation. So who are you really and are you in her majesty's secret service? Or do I have to call my staff at my salon and have them send the news crews and the paparazzi over and tell them exactly what this was? A big secret agent con job!"

Masha struggled, "What assurances do I have that after I tell you that you won't do exactly that? Call the world media over here, expose our mission and you'll probably get me killed?"

He gave her a disdainful look. "I haven't given you any assurances. But I'd like to think that you know I'm an honorable man. Please give me that benefit of the doubt."

Masha sat silent for a few minutes, then she began in a somber tone of voice. "Among the first lessons I learned about the Intelligence profession. First and foremost, it's the second oldest profession with certainly less morals than the first and oldest profession. I also learned that to do this sort of job, one must be grounded in the credo that this work benefits the wellbeing of one's homeland."

She paused, and took a sip of coffee, then stated, "We learned that anonymity is a foundational principle. Which means I will go to my grave without loved ones, relatives and friends ever knowing what I did for my country. Also, knowing that some member of my team has a bullet with my name on it in case of imminent capture. I also had to accept that my home country's government will disavow me if I am ever caught or killed. Last, I had to accept I can never retire from the Intelligence business. Oh, I can retire from my day-to-day duties, but the truth is I am in the business until my dying day. That Mr. Perez is who and what I am. To tell you more would be a serious risk to your health and wellbeing and would probably be a certain death sentence for me. My Russian friend, Mr. Baranov, knows I am a heroine who helped save his country during a deadly nuclear disaster. Beyond that, he respects my anonymity."

"So you won't tell me your real-world name? Luis asked.

She gave him a serious look. "That real world name that you think is so important is the real con job. When I'm not on a mission as Masha, I am a corporate contractor. I sit in a lonely cube reading and drafting reports. Reports which I question whether anybody reads. I come to work, I do my job alone, I drink crappy coffee from a coin-operated coffee machine. After work I sit in evening traffic hoping my old beater car won't overheat. I get home from work, I feed my parakeet. I fix some supper and read my subscription magazines. Perhaps I'll listen to a baseball game on the radio during the season. That is the off-duty hours' role I must pretend to be. I literally must fade into the wallpaper version of me. Luis, you know Masha, who is the real me and yes, it's a deep cover identity. I'm going to Russia to teach for a year. We call that cover identity maintenance. They invited Masha to do this, so to keep up appearances, I'm going to spend a year in a Russian theater arts academy teaching stage craft. Sometimes I live my life on the bleeding edge. I wouldn't have it any other way. Luis, whom would you rather know? Would you rather know that sassy woman who dragged you down to a basketball court and danced your ass off or the quiet corporate contractor cube monkey?"

Luis pondered for a moment. "Are you qualified to teach theater arts?" He asked. She smirked, "Yes, I am! I have a BA in Theater Performing arts. Sort of like you, a legal eagle on one hand, a brilliant hair stylist on the other!" She was quiet for a few minutes. Luis said nothing.

After a few minutes of deafening silence, she stated, "What I did last night just exposed me to an awful lot of danger. Field operations people rarely go around purposely getting themselves on global network news feeds, presenting themselves as high-profile performers and getting themselves banned for life by some world government's diplomatic service. What I did was key to launching the mission. If the mission required a name, it would probably be, 'Charm the Pants off the Russians!' Luis, I am getting to do the royal family relative thing. They assigned me to become Russia's American darling. Literally miss charming with a sassy edge. There, you completely know the mission. If you want to out me! That's your choice. But if you do, please know that will kill the mission and with that, I will disappear back into the wallpaper and become that corporate cube monkey again and you will never know what has become of me."

1:20 pm May 22-Breaking News

The burner flip phone rang in Masha's hotel suite. Masha answered. It was Mrs. Campbell. "Masha, turn on CNN." Masha changed the channel from the program she was watching. The CNN feed was currently in a set of commercials. "Masha just remarked they're currently running commercials." Mrs. Campbell responded, "The Russian Embassy is about to make an announcement!"

Masha hollered, "Luis, turn on CNN ASAP. The Russians are about to make an announcement."

As the commercial block finished, CNN displayed an animated Breaking News Banner with a music bed. The video cut to an anchor. "The Russian Federation Embassy in Washington, DC, has called a news conference. We're breaking away to our correspondent at the Russian Embassy."

A woman's voice, "We're here at the Russian Embassy where we've been told the staff wants to make a special announcement. Here come two representatives." The camera feed cut from the correspondent to two embassy representatives: a professionally dressed woman and a handsome middle-aged man in a suit. The two embassy representatives stepped out onto a patio area behind a collection of microphones.

Masha saw the two and remarked, "Oh, my god it's Pavel, I mean Mr. Baranov!"

The woman began, "I am Galina Sokolova. I am the Arts Attaché. Throughout Russian history, Russia has been a vigorous supporter of the arts and, most especially, the dancing arts. Last evening, the British Embassy hosted their Spring Ball here in the District of Columbia. During the Ball, I witnessed two guests that were very talented dancers. During the last set of the evening, the couple performed a tango. Their execution of the tango was incredible, with an unbelievably original approach and a passion that truly captured the essence of a tango."

"British Embassy security personnel detained the two dancers at the end of the dance number because some members of the audience judged the performance lewd and indecent."

"The news media and the public at large should clearly understand that this was an adult event, and the dance took place during the last number of the evening. I was there and witnessed this amazing dance performance. Today the media has been unjustly slanting and sensationally reporting this performance of a tango. We here at the Russian Embassy strongly object to the persecution of these two dancers, Mr. Javier Perez a noted professional hair stylist in the District of Columbia and Professor Mashenka Petrova, a Theater Arts Professor at Cornell University. Here with me is our acting Air Attaché Boris Baranov, who wishes to say a few words about Professor Petrova."

Baranov stepped up to the microphone.

Baranov considerately spoke, "In 1986 during the Chernobyl disaster there was a small team of American Nuclear experts who were on the ground near the disaster consulting with the Soviet Scientists of the time. I know because I was there as a junior officer of the Soviet Emergency Bureau. Junior Professor Mashenka Petrova was one of two American academics who acted as expert translators between the American scientific advisor team and those Soviet era scientists. Those two-women translators bravely took incredible risks during their duties. Professor Petrova is a levelheaded and professional woman and the grateful Soviet people decorated her for her service. Recently, the St. Petersburg State Theatre Arts Academy invited Dr. Petrova to be a guest professor for this upcoming academic school year. Today I have spoken with the St. Petersburg State Theatre Arts Academy, Dean. Both her and her school's academics are excited and looking forward to Dr. Petrova joining their faculty for this school year. In my humble opinion, she and her dinner-dance guest deserve a sincere apology from the British Diplomatic Service and equally an apology by the news services that have been attempting to tarnish the reputation of these two splendid artists." Baranov stepped back from the microphone.

Galina Sokolova, returned to the microphone, "As the Embassy Arts Attaché, and on behalf of our Ambassador and staff of our Embassy. I am pleased to invite Dr. Mashenka Petrova, and Mr. Javier Perez as Honored Guests, to the Russian Embassy Spring Ball next month. Thank You."

The press pool began shouting questions. Both Sokolova and Baranov left the patio without further comment. (The CNN feed cut back to the studio; the anchor remarked) "We'll be back after these messages."

Mrs. Campbell, still on the phone with Masha, said in an excited voice, "You two did it! Well Done!"

Masha saw Luis walk into her suite and stood looking at her. Masha remarked to Campbell, "Olivia, hold on a minute, please." She held the phone receiver to her chest.

Speaking to Luis, "Are you in or out, Mr. Perez?"

He just stared at her with a stunned expression. He stood, considering the ceiling for several moments. "Sure I'm in! Let's go Charm the Pants off those Russians!"

Masha excitedly put the phone receiver to her ear, "Olivia, Luis and I wouldn't miss this gig for all the vodka in Russia! We'll see you in the morning at the warehouse!" Masha hung up.

"Luis, what made you change your mind?" She asked. Luis pulled out the room's desk chair and sat down. "All my friends and clients would think me an idiot for not accepting an honored guest invitation to a major world powers embassy. Add to that, they would think me a cad for the rest of my days if I left you on the dance floor without a suitable dance partner."

Masha looked touched and remarked, (Speaking Spanish) "Mr. Javier Perez, you are a very honorable man!"

9:00 am May 24-The News Crew

Javier Perez drove into the parking lot of his hair salon. Milling around were several men and women with cameras with big lenses. As Perez got out of his car, a network television news crew approached. A young TV news woman came over to him. "A couple of quick questions, please?" She asked.

He gave her a charming professional smile and simply said, "Keep it all respectful and to the facts and I'll do my best to answer your questions."

The young reporter lit up with a bright smile.

"Ok, respectfully!" Then she asked, "What are your thoughts about the British Embassy banning you for life globally?"

They just smiled. "They did what they thought they needed to do. It is what it is. Perhaps the Queen will grant us clemency."

The reporter continued, "What did you think when the Russians announced they were inviting you and Professor Petrova as honored guests to their Spring Embassy Ball?"

He was silent for a moment, seemingly thoughtful. Then Perez perked up, "Hey I'm just some guy from Albuquerque, New Mexico and I run a beauty salon in the District cutting ladies' hair. The Russian Embassy's gracious invitation shocked and overwhelmed me. And I might add, I'm looking forward to it!"

Then she asked, "How do you know Professor Petrova?"

He gave her an aw shucks look and a shoulder shrug. "They hired me to style Ms. Petrova's hair for the British Ball. Apparently, her dinner dance partner had to drop out at the last minute. She asked me if I'd like to attend the Brit event as her plus one. As they say, the rest is history."

The reporter gave him an odd look. "Where did you two learn to dance like you both did?"

He smiled and rolled his eyes. "I learned in college. I wasn't exactly the baseball or football type, so I danced as my athletic credit."

The reporter added, "And Dr. Petrova?"

He had a momentary vacant look on his face, "Well, she's a college theater professor some place. I suppose she learned all of that song and dance stuff, training to do what she does professionally."

Several photographers quietly snapped photos of the TV reporter's interview with Perez. The news woman, politely asked, "Are you and Petrova romantically involved?"

Perez broke out laughing briefly. Then he composed himself, smiled at the reporter and commented, "Professor Petrova and I are from vastly different worlds. I can honestly say. We certainly don't run in the same circles. Besides, professionally, I have a policy to not become romantically involved with my clients!"

The reporter then asked, "What do you think about Professor Petrova's teaching for a year in Russia?"

Perez took a deep breath and presented a thoughtful look. "Professor Petrova is a smart and talented woman. It surprised me as much as anyone to hear that embassy official say that she is a heroine of some sort in his homeland. That revelation just shook me. I believe anyone who knows her as a friend, colleague, or even a humble hair salon client would feel honored." He paused. "Last question, please."

The field journalist acknowledged with a nod. "Do you think the two of you will dance a tango at the Russian Ball?"

Again, he looked thoughtful for a moment, then broke into a broad smile. "I dare say if the orchestra plays a tango, Mashenka and I will dance a tango that they will never forget!" After a moment, he simply said, "I must go attend to my beauty business."

The reporter tagged along with him but without the camera crew. "We went to her apartment. It was empty. Do you know how we can contact Professor Petrova?" She asked.

Perez stopped and thought for a moment. "Well, I suspect her apartment is empty because she's going to Russia for a year, in the next month. I'd guess her household effects were probably all in storage. Give me your business card and I'll ask her to call you. Likewise, I'll tell her you were polite. Perhaps she'll give you an interview. But please know that she is a very shy and private person. I recommend you tread carefully with your questions!"

She gave him a curious look. "Does she get hostile?"

Perez shook his head in the negative gently. "No, nothing of that sort. She's a polite lady in every sense. But that said. Be aware that she certainly doesn't tolerate fools. If you interview her like you did me, with respectful questions. I suspect she will be forthcoming and answer you honestly. Try to intrude on her privacy, she'll shut down the interview," he advised her.

The reporter nodded. She understood.

10:10 am May 23- Telephone Tea with Mrs. Campbell

"Masha, your agency answering service for your Petrova phone number took a message," Mrs. Campbell remarked. Then added, "The Russian Embassy is trying to contact you and formally deliver your invitations for the Russian Spring Ball. The service told them you were planning to have lunch at the American Café around noon. You need to go up to Ms. Hamilton's shop, dress casual and presentable and be there a bit before noon. I'll have people there to watch your back!"

"Good grief Olivia, do you expect the FSB to put a sack over my head and kidnap me?" Masha asked. Campbell spoke calmly. "No, I'm not worried about the FSB. I'm concerned about your public notoriety. After all, your public notoriety has been spreading all over local and network news for two days. I'm being cautious. Some fan or some crackpot might take a swing at you. There are plenty of nuts in this town, as you know. Besides, I know you can handle yourself, but in a public bistro, if you have to go into a defensive posture, you might use skills the good professor would have a hard time explaining."

"Okay, I get it! Thank you for the guardian angels. When are they sending a courier?" Masha asked. Campbell casually remarked, "The answering service told the Embassy that you would be there between noon and 1pm. It will either be a diplomatic courier, some local commercial delivery service or possibly someone from the Embassy. Which I doubt, embassy people have better things to do than deliver invitations. Have the town car take you over to the bistro and be punctual."

After the phone call, Masha went to the eighth floor and asked for an outfit that was a bit more business wear. After she changed clothes, she called the black car that was at her disposal.

11:55 May 23-Capitol Hill at the American Café

The black town car delivered Masha to the very chic restaurant. There was a small lunch time waiting line outside the main entrance. She knew that a reservation had been made. As she entered the eatery, the daytime headwaiter immediately recognized her from television news and led her over to a table for two next to a window.

Another server brought a glass of ice water and a menu to her. Masha didn't look at the menu and simply told the server, "I'd like some unsweetened iced tea and a Cobb Salad." Then she added, "I'm expecting someone from the Russian Embassy asking for Mashenka Petrova." The server acknowledged, "I know, I saw you on the news! I will bring whomever to you." The server left and Masha reached in her purse and withdrew her phone and made sure it was on in case she needed to take a call.

A few minutes later, she heard a man's gravelly voice (Speaking Russian). "You are always working, aren't you Masha?" Startled, she looked up, and there was Boris Pavel Baranov. He smiled at her. She immediately stood and gave him an endearing hug and turned her right cheek to him, and Baranov gave her a kiss.

Masha asked excitedly, "Can you join me for lunch?" He nodded, "Most certainly. It would be my pleasure." He pulled out the other chair and took a seat. Masha gestured to her server, who returned with a menu for Baranov. "So, what is good here in the American Café?" Baranov queried.

Masha smiled. "I've only eaten here once, but I'm told everything is wonderful. But I'm simply having a Cobb salad." Baranov raised an eyebrow. "My doctor says I should eat more salads." The server returned to the table to take his order. "Are you ready to order?" Baranov smiled at the server, "I'm going to have a Cobb salad." The server asked, "Your beverage, sir." He looked at Masha with a queried look. She spoke up, "He'll have an unsweetened iced tea." The server nodded, picked up the menu, and left them.

Masha folded her arms and leaned on the table. "So, Pavel, to what do I owe this delightful visit?" He reached into his suit jacket and withdrew an envelope. "I am officially delivering your invitation to the Spring Ball of the Embassy of the Russian Federation. It is for you and Mr. Perez. You both are to be our honored guests." Masha gave him a curious look as he handed her the invitation. She quietly stared at the envelope for a moment and asked, "Pavel, you are the acting Air Attaché at the Embassy. Why are you delivering an invitation?"

He took on a stuffy expression. "As an honored guest, it's a customary protocol for an official to deliver it personally. After all, we announced we were inviting you to the Ball during a global television news conference. We could do no less." He relaxed his stuffy posture and grinned, "In the words of the Moscow Municipal Militsiya, consider yourself served!" She grinned at him. "On behalf of both Mr. Perez and me, we are deeply honored to accept this invitation."

A server interrupted the tender moment by delivering two Cobb salads and two large glasses of unsweetened iced tea. After the server left, he remarked, "I saw a brief interview with Mr. Perez on this morning's television." Masha, who was taking a mouthful of her salad, stopped with a fork in her mouth. She chewed for a few moments, staring at her old friend, and swallowed. "What exactly did he say?"

Pavel grinned, "They asked him, if the orchestra played a tango, whether you both would dance the tango." Masha rolled her eyes. "What was his reply?" Pavel gave her a nonchalant look. Perez said, "Mashenka and I will dance a tango. They will never forget!" She stared at her old friend with a vacant look. "I must be frank. I don't wish to embarrass your embassy like we did the British." "Nyet," he remarked. "Masha, you and Mr. Perez dance your tango every bit as good or better than you did at the British Embassy. We Russians love a nice passionate tango. You'll have no complaints from us!"

Mashenka and Pavel Baranov continued to exchange small talk as they finished their lunches. The server approached them and asked if she could remove their salad plate. They both replied that they were done, and then Pavel stated, "This has been a delightful lunch. I would like to have a dessert." The server smiled. "I'll get you a dessert menu."

Masha gave him a troubled look. "Pavel, I want to get into my dress for that Tango, you want me and Luis to dance for the Embassy guests." He smirked, "Anything you say, Masha." When the dessert menu came, they both studied it carefully. Pavel moaned, "My doctor says no more Black Forrest cake and no ice cream." She gave him a saddened look. "Me too." After a few more moments browsing the dessert menu. Masha proposed, "What would you say to custard or a cheesecake?" Pavel reached into the inside of the besom pocket of his suit jacket and withdrew a small pocket notebook. He peeked at a particular page and winced. "Perhaps we could split a cheesecake," Pavel remarked.

Mashenka soberly asked, "Diabetes?" He quickly slipped the little booklet back into his suit pocket, softly answering, "Yes." Masha nodded, "Me too."

The server returned to get the dessert order. Pavel smiled at her. "We'd like to split a cheesecake, please."

The server smiled and left the two of them. He gave Masha a thoughtful look, "Perhaps we both spent too much time at Chernobyl and took too many atomic rays." Masha somberly nodded. "I think we both did. I think some people we were with have passed away."

"Too many," Pavel remarked softly. Then he asked, "How do you manage the diabetes?" Masha frowned. "Pills and diet."

He nodded. "The same for me. My doctor wants me to lose more weight. The way he talks, I think he wants me to look like some damned Olympic runner or something." The two of them chuckled as the server brought their piece of cheesecake on a single plate and set it down between them and gave them each a fresh fork. She smiled and said, "Enjoy."

After each of them had had their first morsel, Pavel asked. "How did you come to get invited to St. Petersburg State Theatre Arts Academy? Did you request it?"

She shook her head in the negative. "No, the invitation came unexpectedly. As I understand it, the chair of the performing arts department read about me in the Russian press back during Chernobyl. He told the Dean of the college he always wanted to work with me."

Pavel gave her a very serious look, "Please assure me you are just going to be a flashy and colorful university performing arts professor and nothing more."

She knew what he was hinting at. She gave him an earnest look. "Old friend, I am planning to teach my students to the best of my ability, produce memorable stage shows, regularly visit you and Natalya and enjoy the rich St. Petersburg symphony and performing arts scene, nothing more. And I assure you no shutki! (hijinks)"

The two looked down at the last morsel of the cheesecake. Masha reached over with her fork and cut the piece in two and remarked, (Speaking Russian) "I promise to you, my friend, one diabetic to another. No hijinks! Let us toast that promise and share this last poisonous piece of cheesecake together." Pavel smiled, "Da, a toast of poison."

1 pm May 23-Masha's Network News Interview

Mashenka entered the lobby of the global news network whose reporter had interviewed Javier Perez. A uniformed guard was sitting behind the reception counter.

"How may I help you, miss?" The Guard asked. She handed the business card of the field reporter to the guard.

"Ms. Blake has requested an interview with me." The guard looked at the card. "Whom shall I say is calling for her?" He asked. Masha simply said, "Professor Petrova."

The guard paused for a moment. "Aren't you that dancer that upset the British embassy?"

Masha smirked. "Guilty as charged!" The guard stood up and extended a handshake. "Ma'am, it's a pleasure to meet you. They say the Russians want you at their ball event." She took on a reserved expression.

"Yes, they do." The guard reached down and picked up a telephone receiver, then paused.

"Ma'am, good for you. You go over and show them Russkies how Americans dance. Please have a seat. I'll call the assignment desk and arrange for Ms. Blake."

Masha walked over to a couch in the lobby area and took a seat. After a few minutes, a woman entered the lobby. The guard gestured toward Petrova. Dressed in slacks and a golf shirt with the television network's logo emblazoned on it, she walked over to Masha.

"Professor Petrova, I'm Mary Allen, the assignment desk supervisor. Ms. Blake has just finished a remote news story. We expect her back here in perhaps fifteen or twenty minutes. Is a brief wait acceptable to you?"

Masha simply nodded. "That's fine. My calendar is clear for the rest of the day."

Then Ms. Mary Allen offered, "Can I get you some coffee, or perhaps a bottle of water?"

Masha politely smiled. "A bottle of water would be nice, thank you."

Ms. Allen left the lobby for a few minutes.

When she returned, she was carrying two water bottles. Behind her, two young camera operators were carrying field news cameras. Each of the two young women clipped a microphone onto Masha's jacket. Then each of them clipped a microphone on Ms. Allen's shirt and sat down on the lobby carpet and prepared to video record her from two angles. Then Ms. Allen remarked, "Since I'm the boss. I have decided to do this interview myself."

Allen handed a water bottle to Masha. Then she took a seat in a lobby chair. "Roll the cameras, ladies! After counting out loud one, two, three, she paused and addressed Professor Petrova..." Masha interjected, "Masha Please." Allen started again, "Masha, we understand you are going to be teaching abroad in Russia. Would you be willing to talk more about that, versus all that nonsense at the British embassy?"

Masha smiled, "Yes, please. I would appreciate a little less sensation and a bit more dignified content." Ms. Allen nodded, "Wonderful! Various callers to our response phone line have suggested that you should be ashamed of yourself for dancing that lewd dance. Your thoughts?"

"As a performing arts professor, I'm in the proverbial song and dance business. A tango dance is classically supposed to be a passionate and suggestive dance, it's an expressive art form. Calling it lewd is simply someone's personal sense abilities." Masha added, "When I was in grade school, I can remember when Elvis Presley first appeared on Ed Sullivan. My mom pointed out that the camera shots were avoiding showing him swaying his hips. Critical people thought Presley's dancing was being lewd."

Allen added. "Since I've been a news producer, I've seen and heard no end to the things our viewers get annoyed about."

Then she asked, "I don't think I've ever heard of American professors going to Russia to teach. How did that come about?"

Masha took a sip of water from the water bottle and then began. "First off, the communist party had led Russia for over seventy years. Add to that Russia has only been the Russian Federation for the past few years. I think they are still finding their way in terms of things like student and teacher exchange programs."

"How did this all come about for you, Masha?" Allen asked. Masha sat seemingly distant for a few moments. "I was a junior member of the Cornell University's Performing arts department. The Chernobyl accident happened. There was an urgent call for some top American Nuclear physics people to travel over there quietly and consult. They needed a couple of translators for the team. I volunteered, as did another junior academic from another school. They cautioned the free world press to never mention that our team was there. The Soviet media of the era, however, wrote profiles about all the western consulting team members. A young professor at the St. Petersburg State Theatre Arts Academy read my profile. He remembered reading about me in the Soviet press of that time. As I understand it, he's now the Chair of one of the departments and invited me to teach there for a year or two."

Allen gave her a curious look. "So how did you come to be dancing at the British Embassy?" Masha gave the news producer a coy look. "The honest answer, my etiquette was lacking. Oh, it was passable by American standards. But my mentoring academic friends felt my understanding of customs and etiquette by European standards was seriously deficient! They hooked me up with a British Lady who specializes in teaching old school etiquette to corporate executives and people joining the Diplomatic service. So I spent a couple of months with her and she was my proverbial Professor Higgins. The dance at the British Embassy was effectively my International Society Debut."

Ms. Allen grinned. "So the Brit ball was your 'I could have danced all night moment'?" Masha sheepishly nodded.

"Can you tell me your Charm School tutor's name? I'd love to interview her." Allen asked with excitement. Masha frowned. "I am afraid I can't disclose that. Her charm school consulting and tutoring is exceedingly private, and by referral only. I had to sign a non-disclosure agreement in order for her to tutor me." Masha explained.

"How does the Russian Embassy fit into this?" Allen asked. Masha rolled her eyes. "It's as much a surprise to me as it was for everyone else. My visa is being processed there apparently, and with all the high visibility media coverage of the British ball nonsense. It drew attention and apparently a few old timers in the diplomatic staff remember me. There it is."

Ms. Allen seemed to study Masha for a few moments. "I'm going to just focus on the American Professor in St. Petersburg angle."

Masha replied simply, "I see my exchange teaching year or perhaps years as a sort of hands-across-the-water good will effort. With global terrorism growing around the world. I think we could use all the international friends we can get. It's my hope that Russia will be one of those friends."

"Professor Petrova, it is indeed an honor to meet someone like you. I'm going to make this news piece charming and friendly." Ms. Allen said with enthusiasm.

Ten minutes later, Masha got into a cab that the reception guard had called for her. She asked the cab to drop her off at Metro Center. As she relaxed in the back of the taxi, she thought to herself. *There we have it. Good spy craft, a great cover story planted and part of the global news record. I hope this teaching gig in St. Petersburg works out. I'd really like to stay there for a couple of years and have people here forget my face.*

6:30pm June 14   The Basketball Warehouse

Luis Perez exited the elevator on the sixth floor of the warehouse building. Mashenka was sitting on the floor of the Basketball court reading the cover of a CD case and sitting next to a new boom box. "Hello Mashenka, how have you been, sweetie?" She turned and looked back at him. "I'm delighted to see you, Luis.

Are you pumped to do the Russian embassy ball?" He seemed to put a swagger in his step as he walked toward her. "Who wouldn't be? This is going to be exciting!" As he got closer to her. "Hey, I saw that interview you did with the news network. Holy heck, that whole an American in St. Petersburg slant was terrific. I was stunned to see that uncensored video of us doing that last tango! I wonder how they got that footage?" Masha giggled. "Don't ask!"

He stopped walking. "You'd probably have to kill me, right?" She smirked and nodded.

"I don't want to know," He jokingly remarked. Masha got off the floor and gave him a friendly hug. "I've got a surprise for you."

Perez raised an eyebrow, remarking, "What the Martians have landed and they want us to dance at their ball too?"

"No, silly! Management has flown in my dance instructor from Miami, and he's going to whip us into shape for the Russian gig." She explained.

Perez gave her a puzzled look. "I thought we'd do like we did with the Brits. Take it easy for the earlier set and save the hot stuff for the later set."

"Management wants us to explore doing the hot stuff we already did in the second set and do something boiling for the final set and really blow the doors off the place!" Masha explained.

He gave her a troubled look. "Hey, I don't want to spoil your chances of going to Russia and the teaching gig!"

She waved a dismissive hand. "Do not sweat the Russians. I have it on expert authority that they love a hot, passionate tango. Besides, figure it this way. From the Russian political view, it will embarrass the British and shame them into lifting the ban on us."

"But we only have a few days." Perez said in a concerned tone.

Suddenly, another man's voice echoed into the court area, (Speaking Spanish) "That's my job, senor Perez." Luis turned and saw a muscular, clean-cut Latin man who had exited from the stairwell and was walking toward the center of the court. As the man reached Perez, he extended a firm handshake. (Speaking Spanish) "Ernesto Torres, at your service."

Torres turned to Masha, who ran over and jumped into his arms. (Speaking Spanish) Torres remarked, "How are you, my little media star?"

Luis Perez gave Masha and Ernesto Torres a curious look. "With respect, Mr. Torres, are you Mashenka's boyfriend, fiancé, or perhaps husband?" Torres grinned, looking down into Masha's face and her bright smile.

"No Sir, I am her dance instructor. Hired by Mrs. Campbell." Torres gently lowered Masha to the floor. Again Perez queried. "So are you the dancer who walked out on her the day before the British Embassy Ball?"

Torres responded, "I did not walk out on Masha. I had a contractual problem that doesn't permit me to dance at either of these events. Nothing more."

"Ernesto," Masha commented, "He knows this is a mission! He knows what I am, but only knows me as Masha! He also knows the intent of the mission, but none of the private details." Torres first looked at Masha with a smile and then a polite nod to Perez, "Ah, my respects honored partisan."

Torres gave them both an amused look. "The Miami newspaper said the two of you tore up the floor! The conservative news network had traditionalist ministers from coast to coast calling you both lewd and indecent. One thumper called in and referred to you, Mr. Perez, as a tempting minion of Satan and you, Ms. Masha the Harlot predicted in the scriptures."

He walked over to a plastic tub with iced bottles of water and took one. As he walked back to them, he remarked.

"The staff at my dancing school watched the video of your late-night dance several dozen times and they made a small list of moves we can add to take your next late-night dance up a few notches."

"What if we're content with our dance as it is now?" Perez commented. Torres took a small swig of water. "That hot late night dance act is yesterday's news! If you are both happy with it and simply want to dance to the goal posts, that's fine by me. But if you want to kick it out into the stands. I've got a few moves that can make it that much hotter!" Torres comments.

Perez gave Torres an amused look. "Do you really think it will make that much difference?" Torres shrugged his shoulders. "Hey, if you do what you did at the British Ball, Masha will be in the St. Petersburg newspaper the day she arrives." Torres remarked. Then he stated, "But if you two do as I suggest, you both will cause the conservative network fans to scream for your skins and Ms. Masha will arrive at Pulkovo International Airport and get a popular reception in St. Petersburg akin to the Beatles arriving in New York in 1964." Torres said as he folded his arms and smirked.

Masha sat down on the floor and covered her blush with her hand. Torres looked down at her. "Mashenka, doesn't every girl dream of such a thing, eventually?" She had both hands over her face at this point.

Perez gave Torres a questioning look. "Good sir, is this for her ego or for the mission?" Torres immediately remarked. "Both!" Then he added, "Sometimes inserting an operative into a mission needs to have some pomp. It serves the purpose of impressing the natives and reinforcing the persona of the operative."

Perez asked, "Is it really that important? He winced. I mean, she's a glorified actress for all intents!" Torres walked over to Perez and stated softly, "My friend, she's so deep into her field identity, she barely remembers who she really is and anything we can do to reinforce that identity is icing on the cake!"

Perez seemed considerate for a few moments. "Ok, what do you want us to do?"

Torres smiled, "Just work your asses off over the weekend so you are both sharp as a tack for the Russian Ball on the 19th. That's all! I want you both ready to rock that embassy so they feel it in St. Petersburg!"

8:47am June 19-Hope for the best. Expect the Worst.

Mashenka was making a pot of coffee in her pre-mission seclusion quarters on Capitol Hill. It had been an exhausting weekend of taking instruction from Ernesto Torres and rehearsing with her dance partner, Luis Perez. She had just poured her first cup of coffee and was ceremoniously sniffing the aroma of her morning, Joe. Her seclusion quarters house phone rang. She rolled her eyes, wondering who the hell was bothering her before noon when her duty day was supposed to begin. She picked up the telephone receiver. "Petrova here! This better be important!"

The voice at the other end of the phone sounded strained. "Masha it's Barbara Hamilton."

Masha remarked. "Geez Barb, that's sounds like a hell of a cold." Barbara said nothing. Masha could hear her blowing her nose. "Hey, Barb, you sound like you need to stay home today."

"Masha, it's Luis Perez. He was in an accident last night." Masha heard Barbara coughing.

"What hospital is he at?" Masha asked urgently.

Barbara continued explaining. "Masha, a drunk driver, ran a red light and broadsided Luis's taxi last evening on K Street and Eleventh Street. The crash killed Luis and his cab driver."

Mashenka stood silently for a few moments, trying to process what had just been said to her. After a few moments, reality sunk in. As the shock overtook her. The fingers on the hand holding the phone spontaneously relaxed, and the phone receiver fell to the floor. She stomped her feet several times on the vinyl tiles while cursing in Russian, louder and louder. After a brief episode of cussing, her deep training took over. Masha picked up the phone and simply said to Barbara Hamilton.

"Ok, the mission model has changed. We must adapt. When can I come in and meet with Mrs. Campbell?" Barbara answered back, "Masha, she's flying to San Francisco with Mr. Torres. She's in the air and we can't reach her until she's on the ground many hours from now."

Masha griped, remarking. "Der'mo," (shit). Then she directed, "Barbara, please contact my handler Laura Boyce and get her to meet me at the warehouse around noon. Make sure she knows it's seriously important. I'll call for the black car within the hour. Barbara, I will manage this!"

10:15 am Eighth floor at the warehouse building. Mashenka walked out of the elevator and approached Barbara Hamilton. Barbara's eyes were all puffy from crying. In a business manner, Masha asked. "What's the situation with my handler, Laura Boyce?"

Barbara blew her nose on a tissue. Then answered. "They told me she's in London on business related to your mission."

Mashenka muttered, "The squads wiped out. No one can find any living officers or contact them. Adapt and adapt some more and take command!"

She looked at Barbara. "I need an untraceable cell phone as soon as possible." Masha requested.

Barbara nodded. "I'll have one activated in about ten minutes. Don't you need to chill?"

Masha gave her a harsh expression. "I'll chill and probably cry a little with you, but I must manage the mission needs first! I need that phone asap."

While Barbara was activating a burner phone, Masha was on Barbara's laptop, looking up a phone number.

When the phone was active, Mashenka walked over to a wing-back chair, sat down, and dialed the phone number. She heard the phone ring three times at the other end before someone answered it. A woman's voice announced, "Good morning. You have reached the Russian Federation Embassy in Washington, DC, USA. How can I help you?" Masha (Speaking Russian) "I'm Professor Mashenka Petrova and I'm scheduled to be an honored guest at your Embassy Spring Ball this evening. I have a pressing matter that needs immediate attention. I need to speak to Boris Baranov, your Air Attaché, immediately."

There was a pause. "I'll see if he's available. Please hold." Masha heard a selection from Tchaikovsky's Serenade for Strings. After a few moments, Masha heard a connection sound being made. "Boris Baranov, acting Air Attaché speaking, how may I help you?"

Masha found it amusing that the switchboard didn't tell him who was calling. "Pavel, my old friend, this is Mashenka. I have a serious problem. I need your help." There was a pause, then he spoke up, "Mashenka, what is your problem?"

"I do not have a dinner date and dance partner for the Ball tonight." Baranov groaned, "What did this Mr. Perez do? Get the cold feet?" Masha waited a few moments, doing her best to hold back tears and a crying and choking voice. "Pavel, a drunk driver ran a traffic signal light and killed both Perez and his taxi driver in an auto accident last evening."

"Mashenka, I am so sorry to hear this. What do you need from me?" Baranov compassionately replied. Masha explained her need. "Pavel, I'm an honored guest and I need a dinner date who's a superb dancer, who perhaps knows how to tango!"

Baranov laughed. "Masha, my dear, it just so happens you are in luck. A member of our Arts Attaché staff is a former performer from the Bolshoi Ballet. His name is Nikolai Antonov, and madame, he certainly knows how to tango! But I warn you, he speaks absolutely no English." Masha giggled, "No worries, I'll manage." Then she completed her conversation. "Pavel, I am in your debt. I look forward to seeing both you and Natalya this evening. Bye for now! Mr. Baranov."

Masha turned off the cellular phone. She left the device on the corner of Barbara's desk. Looking at Barbara, "I've managed the problem. I have a talented dancer for a dinner date for this evening's ball. The mission will go forward using a former dancer from the Bolshoi."

Barbara's eyes got wide. "The Bolshoi Ballet!"

Masha looked at Barbara. "Please arrange a hair stylist for this evening and someone to do my makeup."

She paused. "I think I need a cold bottle of water and a fresh box of tissues and a quiet place to go have a cry!"

Barbara grabbed an unopened box and pointed at the cooler and remarked, "Fourth floor warehouse space, nobody will disturb you there...Go get it out of your system, sister."

Ten minutes later, Masha walked down the rows of the fourth-floor fabric warehouse shelves. She sat down on the floor and leaned up against a big-roll of tweed. After a few minutes, only the mice could hear the wailing sounds of a human being in intense pain and sorrow.

7:47pm June 19-The Russian Embassy Spring Ball
(All Conversation is in Russian)

Mashenka, dressed in a red, long-sleeved silk ball gown, had just passed through a security checkpoint. A woman usher asked for Mashenka's invitation. Upon reading it, the woman asked, "Madame, do you have a guest with you?"

Masha simply answered, Mr. Nikolai Antonov from the Arts Attaché staff is going to be my dinner guest and my dancing partner. The usher gave Masha a surprised look. "Mr. Antonov is waiting for you at the Honored guest's table." The woman gestured to a young male usher. "Please take Dr. Petrova to the Honored guest's table."

The young usher offered his right arm to escort her to the awaiting table. Masha placed her hand on the usher's arm. The two walked toward a special group of tables in the ballroom's heart. As they approached one particular table with a single handsome man attired in a white tie dress suit.

The usher addressed the gentleman. "May I present a guest of honor, Dr. Mashenka Petrova." Masha extended her right hand and Antonov accepted it and kissed it.

"Nikolai Antonov at your service, madame. I hold the

position of 1st Assistant Arts attaché here at the embassy. It is indeed a delight to meet you. Acting Air Attaché Boris Baranov has told me a great deal about you."

He took a step towards her. Masha turned her right cheek toward him. He kissed it gently before returning to an attentive posture. Masha gave him a pleasant smile. "Were you informed that we are to be dance partners this evening?"

He smiled and nodded. "Yes, madame. Mr. Baranov told me we are free to dance a provocative tango."

"Mr. Antonov. Did he use those exact words?" Masha asked.

He seemed to relax and let down his rigid posture. "Professor Petrova, this is a formal occasion. I didn't want to use his exact words in front of a lady."

She smirked slightly. "Nikolai, tell me exactly what he told you." The gentleman stepped closer to her and whispered. "He said we are free to dance a provocative tango during the second set and to dance *a* highly libidinous tango in the final set of the evening."

Masha got wide eyed for a few moments. "He said that truly?"

Then Nikolai added. "Yes. He told me he wanted to see a dance they'll hear about in Siberia and will be talking about in St. Petersburg and Moscow for years."

Masha giggled. "Now that sounds like Pavel, I mean Boris." He gave her a curious look. "You know Mr. Baranov well enough to call him by his middle name?"

Masha simply commented, "We are old friends. Let's not speak of it further. Can we sit down and discuss our two very different tangos since we've never danced together?"

Mr. Antonov pulled out Mashenka's chair and assisted her with it. Then he gestured to a server to approach them.

"Madame, would you like a drink?" Nikolai asked. She looked at the server and said, "I would like ice water with lemon or lime throughout the evening. But please bring us two glasses of champagne now." The server nodded and left. "Two glasses of champagne on an empty stomach?" Nikolai queried.

Masha looked at him. "I was hoping you would join me in a toast to our performing partnership tonight." He looked at her with an apologetic expression.

"Madame, my apologies. I assumed you were going to start the night off drunk."

She looked at him, amused. "I never drink when I'm performing." She paused, then added. "And tonight, my friend, we are giving a grand performance and I'm deeply honored to be dancing with a former member of the esteemed Bolshoi Ballet."

He cast his gaze downwards, almost giving off an embarrassed impression. Masha gave him a concerned look. "Nikolai, did I say something wrong?"

"Mashenka, you make being a member of the Bolshoi Ballet seem like it's this profound, lifelong career." He paused and considered his comment. She whispered to him, "Please continue, please share your heart."

"Mr. Baranov told me you are a performing arts professor and that you are going to be a guest professor at St. Petersburg State Theatre Arts Academy. You'll be teaching someplace until you choose to retire at a ripe age."

He paused and took a sip of water. "I started training with the Ballet when I was six years old. I spent thirty years with them, then they retired me. Thirty-Six is pretty old for a professional dancer, as you probably know. They retired me out of the Ballet a few years ago. They gave me this position because my former profession and Bolshoi Ballet heritage still carry some prestige. I worry that eventually that will be irrelevant."

Masha gave him a smile, "Nikolai, if we rock this place tonight, so that they're talking about us in Siberia. Honey, you'll be back in the game. I believe opportunity will come knocking at your door! Do not consider this dancing tonight as a favor to me and Baranov. Try to view it as a bigger world audition."

Antonov gave her an intriguing look, "Ok Professor Petrova, as Americans sometimes say, let us both go for broke tonight!"

9pm June 19-Planning a tango on the Fly!
(All Conversation is in Russian)

At the Honored guest's table, Nikolai and Mashenka decided on a private dinner in order to discuss tango.

Nikolai remarked, "I'm told that at the British Embassy that you and your previous dance partner danced the tango relatively tamely."

Masha swallowed a bite of her dessert. "We both presented ourselves in a sort of pantomime manner. Luis took his cat-like steps with a bravado that made it easy to follow him. With each step that he made; he displayed very punctuated contra-shoulder movements. Yet, through all of it, he beautifully improvised but was still playful at the same time. I simply followed his lead and interspersed my own lustful teases and shameless struts."

Nikolai took a sip of water. "That sounds straightforward enough. You sound like a good follower. Tell me about that late night last set dance." He gave her a probing look. "What style?"

"Nuevo style!" She remarked. "Upon the first opening of the musical movements. I made aggressive, almost threatening motions. Finally, I grabbed him like a cat snagging a mouse! He followed me, almost fighting me off with his moves and gestures. With each of his efforts to escape me, I would drag him back. Like I said, in a cat playing with a mouse manner, finally I executed a molinete, as a coiled spin with him. After his sharp turn, we traded roles, at which point, he aggressively took the lead."

She paused for a sip of water. "From that point, with him leading and me following, I took on a passionate and lustful manner and flaunted my ravenous desire for him. As the music was hitting its ending climax, I finally fell dead into his arms and he dragged me off the dance floor as the music was ending as a conquest." She paused. "That's when the audience erupted in applause and a war of opinions."

The Bolshoi dancer assumed a devilish grin. "I love it." He seemed to think for a few more moments. Then Nikolai perked up and smiled at her. "Are you willing to be a bit more *showy* in your style as well? After all, we're not just ballroom dancers, we'll be performing! We might as well do a bit of **Fantasia style** and be over the top and flamboyant!" Masha gave him a troubled look. "Without practice or rehearsal?" He lifted his glass with the last of his champagne toward her.

"Mashenka, I will follow you as initially stated. After I become the lead, I want you to do everything I do, but I want you to do it bigger and grander!" He paused, looking deep into her eyes. "Are you game?"

Masha had a reserved look. "What if we fall on our asses?"

"So what, if we fall, Nikolai cracked! Be a clown about it and roll with it and make it look like part of the performance! They'll just think we're a little drunk. If we laugh at it, they will too!" In the back of Masha's mind, her inner dialog echoed, *adapt!*

"Yes, Nikolai, I am game for this. Let's have fun with this." They toasted the remains of their champagne. Then he commented, "The first set is ending. Let's find restrooms and ready ourselves for the second set."

Late Evening Wednesday June 19-Last Tango in DC!

It was the last dance number of the last musical set of the evening. This was the most highly anticipated dance of the ball. Everyone knew that the last number was going to be a tango. The buzz in the ballroom was that Professor Mashenka Petrova had made global news headlines by dancing an exotic and enticing tango with her dance partner at the British Embassy ball a month previous. It was an over-the-top performance that captured the news cycle for three days.

The peculiar twitter in the Russian Embassy ballroom was that renown Bolshoi Ballet dancer Nikolai Antonov was Petrova's dinner guest and her dance partner. They danced waltzes with admirable grace and style earlier in the evening. Likewise, some believed that the second set, tango, surpassed even seasoned

Argentine dancers in its execution with animated and punctuated style. The Argentine Ambassadorial party visited Antonov and Petrova graciously, offered their warmest of compliments upon the two dancers. As well as offering invitations for them to both visit Argentina in the future.

But among the larger guest attendance, the conundrum on most everyone's minds was how Antonov and Petrova might take their tango performance above and beyond. In the last musical piece in the last set. In odd anticipation, only Antonov and Petrova walked onto the dance floor. No one else even hinted that they intended to share the floor with them. Alone on the dance floor, both Antonov and Petrova grinned at each other. Both of them quickly realized they were the center of attention.

When the music began, Petrova took the lead and started her rough, aggressive, almost attacking style. She was a cat that was clear to see with her cat-like steps. She had caught herself a mouse and was insistently teasing and playing with her prey. Petrova pantomimed a playful cat tail wagging as she repeatedly pounced on the mouse. Suddenly the cat and the mouse were mixing it up and after a spin, Antonov's mouse led and gave the cat a run for her money. What wasn't expected was Antonov unexpectedly giving his mouse a personality and making his moves with tango timing but incorporating classic ballet moves?

Petrova's cat, unaccustomed to this mouses moves, did her best to counter his actions with grand and exaggerated moves trying to mimic the mouse. She fell and rolled on the floor comically. The mouse, still in tango timing, but ballet style, pranced around his fallen predator. As the music was in its last measure, the mouse danced to the edge of the dance floor with tango timing, turned and gracefully bowed in ballet style and stuck his tongue out at the frustrated and defeated cat and pranced off the dance floor. People in the ballroom clapped and roared, as a few individuals shouted "Bravo!" and "Brava!" Several gentlemen stepped on the dance floor to help Petrova up, concerned that she had hurt herself. It became quickly apparent that her dance character fall was a calculated stage fall.

Within moments, the media that was attending the ball was on the dance floor, begging for interviews. With the Russian media, the two spoke in Russian.

With the English-speaking media, Petrova led the interview and translated for Antonov.

The two of them spoke French for the media feed in French-speaking countries.

Finally, a small Argentine news crew approach the two perspiration-soaked dancers. Antonov didn't speak Spanish. Again, Petrova graciously translated his remarks for the Argentine team.

As the news people dispersed, Pavel and Natalya Baranov came over and offered well wishes and introduced the two to the Russian ambassador Anatoly I. Antonov, who graciously told Petrova he was no relation to Nikolai.

Nikolai Antonov and Mashenka Petrova shared a last glass of champagne with Boris and Natalya Baranov. As Petrova waited for her town car, Nikolai told her how very much he enjoyed the challenge of doing what they had done with no rehearsal. She invited him to look her up at the Theatre Arts Academy in St. Petersburg. He told her he would welcome such a visit.

Petrova's Town car arrived. There were a few last minutes' hugs and goodbyes. As Pavel closed her door, she covered herself up with a comforter she had staged in the car before she left. She asked her driver to just drive around downtown DC so she could unwind from an intense evening. The driver asked her what kind of music she wanted. She remarked to him, "Put on Oldies 100."

The Town Car driver drove her around the well-lit monument region of downtown DC. For the better part of an hour until finally taking her to her pre-mission quarters on Capitol Hill. She thanked the driver for the meandering ride around downtown DC. After showering, she curled up in her bed and quietly whispered. "Mission accomplished."

Six weeks later!

July 8-Pulkovo International Airport, St. Petersburg, Russia
(All conversation is in Russian unless otherwise noted.)

Mashenka calmly and patiently watched the Russian countryside as her Rossiya Airlines flight descended toward a landing at Pulkovo International Airport. As the aircraft was making its final approach, she reached in her blazer pocket and withdrew a string of Buddhist mala beads and quietly repeated a mantra, as she had done for many years. Suddenly, she felt the familiar sinking feeling just a heartbeat before touching down. A moment later, the Rossiya Airlines aircraft touched down on runway 10L/28R at Pulkovo International Airport, St. Petersburg, Russia.

After a long, boring aircraft taxiing to the International terminal, processing through immigration passport and visa examination, baggage claim and finally customs, Masha walked into the main airport terminal arrival gate. She was overwhelmed to see a crowd of perhaps two hundred people that suddenly erupted in cheers. College aged people wearing St. Petersburg State Theatre Arts Academy tee shirts shouted "Masha! Masha!" Among the enormous crowd of well-wishers and greeters were television news camera teams.

Her first thought was *Torres was right!* In the front row was a man, perhaps in his fifties, in a suit holding a sign that simply read ПЕТРОВА- ТЕАТРАЛЬНАЯ АКАДЕМИЯ (PETROVA- THEATRE ACADEMY). Masha recognized him immediately. It was Dimitri Lebedev, her Department chairman whom she had been corresponding with for months since the first invitation letter.

As she approached Professor Dimitri Lebedev, two young men wearing St. Petersburg State Theatre Arts Academy tee shirts approached her beaming smiles. "We're Professor Lebedev's Assistants. Let us take your suitcases." Masha looked over at Dimitri before she let go of her suitcase tow straps. She gestured toward the two young men. Dimitri nodded his head. The young men dragged her bags over to near Dimitri. She held a finger up and pointed at the three news teams on the edge of the line. Dimitri gestured to her to speak to the media.

Masha spoke up loudly, "Who is Global Network?" A middle-aged man raised his hand and spoke up. "Me, I'm Igor Kozlov, I'm the CNN Russian correspondent!"

"Who works for the Russian network?" Masha said loudly. A woman in her twenties yells, "I'm Cristina Efremova with All-Russia State Television!"

"Who's local television?" The same woman shouts, "All-Russia State Television! We are national and local." Petrova nodded. "Ok I understand. Let me speak to CNN first!"

Petrova told them, "I want your business cards and you each get three questions now. I'll offer deeper interviews after I'm settled. Okay!" The news people shouted, "Yes!"

Global Network-Igor Kozlov, the CNN Russian correspondent.

1: "What do you think of this welcome St. Petersburg style?"

Masha answers, "I'm overwhelmed with the joy and well wishes."

2: "What will you be teaching at St. Petersburg State Theatre Arts Academy?"

Masha answers, "Theater Arts! And whatever the Dean wants me to teach."

3: "Where did you learn to speak Russian?"

Masha answers, "On my mother's knee! THANK YOU."

Russian Network-Cristina Efremova with All-Russia State Television!

1: "How do you feel about being alone here in St. Petersburg for a year?"

Masha answers, "I know the Russian people are warm and friendly. I expect to make many friends. Between all the wonderful academics and all the wonderful students!"

2: "Do you plan to do tango dancing here in St. Petersburg?"

Masha answers, "Perhaps. Given the right venue and the right dance partner, perhaps!"

3: "What are you most looking forward to during this academic year?"

Masha answers, "I am not married and therefore I have no children that a marriage would have brought. But I've been teaching for a long time and I consider every one of my students over the years as my beloved children! THANK YOU."

Masha gave Dimitri Lebedev a thumbs up. He walked over to her. They shook hands. Dimitri gestured the direction he wanted her to move in. Far in front of them were his two youthful assistants towing Mashenka's suitcases.

Dimitri spoke up. "We borrowed a limousine to pick you up. Your guest faculty quarters are within easy walking distance from the Theatre Arts Academy. I am so delighted to have you here. I'll fill you in on other details once we get to the limo."

Masha spoke up, "I've been looking forward to coming here to teach."

Dimitri remarked, "Ever since you made the news feeds with your tango dancing, we've had international print and television media asking for interviews. The academy has had more media visibility in the past two months than we've had in the past ten years. All of this has thrilled our dean! Thank You for promoting us."

Masha remarked in a surprised tone, "My goodness." As they made their way to the limo. She thought to herself, *Mrs. Campbell, I really wish I could have a pot of tea with you right now. This is even bigger than I imagined!*

July 8-St. Petersburg, Russia -The Limo Ride.

Professor Dimitri Lebedev's training assistants, Akim Garin

and Sasha Isayev, loaded Masha's suitcases into the trunk of the vehicle. Both young men got into the front seats. Akim got into the driver's seat and Sasha joined him on the front passenger side. As Petrova got into the rearmost seats, she noted two young women waiting in the car. Both of the women were in their early twenties. They were smiling, and both looked nervous. Dimitri got in and closed the door.

A moment later, someone knocked on the window of the rear door. Dimitri looked out the window. "Goodness, we almost forgot, Tamara!" He opened the door and a woman in her mid-thirties entered the vehicle. After the woman comfortably sat down. Dimitri spoke up loudly, "Mr. Garin, let's take Professor Petrova to her quarters." The young man started the car and carefully merged into the traffic exiting the airport.

Dimitri turned to Masha as he gestured toward the woman who got in last, "Mashenka, this is Professor Tamara Koltsova. She teaches Theater History and Theater Management and she is the Staff Stage manager for our performance spaces."

Masha spoke up, "I'm delighted to meet you, Professor Koltsova. I foresee we will work closely together this year." Dimitri added in a humorous manner, "Mashenka, I feel I should warn you Tamara served in the armed forces before becoming an academic. She's not to be messed with!" Masha tapped two fingers from her right hand to her right eyebrow in a subtle salute and asked, "What did you do in the military, Professor Koltsova?"

Koltsova smiled and caught the hint of a salute and returns it, similarly, answered simply with a tone of pride, "I was **Spetsnaz!**" Petrova nodded with a smile, thinking. *Holy shit, she was an elite special forces soldier. This woman could kill me with one hand tied behind her back! I must keep a distance.*

Masha replies, "I'll do my best to not disrupt your house operations." Professor Koltsova nodded with a smirk.

Then Dimitri pointed at the two young women who had been exceedingly quiet all this time. "Professor Petrova, these two quiet nervous little mice over here are your training assistants. Vera Koneva and Susanna Pankova. They both had exemplary grades as

196

undergraduates and both of them minored in English. They each petitioned me to be your assistants, hoping to chat regularly in English with them instead of their mother tongue."

(Speaking English) The two women addressed Petrova, "Pleased to meet you, Professor." Masha grinned, thinking. *My goddess, they've both got British accents like their teacher.* (Speaking English) Masha remarked, "Ladies, I do not speak the Queen's English, but I would be delighted to chat American English with you." The two training assistants remarked with excited expressions. (Speaking English) "Thank You Professor."

So much for total immersion in Russian. Masha thought to herself. Now, I've got two TAs who are going to be like two puppies, always wanting me to speak English to them. At least I can have private chats with them without my other students understanding every side comment that I might mutter.

Aug 8   **Mashenka's Living Quarters**

Mashenka was exhausted. The past four weeks since arriving in St. Petersburg had been very busy for her at the academy. While the syllabuses for her class were all in order, she had to adjust her topic matters with her available teaching days. She is looking forward to having Tamara Koltsova drop over with some sort of local fast food. The truth, in fact, they were becoming gal pals. Masha mused about her first impression of Tamara was that she resembled some serious goth friends she knew back in DC. Then she whispered to herself, "She's a very sweet woman!"

The two were planning to work out rehearsal space needs for Petrova's junior class production of 'A Funny Thing Happened on the Way to the Forum' and her post grad student's Russian adaptation of 'Charles Dickens–A Christmas Carol.' Masha figured that after working out the scheduling issue over dinner, the two of them might settle back for some popcorn and perhaps a few drinks and perhaps watch the Bruce Willis movie <u>Die Hard</u> dubbed in Russian.

When Tamara arrived, she came in with a bucket of KFC fried chicken, a box of biscuits, and coleslaw. Masha stared at the bucket of fried chicken and mused to herself. *Good grief, I could have gotten KFC two blocks from my old apartment in Silver Spring, Maryland.* Masha queries, "When did they open KFC in Russia?" Tamara nonchalantly remarked '93.

During their meal, they worked out the bugs in the rehearsal space log jam and settled on the use of alternative open spaces that the theater students could use for rehearsals.

Tamara remarked at one point, "A facilities guy I know. He lets me use some vacant warehouse spaces he has on the books. It was a great mutual deal. If he can show he's using it, no other department would try to take it away from him." She took a drink of her Efes' beer and remarked. "If we use it enough eventually, we could make a case to gain the warehouse strictly for performance arts!"

After the two women had their fill of KFC, they discussed what movie they were going to watch. Masha suggested <u>Die Hard</u>.

"I've got a new Arnold Schwarzenegger movie called <u>True Lies</u>." Tamara suggested.

Masha thought for a moment, *I'm sick of Bruce Willis.* "I like Arnold. Let's see what he's got! It must be a new movie?"

Tamara answered, "It just came out!"

Five minutes into the movie, there was Arnold Schwarzenegger dancing a tango. Masha sat stunned, watching the two spies dancing a tango. *Holy shit, that's my life!* She thought to herself.

As the movie played out, Arnold's character was a spy and none of his family or friends knew what he really did for a living. This was too close to reality for Masha. She broke into a cold sweat and did her best to stay calm. Finally she had to run to the bathroom, and she lost the whole of her dinner. After about twenty minutes, Masha told Tamara she was "Feeling better." And was showing her usual perky self.

Tamara excused herself to the bathroom. After about ten minutes, Masha heard Tamara call her name. Masha stepped over by the bathroom door and simply asked, "Tamara, are you ok?"

Suddenly Tamara pulled the bathroom door open, grabbed Masha and shoved her up against the wall across from the bathroom, hard! Tamara began madly and passionately kissing her. Masha went with the moment. Within minutes, their passions whipped both of them into a frenzy.

Tamara blurted out between two long, passionate, deep throated kisses, "Bed...room."

Masha took a breath. "Hang on." Tamara wrapped her legs around Masha. At which time, Masha walked toward her tiny bedroom, carrying Tamara wrapped around her. As Masha walked into the room, she hit the front room light switch. The room plunged into darkness as she closed the door behind them.

7am-Aug 9-Mashenka's Living Quarters

Mashenka awakened. It was morning. Next to her, in bed, was Tamara. Masha thought to herself, *my goddess, I didn't dream it!* She took a deep breath. *At least it was another professor and not a student that would be taboo.* She turned over. As she did, she noted a bit of discomfort. She lifted the blanket and noted that her hip was black and blue. *Oh my, it must have happened when she shoved me up against the wall. Hmmm, battle bruises!* She smirked, trying not to giggle at the concern of waking the slumbering Tamara.

As Masha studied her nocturn lover from the night before. She again found herself amused by how much Tamara bore a remarkable resemblance to a Wiccan goth woman Masha used to be intimate with in DC. She whispered to herself, "Tamara, you commando, you bagged me?" Masha shook her head at that thought. Masha laid her head back on her pillow and considered in her thoughts. *What was the brit term Olivia used? Oh, yeah shagged!* "Tamara, you shagged me!" Masha whispered.

Tamara moved slightly, seeming to stretch a little. She opened her eyes and seemed startled. "What are you doing here?" She asked, wide eyed. Masha quietly remarked. "It's my bed?" Tamara looked around the room quickly. "So it is. Did I hurt you?" Masha smirked. "A little, but it will fade in a week or two."

Tamara sat up in bed. "Show me!" Masha lifted the lightweight blanket and revealed a large black and blue mark on her hip. Tamara blurted out. "Mashenka, I'm so sorry!"

Masha grinned at her, "Well, you are my first Spetsnaz commando. So I guess it goes with the operational experience."

There was an odd silence between them for a few moments, then they broke out laughing. "So I'm still welcome here?" Masha gave her a big smile, "Sweetie, you're welcome to my humble quarters and my bed anytime. You, my dear, are a wonderful spirit and you make me smile!" They hugged for a few moments.

"Let's make breakfast or go find breakfast somewhere." Mashenka stated. Tamara considered the suggestion for a few moments. "I know a new place!" Tamara commented as she rolled out of bed. "Come on, let's shower and be out of here in twenty minutes!" Tamara remarked strongly. Masha, responding to the command tone, simply answers, "Aye, aye ma'am!"

Tamara stopped in her tracks. "You've been in the military?" Masha nonchalantly rolled her eyes. "A long time ago, old habits die hard!"

9:30 am-Aug 9 -Tandoor Restaurant St. Petersburg

Tamara and Mashenka got into a moderate line of people waiting to get a table at the *Tandoor Restaurant*, a Russian-style diner. A server came outside and told the line there was about a twenty-minute wait to be seated. A couple of patrons left. Tamara and Mashenka stayed at Tamara's recommendation.

While waiting, Tamara pressed Masha about her military background. Masha kept the conversation very general and low key in her descriptions. "I was in the Air Force for a few years and did telephone construction work in southeast Asia. After that I was in the Navy. It was boring months at sea with the occasional visit to an exotic port of call."

Tamara looked at Masha with a curious look. "You were on the ground in Vietnam?" Tamara asked.

Masha nodded in the affirmative. Tamara seemed to tilt her head a little in a questioning look. "I didn't think the American military allowed women in frontline combat back then?"

Masha coolly thought to herself. *Share the truth now. Face the rejection now rather than later.* Masha leaned into her and said softly, "Tamara, I was born a boy and I was a guy when I served in the military. I always felt myself to be a woman and became one in the mid-1980s. I've been Mashenka for eight years."

Masha patiently waited for acceptance or rejection. Tamara stepped back away from Masha, seeming to study her from head to toe for a few moments. She had a troubled look on her face.

"So are you into men and you changed to be with men?" Masha shook her head.

"Truth be told, women are my cup of tea. I know it confuses everybody." Masha still wasn't getting a vibe as to Tamara's feelings. Tamara seemed distant for the next five minutes.

Then Tamara's expression broke into a smile. She leaned into Masha.

"Honey, I've been with many men and women since I was in the military. But Mashenka, you've been the most pleasant and sensitive person I've known in years..." She paused, seeming to collect her thoughts. "...and the most fun in the bedroom, too!" She reached up and threw her arms around Masha. "You are who you are now, this minute, and I like you and respect you as you are now!"

A moment later, a server came out and remarked, "A table for two." The server gave the embraced two women a devious look. "Or do you two need to go find a room?"

Masha spoke up, "A table for two, please."

Afternoon-Aug 15-New Vision and Mission

A staff meeting was called by the office of the Dean of the St. Petersburg State Theatre Arts Academy. The staff of the academy gathered in one of the school's smaller performance spaces.

At the appointed time, the Dean of the Academy, Ms. Roza Agapova, approached a podium and microphone. She seemed to collect her thoughts for a few moments before speaking.

"Fellow performing arts colleagues. As many of you know, the school's founders established it in 1779 and named it the Emperor's Theatre. In the school's 215-year history, the name of this institution has changed many times. It changed with the revolution and it changed several more times after the patriotic war of the second World War. The school has developed with changes in the art of performance and with new methods and technologies as they came along."

She paused. Considered her words and resumed. "There is a performance heritage that all of us have grown up with that has been slowly atrophying because of the lack of fresh talent blood coming into its traditions. I speak of the deteriorating Circus performing arts community."

The dean of the academy stopped to accommodate a rich round of applause from the faculty and staff.

"It does my heart good to hear your enthusiasm and that you all feel the same way I do. I take great pleasure in announcing that we have joined forces with the St. Petersburg Circus to recruit and develop new talent to refresh all the circuses of Russia and perhaps the circuses of Europe. We have added St. Petersburg Circus leadership Anton Vasilyev and Polina Volkova to our board of directors. In addition, I wish to announce the next name change of our institution. Starting today, we will be called, The St. Petersburg Circus and Theatre Arts Academy."

The Faculty and Staff erupted in loud applause and cheering. Dimitri Lebedev, department chair, pointed at Tamara and Mashenka and gestured for them to stay put.

Once most of the staff and faculty had left the room. All that remained were several department chairs and perhaps half a dozen faculty from various departments. Ms. Roza Agapova, the Dean of the Academy, approached the podium once more and addressed the teaching staff members who were asked to stay by their chairs. Roza Agapova stated,

"Each of you is being asked to consider being part of a core team of school recruiters who will travel around Russia. The job will be to promote the program, audition potential new talent and to recruit talent that you identify."

"Dr. Petrova, before you came to us from the United States. We came to know you better because of the global news feeds that showed us the outstanding dancing that you and your two male dance partners performed at two embassy balls. Few performers can dance a passionate tango and get banned from a major nation's embassies for life. That takes a very special performance heart!"

The small party of academics applauded loudly. Then Dean Agapova added. "Your gracious sharing of the fact that you were getting ready to come to this academy has literally rained media attention upon us. This has opened up additional funding and has facilitated our union with the circus. I know you had planned to direct plays this year. If you still want to do that, you may. But I would respectfully like to ask you to be our spokesperson for this talent search and recruiting challenge. What do you say?"

Masha was sitting between her Chairperson Dimitri Lebedev and Tamara Koltsova. Each of them could see that she was trembling. Both carefully reached over and held one of her hands for encouragement.

After a few moments, she stood up. "Dean Agapova, I would be deeply honored to mount this noble effort. I have a request. One of my dance partners is deceased. But the artist I danced with at the Russian embassy was the retired Bolshoi Ballet dancer Nikolai Antonov. Could you use your considerable new influence to bring him back to Mother Russia to be part of this promotion and recruiting effort for the academy?"

Dean Agapova just stared at her with an expressionless

face.

Then she commented. "My dear, that is a most generous thing and a most compassionate request. I will make the phone calls when I leave this meeting!" There was applause for her from the remaining staff and chairs. Dean Agapova dismissed the proposed recruiting team members.

Mashenka sat down in her chair and did her best to settle herself.

Dimitri leaned into her. "Masha, that was a brilliant request to ask for Antonov. Between the two of you, we're talking about some real star power for this team, not to mention more visibility for the initiative!" Masha did her best to relax and settle herself. In the back of her mind a little voice cried out, *'a spy is supposed to be anonymous.'*

Tamara Koltsova addressed her boss, "Dimitri, I'd like to be part of Dr. Petrova's team."

Dr. Dimitri Lebedev grinned. "Tamara, thank you for your support. Looking at Masha here, I think she's had enough for the day. Please take her some place and buy her a couple of stiff drinks."

"I will," Professor Koltsova remarked. She reached over to Mashenka, taking her hand. "Masha, let's go find a quiet cozy bar and decompress from the meeting and have a few serious drinks."

Masha slowly got up and, for a few moments, she had a bit of a vacant look in her eyes. She pondered. *Holy Hell! More visibility! When am I going to be out of the spotlight?*

Then suddenly Tamara realized the light had come back to her eyes. Masha spoke up, "Good night, Dimitri. We'll talk tomorrow."

Tamara led Masha from the room. Within an hour, they had changed clothes and were hiding in a small, dark bar near the port. The two of them talked about everything and nothing, but certainly not work.

Afternoon-Aug 19-St. Petersburg Circus and Theatre Arts Academy - A Meeting.

Dimitri Lebedev, Mashenka's chair, and Masha entered the conference room next to the academy dean's office. The dean, Ms. Roza Agapova, was already there and was on the conference room phone. A few moments later, the Circus leadership, Anton Vasilyev and Polina Volkova, arrived and exchanged pleasantries with Dimitri and Mashenka.

When the academy dean hung up the phone. "Sorry, that was important." Dean Agapova said. No one commented. Agapova looked over at Mashenka. "Professor Petrova, what are your thoughts about how we promote our new talent recruiting effort?"

Mashenka looked considerate for a few moments. "In my opinion, I see two approaches and several problems that we must overcome." Dean Agapova nodded and gestured for Mashenka to share her thoughts.

Masha began, "When I taught performing arts in the United States, I always encountered students who had stars in their eyes and solely aimed themselves at becoming a famous stage actor or a glamorous television or movie star. So many graduated with theater arts degrees and now spend their lives delivering pizzas."

She paused and added. "Regarding circus performing. It was old school, something that was only done hundreds of years ago. But here in Europe, the circuses are a live and still out there on the road and traveling." Around the table, there were nods. Anton Vasilyev and Polina Volkova made polite affirming and supportive comments.

Masha continued. "After you invited me to come here to teach for this year, I was prepared to present the best examples of American musical theater."

Dimitri Lebedev interjected, "We hoped you would do exactly that."

Dean Agapova added, "Yes, I was very excited about that prospect as well. I will support you in that endeavor if you wish."

"But Dean Agapova, the landscape has changed." Masha remarked. "This academy has joined forces with the Circus community and has experienced a windfall of public visibility and financial support due, in part, to my outrageous embassy team dancing. I think it would be foolish of us as producers and entertainers to not exploit these rare resources. I propose we dedicate this school year and perhaps the next, to both faculty and students alike, forming production teams. Teams that will literally go out on the road and strut our stuff. In order to recruit new up-and-coming talent for the technical and performance aspects with an emphasis on the circus arts."

Mashenka paused for a moment's thought, "Many people think that the entertainment business is a closed shop. All of you, as well as I, know that entertainment isn't the perceived closed shop that most people think it is. Let's go find that talent and audition them and give them the opportunity to show us their best!"

Masha paused for a moment, holding one hand in the air, obviously grasping a thought. "Let us change the academy's curriculum for the next year or two and become an army of smaller traveling road shows...and change the public view of teaching our craft from the classroom to that of on the road apprenticeship. Pointing out it's not just for elite performers and the glamorous of the movie screen! Let us take some of the faculty and students out on the road and tour and let our students experience the glamor and the love of the audience. As well as the challenge of the demanding realities of life on the road as part of a touring company!"

The members of the meeting cheered and pounded on the conference room table.

Dean Agapova looked around the table. "Thoughts? Opinions?"

Dimitri Lebedev remarked, "I can't think of a single faculty member that won't want to be part of the effort and spend some time on the road both onstage and backstage."

Polina Volkova rose, looking at her colleague Anton

Vasilyev. "I think I can speak for both of us when I say we should be able to recruit plenty of retired Circus talent for this grand effort." Anton simply nodded his head in the affirmative. "Unquestionably!"

Dean Agapova looked around the table. "I will put the word out to faculty what we're planning. I want the rest of you to team up with Mashenka and start outlining proposed traveling-show concepts and tour acts that the circus and our staff can readily present. All of us served in the armed forces at one time or another. We all know how to plan, mount, and launch a mission. A performing tour is no different. I'll organize a team to focus on just the logistics of moving one or many traveling shows."

Anton Vasilyev addressed Dean Agapova. "I'm plugged into those kinds of experienced travel managers and advance team people."

Dean Agapova greeted his offer with a nod and a smile! Then she sat back with a thoughtful look.

"I'm pleased to inform you that former Bolshoi dancer Nikolai Antonov, has received indefinite leave from the diplomatic service, will join us within the week...and he's most certainly accustomed to life on the road." She paused and added with a broad grin, "Using the star power momentum that Mashenka and Nikolai have started, I believe we can start a wave that will capture Russia's attention and perhaps that of the world. You are all excused. Let's get to work!"

Dean Agapova and the circus folks rose and left the conference room. Dimitri Lebedev had put his hand on Masha's arm so that she didn't rise. After the others had left.

Dimitri remarked, "Mashenka, that was a bold speech. Can I assume you might stay here for more than one school year?"

Masha stared at the conference table for a few minutes and said nothing. Dimitri could see that his colleague was in deep thought. Finally, she turned to face him. He clearly saw tears streaming down her face.

"Have I upset you, Mashenka?" He asked.

Masha took a deep breath and, with a little bit of choking in her voice.

"Many a child has thought about running away and joining a circus...it's an old whimsical notion. I entertained those closely guarded thoughts during my childhood and late adolescence."

She giggled slightly. "It seems the Fates are offering me another chance to pursue that dream."

Dimitri gave her a quizzical grin. "Are you going to accept their offer this time?"

He could see that her tears were flowing even more strongly now. He removed a handkerchief from his jacket pocket and handed it to her. Masha took it and blotted her tears.

"My theatrical brother. I am here for the duration of the project. Whether this road show last's a few months or perhaps conceivably years. Dimitri, you are my witness. I hereby stand before the Fates and I freely accept this call to adventure and to the grand stage of happenstances! I declare I am running away and joining the circus!"

With a mutual look of resolve, the two thespian professors rose and left the conference room. As the two of them made their way to their respective offices, Masha excused herself and entered a women's restroom. Using some tissues, she carefully wiped away her runny mascara. After she was satisfied that all was in order, she whispered to herself.

"Rule number one, you are anonymous. Field officers aren't supposed to make a spectacle of themselves or draw attention to themselves." As she stared at herself in the mirror, she whispered again, "But you are the impossible gal!"

2:15pm-Aug 21-Theater Department Faculty Offices

Cloistered in her office, Mashenka was head down, outlining a plan for her and other Academy instructors to tour the country and begin presenting free shows to draw prospective young and adult talent to the academy for training in the Circus and theatrical arts.

At the core of her project, there would be a group of traveling teams of exotic acts that would use a mix of performing talent from the academy's faculty and students. But the centerpiece in her plan would draw upon a pool of retired St. Petersburg circus performers to place an emphasis on classic circus craft.

Her eyes were tired. She took off her reading glasses. She closed her eyes and quietly and gently meditated to clear her thoughts. *I wonder if Mrs. Campbell ever imagined that her protégé would make a splash in Russia and be leading an effort to revitalize the Russian culture of circus performance arts. Perhaps this will make the desired splash she hoped for on both sides of the Neva river.*

From behind her, Masha heard a knock at the door. She remained with her eyes closed and asked, "Enter, friend! Whom do I have the pleasure of this afternoon?"

A man's voice sang out to her, "Madame pussy cat, it is I your playful dancing mouse!" Masha sat up straight and immediately swung around in her office chair and looked into the happy face and eyes of her Russian embassy dance partner Monsieur Nikolai Antonov.

"Nikolai!" she shouted, as she leaped from her chair and gave him a warm embrace. As she stood back, she asked, "Monsieur mouse I wasn't sure if you would accept our offer to come to be part of our project. After all, you had an important arts position at the embassy!"

"Madame pussy cat, I am in your debt. I am now going to have the opportunity to teach young people again, perhaps in a new context, which I am very excited about," Nikolai explained.

Mashenka gave the retired Bolshoi Ballet dancer a business look. "Nikolai, you realize that you and I will have to dance at some of the bigger recruiting events, as we will be the flashy draw?"

Nikolai laughed and expressed, "Madame pussy cat, I would be honored and happily dance with you anytime, anywhere!"

Mashenka put her hands together as if she was clapping, "Have you checked in with the dance department yet?" Nikolai shook his head. Masha spoke up, "Please do them with the honor of your cheery face. You and I will start planning our child friendly version of our dance routine in a few days." Nikolai nodded politely and blew her a kiss before turning and exiting her office.

Masha returned to her office chair and turned it back to facing her planning work on her desk. After about ten minutes, from behind her, she heard a woman's voice. "Knock Knock is this Professor Petrova's office?"

Masha didn't turn to speak to the woman. "Who's asking?" Masha remarked nonchalantly. The woman's voice replied politely. "Katherine Van Helsing."

Masha sat up straight. "I suppose you are here to stake me through the heart, Ms. Van Helsing? Very well, I yield to your sacred quest, madame. I'll surrender quietly. I am curious who sent you." Masha countered politely, without turning around.

The woman stood grinning. "Lady Anna Lloyd sent me. I'm your shadow reporter from 'Notable People Magazine.'"

Still not turning around to meet her guest. "Oh, dear me, a fate worse than being staked through the heart. Hence, forth I am to be haunted by a special correspondent!"

Masha swung around in her desk chair with a bright smile. "Pardon my theatrics. Your surname was too much of a sweet morsel to not indulge in a sweet flight of dramatic fantasy."

Van Helsing grinned. "It sure beats what people usually call me."

Masha gave the young woman a probed look. "What do people usually say to you?"

Van Helsing seemed to wince. "Usually something like, Get out of here, you hackette!"

"Oh, my," Masha responded, gesturing to the woman to take a seat in a comfortable chair. After a pause in conversation,

Masha asked, "Katherine, how does this shadow reporter thing work?"

The reporter spoke up. "Our working relationship is best kept very informal. If you must introduce me to someone, then I'm Katherine, otherwise between us I'm simply Kate. My presence is something like that of a translator. Their business and conversation are always with you. I'm just a trusted observer, nothing more. Likewise, her ladyship Mrs. Campbell sends her regards."

Mashenka knew that was code for Van Helsing's dispatches were an informal in the clear back channel to Mrs. Campbell.

Then Masha mused, "Hmm, I've known a few Kates in my time. All of them were precise and reliable." Masha said and nodding with a bit of a distracted expression. *Thinking briefly about the Bravo-51 sniper rifle she had once trained on. Often referred to as Kate.*

Then Masha asked, "What do I say you are doing?" Van Helsing just grinned. "Tell them I am your biographer. It will make the other professors insanely jealous."

Mid-morning Sept 14-A Meeting at the Circus of St. Petersburg
(The conversation in this passage is entirely in French)

Mashenka exited a taxi in front of the Circus of St. Petersburg, the world's first "Museum of Circus Arts." She had received an invitation to join a colleague for a stroll through the over 160-year-old first brick-built circus in Russia. Enclosed in the invitation envelope was a small piece of decorative stationery that had a fruity aroma to it.

A typed message read simply:

Join me for a casual stroll through the Circus Museum. N. Brunner

Paper clipped to the stationary was the Vatican Guardia Svizzera business card for Noah Brunner and a pre-paid ticket to the Museum.

Masha wondered why an officer of the Vatican's Swiss Guard wanted to meet with her. After all, she really wasn't on a covert or tactical mission. Masha found it amusing that Noah

THE SECOND OLDEST PROFESSION

Brunner had chosen the St. Petersburg Circus as a meeting place. Since becoming a faculty member of the Circus and Theatre Arts Academy, she and most of the academy of faculty and students were currently involved with mounting a small army of touring road shows intended for recruitment of students for the circus and theater performing arts. It was something that she found most rewarding and had never imagined for herself.

She really didn't need the enclosed ticket, as her academy faculty badge was enough to get her in. But she decided to just go through the motions of being a paying patron of the St. Petersburg Circus. As she quietly strolled into the museum portion of the facility, she began looking at the exhibits. After a few minutes, a man's voice from behind greeted her, speaking French.

"Good afternoon, Professor Petrova!"

Masha turned to see Noah Brunner. He extended a handshake, which she graciously accepted. Masha returned a cordial greeting and continued the conversation in French.

"Mr. Brunner, what an unexpected surprise. It's been a few years since our last meeting. What brings you to St. Petersburg?"

Brunner gestured for them to keep walking slowly. "Professor, one thing I love about working in Italy is the considerable variety of traveling circuses during the warmer season. In fact, I've always wanted to visit the St. Petersburg Circus."

Masha remarked, "As a matter of fact, I'm helping recruit performing arts students to train and become some fresh blood in the Russian circus community."

Brunner stopped and gave her a quizzical expression. "Are you really?" She just nodded in the affirmative. He began slowly strolling again, seeming to show an interest in some antique horse-drawn circus carriages.

"I'm surprised that your superiors don't have you engaged in more serious duties," Brunner commented.

Masha simply answered, "You know as well as I do, appearances are everything in our business."

Brunner nodded and replied, "I most certainly do."

She stopped and looked at him.

"As a theater arts professor, they invited me to teach over here for the foreseeable future." She looked at him with a bright smile.

Brunner began walking again. Masha followed suit. Brunner then commented,

"Your tango dancing at those embassy balls impressed me on the global news feeds. I felt deep sadness when the news reported that Mr. Perez, your dance partner, lost his life in that tragic auto accident. You showed great resolve to still perform at the Russian embassy."

Then Mr. Brunner stopped and remarked after a moment. "Any other woman would have felt devastated and would not have attended the embassy event, let alone perform brilliantly in-front of a huge diplomatic audience. That's when I knew you were functioning in a professional capacity. You carried on like a warrior and a well-trained field officer."

Masha stopped, faced him and remarked. "Your point, sir?"

Brunner leaned into her, stating, "They sanctioned your dance partner!" Masha stood transfixed, staring at him. Her eyes began to tear up.

Brunner continued, "Didn't you think it strange that all your mission handlers were oddly incommunicado when you needed them? I know you must have gone into improvise mode and focused on the mission and focused on finding another suitable dance partner and dancing at the embassy that night. You clearly had contacts at the Russian embassy to arrange for that Bolshoi fellow to dance with you. That was brilliant." Masha began weeping. Brunner gave her his handkerchief. He gestured toward an obscure museum bench amongst the circus artifact exhibits. After a few minutes of sitting, she simply asked,

"Why are you sharing all of this with me?"

"Simple," Brunner said. "Consider it a professional courtesy." She finished blotting her tears and asked him.

"Do you know who was responsible for arranging Mr. Perez's death?"

He nodded his head. "It's my understanding that when you were being considered for the Field Director's job. The selection committee had to use their second choice, Mrs. Boyce, because Director Kramer stomped into the committee and told them in no uncertain terms why he wouldn't accept you as the new Field Director."

"I also heard that when Olivia Campbell pitched your current mission to your superiors, Mrs. Boyce and Director Kramer. He wouldn't sign off on it, objecting to Campbell using you on the mission. I suspect Boyce went on detached duty with you in order to support Olivia Campbell's project." Brunner explained.

Masha remarked, "Kramer doesn't like me."

Brunner shook his head. "My dear professor, it's a bigger game than just you. In the world's whole of clandestine services. There are a bunch of Kramer types who privately want the Cold War to come back and for gay, lesbian and trans folks to have no role in it."

She looked at Brunner. "You know I'm a transwoman?"

Brunner nodded and added. "Mashenka, Kramer wants to get rid of you, and I think he's going to keep trying until he manages it. My advice is to watch your back. I wouldn't put it past him to tip off the FSB and get you locked away in Siberia some place or worse. Some cell we're monitoring mentioned your name and the Russian term 'mokrie dela' in the same breath."

Masha had a shocked look and after a moment she commented, "It's Russian slang, it means 'Wet Affairs.' I'm marked for assassination."

Again Brunner spoke up. "Professor Petrova, I chose this circus museum on purpose. The whole clandestine business is a big circus when you really consider it. All of us are out there performing like trained monkeys in an enormous show. The best any of us can do is perform our little dance and take our humble reward."

The two field officers sat quietly for a few minutes. Both were strangely comfortable in each other's company. After about ten minutes.

Brunner asked, "I assume you have a secure method to get

messages back to your Field Director or to Olivia Campbell?"

"Actually, no! Masha commented. I'm simply an exchange professor for a year or two in the interest of goodwill between the USA and the Russian Federation. I have no mission directives and no standing orders for observation and report. This mission has always been informally to charm the pants off the Russians."

Brunner studied her face. "...and the dancing?"

"Some media splash to give the arts academy I'm teaching at, some media exposure." She explained.

He grinned. "So, you are really taking a vacation from being a spymaster and just being another exchange academic?"

She nodded her head. "I have absolutely no comm channel, no backup and certainly no dead drop. I'm 'naked', as we say in this business."

He moaned, "That's interesting and troubling." Brunner reached into his pocket and retrieved a couple of more of his business cards.

Then he remarked. "Professor, if you find yourself cornered without a friend to turn to, I want you to go to the Swiss embassy in Moscow or The Consulate General of Switzerland in St. Petersburg, and tell them I have offered you safe refuge and secure transport out of Russia."

Masha accepted the business cards graciously. "Thank You Mr. Brunner. That is very kind of you."

Brunner added. "Professor, I'll pass a note to Olivia Campell and let her know you are exposed over here and by who." Masha simply nodded.

Brunner cracked. "We spymaster monkeys have to stick together."

Mashenka rose and offered her right hand. Still speaking French. "Until we meet again! Mr. Brunner."

Brunner rose from the bench, took her right hand and kissed it. "Goodbye madame professor, until we meet again!" Then he turned and left the St. Petersburg Circus. Masha took her seat again and seemed to just quietly study the fine collection of antique Circus carriages near where she was sitting.

Apr 24-Ural Mountains-Me and my Shadow
Mashenka's Road Show Journal

For the past eight months, our troupe of Academy Faculty and student performers and a prestigious team of retired Circus performing elite have been on tour. We've been in cities big and small all over Russia to audition and recruit a new generation of performance and production talent. In addition, we've been carefully searching for a special sort of talent for apprenticeships within the Circus arts aspect of the academy. It's been a grand effort full of joys, some disappointments and certainly its own form of weariness that living 'on the road on tour' as it's said, brings.

Likewise, for me personally, it's also had a creepy movie form of weirdness, to boot. From our first tour performance, thirty-five weeks ago, there's been this very visible guy in the seats. Everywhere we go, there he is somewhere in the front three rows of seating.

Our traveling tour is presently in the City of Orenburg, in the Ural mountains range. We have three performances scheduled over the next three days. If this guy is in the audience tonight, I'm going to confront him.

Post Journal Performance entry.

We had a fantastic company performance. As I half expected, my shadow gentleman was here tonight, second row stage left. I observed him from backstage. I politely asked theater security to invite the man back to my dressing room after the performance for a cup of tea and a brief word. After the final curtain, they informed me that the man expressed surprise but peacefully complied with security.

I had just gotten out of my belly dancing costume from our entire touring company's finale using eastern dance as a theme. My costume was soaked in sweat, as usual, and I was glistening, just like my old eastern dancing teacher Lady Artemis used to say.

I was now out of costume with my robe on; and seated in a wooden rocking chair. When security brought him into my dressing room, they gave him a seat on a small couch behind a small coffee table. I introduced myself and congratulated him on his 35th performance of our traveling road show. I asked him his name, and he got all shifty eyed. Then I whispered to him, "Come now, my friend. You must be either an underworld contractor or an FSB agent." He shook his head wildly, remarking, "Not FSB, Not FSB. Contractor with Bratva!" (братва)

I poured him some tea. "As a member of the Bratva underworld network, you're a member of 'The Brotherhood.' Which family or network?" The poor man shook his head. He looked like he was being chased by hell dogs. "Ok my friend, I won't challenge your Brotherhood Oaths." He seemed to relax. "What is your name?" The man winced. "Then have some tea!" I politely told him.

He looked at the teacup and whispered. "No, you poisoned it."

I reached over and took a drink from his teacup. "No poison!" I remarked. I topped off his cup. And told him, "I am a member of an American Sisterhood. I respect your oaths!"

He seemed to relax and picked up his teacup and carefully sipped from it. "It's good, thank you." Then he asked, "Are you Lady-355?" I wasn't expecting him to ask about the 355 folks. But since I was technically a member from a few years back, I simply told him, "Yes." He took another sip of his tea, remarking, "I am Yuri." I lifted my teacup and replied, "I'm Masha."

After a few minutes of silence, I asked the tough question. "Yuri, are you here to kill me?" With a sad look on his face, he nodded once and commented. "It's not right! You are a good woman. By dancing, you bring smiles and laughter to people. You are also inviting young people to join the theaters and circuses. And offering to teach kids the Circus arts. It's just wrong to kill you." Then he added, "Also, I'm oath bound not to kill a brother or sister."

In the back of my mind, I suddenly realized, this poor man is in a serious predicament. "Would the brotherhood unburden you if you told them, you couldn't kill someone from the 355 sisterhood?" I asked. Yuri assumed a sincere, business expression. "Masha, you are Lady-355. That is a recognized sisterhood and part of the networks. We live by rules and covenants within the Bratva. We don't kill brothers or sisters."

I poured him some more tea. Then I asked him, "Do you know who put a contract on me?" Yuri nodded, "Yes." I gave him a pleasant, sincere look. "Please tell me." Yuri looked thoughtful for a few moments. "Since you are sisterhood. I'll tell you. Apparently, you pissed off the czar at an American spy network."

I remained calm and smiled. The first thought in the back of my mind, *Daniel Kramer*. I simply commented, "Its seems some people can't take a joke." Yuri's expression clearly showed he appreciated the irony. "Miss Masha." He said, "Please remember, I'm not the only person in this business. If that czar really wants you dead, he can just as easily go out of the brotherhood and sisterhood networks."

I stood up. "Yuri, it's been a pleasure to meet you, a brother in the business. Thank You for coming to our shows and good luck explaining the situation to the family. Why don't you report back that you saw me arrested by the FSB and they carted me away to Siberia." Yuri grinned, "FSB and Siberia, you'd be as good as dead. I will report this back." I offered a handshake, in brotherhood and sisterhood style. He grabbed my arm, and I grabbed his. "To family Miss Masha."
I reached over and opened the door to the dressing room. I looked at my security guard. "Please see my cousin Yuri safely out to the parking lot." I looked at Yuri and gave him a bright smile. "Cousin Yuri, give my regards to the family. It was so good to see you again after all this time." He brightened up. "Of course, my dear cousin." Yuri exited my dressing room. After I closed the dressing room door, I sat for a few minutes pondering my situation regarding Daniel Kramer.

There was a knock at the door. I simply asked who's that knocking at my door? A voice said, "Monsieur Mouse." I grinned, "Come in, Nikolai," I exclaimed. "I suppose it's time to go have our evening meal. Please give me a few minutes in the shower."
End of Entry.

May 25 -A Terrace Café -Moscow, Russia

It was a lovely day in the middle of May and the best time to witness Moscow in full late spring bloom, flowers everywhere. Professor Tamara Koltsova, retired Bolshoi dancer Nikolai Antonov and Professor Mashenka Petrova were enjoying the warmth and beauty of spring.

As members of the principle touring group of the St. Petersburg Circus and Theatre Arts Academy, they were in Moscow for a Command Performance after nearly seven months on tour throughout Russia. All three of them were looking forward to the coming summer months to rest and relax before mounting a new fall season of touring.

When the waiter came to take their orders, Monsieur Antonov took the gentlemanly role of communicating the wishes of his two lovely women guests.

Their relaxed conversation was simple and light. Nearly a year on tour together had made them the closest of friends. Tamara and Nikolai cracked lighthearted jokes that Mashenka, who was always the clueless one, never got.

When the server brought their glasses of wine. They raised their glasses in a toast. Nikolai did the honors of the toast.

"To a splendid performance tour and to a successful Command Performance Tonight, To Our Friendship." They clicked their glasses together.

Before Masha could sip her wine, she felt a spring allergy sneeze and bent over to the right and sneezed away from her party. As she sat up, Masha heard women screaming. Masha glanced at the table and saw two broken wine glasses and spilled wine. She looked up towards Tamara and Nikolai and saw them slumped in their chairs, each with a trickle of blood oozing from their foreheads.

She ducked down, throwing herself toward the patio stones below. As she did, she heard the crack of a whip sound of a high velocity rifle round over her head. She went spread eagle on the patio stones and went dead still. Hoping the assailant would think she was dead and leave his or her perch. The cafe was in pandemonium.

A minute later, she got up and ran out to the back entrance of the cafe. She quickly made her way up the street behind the establishment. Using several parked cars along the street as shielding. A few blocks away, she flagged down an empty passing taxi. Once in the cab, she shouted,

"Embassy of Switzerland, Ogorodnaya Sloboda 2/5."

In the taxi, she breathed a sigh of relief. She glanced down at her side and breathed another sigh of relief that her purse strap was still slung over her shoulder and her purse was resting safely on her right hip. In her mind she repeated over and over, *I must focus. Keep your mind on the ball. One mind, stay focused, get to safety with the Swiss. Cry and mourn later.*

{All conversation at the Swiss Embassy was in French}

As the taxi approached the Embassy of Switzerland, the driver spoke the fare. She gave him twice the amount and thanked him. She exited the cab. Masha walked up to the guards at the gate and handed one of them her American passport and Noah Brunner's business card.

"Mr. Brunner offered me emergency safe refuge and safe transport out of Russia."

A moment later, the guard blew his police style whistle and the duty officer came over and looked at the Mashenka Petrova passport and the Vatican Guardia Svizzera business card for Noah Brunner.

Again Mashenka spoke up, "Mr. Brunner offered me refuge and safe transport. Someone is trying to kill me."

220

The duty officer nodded and ordered loudly, "Get her in here and out of sight now!"

A few minutes later, an officer from the facility's security team escorted Mashenka inside the embassy and took her to the embassy Security Office. As she sat quietly waiting, she noted the crest on the wall in the office. Thinking, *My goddess, this is the office of the site commandant of the Swiss Federal Intelligence Service (FIS). I sure hope Noah Brunner's name carries some weight around here.*

A short middle-aged man in a double-breasted suit came into the office carrying her passport.

"Good afternoon, Miss Petrova. Your arrival here certainly surprised us. My name is Jakob Caspari and I am the Federal Intelligence Service director for the Swiss Embassy here in Moscow. Could you explain how you know the Deputy Commandant of Vatican Guardia Svizzera?"

Mashenka simply answered, "Mr. Brunner and I have had quiet business dealings in the past." Mr. Caspari seemed to study Petrova silently for a few minutes.

"When did he give you his card and offer you refuge and safe transport?"

Petrova simply stated, "He met me last September in the Circus Museum in St. Petersburg. He told me my life was in danger and offered me refuge and safe transport out of Russia if I needed it. My circumstances have changed, and I most certainly need your help."

Mr. Caspari extended his arm.

"Please let me examine your purse." Petrova handed over her purse. Masha watched as he poured the contents on his desk blotter. He picked up a plastic laminated clip-on badge.

"So you are an American and serve as faculty at a Russian Theater Arts Academy in St. Petersburg?"

"They invited me to be guest faculty," Petrova answered casually. The security director seemed to examine every item of ID in the purse.

"Where do you teach in the United States?" Masha

responded, "Cornell University." Director Caspari took a seat and continued to studying all of Petrova's identification.

"For some odd reason, I think I know your name. Why is that, Miss Petrova?"

Masha grinned. "My colleagues and I have been on a performance tour for the past seven months all over Russia, recruiting talent for our theater arts and circus school. We've had a lot of media visibility over the past year in magazines, newspapers and on television. Our team was supposed to present a command performance tonight here in Moscow."

"And why are you sitting in my office and not preparing to perform tonight?" Caspari asked.

She started to tear up. "A sniper shot and killed two of my colleagues about an hour ago in a cafe on the other side of Moscow. Based on what Mr. Brunner had told me, I was probably the principal target."

Director Caspari, with an expressionless face, simply asked, "In my wildest imagination, I can't fathom why someone would hire a Bratva contract killer to murder a few innocent traveling performers or you an esteemed university drama professor."

Petrova said nothing. There was a deafening silence in the office for a few minutes. Then she spoke up.

"In a very private side of my life, I know things. Things I must take to my grave. Let's just say there are people who wish to put me there sooner than I would hope." Caspari nodded with a knowing look.

"I suppose theater critics must be absolute killers in your business?" Petrova relaxed and smirked.

"They are the worst, sir!"

Director Caspari stroked his chin, clearly in deep thought.

"We must get the wolves off of your trail, before we can move you out of the country, it would be advantageous to have the Moscow Municipal Militsiya find your dead body and your purse with all your ID washed up on the banks of the Moskva river tomorrow."

Masha shook her head slightly and commented, "That is the

shame of it. Floaters are so very difficult to identify. Aren't they?"

Mr. Caspari nodded with a smirk.

"I'll arrange for some Swiss credentials and a Swiss passport. Of course, we'll have to change your appearance a bit, hair color, a new haircut and perhaps some studious glasses. We'll probably move you out of Moscow in a about a week and fly you to Geneva and then back to the United States. But in the meantime, welcome to Switzerland and congratulations on becoming a Swiss citizen, Madame Sophia Heffelfinger."

May 28 -Embassy of Switzerland in Moscow, Russia

Guest Visitors cafeteria

Mr. Caspari came to the embassy cafeteria and found Madame Sophia Heffelfinger quietly eating breakfast. He greeted her.

"Good morning, Madame Heffelfinger. May I join you for breakfast?" She smiled at him and nodded politely and silently since she was chewing on a morsel of her breakfast. Then Mr. Caspari remarked,

"I think you will find the morning edition of Pravda quite interesting." Madame Heffelfinger picked up the newspaper and read the bold headline.

Russian Embassy Tango Dancer Petrova Found Dead
Moscow Municipal Militsiya calls it Foul Play

She swallowed hard.

"Goodness to see such a familiar name in a bold, heart-breaking headline is most distressing."

Mr. Caspari commented, "Oh Yes, it's very tragic." He further expressed his surprise upon reading that the old Soviet Union considered Dr. Petrova to be a hero, and the Soviets decorated her.

"Very unusual for an American to be decorated."

"I read about her. It's my understanding she was simply a

translator for some American scientists." Madame Heffelfinger remarked before taking another morsel of her breakfast. Caspari considered,

"I suppose Dr. Petrova's critics are happy she's dead." Madame Heffelfinger swallowed her food. Then, after she sipped a bit of her coffee.

She uttered, "I suspect her critics are dancing in the aisles."

"Mr. Brunner has requested that we fly you to Rome in a few days. Then his people will give you safe refuge." Caspari explained. He studied her for a few moments as a server brought his breakfast.

"How do you think it's going to play out?" Madame Heffelfinger simply said,

"Trust me. There will be a reckoning. Not today, certainly not tomorrow, but a day will come and there will be a reckoning."

May 31-TELEX Message

Olivia Campbell c/o Lord Walker British Embassy, Washington, DC
Please send William Taylor as a diplomatic courier. Purpose, pick up the remains of your tango dancer. Mr. Taylor must have proof of her British citizenship: passport, driver's license and government ID etc. and any other supportive items of her British identity with him.
Noah Brunner, Deputy Commandant
Guardia Svizzera Pontificia
Città del Vaticano, Vatican City

Jun 22-Vatican City- Guardia Svizzera Pontificia

William Taylor was quiet as he gazed at the historic architectures as his taxicab entered the gates of Vatican City. Once the taxi was through the gates, he commented to the driver, Speaking Italian,

"Guardia Svizzera Pontificia, please." The driver acknowledged he understood.

Then William looked at her ladyship.

"Ma'am, do you want me to accompany you to speak to Mr. Brunner?" Olivia Campbell silently shook her head.

"No! On the off chance she is still alive, I want to see her first. If Brunner just has a box of ashes, I want him to provide me with a thorough briefing on what transpired. To be very honest with you, I clearly want to know how the bloody Swiss Guard is involved."

William simply remarked,

"I understand your ladyship. It is puzzling, isn't it?" The taxi stopped in front of the barracks for the Guardia Svizzera Pontificia. The taxi driver got out of the car and opened the door for Mrs. Campbell. She exited the taxi, carrying her purse in one hand and a small attaché case in the other. She looked at the Corporal Guard at the door. Speaking German,

"I am here to meet with Lieutenant Colonel Brunner."

The guard pressed a button similar to a doorbell. A few moments later, a junior Non-commissioned officer (NCO) exited the building. The guard spoke to the junior NCO in German. The young man crisply and politely open the door for Mrs. Campbell. Then he led her down a corridor to a door that had a nameplate that read Oberstleutnant Brunner. (Lieutenant Colonel Brunner) The young NCO gestured for her to knock. Campbell knocked. From inside, a man's voice spoke loudly in German.

"Eingeben" (Enter) Campbell nodded politely to her escort and opened the door.

As she entered the office, Brunner stood and grinned. Speaking English,

"Your Ladyship, it is indeed a pleasure to meet you at last. Please have a seat." As she sat down, she abruptly got to the point.

"Mr. Brunner, If I read your message correctly, you either have a box of cremation ashes for me or you have my field officer in protective custody."

Brunner responded with a banker's business-like expression.

"Your ladyship, the officers of the Guardia Svizzera Pontificia, pride ourselves on attentiveness to proper procedures. Do you have the requested identity documents?"

Campbell lifted the attaché case onto her lap and opened it. She removed a large manilla envelope and handed it to Brunner. He opened the envelope and gently poured the contents onto his desk. One by one, he began inspecting each item of the documents.

"A British passport current and in order. Her current British photo ID driver's license is all properly in order. A certified copy of her birth certificate, impressive, an aristocratic family."

"Respected nobles!" Campbell replied. Brunner gave her a frown. "She didn't sound British!"

Campbell curtly responded, "She spent a long time living in the United States and sadly picked up an American accent."

Brunner looked at another document. "Graduated from Cambridge and with a master's degree, no less."

Campbell, stone faced, replied, "She's a smart woman."

Finally, Brunner held up two British credit cards, smiled and simply nodded. He scooped up everything and returned it to the original envelope and handed the packet full of documents back to Campbell.

"Mrs. Campbell, it seems everything is in order." Brunner happily stated.

Then he explained. "She approached the Swiss Embassy in Moscow, seeking refuge, stating that someone was trying to kill her. We sheltered her."

Campbell queried. "What about the body found in the Moskva river?" Brunner smirked and shrugged his shoulders.

"An indigent from the Moscow morgue. Used as a ruse to get the wolves off her scent. Someone wanted her dead and forgotten." Campbell gave Brunner a coy look.

"Where is she now?" she asked. Brunner grinned.

"In the care and safety of the Carmelite Nuns." Campbell gave him a troubled look. Brunner simply remarked,

"Trust me, she's very protected."

Jun 22-Vatican City-The Cloister

After twenty minutes, an out of uniform Swiss guard soldier led Mrs. Campbell to the front entrance of the Mariae Monasterii Sororum Carmelitarum, a cloistered facility for Carmelite Sisters within Vatican City. She knocked on the door and after a few minutes, a young nun answered the door. Campbell handed the woman a note given to her by Brunner. The nun read the note and invited the British woman inside. With a British accent, the nun told Campbell,

"I will take you to your niece." The young nun led Campbell to a small chapel. The nun gestured for Campbell to enter.

"Will she meet me here?" The young nun pointed at a solitary nun at prayer in a front pew. Campbell slowly walked toward the front pew. She carefully genuflected and slid into the pew, and sat quietly. Glancing over at the nun, Olivia could clearly see it was Moira, bare faced and dressed in a customary Carmelite Nun's habit. She was kneeling and saying a rosary. After approximately ten minutes, Moira moved off the kneeler and slid back onto the pew, and said nothing.

Finally, Campbell broke the silence with a soft voice.

"I'm here to take you home." Moira, still expressionless, whispered,

"Masha is dead. They pulled her from the river with all of her ID. From what Mr. Brunner told me, nobody from the USA even tried to claim her body or confirm its real identity. Not the State department nor OSS62. They followed protocol to the letter and then some. That poor destitute woman they pulled from the Moskva river who was supposed to be me will go to her grave with my cover identity. Here I sit, simply known as Sister Bridget and officially a woman without a country."

"I can get you out of here to safety." Mrs. Campbell stated. Moira scoffed.

"I'm actually quite safe here. The nun who led you in is former British SAS. This convent has two former SAS. The mother superior was formerly with Spain's Centro Nacional de Inteligencia the CNI. This convent is very special. It's for all nuns who wish to live and do work here in Vatican City. Also, there are a handful of women who requested refuge from the spy business. They sought redemption and a quiet anonymous life here protected by the church and the Guardia Svizzera Pontificia."

Moira paused. "I have half a mind to stay here. The food is terrific. The nun who runs the kitchen used to be with the French DGSE, the French secret service."

Olivia had a stressed expression on her face. "Moira, if you come with me, you'll have a new identity! You will have a good life in England. You will receive treatment as a genuine lady and earn people's respect. There's a position in MI6, if you want it. Your skills and insights would be invaluable to us." Olivia paused. "Come with me, Moira, please."

Moira sat silently, obviously in deep thought. She spoke up,

"The Russian criminal network told me it was Daniel Kramer who put the contract out for my life." Olivia quietly concurred.

"That is our understanding. Laura Boyce informed me of Masha's reported death. She was understandably upset. Then she quietly told me she overheard Daniel Kramer cheerfully tell some upper management colleagues, 'Ding Dong, the Witch is dead!' So it's certainly not safe for you to go back to the United States for the foreseeable future."

Moira whispered.

"That's about what I would expect from that bigoted bastard." After a few moments, she turned and looked at Campbell.

"So, who would I become?" Olivia smiled.

"To begin with, you're going to be my niece!" Olivia reached down and retrieved her attaché case on the chapel floor and set it on her lap and opened it and removed a large manilla envelope. Olivia handed Moira the envelope.

Moira poured the contents onto the pew next to her. She picked up the British passport. After opening it, she smirked at her photo inside. She cocked her head slightly.

"Cora Elizabeth Waldegrave? Are you kidding me?"

Olivia shook her head and explained. "The new identity is as the youngest daughter of Lord Alistair George Waldegrave and Lady Ernestine Victoria Waldegrave. You are Cora Elizabeth Waldegrave. You were born in Somerset, England, on September 23, 1952. Your eldest siblings are Paul, Esther, and Chauncey. You'll meet them soon."

Moira gave Olivia a questioning look.

"I don't sound like a Brit?"

Campbell smirked; "Nonsense, you used to, but you've lived in the United States since you finished your education at Cambridge. During those eighteen years of being exposed to the Americans, you've picked up an American accent. It happens all the time with expatriates."

Moira just stared at the diploma from Cambridge. "What happens if OSS62 finds out?"

"They pulled Masha's body, a floater, from the Moskva river. Health authorities cremated the body. There is nothing left for anyone to make that connection. Cora Waldegrave can be your real identity from now on if you wish or your cover identity if you wish that. But if Moira were to suddenly become visible again. You'd find yourself with a target on your back. A few minutes ago, you suggested you might be comfortable remaining a Carmelite nun, invisible and anonymous. You could just as easily be my niece and that graceful lady I've trained you to be and have a profession working for MI6. After all, you are seriously familiar with Russian culture. You'd be one hell of an asset to us! It's your choice."

After a moment, she added. "I'll arrange for a dialect coach to give you lessons and we'll have you sounding like a member of the family in no time."

"I understand your point," Moira nodded her head. "Especially while Daniel Kramer is still alive."

Moira placed all the documents back in the envelope they

came in. She seemed to be in deep thought for a few minutes before speaking. Then, in her contralto voice, Moira sang a musical verse.

"Bring me my bow of burning gold."
"Bring me my arrows of desire."
"Bring me my spear. O clouds unfold!"
"Bring me my chariot of fire."

"My dear auntie Olivia, please take me home to England." An emotionally moved Campbell gave Moira a beaming smile.

"Cora Elizabeth, my lovely niece, it would be my pleasure."

PART FIVE

THE ZOMBIE

23 September 2011- John F. Kennedy International Airport

A British Airways jet landed at John F. Kennedy International Airport at 10:50am. It had been on a seven-hour, 55-minute flight, which most of the passengers slept through.

In US customs, an elegantly dressed first-class passenger handed her British passport to the US Customs agent who looked at her photo and her name, Cora Elizabeth Waldegrave.

"What is your purpose in visiting the United States?" The officer asked. She smiled and answered in a clearly British accent.

"A little business and hopefully a little bit of pleasure. To visit old friends and old haunts."

The agent smiled and placed her passport on his scanner. It dinged, then it triple dinged. He looked at her with an odd look.

"Lady, could you please step over there?" He gestured to another officer. The other officer stepped over to the customs guard with the woman's passport, took it and asked Miss Waldegrave to come with him.

He guided her to an interview room with beige walls and simply said,

"Please take a seat. Someone will be with you shortly."

Cora leaned her suitcase with rollers up against the table. She glanced up at two CCTV cameras mounted on the wall. In the back of her mind, she knew that someone, somewhere, was watching. She smirked and turned and faced one camera and waved, then she turned and waved at the other camera and blew that camera a kiss. Beyond that, she sat quietly with her legs tucked together, with one leg behind the other with her hands resting on her lap.

After about ten minutes, a female airport officer came in and said nothing and assumed a parade rest posture next to the wall. A few minutes later, a heavy-set middle-aged man in a suit entered the room, followed by a young woman carrying a device in a black leather case.

The man was holding her British passport in one hand and several pages of printouts in his other hand. He opened the passport and addressed her,

"Miss Waldegrave, do you have any idea why we have detained you?" She smiled at him and politely said.

"I suspect your national security apparatus flagged me." He nodded.

"Do you understand why?" he asked.

Again, she gave him a pleasant smile. "Perhaps because I'm a Zombie. I suppose I'm listed as missing-in-action and/or dead." The man nodded his head.

"Indeed, you are. We received a request to take your fingerprints. If you refuse, we will detain you for a longer period."

Cora smiled graciously.

"As I am not a criminal, I have nothing to hide. I will happily cooperate." The woman with the handheld device opened the leather carrying case. She took a moment to boot the device. Then the woman asked Cora to place her right thumb on the device's glass screen. As she did, the technician pressed a button. An instant later, the technician nodded and simply said,

"Thank You ma'am." A few moments after that, there was a squeaking beep, and the technician looked at the device's display screen. Suddenly, she had a shocked look.

The interviewing man asked the technician to read the name. The tech, with a surprised expression, spoke up.

"It lists four names. Air Force Sergeant Charles Stewart, Navy Petty Officer 1st class SS Charles Stewart, Moira Stewart and Dr. Mashenka Petrova."

Cora closed her eyes and remarked,

"In the first Star Wars movie, Jedi Obi-Wan has an impressive line that seems to fit our moment. Those are names I've not heard for a long time." There was another beep on the handheld fingerprint device. The Technician spoke up again,

"It also lists a British citizen, the Honourable Cora Elizabeth Waldegrave." Cora closed her eyes for a moment as she experienced a subtle sense of feeling naked.

The interviewing officer asked,

"Why have you had so many names?" Cora looked at him and just commented, gesturing toward the two young women,

"I was defending this country before either of them was born." She looked at the interviewer and added.

"And when you were probably in diapers, sir."

Cora addressed the Technician. "Miss, are there any warrants?" The Fingerprint tech shook her head.

The investigator asked, "Those male names and then a woman's name? Why?" Cora smiled gently.

"Those gentlemen's names were given at birth," Cora gently explained. "Later I renamed myself as Moira, as I developed into my authentic self."

"...And that Russian name. What about that?" The

investigator asked. Cora just smiled. "My friends, that name and all that concerns her is well above your pay grades and most certainly above your clearance levels. And for what it's worth, I was never here."

She reached into her purse and withdrew her British MI6 identification. And showed it to the investigating officer. He focused on it, read it and remarked to his associates. "Do not speak of this, as per my instructions. Ladies, she was never here!"

The investigator stood up and addressed her. "Ms. Waldegrave, I'm very sorry for the inconvenience this has caused." He offered a handshake. She simply grasped his hand and shook gently. She commented, "You and your team were professional and courteous. Can you arrange a golf cart? I really need to find my limo driver." The investigator looked at the uniformed woman. "Please get a golf cart and take her to find her limo driver."

After Cora reached her driving service, she gave the driver the address to New York's Mount Sinai Hospital on Madison Ave. After about a thirty-minute drive. Cora entered the main lobby of the Mount Sinai hospital; she approached the information desk. Cora asked after the patient, Alexi Sidorov. The desk gave her a visitor's pass and was told what floor to go to. After taking an elevator to the desired floor, she approached the nurse's station.

They directed her to Sidorov's room. The nurse informed her that his sight was gone. She told Cora speaking to him was the only way he would know she was there. Cora thanked her for the information. Cora quietly entered the private hospital room. Eighty-two-year-old Alexi Sidorov was lying in his hospital bed listening to classical music on the radio. He sensed someone in the room and called out,
"Greetings. Who do I have the pleasure of?"
With her deeply British-accented voice, she addressed him. "Greetings Dr. Sidorov. My name is Cora Elizabeth Waldegrave. I

am the youngest daughter of Lord Alistair George Waldegrave and Lady Ernestine Victoria Waldegrave. I bid you greetings from the Realm of Her Majesty, Queen Elizabeth the second."

Sidorov responded curiously. "My goodness to what do I owe your, visit? After all, I've never heard of them, nor made your acquaintance?"

"Dr. Sidorov, may I close the door? What I have to say to you is secret and compartmented."

The old man's facial expression and vocal tone perked up.

"Please know that my clearance has long since lapsed."

Cora simply answered, "No worries, Professor. What I have to tell you is well within your realm of Need-to-Know."

After closing and locking the door. Cora answered him as she brought a chair over to sit by his bedside.

"Come now Alexi, you know that we in the clandestine services are in the business until the day we die."

The old man seemed to twitch. "Madame, you addressed me by my first name. That is very informal for someone I have just met. Why would you presume to do so? Your British accent suggests that you are a woman of fine breeding and culture."

She leaned into him and changed the conversation to Russian. "Alexi, my old tutor. I was always formal with you when I was under your tutelage. Only at places like visits to the Abramov residence in Brighton Beach was I allowed to be so informal."

Sidorov replied in Russian. "Madame, I have never had a British student. Who the fuck are you?"

Cora grinned and responded and stated gently. "Once upon a time, I was Leytenant Charl'z Mikhailovich Sidorov, your nephew from Murmansk."

Sidorov took a deep breath and was silent for a few moments. When the Russian cultural tutor spoke again, he remarked.

"I must be dying, and you are the soul of my old friend Moira Stewart, and you have come to guide me to heaven. Because

Mashenka has been long dead, nearly twenty years! I read about her demise in Pravda long ago."

"Alexi, I am not dead and you are not dying. That body found in the Moskva river with Mashenka's ID was a ruse by the Swiss FIS to get assassins off my trail. The Swiss spirited me to Vatican City and put me under the protective care of the Swiss Guard. Olivia Campbell, my other tutor from MI6, rescued me and gave me a new identity and a new life in England." Cora explained.

Sidorov laid quietly, obviously trying to process what had just been told to him. When he finally spoke, he simply asked. "Over the years, we heard odd stories. People claiming to have seen you. For a time, you were like the intelligence business's version of Elvis Presley and his supposed sightings."

Cora explained. "Most of it was by design to maintain a level of absurdity. It's sort of like the distractions used to keep the UFO topic matter from being taken seriously. You must remember how it all works."

"So have you had a good life in England, my dear?" Alexi asked.

"The best! An aristocratic family adopted me and gave me, in adulthood, a loving family. The family I should have had after my birth family abandoned me after I became Moira. I'm still in the business and have been working at MI6 since I disappeared. They've even had me teach modules in their field officer school." Cora clarified.

"I have one serious question for you, my dear." Alexi requested.

"Ask it of me, Alexi!" She whispered.

"Were you the one who assassinated Daniel Kramer?" Alexi queried. She replied immediately and frankly.

"My regius professor. Outside of my time in combat, I have never intentionally taken a life. Daniel Kramer was a nasty piece of work, but no, I didn't kill him. But when I heard of his demise, I certainly popped a cork and raised a toast to whoever did it."

She paused. "Alexi, you once shared with me a quote from old Joe Stalin, 'Sleep is the sweetest after you have settled an account with your enemy.'" Then she added. "I must admit to you, my teacher. I certainly fantasized, taking him out with the heavy end of a champagne bottle with simple blunt force trauma to his head. But it was merely an idle fantasy. That anonymous sniper, whomever he or she was, did the world a favor, in my humble opinion."

She was quiet for a few moments before she added. "But I must admit to you, my sleep has been the sweetest since his demise."

Alexi smiled. "I completely understand, my dear. That pleases me. You never had to tarnish your soul with that aspect of our business."

"My dear Alexi, I was told an orderly was going to bring your supper soon. I must take leave of you. Thank you for all the things you taught me and for your deep respect for my blossoming authentic self-long ago."

Cora leaned into him and kissed him on the cheek. "Goodbye, Alexi, my dear teacher." Alexi Sidorov, replied to her speaking English, "Goodbye Moira!"

She stepped over to the door and unlocked it. "Goodbye, old friend," Cora said.

As she exited the room, she passed an orderly with a cart of meals and remarked,

"Professor Sidorov is ready for his supper."

A few minutes later, Cora exited the hospital and disappeared into the masses of New York City office workers who were filling the streets on their way home.

Two days later.
Union Station, Washington DC

Mid-morning, Cora Waldegrave exited an Amtrak Commuter train, pulling a suitcase on rollers behind her. She made her way to the Metro's red line stop within the train station. With a twenty-dollar bill, she purchased a paper metro pass and boarded the next red line train going toward the Metro center. At Metro center, she boarded a yellow line bound for Ronald Reagan Washington National Airport. Cora exited at the Pentagon City Station.

She took the escalator to the surface level from the Pentagon City Metro and walked a block west until she came upon a commercial office building. She took an elevator to the top floor. The elevator car doors opened across from a pair of mahogany doors with an engraved brass plate on the door that read, "North American Surveying."

Upon entering the apparent business, a well-dressed young woman sitting behind a reception desk greeted Cora,

"Welcome to North American Surveying. How can I help you?"

Cora could clearly see that the young woman had one arm on the top of the desk and one arm under the desk. She obviously knew that the receptionist had her hand on an automatic pistol holstered under the file drawer. Cora thought to herself. *I have no clue to what this week's pass phrase is.*

Cora stated plainly, "I'm here to see Doctor Kevin Rice or General Director Laura Boyce."

The young woman said nothing. A moment later, Cora heard a distant buzzing sound. Cora thought. *She pressed the panic button.* A moment later, a man and a woman exited doors from either side of her and each were pointing Glock 17s at her head. The woman standing to her right said in a command tone,

"Slowly raise your hands. Who are you? What do you want?"

Cora simply said in her clearly British accent.
"I'm a long-lost family member and I want to come in out of

the cold?" The agents gave each other questioning looks.

"I'd like to speak to Doctor Kevin Rice or General Director Laura Boyce." Cora said, speaking up.

The woman pointing a gun at her seemed to study Cora for a moment, then ordered.

"Get Doc up here, now!" Obediently, the receptionist pressed a button on her desk phone and simply said,

"Doc, you're needed at reception, stat."

A few minutes later, a salt and pepper-haired Dr. Kevin Rice appeared behind the receptionist carrying his doctor's bag. Upon seeing the two agents pointing weapons at a woman's head, remarked.

"Whoa, what's going on here?"

"This Brit woman asked for you, doctor!" The woman agent remarked in a command tone. Dr. Rice looked at Cora with a puzzled look and answered,

"I don't have a clue who this is!" Cora smirked.

"Kevin, I once told you I couldn't date you because women are my cup of tea." She said in her clear Moira Stewart Virginia accent.

Dr. Rice winced and studied her again, and after a moment. With a stunned look of recognition uttered,

"Bless my soul, it's Moira Stewart!" Cora spoke up,

"What's wrong doc haven't you ever seen a zombie before?"

Kevin gestured with his hand for the agents to lower their weapons and commented,

"Folks, she is one of our missing-in-action and long thought dead sisters of this outfit...She's family!" Dr. Rice directed the receptionist.

"Call Director Boyce. Tell her the Tango Dancer has returned from the dead!"

An hour later, after plenty of hugs and tears with longtime OSS62 management and support team members. Moira Stewart/Cora Waldegrave found herself in a debriefing room with

Director Boyce, Dr. Rice, a duty stenographer and a handful of senior staffers who all wanted to hear the firsthand account of Mashenka Petrova's yearlong mission in St. Petersburg. Her escape for her life with the Swiss, sheltered for nearly a month with Carmelite nuns in Vatican city under the watchful protection of the Guardia Svizzera Pontificia. Finally, being rescued by Mrs. Campbell and British Diplomatic officer William Taylor.

Finally, they asked her to discuss her life in an aristocratic family in England and the non-classified aspects of working for MI6. Of course, OSS62 was respectful of her oath bound MI6 duties.

General Director Laura Boyce sat pondering. Then she asked Moira,

"How did you check to know it was safe to return to the USA? How did you know there was no longer a contract out on your life?"

Moira nodded. "In the early nineties, I used to work for old Bob Akron. During my duties, I was required to join the Lady-355 sisterhood. That membership saved my life in Russia at one point. Before I returned home to the states, I checked with the Sisterhood to see if there were still any outstanding contracts in force for sanctioning my life. They confirmed that the slate was clear."

At the end of all of it, Director Laura Boyce explained to her staff that she had assigned Moira to a detached-duty assignment with MI6 for the Russian Theater Professor mission. Finally, Boyce asserted that all of Moira's protected deep cover duties with MI6 were still part of the detached duty assignment. Director Laura Boyce finally declared that Field Officer Moira Stewart deserved sixteen years of back pay and benefits and that she was due for her retirement.

They took Moira Stewart to OSS62 personnel and processed her out like any other retiree. Provisioning provided her with up-to-date American identification documents.

Moira Stewart settled in upstate New York, became a newspaper columnist and wrote a lot of books about Unidentified Flying Objects and began speaking on the UFO circuit.

PART SIX

OLD FRIENDS

Sometime after the Covid Pandemic...
Late Morning in August-The Reunion

It had been 34 years since the two women had been in each other's physical presence. While their respective lives had been distant from each other, they had remained in casual, friendly contact. The two caught sight of each other and just stood staring across an expanse of parking lot. The nature of their former work and adventures sensibly dictated that neither of them should ever be in the same state, county, or city ever again. Yet, somehow fate or circumstance had put to two of them in the same Bed and Breakfast in the middle of nowhere in rural Illinois.

Moira Stewart was the first to break protocol, and began walking. Leila Blakely took the cue and the two old colleagues met in the middle of the parking lot and gave each other a friendly embrace. Moira whispered, "It's been too long, old friend." Leila simply moaned, "Most certainly too long."

After a lingering moment, Moira remarked quietly, "The other guests are staring. Let's go walk in the garden. It will get us both out of public view." Leila released her hug, glanced over her shoulder at several gawking on lookers among the other guests.

"Yes, let's get out of open view."

Moira led Leila over to a small footbridge and into a maze-like garden of shrubs. Once obscured by dense shrubbery,

Leila spoke up. "How did we both end up here?"

Moira began, "Out of nowhere, DC people got in touch with me," Moira explained and added, "They told me I was being booked to speak at 'The Worldwide Metaphysical Tribe' and that I must go. I hadn't a clue why, but here I am, a guest speaker. They even gave me paroles."

Leila Blakely nodded. "The same here. They contacted me too! They told me I needed to come to this event and attend as a one-day attendee on this date and they even gave me parole pass phrases as well," Leila added.

Moira groaned, "You don't think that we're being retreaded and pressed back into service? A couple of old farts like us?"

Leila closed her eyes, seeming to digest what Moira had said.

"It's a distinct but remote possibility." Leila casually remarked, while she admired some flora. Then, after a prolonged thoughtful moment, she simply stated in a hushed manner,

"Remember what they taught us in spy school? We're in the business until the day we die."

Moira sat down on a weathered bench. "Leila, we're both pensioners, for God's sakes. We're elderly, out of physical shape, and literally everything hurts."

Leila answered, "Perhaps that's the cover. We're just two old ladies on a sightseeing tour some place. A simple observe and report mission."

"... Yeah, and as old women, we're virtually invisible." Moira added.

Seated in the nook of shrubs, the two women enjoyed the peace and quiet, sitting quietly in each other's company for perhaps ten minutes. Leila casually changed the subject.

"Are your UFO books selling well?"

Moira snorted a laugh. "Yes, of course they are. It's always a hot topic." Leila turned and gave Moira a devilish grin.

"We should author a book about our team visiting that Lost city in Antarctica. It would be an over-the-top best seller!"

"Good grief, we'd never see a cent, and we'd quickly have adjoining cells in Leavenworth."

Stewart sneezed, then added, "Besides being a whistleblower, it is a game for folks younger than us."

Then Leila's jovial moment turned serious.

"Do you really think we're being retreaded?" Moira leaned forward and turned to her old pal. Speaking Russian.

"Yes, my friend. I think it might be old Cold War nonsense."

Leila simply sighed, Speaking Russian. "Yep, the old cat-and-mouse game."

An August afternoon-A Mystical Presentation by Moira

Moira and Leila had a quiet lunch where they discussed mundane aspects of their public lives. As a newspaper columnist, novelist, UFO researcher/speaker, and noted Mystic, Moira had become quite accomplished.

Leila was still a software engineer and scientist tornado researcher/chaser.

After lunch, Moira changed into her Tibetan Yogini robes to prepare for her afternoon 'Mystical Physics lecture.' Leila found Moira amusing but respectful when she saw her in her cleric vestments.

"When I heard they ordained you as some sort of Tantric shaman, I about died laughing." Leila said with a grin.

Moira moaned, "You wouldn't believe the vetting they put that poor Tibetan lama who recognized me through, to see if he was a Chinese spy. In the end, everything was legit!"

Then Moira changed the subject.

"Leila, would it embarrass you if I introduced you and briefly told my audience that you are a hero of the 1999 Antarctic incident with your doctor friend?"

Leila closed her eyes and blushed, "Sure it's ok, hell they made a television movie about it."

Deb, the esteemed curator of The Worldwide Metaphysical Tribe Conference, introduced Moira Stewart to the audience of seasoned and aspiring mystics. Yogini Moira began her talk with a brief talk about being in the right place at the right time. She began by briefly telling the audience a short story about a 1999, southern winter remote *Antarctic* research station.

During that time, the Antarctic explorers and crew were isolated from the rest of the world. In that period, the only medical doctor at the station discovered she had breast cancer. Moira explained that the only communication link to the outside world was a narrow band satellite link facilitated by a colleague scientist who was the IT manager for the wintering over expedition. She pointed to her long-time friend, Leila Blakely, and introduced her to the gathering. Leila politely arose from her seat, the audience erupted in loud applause.

After everything quieted down. Moira told the gathering that she is a seasoned public speaker about many other topics. She felt slightly timid about speaking about her mystical knowledge and her intimacy with Magickal Mechanics. Gradually, she loosened up and set her notes aside and spoke extemporaneously and expertly about her beloved subject. She requested a penny from an audience member during her talk. She suspended that penny from the side of her finger; to the amusement of the gathered mystics. Leila, always the pragmatic scientist, spoke up loudly and exclaimed, "My God, that's quantum entanglement!"

Moira mesmerized the audience for the next ninety minutes with deep meta-physical teaching and mystical conversation at the gathering. When Moira was done, she modestly bowed to an applauding crowd.

Moira, drenched in perspiration from her energetic presentation, departed the presentation space to the sound of rich applause. Leila escorted Moira to her room on the second floor of the B&B. As they climbed the stairs, Leila asked her old friend, "Does Langley know you can do that stuff?" Moira put her finger to her lips before inserting the combination on her room's door lock. Inside her B&B quarters, she quickly laid out a change of clothing. As she removed her sweat soaked yogini garb in the bathroom, she and Leila conversed through the slightly open door.

"Regarding your question about the company. Yes, they took an interest a long time ago. Those clowns wanted me to teach them how to kill someone at a distance using magick. I refused; I haven't heard from them since." Then she remarked, "I'm going to run through the shower. I'll meet you downstairs," Leila acknowledged and quietly left the room, grinning at the sound of Moira singing in her Contralto voice in the shower.

Aug 12-A visit to the Log Cabin

A refreshed Moira met with Leila and Deb, the Worldwide Metaphysical Tribe curator, in order to ride with her in a small convoy of attendee cars to visit the new site for the following year's Tribe Conference event. When the tribe arrived, the new venue turned out to be a facility called **The Lodge.** The log cabin lodging and conference facility were equal to or greater than the number of attendees at the current event.

After an impressive tour of the principal lodging building, Moira and Leila rode in a golf cart with a grounds keeper to visit the additional outer individual group mini cabins. Many members of the Tribes' groups were wandering around the various mini cabins.

Moira and Leila were standing behind one particular unique cabin that had a splendid view of a lovely stream valley. Leila wondered out loud if the stream perchance had trout for stream fishing. Moira just shook her head. "I haven't been stream fishing in over twenty years."

From behind them a woman's voice spoke, "They say from the observation deck on the Empire State Building you can see for miles." Moira and Leila paused and glanced at each other, then turned to see a middle-aged woman in resort casual attire. Moira replied to the woman, "But King Kong had a better view..." Leila chimed in and added, "from the blimp terminal on the very top."

The woman grinned and nodded. She looked over at Leila. "Hex, and Leila Blakely, I presume?" Leila nodded and countersigned the woman. "We're just a couple of long-distance voyagers." The woman replied, "I'm moody for the blues."

The woman gazed at Moira and asked, "Hmmm, this is complicated. Should I address you as Zombie and Moira Stewart or would Artifact and Cora Waldegrave be more suitable?" Moira smirked. "Moira Stewart is suitable in this setting." Leila gave Moira an odd look, and a questioned look. Moira simply remarked to Leila, "Later."

All three women politely nodded acknowledgement to each other. The Handler woman simply offered Siobhan as a name. Neither Moira nor Leila knew if it was her real name or a field cover name, only that she would be their Controller. Moira raised her voice and asked, "Can you please explain why we ended up in Lost Nation, Illinois?"

"We didn't want both of you traveling via air travel at the same time. Since Moira is a somewhat active public speaker, it made more sense to bring her here, where it would appear relatively routine and merely a few hours' drive for Leila." Siobhan explained. Leila queried, "Why didn't you want us both traveling by air?" Siobhan curtly answered, "Resource protection!"

"Resource Protection!" Both Moira and Leila busted out laughing.

Leila calmed down, "Honey, neither of us has worked together since the 80s or individually active since the mid-90s. We're both more or less retired and only working vocational interests. Didn't you people get the memo?"

Moira just bit her lip and let Leila do the heavy lifting of the conversation. Siobhan looked at Moira. "Are you going to jump down my throat too?" Moira just shook her head in the negative. "Nope, but I'd like to know why you are reaching out to us?" The field handler paused and simply remarked, "You both are still breathing!"

"Of course we're still breathing," Leila barked, "And we'd both like to stay that way!"

The two women gave Siobhan a questioning look. "Both of you had regular contact with Boris Pavel Baranov back in the day. You are the last living operatives to have had frequent contact with him and know him and can recognize him. As well as have him know and perhaps trust either of you or both of you as a friendly face."

Leila and Moira gave each other the proverbial odd looks. Leila struggled to put words to her feelings. "I haven't been active as Anya Gusev since 2001," she whispered. Siobhan looked at Moira for her thoughts.

Moira seemed to have a lump in her throat as well, as she slowly spoke up, "Technically, as a matter of public record, my cover persona as Mashenka Petrova has been dead since 1995. All the news wires reported it back in the day! I wouldn't want to scare the hell out of Pavel by showing up alive."

Leila spoke up, "Look, I think I can speak for both of us when I say with a war going on between the Russian Federation and Ukraine, neither of us are jumping up and down about travel to Russia. In the same way, I'm still relatively unknown, but Moira has gained popularity as a UFO researcher. UFO and mystical podcasts plaster her face all over the internet. If someone does a simple web search, they can easily verify her identity and blow her cover." Moira simply nodded her head in agreement.

Siobhan smiled. "I clearly understand your concerns. Let me assure you both that neither of you has to go to Russia. That won't be necessary. Baranov comes to Canada regularly on diplomatic credentials as a commerce attaché. All you have to do is to be a classic escort. Simply pick him up at the Ontario airport, make him feel welcome and shepherd him across the border and to a safe house on the American side in Morristown, NY, south of Ogdensburg. Think of yourselves as a welcome wagon."

"Does Pavel want to come and defect to the USA?" Moira

asked thoughtfully.

"Yes! He's passed several notes to the Canadians asking for a life in the United States," Siobhan answered.

Leila started shaking her head. "This feels too easy. There's got to be Russian Federal Security Service (FSB) agents attached to the embassy in Ottawa. How do we know they won't be shadowing him at the Ontario Airport?"

Moira piped up as well. "Pavel will know me the best. But if there are FSB operatives in the Ontario airport, I mean, I'm no match for those thugs. I'm a freaking old lady, for god sakes."

Siobhan commented reassuringly, "Don't worry, we'll have a Plan A, a Plan B and C if needed. All you need to do is have a friendly face and invite him to come with you to the United States. We'll work with the Canadians to get you out of the airport and into an awaiting car safely." Siobhan explained and added.

"All you have to do is greet him, make him feel at ease with you. Then get him across the border and to a safe house and chill."

Leila had by this time shifted to a pragmatic business mode. "When's all this supposed to go down?"

"Either the last week of September or the first week of October." Siobhan answered.

"We'll have up-to-date ID packages for both of your operative personas. You will both be them on paper and bold as life if someone web searches either of them." Siobhan explained.

Moira simply nodded. "I remember Pavel as a gentleman. Ok I'll help."

Leila raised her hand. "I can't have her having all the fun. I'm in too."

Siobhan took on a reserved look. "You both know the drill. We will disavow your actions if they catch you or kill you. We will give your designated dependents a sizable death benefit package and a suitable cover story."

"OK, if that's the case, I want my real identity to get a sizable obituary in the New York Times," Moira declared! Upon hearing that.

Leila seconded that! "Me too. I want that too if the worst

happens."

Siobhan grinned. "Geesh, consider it done if something goes horribly wrong. But you gals are both talented experienced operatives and your records say you are both fast and adaptable." Leila groaned,

"Fast is an exaggeration these days, adaptable perhaps." Siobhan continued with some briefing detail. Then she led the two women over to an outlying cabin marked private. Inside were two agency ID technicians who took varied photos of both women with an assortment of tops, with slight changes to their hairstyles. As well as some photos with makeup, others without, still others very dressed down.

As the two women left the cabin, Siobhan handed each of them a business card for a real estate company. "The address of the safe house is on the back. When you each get to the Morristown–Ogdensburg area, either call the number on the card and tell them you want to tour this address or just drive to it and meet your local team who will meet you and trade pass phrases with you."

Later, after the evening dinner with the Mystical Tribe participants, everybody was back at the B&B, having quiet time before the evening's events. Leila and Moira were sitting quietly in Leila's car, that was parked across from the B&B. Leila was preparing to drive home a few hours away.

Moira fixated her gaze on the large cemetery next to the parking lot, which she could see through the windshield of the parked car.

Finally, Moira spoke up, "Is that what awaits us, Leila? An enormous piece of granite with our names sand-blasted into it and our bodies tucked neatly into a couple of coffins beneath it."

Leila gave her longtime colleague a perturbed look.

"Gad, haven't you gotten morbid suddenly?" Leila remarked with a questioned tone.

"Weren't you the one who told us this afternoon we reincarnate again and again?" Moira just mumbled something about not looking forward to being a toddler or a teenager again.

Then Leila asked,

"What was that, Artifact, and Cora Waldegrave nonsense?" Moira continued to stare out at the tombstones.

"Leila, OSS62 technically listed me as missing-in-action and presumed dead for sixteen years between 1995 thru 2011."

Leila softly remarked, "I had assumed you were on a long-term mission. Where the heck were you?"

"I had been on a cover identity mission in St. Petersburg, Russia 1994-1995, the mission rolled-up and I was on the run for my life. The Guardia Svizzera Pontificia rescued and sheltered me until MI6 gave me a new identity and gave me gainful employment. For sixteen years, I was quietly living under a British identity. Until I showed up in 2011 at OSS62 HQ reappearing as Moira Stewart. They debriefed and retired me."

"Holy shit, that's when you reconnected with me in 2011. Why didn't you tell me where you'd been?" Leila asked in earnest.

Moira simply answered, "Britain was my backup plan and haven if I was still being hunted, I needed to keep that option open if I was still being hunted."

Neither woman said anything further for a few minutes.

Then Moira spoke up. "Leila, did we just screw up by volunteering to do this?"

Leila just shook her head in the negative. "Nah, we've got this. It's easy. Besides, we've both been through rougher stuff than this during the Cold War."

Moira rolled her eyes. "We were thirty or forty years younger than we are now, sweetie. But we've both volunteered, so we're committed."

Moira reached over and gave her old friend an endearing hug. "Drive safe going home."

(Speaking Russian) "Anya, I'll see you in upstate New York in a few weeks."

Oct 2-Moira Mission Prep

Saturday afternoon, in North Olmsted, Ohio; Moira Stewart received an email reminding her of a doctor's appointment. She knew full well the doctor's office, while real, was going to be an agency credentials drop and mission prep for her as well.

At close to the appointed time in the afternoon, she got into an Uber ride and rode it to the physician's office and checked in as Moira Stewart. After about 10-minutes in the sparsely occupied waiting room. She was called to an exam room. After another brief wait in the exam room, a nurse wearing scrubs entered the room.

"Good afternoon, Moira. I'm Sally from provisioning. Let's do this." The nurse held up two casual outfits.

"What's your favorite for today?"

"I'll take the slacks and fall blouse," Moira said cheerfully. The nurse handed her a large Ziploc bag.

"Here's a change of underwear. I'll be back in five, after you change. Have you had your Flu and Covid shot yet?"

Moira answered, "No."

The nurse nodded. "Okay, when I bring your travel bags and credentials package. I'll give you your Flu and Covid shots."

Moira smirked, "Okay."

The nurse left the exam room. Moira wondered to herself if the agency prep tech was really a nurse. Moira stripped and dropped each personal item of her clothing into a banker's box sitting on the counter. She turned off her cell phone, picked up her purse and placed them both in the same box.

Then she opened the package containing panties and bra and donned them. She put on the slacks and the blouse she had chosen. She took off her wedding ring and a couple of other rings and a Wiccan necklace and placed them into the Ziploc bag that had contained fresh underwear, sealed the bag, and stowed it in the banker's box. There was a knock at the door.

She answered, "Come in."

The nurse entered, carrying another purse and pulling a

carry-on suitcase on rollers. From this point on, the nurse addressed her by her mission identity.

"Masha, the travel case has a week's worth of resort casual clothing. There is one dress outfit that's a little more elegant. Just in case you need something a tad more evening wear. I threw in some cosmetics but I had my intern make them look slightly used as well. Should you choose to wear any makeup."

"Okáy." Masha answered back with a slight accent in her voice. The nurse continued,

"Your purse has all of your Petrova ID credentials, passport, travel card, driver's license, credit cards, medical plan card, library card, pocket litter, and other suitable items that fill out your life. You've got business cards for our front realty company. You are a real estate broker these days."

"My father was a Real Estate guy. I know the language and lingo," Moira remarked with a slightly stronger accent.

The nurse continued,

"Next, your cover identity cell phone has plenty of casual texts and phone numbers. Going back at least five years. There are car keys and apartment keys."

Masha asked in an accented voice,

"Are they real? Is there a car and an apartment?"

The nurse answered, "Yes to both, and they looked lived in. Your Masha car is in the rear and you should sleep in the Kamm's Corners apartment tonight and tomorrow night to help you settle into your field identity. You are to drive to the cottage safe house on Oct 3rd. We have programmed your car's GPS with all the places you need to go, including a couple of pubs and good pizza joints, on both the Canadian and American side. There is a light duty jacket and a winter coat with gloves in the back seat of the car. It's October weather up north, it can be a little weird. It might be 30 degrees and snowing or 80 degrees. Who knows?"

Masha made a thoughtful calculation in her head. Then speaking with a thicker accent,

"Da, that's going to be an all-day road trip." The nurse answered plainly.

"The front office is trying to minimize your travel footprint. Air travel would leave a significant paper trail. Besides, you'll be crossing over to Canada in this car. We wanted it to appear to be just another family car." Masha nodded in concurrence.

She thought for a moment and asked in a thicker accent and broken language, "Is the safe house provisioned with plenty of food?"

The nurse simply gave Masha a pronounced nod! To which Masha answered in Russian, "Spasibo." (Thank You)

The nurse at this point simply commented, "I'll get your shots." Then Masha asked, "What if I have a reaction to the shot while on the job?" The nurse looked at her.

"Have you had reactions to flu shots & Covid shots before?"

"Nyet!" (No) Masha answered.

The nurse shrugged her shoulders.

"I doubt you'll have a reaction to this beyond perhaps a slight fever and perhaps be a little peaked. An analgesic like aspirin should do the trick." And she added, "All the information for your guest's arrival is on your phone and should be easy to find."

The nurse walked out of the exam room, and Mashenka waited patiently. After a few minutes, the nurse returned carrying two pre-packaged syringes. She lifted the sleeve of Mashenka's shirt. She wiped a spot on the left arm with an alcohol pad and gave Masha the first injection of the flu vaccine for seniors. Then the nurse wiped a similar area on Masha's right arm with another alcohol pad and jabbed that arm with the remaining syringe with the Covid vaccine.

Finished with her chores, the nurse spoke up.

"Dr. Petrova, I believe you are all set to go on your trip. Have a safe trip, my friend. Goodbye and good luck."

Masha simply smiled and said politely, speaking Russian, "Goodbye."

The nurse left the exam room and Moira Stewart, a.k.a. Dr. Mashenka Petrova sat quietly for a few minutes and just settled herself. As she rose from her seat, she whispered to herself, speaking Russian, "Once more into the breach."

Oct 3-A Day to Kill

Mashenka slept relatively well overnight. Which is unusual, especially before a business trip. She believed that the stronger flu vaccine she got during mission preparation was causing her to sleep more deeply. Masha curled up quietly in a large, overstuffed armchair to nurse her morning coffee. She wondered how Anya was coping, especially if her colleague got the same inoculations that she did.

With her second cup of coffee, she quietly read a briefing dossier on Boris Pavel Baranov. Also in the package was a 'Shoe', a false American passport for her to give Pavel for crossing the border from Canada.

She noted that during and after the collapse of the Soviet Union from 1989 through 1992, Pavel Baranov was one of those few people who landed on his feet in the scheme of things. Of course, in the back of her mind, she suspected former bureaucrats like Baranov did better than most because they were on the inside of things and had substantial connections. He rose in the diplomatic ranks and finally settled into a secure position as an international commerce envoy.

Masha struggled to understand why someone in Baranov's position wanted to give it all up and move to the west. As her pod coffee maker hummed and buzzed, she turned a page in Baranov's dossier and saw the unvarnished truth. On the 5th of May 2019, while Pavel was in France on a trade mission. His wife, Natalya, his adult daughter, and her family died in the crash of an Aeroflot flight bound from Moscow to Murmansk. The crash event claimed the lives of 41 passengers and crew members, including them.

Masha carefully noted that state media photos of Baranov spanning four years since the accident and to the present illustrated a progressively broken man. His face, that was once happy and full of optimism, was lacking the light she had once seen in his eyes and smile. Recent media photos showed the face of a man who had lost everything he had held dear. Masha quietly sobbed for this man she once knew as she finished reading the briefing report and examining all the photos.

Later, while she showered, Masha did her best to release her sense of grief that she felt for poor Pavel. After her shower, as she sat wrapped in a terrycloth bathrobe, she resolved she was going to do her best to help her old acquaintance come to the west. But the more she thought about the situation, the more she came to her senses. She was aware of her significant limitations in terms of what she could actually accomplish.

Apart from encountering Pavel Baranov at the Ontario airport and transporting him to a secure agency hideout across the border, she realized she couldn't be more involved than that. Her Mashenka Petrova persona differed significantly from her real life. Baranov could never and would at no time know Moira Stewart, which was the reality of the situation.

Masha spent the afternoon reading a book she found in the apartment. In the early evening, she went to an online mapping website and planned her drive for her all-day road trip to Morristown, New York. She was looking forward to seeing Leila again, though it would be in her Anya Gusev persona. After she had turned the light out. She lay still in her bed. But before she rolled over to embrace slumber, she whispered a simple prayer, "Dearest Goddess, please don't let me screw up."

4 Oct-The Road Trip

Masha was up bright and early and ready to mount her road trip to upstate New York. She showered and dressed, then brewed a tall travel cup of black coffee in the pod coffee maker. She downed her morning regimen of old lady medications and a couple of full-strength aspirins since she was still feeling rough around the edges, the aftereffects of her inoculations that hit her unusually hard.

Masha, who had stayed at the apartment for two days, picked up her trash and threw the trash bag into the dumpster near the parked car. She put her bag in the trunk, along with the winter coat she was given. She also placed a tote bag for her real-life prescriptions that now reflected her field identity. Masha mumbled to herself as she opened the car door, "Here we go, back into the spy business. We're probably the first spies with Medicare cards!"

She put her travel cup in a cup holder. Likewise, she positioned a frozen bottle of water in the second cup holder. *Chilled water for later on the road*, she thought to herself.

The travel plan was straightforward enough: Interstate 90 to central New York State and then North on I-81 up to either state Route 37 or Route 12 over to Morristown.

Initially, she programed the car's GPS for Irving, NY. It's a native American reservation, an easy off ramp off of I-90. Gasoline is cheaper there, and it's the home of one of the best diners along the Interstate 90 corridor. Aunt Millie's Family Restaurant. She figured that she could have a substantial brunch there and buy a few of their impressive baked goods to take with her and top off the car's fuel supply.

The entire trip would be about six hours. After the stop at Aunt Millie's, she'd have about a four-hour drive to Morristown. She considered depending upon how hungry she was in the early evening she might stop off in Watertown, NY for a bite to eat.

As she began driving across Cleveland, she realized that the car's only radio was a combination AM/FM and satellite system. Despite her lack of enthusiasm, it functioned as a government rented vehicle. She found a couple of talk channels on the Satellite radio that kept her mind occupied as she drove. She set the cruise control for the speed limit and just stayed in the right-hand lane.

Towards evening, the auto's GPS took her off of I-81 and up the state road RT-37 to Morristown, arriving at about 6pm. Once in Morristown, she reprogramed the GPS for 17 River Launch Road. The cottage safe house was supposed to be on the St. Lawrence river.

Masha pulled into the paved parking area of the cottage; she left the motor running. She thought to herself; *it wasn't the fanciest cottage, but it was big enough to accommodate her and Anya and a couple of agencies' security folks. Of course Pavel Baranov after they bring him into the states.*

There was a large sport utility vehicle already parked there.

She wondered if she had the correct cottage. She honked the horn twice. After a couple of minutes, a man and a woman exited the house. They were perhaps in their thirties and rather athletic looking. She wondered if these were the two agency security people or perhaps someone else?

Can we help you? The man politely said. Masha spoke up, "I'm a Real Estate agent. I'm looking for number 17 River Launch road." The woman spoke up, "This is number 17, but we're renting this place for the weekend. We're expecting out-of-town friends."

Masha answered back, "Hmmm, I was supposed to stay here this weekend. Perhaps they double booked the place."

Again the woman spoke up, "Remington was told to send the pictures..."

Masha answered back, "...and Hearst sent him the war!" The man and woman grinned. The man spoke up, "Dr. Petrova I presume?"

"Yes," she said, "But Masha is fine. Whom do I have the pleasure of?"

The woman spoke up, "I'm Tuesday, and he's Thursday."

Masha giggled, "This feels like the Addams family."

Thursday spoke up, "Let me help you with your bags." Masha triggered the trunk release. Thursday promptly removed her two bags and carried them into the cottage. As Masha got out of the car, Tuesday walked over to her and began giving her the layout. "There is a large bedroom on the ground floor. We've taken that for obvious reasons. Upstairs there's a main bedroom and two nicely appointed single bedrooms down the hall. We suggest that you and Ms. Gusev take the two singles and let your esteemed guest have the main bedroom."

Tuesday gestured to Masha to follow her. The two women walked down a long private pier to a boathouse. Tuesday opened the door and led the way in. Within the boathouse there was an exquisite speedboat moored to the pier cleats on the boathouse deck.

Tuesday spoke up, "If for any reason things God forbid roll-up and it goes to hell, this is your emergency escape route. Jump in and go fast. Go down to Alex Bay, tie up at a hotel pier, and call for backup with the burner phones that are stowed in the boat."

Masha nodded. "Any weapons onboard?" Tuesday pointed at the seat next to the driver's position.

"There's a pair of Glocks in a box under the seat with extra clips and a substantial first aid kit and the burner phones to call for backup."

Masha cocked her head slightly. "Do we have a backup team in Alex Bay?"

Tuesday gave Masha an expressionless business look. "Yes, we've been told your guest is a high value asset. We're not taking any chances." Tuesday paused and then said, "If things go sideways, don't wait for me and Thursday. Get the asset out of here and to safety in Alex Bay."

Masha, expressionless, simply nodded, "Got it."

The two women left the boathouse. While walking back to the cottage, Tuesday spoke up again.

"After you pick up Ms. Gusev at the Airport, come back here promptly and I'll give her the boat instructions. Both of you must leave me and Thursday behind and get the asset to safety."

Masha simply answered, "I know the routine and have the damned tee shirt."

Upstairs in her room, Masha thought to herself. *I hope this is the cake walk that Anya had suggested it might be. Time and circumstance will tell. I'll pick up Anya at the Airport, first thing tomorrow afternoon.* She sat on the side of her bed and performed a meditation to clear her head of mission duties. Afterwards, she brushed her teeth and crawled into bed.

Oct 5-Deeds to Do, People to Meet and Anya to pick up.

Masha awoke rested! The safe house cottage was as quiet as a tomb. Masha slept soundly, no doubt because of being exhausted from a seven-hour drive. Not to mention still burning off a post inoculation reaction from her combination of Flu and Covid seasonal shots. As she lay comfortably in the bed, she caught a whiff of something in the air. After a moment recognized it as bacon! She whispered to herself, "Oh yum."

She got up and put on a robe that was hanging on the back of the door and descended the stairs and entered the kitchen. Standing at the stove wearing a long chef's apron was Mr. Thursday, attentively making bacon.

He glanced over his shoulder, "Good Morning, Dr. Petrova. I trust you slept well?"

Masha simply remarked, "I slept soundly. Is there any coffee?"

Mr. Thursday gestured toward two coffee makers and commented, "On the left, a robust dark roast. On the right a pot of delicious Kahlua flavored coffee."

Masha warmed up to the idea of a cup of flavored coffee. She walked over to the two coffee pots and opened a cabinet above them and noted a large mug, grabbed it, and poured herself a cup. Mr. Thursday added,

"There's cream and sweeteners on the dining table. Black is my preference," Masha commented and smiled.

The security officer asked, "Doc, I can make you eggs any way you want them. I also have poutine if you are into Canadian fare."

Masha stood thinking for a few moments, carefully smelling the aroma of her Kahlua flavored coffee. "I'll have three scrambled eggs, some of that bacon, and a small side of poutine. Thank you."

She wandered over to the dining room table and took a seat across from Ms. Tuesday, who was picking at her breakfast as she read an online newspaper. Masha said nothing. After perhaps ten minutes, Tuesday put her pad down, took a swig of her coffee.

"Good morning, Doctor."

Masha simply returned the courtesy and asked, "What's on tap for today besides picking up Anya Gusev at the local airport?"

Tuesday nodded a smile.

"Control wants us to go down to Alexandria Bay and introduce you to the backup team, so you are familiar with them, just in case."

Masha just nodded as she sipped her delicious coffee. Tuesday added, "I figured we could have a light lunch there to kill some time and then make our way back here to pick up Ms. Gusev."

In a business tone, Masha asked, "Do we have a firm schedule when Mr. Baranov is arriving at Ontario Airport?"

Tuesday curtly replied, "On the afternoon of Oct 6th around three."

"When do we plan to ship him out?" Masha probed. Tuesday smirked.

"Not until Sunday. Protocol guidelines suggest we keep the defecting asset for 48-72 hours as a sort of cooling-off period in case he or they reconsider and want to go back."

"What are we supposed to do with him?" Masha queried.

Tuesday simply remarked, "He's supposed to be your friend. Why not take him out and do some tourist stuff or take him to an Irish pub and get him trashed? It's your call. My briefing says he's yours and Gusev's handling until we put him on a private jet on Sunday. We're your security team. It's your job to entertain him!"

In Alexandria Bay, Ms. Tuesday and Masha parked in a metered parking place on Rock Street by the American Legion in order to not show up on traffic cameras on James Street. The two women had dressed casually and appeared like any other off-season tourist. They wore sunglasses, carried tote bags, and did their share of window shopping as they casually worked their way toward the end of James Street near Uncles Sams Boat tours. As they walked by Bay View T's, a large store fully dedicated to tee shirts. Masha stopped and stood looking at the window.

"This is my favorite tee shirt shop anywhere," Masha remarked.

Tuesday asked, "Are we going in?" Masha gently shook her head in the negative, "My real identity has been a regular customer for years. Management knows me on a first name basis. As Masha, I can't go in there."

Tuesday gave her a questioning look. "They have to see thousands of people every season. Surely, they won't know you by name."

"Nah!" Masha remarked, "My other self has designed and ordered custom tee shirts from them for years. Trust me, they know me."

Tuesday said with a smirk, "God forbid you blow your cover in a tee shirt shop!" She said, snickering.

Masha simply shifted the conversation. "Where's this pier I'm to use if we have a roll-up and things go badly and where's our backup team?"

Tuesday gestured for Masha to follow her the rest of the way down James Street to the end.

"Over to the left of us is Uncle Sam's Boat tours and the restaurant to your right is Riley's by the River. Both establishments are very visible from the water night or day." Then she pointed to a nearby pier. "If you end up here, tie up on one if these two piers. They are private, then call the backup team on the burner phone."

"Let's go back down the street and have a light lunch on the patio and meet the back-up team." Tuesday said as she walked back down James Street. Masha just smiled and joined her security chief strolling down the street. About a block away was a patio style bistro and pub. There were seven women and men dressed in casual vacation clothing crowded around a couple of tables. They were all happily enjoying each other's company with high joviality, as they all seemed to enjoy a pint of brew.

Masha, upon seeing them all, thought to herself. *My Goddess, I could be their mother and perhaps a grandmother to the two on the end.* Masha had one of those "feeling old" moments.

Both she and Ms. Tuesday grabbed the last two metal deck chairs at the table.

Ms. Tuesday leaned into Masha. "We are an aero club and you are our former flight instructor if we need cover conversation. We all know you are a pilot." Masha just grinned.

Ms. Tuesday spoke up in a loud voice, "Hi everybody. Look who I found window shopping!" All the gathering in a cheering manner yelled, "Masha!"

Before she sat down, Masha stood and seemed to scan their faces one by one. *These kids will be defending me if it all goes south. They might die for me or I might die in their arms.* She thought to herself.

Then Masha spoke up, "Seems I'm the senior pilot at the table. I'll have a half pint of whatever the rest of you, flyboys and fly girls, are drinking!"

There was a moment of silence, then the party all busted out laughing. One young man left the table and gave the server Masha's and Tuesday's order.

Tuesday spoke up. "Briefly introduce yourselves."

A woman in her thirties spoke up.

"I'm Sue, your field surgeon."

The man next to her, "I'm Tom, her field nurse as needed."

An athletic black gentleman spoke up, "I'm Todd. The guy next to me is Lenny. We're your muscle and tactical, if needed."

The next two women announced themselves as Anna and Zena, "We're ground or air transportation as required."

The last woman, perhaps in her forties, smiled, "I'm Lizbeth. I'm the mother hen of this crew. We're here to save your asset and your butts if it all goes to hell! To be perfectly honest, none of us wants to see you ever again, Masha!"

Masha lifted her right arm slightly and tapped two fingers to her right eyebrow as a subtle salute, "I hope to hell I don't see any of you again, either. But my thanks to all of you if we have to dance."

The server returned with two half pints, one for Tuesday and one for Masha. After the server left, Masha spoke up.

"My teammate Anya arrives this afternoon in Ogdensburg." She smirked at Tuesday. "With a good tail wind, and some luck, my colleague Anya and I should pick up the Asset over on the Canadian side on Friday and spirit him back to our soil and keep him safe until he's transported elsewhere."

Ms. Tuesday spoke up, "When we're sure that the Asset has gotten safely to the cottage, we'll let Lizbeth know and from that point until he's safely in the air elsewhere, you will all be on hot standby."

Masha glanced at her watch.

"Anya's flight will land soon. We best get on the road."

Ms. Tuesday nodded her head. "Yes, let's go! Best of luck to all of you."

Morning Oct 6-Mission Day

Masha awoke to the delicious smell of bacon again. She got out of bed, relieved herself, and put a warm washcloth on her face. Then left her room and proceeded downstairs to the kitchen. Again, Mr. Thursday was busy at the stove.

"Good morning, Doc, mission day." He said with a smile, "What would you like for breakfast?"

Masha stood staring at the two coffee pots. She considered the flavored coffee, but after a moment's consideration, she poured herself a generous mugful of the Dark Roast coffee.

After she did, she looked at Mr. Thursday. "I have a tradition. I always have a serious breakfast on mission days."

Thursday just nodded his head. "Sort of that last meal mindset with the unknowns of the day ahead?"

She nodded, "Yeah. Any chance I can have a robust omelet and some toast?"

Thursday simply smiled. "Yep, anything special in it?" Masha seemed distant for a few moments, then simply answered, "Surprise me."

She joined Ms. Tuesday at the dining table.

"Any word about what happened to Anya's flight yesterday?" Masha inquired.

Ms. Tuesday gave Masha a troubled look. "Can you meet Baranov by yourself at Ontario's baggage claim?" Masha rolled her eyes. "Yes, if I must. After all, I'm simply picking up an old friend at the airport! What's the bad news?"

Tuesday gave Masha a perturbed look. "These days, airlines start their equipment out west and route it eastward." "Apparently, the aircraft that was supposed to support Ms. Gusev's flight had mechanical issues and was stuck in Lincoln, Nebraska. The airline canceled the flight, and it was the one and only flight from Chicago to Ogdensburg, and Ms. Gusev was stuck at O'Hare. She got a room for the night and should be with us later today."

Masha sat shaking her head and quietly muttered,

"Der'mo." (shit) She sat nursing her coffee for a few minutes in deep thought. "What's our Plan B?"

Tuesday gave her a troubling look. "There is no plan B for this. We didn't expect Gusev's flight being canceled. We made multiple plans for a variety of upsets at the Ontario airport, but not this."

"Originally, Anya was supposed to be my driver. Why can't you be my driver? You're young enough to be my adult daughter. We could make this a family affair," Masha suggested.

Tuesday looked very pained. "I'm not a field operative like you are. I don't have field operative credentials like you do. With no passport, I can't go across the border."

Thursday walked over to the table with a plate.

Masha looked at the omelet on the plate. "What is it?"

Thursday simply said, "A three-egg omelet with Swiss cheese, bacon, sausage, pepperoni and some zucchini. The toast is sour dough bread with butter and cinnamon."

Tuesday looked at her teammate, "Get yourself a cup of coffee and sit with us and help us think out a fix to our situation." Thursday stepped over to the counter by the stove and retrieved his coffee and rejoined the two women at the table.

Masha looked at Thursday. "I don't suppose you have field credentials?" He shook his head in the negative.

Masha dug into her omelet and sat quietly, thinking as she munched on her breakfast. After a couple of mouthfuls, Masha swallowed and spoke up.

"Ok kids!" Masha remarked to the surprise of both Tuesday

and Thursday. "The name of the game in the spy business is to always give yourself options. Adopt a pessimistic mindset that something will always go wrong and be prepared to adapt, adapt and adapt again to the cards you're dealt."

Masha explained and added, "I've been out of the business so long I had almost forgotten my old cold war mission mantras."

Mr. Thursday gave Masha a raised eyebrow and asked, "What are your old mantras?"

Masha gave her safe house security team a pragmatic look. "First: Nothing Ever Works Right!"

"and Second: Some Problems You Can Throw Money At!"

Afternoon Oct 6-Mission Day-Canada
3:15 pm Ontario International Airport, Canada

Dr. Mashenka Petrova stood patiently near the bottom of an escalator in the Baggage Claim area used by the Russian Airline Aeroflot. She was wearing a snappy fall ensemble of a blouse and skirt. Next to her stood a professionally dressed limousine driver, who held a large white card. The top line of the card read "Баранов" which was the name Baranov in Cyrillic. Below the Cyrillic, it spelled the name Baranov out in English. Both Call-outs of the man's name were in six-inch-high letters.

Finally, after about thirty minutes of watching, over a hundred people descend the escalator. Masha caught sight of the older version of her old friend Pavel Baranov about halfway down the moving staircase. She watched as Baranov finally noticed the limousine driver holding the name card with his name on it. Baranov then seemed to notice a gray-haired woman in a light orange blouse and brown skirt waving at him. Baranov looked puzzled until he suddenly Masha could see a moment of recognition that gave way to light in the old man's eyes and a smile on his face. He walked over to her, speaking Russian, "Masha Petrova, is that you after all this time?"

She flung her arms around her old friend and whispered in

his ear, speaking Russian,

"Yes, it's me Pavel." Baranov pulled back from her a little and questioned,

"Masha, you are supposed to be dead. I read about it in Pravda, I read about it in all the news wire stories, they all said the tango dancer was dead! They pulled your body from the Moskva river almost thirty years ago!"

"Pavel, my old friend from Chernobyl. I'm here to take you to a new life in America!"

He asked speaking Russian, "Truly?"

Masha smiled broadly, speaking Russian, "We danced the last waltz of the first set at the Embassy Ball. I whispered in your ear then that I was real! Now I will tell you again, truly! I am real! Just as real as that last piece of poisonous cheesecake we had in the American Café in Washington."

Baranov spoke up, "I should get my bag."

Masha asked firmly, "Pavel, do you really need that bag? I'll buy you new clothes!"

Baranov gave her an urgent look in the eye and, shaking his head in the negative, spoke Russian, "No!"

Masha broke the friendly embrace and took Baranov's hand firmly and said,

"Go now" to the limousine driver. All three quickly left the baggage claim area outside to the awaiting limousine. Once inside, the driver wasted no time in driving away.

Masha then directed the limousine driver, speaking French,

"Drive around the airport access loop road three times to avoid us being followed, then head to the Bridge to America."

As the limousine driver meandered through the traffic orbiting the airport's departure and arrival gates. Pavel leaned into Masha and softly commented in English,

"You directed that like an expert professional, Masha." Masha briefly grinned at him and winked and directed the driver to head to the Bridge to America. She reached into her purse and removed two American passports. She glanced at both. Masha kept hers and handed Pavel the other American passport.

"My friend for this border crossing, you speak English only if questioned and you are now Yuri Petrov, my older brother! Do you understand?"

Pavel, amused, replied, "I absolutely do, my dear little sister!"

When the limousine driver drove up to the passport check, he handed the border clerk officer his Canadian passport. Then he moved the auto up a few feet and lowered the rear window. Masha said "Hello" and handed both passports to the clerk. The clerk looked at both of them, then the pictures in the passports. She placed both passports on a scan, both of them dinged. Then the clerk looked at both of them and handed the passports back to Masha and commented,

"Welcome home!"

Masha simply smiled and said, "Thanks."

The limousine driver drove on.

Pavel looked at Masha, "Now what?"

Masha smiled, "Now we drive around town for about twenty minutes to be sure we're not being followed and then I will drive you in my car to a secure dwelling."

Pavel winced, "What kind of secure place? A prison? A military base?"

Masha shook her head, "No, my friend, a lovely cottage on the St. Lawerence River. In a few days, my team will take you to a lovely new home."

Evening Oct 6-Mission Day-Unique American Experience

Ogdensburg 5:37 PM–The Frederic Remington Art Museum

The limousine driver drove up State street and turned into a large parking lot behind the Remington Art Museum. The driver got out of the vehicle and opened the rear doors, allowing both Masha Petrova and Pavel Baranov to exit. Masha stepped over to the limousine driver, shook hands with him and simply said, speaking French, "Thank you so much, sir." As she palmed him a tip of two hundred dollars (US). The limousine driver tipped his hat to her, closed the open doors on the limo and drove away.

Pavel gave Masha a perplexed look,

"What's next, Masha?"

She grinned at him, "Pavel my friend, I'm going to give you a uniquely American experience."

She had parked her car behind the Remington Art Museum and led him over to it. As the two got into the car.

Pavel curiously asked, "What is this unique American experience?" She started the car and then she put the car into gear.

"I'm taking you shopping for clothing at Walmart!" she Remarked.

After a short drive, Masha drove into the Walmart plaza on the Ford street extension. The wide selection of clothing fascinated Pavel in the store. After trying on a couple items for size, Masha helped Pavel select several golf shirts, two white button up shirts, a couple of ties and several pairs of pants and two belts. She helped him select a medium-weight jacket and a heavier coat in case the weather turned cold. Pavel decided on plain boxer shorts, tee shirts, and socks for his men's undergarments. Masha selected a suitcase. Then she took him to the toiletries area and selected travel size items suitable for a business trip. She had a feeling the agency hospitality team would properly equip Baranov once they settled him.

Finally, Masha asked Pavel,

"Do you shave with soap, water, and razors, or with an electric shaver?"

He simply commented, "electric."

After a few minutes in the small appliance department, Pavel selected an electric shaver.

Finally, Masha wheeled the cart to the cash out area. As the two waited in line, Pavel leaned into her and whispered,

"I will pay you back once I'm settled."

She smirked. "No need, my friend. This is the least I could do to get you out of the airport safely."

After they cashed all the items out, Masha removed a credit card from her purse and paid the cashier. While her purse was open.

Pavel asked, "May I see your driver's license?" He read it and asked, "It says you live in Cleveland, Ohio. That's a very long way from here, I assume." He queried as he handed the driver's license back to her. As the cashier was bagging up the clothing and other items.

Masha casually remarked, "About five hundred miles."

Back in the parking lot with all Pavel's items.

Masha looked at him. "Now I'm going to take you to a lovely cottage and a really pleasant home cooked meal."

Masha drove the car out on to route 37 and headed back to Morristown. Pavel was quiet and just seemed interested in taking in the countryside's view as they drove back. As they passed a residential area, Pavel observed a large white sport utility vehicle with a large green stripe on the side labeled Border Patrol.

"Oh, my! The border patrol! Masha, are they looking for me?" Pavel asked urgently.

Masha simply said, "No, they are watching for trucks illegally trafficking people."

Finally, in the Morristown area, Masha turned off of route 37 and onto River landing road and proceeded to the cottage. As Masha pulled up and parked the car. Ms. Tuesday and Mr. Thursday exited the cottage.

Tuesday gave Masha a concerned look. "We were getting worried."

Masha shook her head. "We exited baggage claim in a hurry and Pavel had no clothing, so I took him shopping."

Tuesday rolled her eyes. "You should have come straight back here. We could have sent out for his clothes."

Masha shrugged her shoulders, "The shopping trip was just what he needed to get his mind off the stress of what we just accomplished."

Tuesday gave Masha a curious look. "So, the commercial

limo thing worked?"

Masha nodded in the affirmative. Then Masha asked, "Any chance we could get Sue the Field surgeon or the Nurse up here to check him out? He's been under a bit of stress and he's not exactly a spring chicken."

Tuesday nodded, "Sure thing. Dinner will be ready shortly."

Evening Oct 6-Mission Day-A Quiet Dinner Party

Mr. Thursday had spent the day fussing over a serious Welcome to the USA - Thanksgiving meal. He had thawed a 20-pound turkey over the past few days and put the entire works together with all the trimmings to celebrate a successful mission and to welcome Pavel Baranov to the USA.

After a lively dinner party, Masha and Ms. Tuesday did the dishes and put the kitchen in order. In thanks for a wonderful meal, Masha and Ms. Tuesday rewarded Mr. Thursday with a tall glass of wine.

Anya Gusev had finally arrived, and she sat down with Pavel and endured several intense games of chess. Each of which she lost. Which was very embarrassing for her. Especially considering that she had been a championship chess player during her university days. Pavel was very gracious and told everyone that Anya had given him a run for his money. Masha knew full well that Pavel, if he hadn't been so deeply involved with his government career, could have been and should have been one of the prominent Russian chess masters of the seventies and eighties.

Because they gave Mr. Thursday the night off. Anya stayed up and planned to do the overnight security watch until Ms. Tuesday relieved her around 4am.

After they did the dishes, Ms. Tuesday went to bed and Masha sat down with Pavel for a quiet game of chess, a game she expected to lose in under ten moves. She remarked to her old friend, "You have white please begin." As they started their game,

Pavel asked her, "So, are we going to play chess all

weekend?"

"No, I have other plans." She remarked just before Pavel took her rook.

"Please share with me your plans," He requested.

She moved a pawn, then commented, "There's this great bookstore about thirty miles from here and it is very exclusive, in that it's in a barn and is only open on weekends."

Pavel took his eyes off of the chessboard and smiled broadly, "That sounds like a delightful and rustic place."

Again, Masha made a move, and he countered it and took one of her pieces.

"My dear Pavel, it's more rustic than you think. The public toilet is a hole in the ground, inside an outhouse."

Pavel stopped and gave her a serious look. "Truly?"

Masha, with a straight face, nodded in the affirmative. "I've used it many times when I've visited there."

"I'm looking forward to visiting this special bookstore. Checkmate." He stated plainly.

Masha studied the board and realized she had left herself wide open. She nodded and reached across the chessboard for a handshake.

As they shook, Pavel remarked, "You used to play much better. I remember you as a force to be reckoned with."

Masha simply answered, "I haven't had a challenging opponent for decades."

Pavel grinned, "My dear, you just needed a competent Russian master as an opponent!"

"Would you like something soothing before you go to bed?" She asked. He gave her a curious look.

Masha explained, "Its piping hot tea water mixed with a heaping tablespoon of decaf instant coffee and a heaping tablespoon of sugar free powdered chocolate mix. It's called Mocha."

He shrugged, "Most certainly. I've got a new life now! I might as well try new things!"

Masha filled and put a kettle on and put heaping

tablespoons of both decaf instant coffee and sugar free powdered chocolate mix into two coffee mugs. When the teapot whistled, she poured the steaming hot water into both mugs. Then she stirred the contents of each mug.

She handed a mug to Pavel.

He sniffed and sipped the hot brew. "Is good!" He remarked and smiled. Masha raised her mug high.

"Welcome to America, my old friend!"

Pavel clinked his mug gently to Masha's, "Da!" (yes)

Oct 7- Zero dark Thirty-The Patio Party

Masha descended the cottage stairs and entered the kitchen. Mr. Thursday was dutifully working on breakfast for the relatively large party of folks in this cottage. Masha poured herself a cup of coffee and took a seat with Ms. Tuesday.

"How was the security watch?" Masha asked.

The security officer remarked, "It was going fine until Anya had a carload of college kids drive on to the property thinking the place was off season with nobody around and the perfect place for a patio party. They quickly drove off when they saw she was packing a service pistol!"

Masha, blowing on her hot coffee, remarked,

"Hopefully that was that."

Tuesday shook her head. "Not by a long shot. After I came on watch, two sheriff's deputies showed up and when they saw me with my side arm; they drew their weapons and had them pointed at me!"

"Oh, my God!" Masha whispered.

Ms. Tuesday continued, "They ordered me to set my weapon quietly in the grass and show them ID. It shocked them to see my agency badge and my photo ID card."

"Did they apologize?" Masha queried.

"No!" Tuesday griped. "They didn't believe my ID was real and wanted to arrest me for impersonating a federal officer." Masha had a shocked, disbelieving look on her face.

Tuesday continued, "Fortunately, Anya was still up and walked outside holding up her agency badge and ID and announced that they were jeopardizing a National Security operation."

"They both lowered their weapons. The senior of the two officers broke out his cell phone and called the night number on the back of my ID. After he told them my name and Anya's names, the officer got a really sober look on his face and holstered his weapon and told his fellow deputy to follow suit. As he got off his phone, he apologized, as did the other officer."

"My god, are we compromised?" Masha asked in a serious tone.

"No, I simply pointed my finger at them and told them they were to never mention that we were here and to forget they ever saw us because we were never here! They both nodded, appearing extremely scared. They each got in their patrol cars and left the area." Tuesday finished recounting.

Masha gave Tuesday a look as serious as a heart attack. "Hon, we need to move the asset. Like first thing in the morning! I mean, if either of them says something on social media. We'll be up to our butts in FSB operatives tomorrow!"

Ms. Tuesday hung her head for a few moments to ponder Masha's serious concerns.

Then she spoke up, "Let's assume that Andy and Barny are honorable guys and will keep their mouths shut. But to your concern, let's assume that all those kids who reported it all to the sheriff's dept. Posted their adventure on social media an hour or two ago. To your concern, we're going to be up to our asses in teens and others coming down here to have a look-see or FSB agents or both in a few hours. This could be a serious cluster fuck! We need to bug out asap! Masha, go! Get everybody up asap, we're leaving."

As Masha rose and asked, "Where are we bugging out too?"

Tuesday remarked, "Choices, there are plenty of empty off-season motels in Alex Bay or Clayton. We could literally give some ma and pa motel joint a windfall off season booking."

Masha thought for a few moments, "I've got one better! Call down to Fort Drum. They're a half hour or forty minutes away down I-81. Tell their intel people we need to move an asset to a secure location ASAP. Asked them if we can use some of their visiting officers' lodge quarters."

Ms. Tuesday lit up. "Love it. Start waking everybody up. I'll call our operations folks and have them arrange it ASAP." Masha ran upstairs and began rousting everyone. Ms. Tuesday grabbed her secure satellite phone and began dialing.

Morning Oct 7-Cowboys, Oaths

Anya put Pavel's suitcase in the trunk of Masha's car. Masha followed suit and placed her own carry-on style suitcase in the trunk as well. Masha gave Anya a curious look. "Do you want to ride with me and Pavel?"

Anya shook her head. "I think he's feeling nervous with us bugging out and all. You were always a deeper friend to him than I was. I think he needs his friend right now."

She paused, seeming thoughtful, and added, "Besides, I think we should break this conga line up."

Masha gave her scientist friend a curious look. "Conga line?"

Anya nodded. "Let's suppose we're being watched out there on the state road. If we all pull out of here together, six vehicles traveling together convoy fashion. It's going to be noticed for what it is. Why don't we play the shell game? You drive down to one of the other empty cottages and quietly park there for perhaps thirty minutes or maybe an hour. Then you leave and head out a different way. You were talking about taking him to the Remington Museum. Why not do that! Then, when you are done, take the long way around, out towards Canton and Potsdam. You've got a GPS, spend the day admiring the fall leaves, but take all the three-digit minor roads. Use an illogical, off the beaten path route to get to Fort Drum. If, God forbid, we get jumped traveling there, neither of you will be at risk if we have to mix it up with whomever."

Of course, Masha considered what her long-life friend had

suggested for a few moments.

"Good point, my dear. I see the logic in it."

Anya reached over and hugged her friend and colleague. "I heard on the radio that there is trouble in the middle east again and it's pretty vicious stuff. My friend, the world is going to hell in a handbasket as usual and the middle east is leading the way. All we can do is try to keep the peace in our little corner of it."

Anya could see Masha's eyes welling up in tears.

Masha spoke with a choke in her voice, "This mission was supposed to be easy. We both know they never really are, are they?"

Anya released her embrace and shook her head. "Yeah, they always roll-up and go sideways, don't they, Masha? You take care of Pavel, and I'll do my best to protect the rest of the team."

With appreciation, Masha softly said,

"Anya, until our next mission!" Anya put two thumbs up in front of her.

"Until our next mission, Masha!" Anya walked toward the cottage. Masha took a few minutes to compose herself before going into the cottage to get Pavel.

Within ten minutes, Masha and Pavel were in Masha's car and were driving down to the end of the River Landing Road. They sat parked behind some bushes and they watched as five vehicles pulled away and drove out to the state road. Masha started the stopwatch feature on her phone, which was on airplane mode. After thirty minutes, she started the car and drove out of River Landing Road.

She turned left and drove north on state Route 12 toward Ogdensburg. After she got to Ogdensburg proper, she took a couple of odd turns onto lesser used streets to find her way to Washington St. and the Frederic Remington Art Museum.

As Pavel got out of the car, he stood admiring the stately mansion that was the Museum building. He asked Masha. "Did Mr. Remington live here?" Masha smiled, "No, he didn't, but his wife did several years after his death."

During the tour, Pavel got very excited when he realized

that Fredric Remington lived out west in the 19th century and captured the old west in his sketches of Cowboys, Indians, US Army cavalry soldiers, and such. He carefully studied the over a century old artwork of the long-dead Mr. Remington, fascinated by it.

In one nook displaying Remington's work, Pavel noted an inked drawing of Russian soldiers from the era of the Russo-Japanese War, which was fought between the Empire of Japan and the Russian Empire during 1904 and 1905.

"It was a silly war by the Czar, with his foolish imperial ambitions in Manchuria." Pavel grumbled. Masha said nothing, respecting the opinions of her old-time cold war era former Soviet friend.

About twenty minutes later Pavel and Masha were in the second level of the museum studying a display of early 20th century cut glass bowls made by the famous H.P. Sinclaire & Company of Corning, New York.

Out of nowhere, Pavel commented,

"So, my old friend, are you ever going to tell me of your real identity and share with me whom you really are and your real life?"

Masha about choked. "Pavel, you understand the business as well as I do. We both took security oaths."

"Yes, Yes we both entered a life where our loved ones and everyone we hold dear would never know what we did for our respective countries." He casually remarked.

Masha closed her eyes. "Pavel, my old friend, I'm still bound by those oaths. Hell, my blood family doesn't even know that I can play chess or that I speak Russian or where I've been. Pavel, you literally know more about me than my blood family."

Pavel remarked. "Yes, I truly do. I also know you are someone globally known as Moira and you are renown for your research work about UFOs and the little grey fellows from another dimension. I've seen you on countless YouTube videos. You are informative and have a delightful and humorous presentation." Masha stood wordless and thunder struck!

Afternoon Oct 7-Reality of One's Life

Both Masha and Pavel were back in her car and on State route 68 headed toward Canton, NY En route to Potsdam and the Birchbark Bookshop. Pavel regretted revealing that he knew Masha's real identity. Masha hadn't said two words to him since the two had gotten in the car back at the Remington Art Museum.

Masha put on the Satellite radio and kept her thoughts to herself. In Canton, her GPS directed her to a route she hadn't taken before. Thinking this might be a faster route, she went with the GPS suggestion. As she drove, the two-lane state route eventually degraded down to a single lane paved country road. When she was less than four miles from the rural bookstore, the road suddenly turned into a tiny dirt road in the middle of the woods.

Petrova bitched out loud, "I should have driven into downtown Potsdam and taken Ashton Rd. from the city center!" Pavel just looked around at the fall leaves in the thick woods all around them.

"Well, if your plan has been to hide from the Russian FSB or their associates. Then you certainly have done a wonderful job. With these woods, not even satellites could track us."

She stopped the car, frustrated and cussing in Russian.

Pavel remarked, "Thank you for stopping. I need to relieve myself. I'll be right-back, old comrade." He exited the car and walked behind some bushes.

Masha continued to pound in frustration on her steering wheel, still cussing in Russian. Pavel returned and opened the car door and got back in the auto.

"I'm surprised you didn't drive off and leave me stranded in the woods." He joked. Masha said nothing. Pavel then casually offered,

"The bushes are rather thick if you care to relieve yourself.

I promise I won't look."

Masha let out a sigh. "The bookstore's out-house is only about a mile down the road. I think I can hold it until then."

There was a pause. After a few moments, both of them busted out in loud laughter.

After some laughing, Masha put the car back into gear and drove to the end of the dirt county lane that ended at Ashton Rd. About 700 yds down Ashton road was a white sign hanging on a post that read, Birchbark Bookshop. Masha parked the car, gestured for Pavel to follow her behind the Barn-like-building. There was a tiny structure with a weathered white door. Masha looked at Pavel and gave him a grin.

"I'll be right back." She opened the white door to the tiny building and inside was a large bench-like structure with a varnished wooden toilet seat and a seat cover. She stepped inside the structure and closed the door.

When she exited the out-house, she spoke to Pavel in a firm voice, "When we reconnect with the team at the Army base. You must call me Masha or Mashenka. Call me by my real name and I'll be in a lot of trouble. It also might affect your status."

Pavel nodded respectfully. "My dear lady, I understand the game we must play. I have no intention of exposing your cover. Besides, nobody would really care who or what you are these days, especially since you have retired from the bigger game. I simply wanted you to know that you don't have to keep up the charade with me when we're in private."

Masha nodded and accepted him at his word. After all, she held his life in her hands and he had her life in his hands. The bond of trust benefited them both.

Then Masha spoke up, "Come, let me show you the world's coolest bookstore." She walked over to what appeared as a back door to the building and the two entered. Inside, the owner smiled and looked at Moira/Masha and remarked,

"Nice to see you. It's been ages!"

She simply returned the greeting and then walked Pavel through an uncommon bookstore that was heated with a wood stove. Masha showed him all the various rooms and their collections, both on the ground floor and in some upper spaces.

After browsing for an hour, Pavel ended up with two books in his hands, while Masha had three. The proprietor added all the used books up and told Masha the amount; she opened her purse and paid in cash. After they left the building and walked to the car.

Pavel remarked, "It was wise to pay with cash."

She smirked, "The bookstore is a cash only operation! The proprietor is a retired university professor."

Back in the car, Masha looked at a road atlas and made some decisions related to their meandering route down to Fort Drum. I'm going to top off our gas back in Potsdam, then we're going to joy ride through the country roads.

Pavel spoke up, "How far is this Army base?"

Masha simply answered, "about sixty miles straight down Route 11, but I'm going to wander down there on a bunch of minor routes to stay off the grid of the main highways. If I do this right, we'll come to the back gate of the base and away from prying eyes."

Oct 7 21:17 hours -Delivery of the Asset

Masha pulled the car over to the side of the road about two miles from the rear gate to Fort Drum. She turned off the engine.

"Pavel my friend, once we go through that gate, I'll have to hand you off to the base intelligence people who will see that you are comfortable until my agency can fly in and take you to processing and get you resettled."

Pavel gave her a disappointed look.

"You won't be able to go with me?" She shook her head. "My job was to meet and greet you at Ontario airport, spirit you across the border to the USA and to keep you safe and entertained. Until I could deliver you to a competent authority."

Shaking his head slowly, Pavel asked,

"So, they will give me a new identity and a new life?"

Masha, trying to hold back tears, "Yes."

He studied her face. "I suspect we'll never get to see each other again."

Masha choked a bit. "That would break protocol for me. I would get in serious trouble."

He wrinkled his nose, "But you are retired. The USA is supposed to be a free country?"

Masha thought for a minute, then remarked,

"From time to time, I have spoken a few words of Russian on a UFO Podcast or while greeting my UFO conference audience in Russian. If by some chance I were at a UFO conference somewhere and encountered a serious fan of my UFO research who greeted me with a polite 'Privet, tovarishch' (Hello comrade), perhaps I might consider having lunch or dinner with that fan." He smirked at her and gave her a slight nod.

She started the car and silently drove the two miles to the back gate at Fort Drum. A woman army sergeant stepped out of the reception building.

"Good evening, ma'am. Can I help you?"

Mashenka Petrova held up her agency badge and ID card and remarked,

"Base Intelligence is expecting me with a package." The soldier directed her flashlight onto the badge and ID card.

"Ma'am, I need your ID card for a minute." Masha handed it to the sergeant. Both Masha and Pavel watched the woman soldier make a phone call and held the ID in front of herself and read it to someone on the phone. The sergeant seemed to listen, then nodded.

She stepped back out to the car and handed Masha her ID card back.

"Ma'am, they are sending over a protective detail to escort you. They also said to tell you they are so thrilled that you arrived safely. When I open the gate, please drive over to that reserved parking place and wait." The sergeant gestured, and another soldier pushed a lever and the gate opened as Masha drove into the reserved parking slot.

The sergeant blew a police whistle and several soldiers emerged from the building holding automatic weapons, encircling the car that was turned in the opposite direction. Again, the sergeant walked back over to Masha's car window.

"Ma'am, this is a precaution. Hostile forces suspected that the other team had the package. Base intel will fill you in."

Masha rolled up her car window and looked at Pavel with a horrified look. Pavel gave her an equally concerned expression. Neither of them uttered a word. Within minutes, several army jeeps with armed soldiers and an armored personnel carrier drove up. An Army Major walked over to the car.

Masha rolled down the window. "Dr. Petrova and Mr. Baranov, I presume?" Masha held up her badge and ID card again.

The major shined his flashlight on to her credentials and nodded, then the major flashed the flashlight in the car at both of them.

"Dr. Petrova and Mr. Baranov, your other escort team came under serious assault by an armed party of criminal subcontractors, apparently hired by the Russian FSB. We need you both to follow me and ride in the armored vehicle."

Masha and Pavel exited her car and followed the Major to the armored personnel carrier. Once inside, the officer buckled up and gestured for them to fasten their seat belts. The door closed, and the vehicle began moving.

Masha spoke up, "Was anybody hurt?"

The officer hesitated, then spoke, "Of the ten in the escort party, six were killed. Two more are in critical condition. Two more of the team had minor injuries. They successfully neutralized the hostiles but obviously sustained substantial losses themselves. Your agency has directed us to keep you secure and comfortable. We'll put you both up in guarded quarters in the base underground command center until your agency folks fly in first thing in the morning."

08:00 hours Oct 8-The Debriefing

An army corporal had awoken both Pavel and Masha. After both had freshened up, he escorted the two of them to a dining area for both of them to have breakfast.

The Major who had brought them to the underground facility the night before approached Masha and Pavel at their table carrying a steaming cup of coffee. As he did, he greeted them in flawless Russian,

"Dobroye utro." (Good Morning) The two looked up from their meals, smiled and returned the greeting in Russian. Then Masha spoke up,

"We both speak English, Major." He grinned as he sat down. "I'm just trying to keep my language skill sharp."

Pavel spoke up, remarking,

"You have a slight northern accent."

He responded,

"My language teacher was originally from Moscow."

Masha cut right to business.

"Any word about how soon my agency team will arrive?"

The Major nodded.

"They should land in a helo within the hour!"

Masha looked content with that answer. Then she asked,

"Who survived the ambush?"

The Major answered promptly,

"The critically injured were the field surgeon and one of the tactical techs. The two with minor injuries were operatives, Ms. Tuesday and Ms. Anya Gusev."

Pavel put his hand on Masha's shoulder to reassure her.

Masha's eyes were closed, doing her best to fight back tears.

Then the major asked her,

"Ms. Petrova, what made you take off on your own with Mr. Baranov? Wasn't that risky?"

She began,

"Ms. Gusev and I figured someone had blown our location after some college kids visited our cottage. We figured it would be all over social media, so we moved. Ms. Gusev suggested I leave with Mr. Baranov well after the convoy left and sneak around on the north country back roads."

"Obviously, the plan worked." The Major commented.

A private approached the party and whispered to the Major. The officer nodded and addressed Pavel and Masha.

"Your team is here. They are being escorted over to this facility." The Major explained.

Twenty minutes later Pavel Baranov and Mashenka Petrova sat quietly waiting in a secure briefing room. In walked the senior official Masha had only known only as Siobhan from the meeting at The Lodge in Lost Nation, Illinois. With the woman were several other men and women.

Siobhan Allen introduced herself and remarked, "You deserve a medal for getting Mr. Baranov here safely. Especially under the unfortunate circumstances."

Baranov spoke up, "She most certainly does!" Masha shook her head, "It was Anya Gusev's idea to break up into two parties and for me to wander around on the back roads."

Again Baranov spoke up, "Madame, they both deserve a medal!"

Siobhan gave Baranov a serious look, nodded and remarked, "Duly noted, Mr. Commerce Attaché. We have a helo waiting to take you to a secure retreat somewhere in West Virginia, sir. You two should say your goodbyes now."

Pavel Baranov turned to Masha, speaking Russian.

"Goodbye my old Friend" as he extended a handshake. Masha got a disturbed look on her face.

Speaking Russian.

"Oh, forget that protocol nonsense!" She remarked as she stepped over to him and wrapped her arms around him and gave him a kiss on the cheek.

"Farewell, my old friend."

Masha stepped back from him and assumed an attentive posture. Then she rendered Baranov, a former Soviet Fighter Pilot, a crisp salute. He appeared taken aback by her military courtesy. Baranov also assumed an attentive posture and returned her salute. He bowed slightly to Siobhan.

"Madame, I am prepared to leave with your associates."

Siobhan nodded and gestured to her support staff. Baranov left the briefing room with his escorts.

Siobhan turned and looked at Masha, who was quiet but still obviously crying.

"Masha, it's one of the toughest parts about our jobs and the mission relationships we establish." Siobhan commented.

Masha excused herself, went to the women's room, and composed herself. She returned to the briefing room and by this time, an Army Intelligence stenographer had joined Ms. Siobhan. Masha sat down and spent the next ninety minutes being debriefed.

After the stenographer left the room, Ms. Siobhan relaxed and chatted with Masha informally. Finally, after a few minutes of quiet conversation, she opened her briefcase and handed Masha an airline ticket.

"You fly back home and get back to your real life." Ms. Siobhan told her. Then she added.

"I must tell you honestly that I had grave concerns about sending you and Anya on a mission after so many years of retirement. But you both did a brilliant job."

The agency officer paused, then queried,

"Would you be up for some light duty assignments in the

future?"

Masha smirked,

"Yes, I would." She added, "Most certainly no long-term assignments but shorter less than a month assignments. Absolutely, I'd love to be back in the game again!" The two women shook hands.

An hour later, Masha and Anya sat in the back of an Army staff car and quietly and privately shared each other's adventurous moments from this assignment. They were both driven to Syracuse International Airport for flights back to their respective homes.

The agency flew the two women to Washington, DC, six months later and secretly presented them with Medals for their irregular post-retirement mission service.

Sometime later...

Palm Springs, California, Moira Stewart, was signing UFO books in the vendor suite of the huge UFO Convention: 'Contact in the Desert.' As she was finishing autographing one of her books.

A male voice from behind her said,

"Privet, tovarishch." Moira closed her eyes and simply spoke up.

"Hello old friend."

The End

EPILOGUE

Mary Allen, a network news correspondent, won an Emmy for her interview with Professor Mashenka Petrova in 1994.

Fiona McKenzie became the Director of Forensics at L3S in 1998.

Joyce Pemberton Anderson became the Director of L3S in 2005.

Noah Brunner of the Guardia Svizzera became the Commandant-Director of the Sondergarde in 2001.

Deputy Director Maureen Henderson became OSS62 Director, after the assassination of OSS62 Director Daniel Kramer in 1998. The post 911 investigations and reorganization of the intelligence community forced Maureen Henderson of OSS62 into retirement in 2002.

Moira Stewart, An OSS62 promotion selection committee, did not choose Moira Stewart for the position of Controller of Field Operations in 1993. She continued her work as an analyst of Russian culture. In her cover identity as Professor Mashenka Petrova, she went on a multi-year cover identity maintenance assignment to a Circus and Theatrical Arts Academy in St. Petersburg, Russia in 1994. Russian and European media reported she was a manager, instructor and performer in an Academy Traveling Circus 1994-1995. The Russian Newspaper 'Pravda' reported her death prominently on 28 May 1995. The newspaper quoted the Moscow Municipal Militsiya as attributing her death to 'horrific foul play'. They reported that her body was found floating in the Moskva river.

Katherine Van Helsing is a British journalist for 'Notable People Magazine.' Asserted in her 1996 book 'The Cover Up' that retired Bolshoi dancer Nikolai Antonov, and Theater professors Tamara Koltsova, and Mashenka Petrova; were assassinated in a Moscow Café on May 25th, 1995, by a Russian underworld (Bratva) rooftop sniper.

OSS62 and L3S, intelligence sources within the Russian Bratva underworld network, claimed that Petrova was the victim of a kidnapping in the Russian City of Orenburg, in the Ural mountains. Those underworld sources reported that the Russian FSB took Petrova to a Gulag deep in Siberia. OSS62 officials still list her as missing in action and presumed dead.

For decades, there were persistent stories in the intelligence community that she escaped the Gulag and was living in a Buddhist monastery Bylakuppe, India from the late 1990s and later that she was managing a small monastery in the Catskills of New York in the mid-2000s.

Likewise, there were also wild reports that she was living somewhere in Britain. Neither the world media nor any government entity has publicly confirmed or denied any of these wild assertions.

To this day, people have relegated the topic of Professor Mashenka Petrova aka the Tango Dancer to the realm of outrageous conspiracy theory and cold war folk myth.

LIST OF CHARACTERS

Abramov family: Ilya and Galina, their children, daughters are Lara, Nina and Mischa and their young son Kirill.
Alice Pemberton, Director of L3S (circa 1940)
Anna & Zena, Backup team ground or air transportation
Anna Lloyd is a magazine journalist and is married to Harry Lloyd.
Anton Orlon, lawyer at the Consulate General of the USSR, NYC
Anton Vasilyev and Polina Volkova. Circus board members of St. Petersburg State Theatre Arts Academy.
Anya Gusev, Ph.D., Russian cover identity for Leila Blakely.
Barbara Hamilton, Senior costumer contractor to OSS62
Bob Akron, OSS62 field operative's Controller, OSS62, DC office.
Boris Pavel Baranov, Acting Diplomatic Air Attaché at the Russian Federation embassy in DC.
Katherine Van Helsing is a British journalist for 'Notable People Magazine.'
Charles Adam Stewart, Electronics Technician-Radar second class, Qualified in Submarines, Charles Stewart, aka Moira Sovietologist trainee at OSS62.
Cora Elizabeth Waldegrave, a British identity given to Moira Stewart after the apparent death of Mashenka Petrova.
Courtney Malone Davis, Ph.D.- Physicist–Library of Congress (L3S) Deceased 1989

Cristina Efremova, field correspondent with All-Russia State Television.
Daniel Kramer, General Director of OSS62, District of Columbia office, was assassinated in 1998.
Edward J. Clemson, US Navy Admiral-Naval Intelligence—Member L3S (circa 1941)
Ellen Peterson, the manager of the provisioning department at OSS62, Greenwich, CT office.
Emily Taylor, former Member of Parliament, political strategist, married to William Taylor.
Emma, a provisioning Jr. tech at OSS62, Greenwich, CT office.
Ernesto Torres, Dance Instructor—Contract Covert Field Officer
Felipe Romero, Diplomatic Commerce Attaché for the Government of Spain.
Fiona McKenzie, Forensic Archivists L3S
Galina Sokolova, Arts Attaché, Russian Federation embassy, DC.
Harry Lloyd, a commerce attaché in the British Diplomatic Service.
Igor Kozlov, CNN Russian correspondent in Russian Federation
Ishmael, Administrative Assistant from Provisioning @ OSS62
Jakob Caspari, Federal Intelligence Service director for the Swiss Embassy in Moscow.
Javier Luis Perez, Attorney specializes, beauty, modeling and also High-end hairstylist in DC.
Joyce Pemberton Anderson, Official first contact with Ladies' secret Signal Society (L3S)
Katherine Van Helsing, embedded reporter covering Prof. Petrova for Notable People Magazine.
Kevin Rice, MD., Medical Director OSS62, District of Columbia office.
Lady Artemis, Moira Stewart/Mashenka Petrova's former belly dance & eastern dance teacher.
Lady Esther Walker, married to Lord Liam Walker and writes history books.
Laura Boyce, OSS62 field operative's Controller, OSS62, District of Columbia office.

Leila Blakely, Meteorologist & Sovietologist and a field operative for OSS62

Leo Hamilton, site manager for OSS62, Greenwich, CT field office.

Leytenant Charl'z Mikhailovich Sidorov, Charles Stewart impersonating a Soviet Naval Officer.

Lizbeth, Field Backup team Commander "Mother Hen"

Lord Liam Walker, Chargé d'affaires at the British embassy in Washington, DC

Louise Peterson Hamilton,- Director of L3S (circa 1990s)

K. Louise Stewart, Deceased wife to Charles Stewart aka Moira.

Madame Sophia Heffelfinger, a Swiss non-deplume for Mashenka.

Marie Jean-Baptiste, US Navy Admiral-Naval Intelligence– Member L3S (circa 1990s)

Mashenka Irina Petrova, Ph.D. Theater Professor, Russian cover identity for Moira Stewart.

Maureen Henderson, Deputy Director of OSS62, District of Columbia office.

Miss Popov, Russian speaking, INS immigration & naturalization case worker.

Moira Arabella Stewart, Analyst, Sovietologist & Field Officer for OSS62

Mr. Charles Lawerence, protocol officer and diplomatic courier.

Mr. Thursday, Bodyguard at safe House

Mrs. Freya Gardner is a retired Cambridge History Professor.

Ms. Blake, field television reporter with a global television network.

Ms. Mary Allen, Senior News Producer with a global television network.

Ms. Tuesday, Bodyguard at safe House

Natakya Solovyova, owner Rus Uz Tea house in Alexandria, Virginia

Natalya Baranov, a pediatric physician, married to Boris Pavel Baranov.

Nathaniel Green, OSS62 field operative's Controller, OSS62, Greenwich, CT office.

Nikolai Antonov, retired Bolshoi dancer, asst. Arts Attaché Russian Federation embassy in DC.

Noah Brunner, - Guardia Svizzera Pontificia

Olivia Bailey Campbell, Her Ladyship-Etiquette teacher (MI6 official)

Peter Reynolds, an INS case supervisor

Professor Alexi Ivanovich Sidorov, Academic Tutor for Sovietologists at OSS62, Greenwich, CT office.

Professor Dimitri Lebedev, Dept chair St. Petersburg State Theatre Arts Academy, Masha's boss.

Akim Garin and Sasha Isayev, Professor Dimitri Lebedev's training assistants.

Professor Roza Agapova, Dean of the St. Petersburg State Theatre Arts Academy.

Professor Tamara Koltsova, teaches Theater History and Theater Management. Masha's girl Friend.

Sam, a provisioning Sr. tech at OSS62, Greenwich, CT office.

Siobhan Allen, OSS62 Field Director and Controller 2023

Sister Bridget, a Carmelite Nun, non-deplume for Moira Stewart while hiding in a Vatican City Carmelite Monastery.

Sue, Backup team Field Surgeon

Todd & Lenny, Backup team Muscle and Tactical support

Tom, Backup team field nurse

Two Men in suits, recruiters for a clandestine spy agency-OSS62.

Vera Koneva and Susanna Pankova, Prof. Petrova's Teaching Assistants.

Wagner Vincent, - Guardia Svizzera Pontificia & Sondergarde

William Taylor, a foreign service officer in the British Diplomatic Service.

Yuri, a contract assassin in the Russian underworld crime network known as Bratva. (братва)

ABOUT THE AUTHOR

Cheryl Costa is a New York State native and currently lives with her wife and dragon on the north coast of Ohio.

Cheryl learned about the spy business while ███████████████

███████████████████████████████████████

During the Cold War. Cheryl Costa served in the Air Force and the Navy, and for thirty-two years as a government contractor.

Many folks who know her have said, "She has lived more lifetimes in one life than anyone they know!"

Cheryl attended Film School. As well as studied Performance Media Writing at SUNY Binghamton University. She was an Industrial Filmmaker for half a dozen years.

She admits to having worn every outfit the protagonist wore in this novel.

Nowadays, she practices magick, creates universes, teaches Magickal Mechanics, as well as writes and lectures about UFOs.

Cheryl has a BA in Entertainment Writing and Production from SUNY Empire State University. These days she's a writer!

I may have played many roles in my life, but the greatest role I have ever played is being myself.

Mata Hari - born Margaretha Geertruida Zelle

True liberation comes from embracing and celebrating one's own authentic self.

Cheryl Ann Costa

"Fiction is the lie that tells the truth!"

Neil Gaiman

Made in United States
Orlando, FL
22 October 2024

52871746R20181